The Pilots

The Pilots

JAMES SPENCER

G.P. PUTNAM'S SONS

NEW YORK

S

G. P. Putnam's Sons
Publishers Since 1838
a member of
Penguin Putnam Inc.
375 Hudson Street
New York, NY 10014

The following chapters have been published previously:
"Introduction" (as "The Pilots"), in *Topic* magazine
(Cambridge, England), Summer 2002.
"The Hurlingame Trainer," *South Dakota Review,* Spring 1994.
"Famous Aces" (as "The Lufbery Circle"), *Ontario Review,*
Spring/Summer 1992.
"The Jungle—Part I" (as "The Jungle"), *Ontario Review,*
Spring/Summer 1996.
"Flying with Angels," *Ontario Review,* Spring/Summer 1993.

Library of Congress Cataloging-in-Publication Data

Spencer, James, date.
The pilots / James Spencer.
p. cm.
ISBN 0-399-14973-2 (acid-free paper)
1. World War, 1939–1945—Aerial operations, American—Fiction.
2. World War, 1939–1945—Campaigns—Pacific Area—Fiction.
3. Americans—Pacific Area—Fiction. 4. Autobiographical
fiction, American. 5. Air pilots, Military—Fiction.
6. Pacific Area—Fiction. 7. War stories, American. I. Title.
PS3619.P6445 P55   2003   2002073449
813'.6—dc21

Printed in the United States of America

1   3   5   7   9   10   8   6   4   2

This book is printed on acid-free paper. ∞

Book design by Michelle McMillian

To my sons,
Jon and Brian

James Spencer (standing, third from left) *with B-24 crew,
Morotai, Halmaheras, 1944*

CONTENTS

Author's Note

The characters in this book are fictional and are not intended to resemble any persons, living or dead. However, many of the events are taken from real life or are variations of events that actually occurred during the Second World War.

INTRODUCTION

I've been asked why I waited so long to write these stories about combat flying in the Second World War. The first answer, I guess, is that I'd have to face it all again, and for many years I wasn't ready to do so. When I returned to college, hardly anybody talked about the war. Those who did were considered a little cracked, living in the past. They acted as if the war was the biggest thing that ever happened to them, which it was, and had been for all of us, but we weren't about to admit it. A few guys plunged into their studies with the focus of a fighter pilot trying to get a Zero in the ringsight. It may have been their type of self-medication. What most of us did was drown our post-traumatic stress syndrome (at that time lacking a diagnosis) in beer and bourbon and sex. There was still a certain panache attached to the college drunk, who could cut class and party all semester, buy the lecture notes, and crack the text a day before the final and pull a C in the course.

Another reason I held off writing about the war is that I dreaded boring my friends as I'd been bored by old doughboys bragging about their experiences in World War I. Who knows, if any of them had been pilots, I might be giving a different account of myself. By the time I started getting interested in writing about the war, I had a family to support, and not enough time and perhaps still not enough courage to relive my experiences with the clarity I needed in order to write well about them.

What finally got me started was the curiosity of my own sons. They were approaching draft age during the Vietnam War. There were things they wanted and needed to know, not from just anybody but from their father. I was honored. I started cautiously, afraid to bore them as I'd been bored, but my sons wanted more. I saw that it was not just the experiences they wanted, not just the facts. They wanted to know what I felt about those experiences, what values I placed on them, how they affected me, how I came through the war whole and, arguably, sane. They wanted to know what those experiences *meant* to me.

The accounts I gave my sons were as close to the literal facts as I could make them after so many years. But those accounts started a process. It seemed to me that I could give my answers more life by making stories that were partly the literal truth as I remembered it, and partly imagination based on truth. The gift of my children's questions got me to writing about that war in the least boring way I knew—a way intended to reach the heart, mind, and gut simultaneously, which is the way of literature.

During the Second World War, I flew forty missions as a bomber pilot in the South Pacific and Southeast Asia. My unit was the 370th Bombardment Squadron, 307th Bombardment Group, 13th Air Force. I flew a B-24 Liberator, a four-engine bomber carrying a crew of ten. I arrived in combat as a copilot in September 1944, and eventually became a first pilot. My bombardment group was known as the Long Rangers because we specialized in reaching targets as far as 1,500 or 1,600 miles away, where the Japanese thought they were fairly safe from our bombs. My flight log tells me that my longest nonstop mission lasted thirteen hours and thirty minutes, takeoff to landing.

I flew most of my missions from Morotai, a jungle island about halfway between New Guinea and the Philippines. From Morotai we struck oil refineries in Java, Sumatra, and the east coast of Borneo, Japanese shipping in the South China Sea, and enemy bases throughout the Philippines. By making one landing to refuel at Puerto Princesa, Palawan, we could reach Saigon harbor. On one mission, the four squadrons of my group bombed two battleships and their escort ships and caused enough damage to make the fleet turn back to Japan.

Most of the island of Morotai was still held by the Japanese. We occupied just enough territory for our bomber base and the supporting squadrons of U.S. P-38s and Australian Spitfires. For ten months, my home was an open-sided tent with a wooden floor and frame set on six upended fifty-gallon oil drums among the surviving trees of a coconut plantation. The entrance side of the tent looked out across a coral beach and a bay with Navy ships and freighters unloading war supplies. On a clear day, we could see thirty or forty miles across the water to the mainland of the Halmaheras, where it was said that fifty thousand Japanese troops had been isolated as the war bypassed them. Once in a while a suicide mission tried to get across the straits to us at night, but none ever made it past the PT boats that patrolled those waters. Somewhere on the main island, the Japanese had managed to hide a few twin-engine Betty bombers, and with these they bombed us every three or four nights, forcing us to spend part of a sleepless night on a damp coral floor in a palm-log-and-sandbag bomb shelter.

My third mission was my baptism of fire, flown from an island off the coast of New Guinea before we moved to Morotai. Our target was a Japanese base north of Manila. To fly fourteen hours nonstop, we had to install fuel tanks that filled three-fourths of the bomb bay. We became a flying bomb ourselves, needing only an incendiary bullet in one of the tanks to blow us to kingdom come. Also, with this load, the plane was so heavy that we had to use every yard of runway to get off the ground. Fortunately, the runway ended at the edge of a shallow lagoon. Once in a while, a bomber that couldn't get airborne simply shot off the end of the runway and settled into the water while PT boats sped to the rescue.

On that third mission we had no fighter escort because our P-38s and P-51s had not yet developed sufficient range. A half-hour from the target, the sky swarmed with Japanese fighters coming at us from every angle, flashing through our formation so close that I could see canvas helmets, goggles set on high cheekbones, and white scarves around the necks of the pilots. Every so often, I thought a Zero with its guns flickering like little red snake tongues would fly right into my windshield, and my body tensed up for the impact of a kamikaze. I've described a mission much like this one in the story "First Love." My plane came home full of holes and with one tail fin half gone. This was the first of my long-range missions, and as far as I knew at the time, it was about what I could expect on all of them.

At one point in my combat tour, I volunteered for a series of long-range, single-plane missions to fly across Borneo and destroy Japanese ships along the edge of the South China Sea. In order to avoid detection by Japanese radar as we approached Borneo, we had to fly under the beam, which meant an altitude of no more than a few hundred feet. We crossed the coastline and continued at treetop level up over jungle-covered mountain ranges, then down the canyons and river valleys that led to the harbors on the western coast. Spotting a ship, we would level off at two hundred feet above the water, high enough to clear a ship's masts and low enough to skip a bomb into the side of a ship. We had the element of surprise on our side, but a few gunners on the ships usually got to their turrets, and a fighter or two got off the ground. Because the missions were considered unusually hazardous, those of us who volunteered were offered credit for two missions each time we flew. We would get home to the States that much sooner.

In the story "Flying with Angels," I describe two of these strikes. In spite of the occasional terror (or maybe because of it), they soon made the usual mission seem dull. For one thing, a favorite pastime of all the pilots I knew was flying as fast and as low as possible. Prominent in our fantasies was buzzing the girlfriend's house, or roaring down Main Street between the buildings. A few pilots actually got to do it. In training for heavy bombers, I flew a B-17 down into the Grand Canyon. It was forbidden, and my commanding officer must have heard about it, and had probably done similar things himself. Low-altitude flying was a chance to experience speed and to see a world I could not see at safer altitudes. On one flight, my crew and I discovered a perfect Chinese city of pagodas and gardens and narrow cobbled streets and red tile rooftops nested like a jewel in the remote jungle highlands of central Borneo.

That my crew and I survived, I attribute largely to luck. On one low-level mission, a Japanese ship exploded directly under us. Our skip bombs had two-second-delay fuses to let us get away before detonation, but this time the bomb punched through the hull directly into the ship's magazine, where the impact instantly ignited the ship's munitions. We flew through a cloud of wreckage, just as I've described it in "Flying with Angels." On another mission, I nearly killed us all, trying to see down the throat of a volcano newly risen from the Celebes Sea. On yet another flight, we surprised three cruisers steaming north toward the Philippines. My radio operator could get no reply on IFF or voice frequencies to tell us whether they were ours or the enemy's. As a test, I opened the bomb-bay doors, whereupon the sky around us exploded with antiaircraft bursts, some of them close enough to rock the plane. It took four squadrons of B-25 bombers to sink one cruiser and disable the others. Three-quarters of our B-25s were lost.

What were we thinking, volunteering for those missions in the first place? The other pilot was in a hurry to get home to his wife. I was bored, sitting on the ground three or four days between missions. Apart from sex, flying was the most exciting thing I'd run across in my twenty years on this planet. For some reason it hardly occurred to me that this kind of flying greatly increased my chances of not getting home at all. Like the fighter pilots in the story "Doc," when my wheels left the runway I felt the thrill of some godlike power and freedom. Our clever machines defied rules by which humans had been bound for millions of years. No matter that, in a few hours, my plane and crew would be a thousand miles from home, with no hope of rescue if we survived a water landing or a parachute jump.

Lest my passion for flying seem a glorification of war, it is important to distinguish between the flying part and the combat part of the job. The time we spent bombing and shooting and being shot at was over in an hour or less. We spent the rest of the ten or twelve or fourteen hours getting to the target and flying home again. We cruised at an altitude of ten thousand feet, where we could see much that is invisible from the window of today's airliner. We flew around and between backlit clouds like vast sculptured monuments slowly changing shape, over coral islands and turquoise lagoons, volcanoes just emerging from the sea. We studied all the moods of wind on water, and watched the sun rise or sink slowly over tropical oceans. Even after twelve or fourteen hours in the air, I sometimes felt a vague disappointment when I began to hear the faint call signal of home base in my earphones.

• • •

"The Hurlingame Trainer" is a story about a gang of boys in the mid-1930s who built themselves a flight trainer. The story is modeled on my own experience. We knew in our bones that war was coming. We constructed miniature forts and bombarded them with clods from the orchard, and ran around shooting at each other with cap guns, but our serious preparations had to do with airplanes. The aces of World War I and the barnstorming pilots of the thirties were our gods and heroes. Lindbergh had crossed the Atlantic only a few years earlier. Every week, it seemed, some pilot set a new record for speed or distance or altitude. We lived in California, where the dirigible *Akron*, a thousand-foot-long aircraft carrier, rumbled overhead every few days on the way to its hangar at Moffett Field. We lived, breathed, and dreamed flying.

One morning during my senior year in high school, I learned that Pearl Harbor had been bombed. I knew then that I would fly, and that I might be killed, but unlike many soldiers who went to Vietnam, I had some clarity about the reasons. For all we knew, the Japanese warships had paused at Hawaii only long enough to neutralize our Pacific fleet, and were even then steaming toward our beaches with an armada of troopships and landing craft. There was nobody to say it was not so—no global net, no long-range air patrols for early warning. Within a week of Pearl Harbor, gun shops from San Diego to Seattle had sold their entire stock of guns and ammunition. Men in my own family were collecting bottles and rags and kerosene for Molotov cocktails, and preparing to burn their farms and crops the way the Russians were doing as the Germans advanced. We heard of sisters and mothers who said they would commit suicide before they'd let themselves be captured by the Japanese. The invaders were soon in the Aleutian Islands, working their way toward our farms and cities. There was no such thing as resistance or protest, as there was in the Vietnam War. We knew who the enemy was and where he was. He was at our throats.

Though we had no affection for killing or being killed, it is worth noting that in the air our experience of death was different from that of soldiers on the ground. Killing in the air was more impersonal and remote than it was on the ground. In a heavy bomber, we almost never saw the destruction caused by our bombs. We might see black smoke towering three or four miles in the sky from a burning oil refinery, but we did not witness the human suffering on the ground. With rare exceptions, as in the story "Famous Aces," a fighter pilot did not see the effects of his bullets on the body of an enemy. A stricken plane, enemy or friend, usually went into its last dive and crashed far from home. Rarely were there torn, bleeding bodies, as in the infantry. No medics, no stretcher, no ambulance or helicopter. No body bag. Pilots almost never saw death happening. It was easier for them to cling to their youthful illusion of personal immortality. Without it, they might not have been able to do the work they'd been sent to do.

Though I went to war as a bomber pilot, I've written about fighter pilots in many of these stories. Fighter and bomber pilots in the Pacific led a similar kind of life. We both came home to a shower, a hot meal, and a clean bed every night. There was usually a clubhouse, however primitive, where we could drink, play poker, and generally unwind. Often there was a volleyball court on white coral sand, and somebody had a football. For both of us, when we fell from the sky we might be a thousand miles from home without any hope of rescue. If we ditched our plane in the ocean or lived through a parachute jump, we were at the mercy of sharks, headhunters, or the Japanese, who had a habit of executing American and Aussie fliers. "The Jungle—Parts I and II" describes the hazards of bailing out over New Guinea.

The lives of fighter and bomber pilots also differed in important ways. With the help of belly tanks and some advice from Charles Lindbergh, the range of the P-38 was eventually extended so far that a pilot sat cramped in the cockpit for six or seven hours at a stretch. Often, on landing, the crew chief had to pull his pilot from the cockpit and hold him upright until his legs began to work again. A bomber pilot sat in a roomy cockpit, and he could get up and walk back through the bomb bay to the waist section, talk to the gunners, even take a nap while the flight engineer and the other pilot looked after the plane. If a fighter pilot found himself chased by an enemy, he could take evasive action, while bombers had to hold to a sober, steady course much like the flight of an airliner. Antiaircraft cannons on the ground had time to compute the bomber's course and altitude. The only reason I ever found for preferring the life of the bomber pilot over that of the fighter pilot was the comfort of the cockpit and the greater range, which allowed me to see more of this beautiful planet while somebody else paid for gas and maintenance.

Potential fighter pilots made themselves visible in primary flight school by the maneuvers they were willing to try. The standard aerobatics menu of loops and rolls was too unexciting. They taught themselves upside-down spins, snap rolls beginning and ending upside down, inverted loops, vertical snap rolls with three or four rotations. A few of us believed we could actually fly backward for a few feet by cutting power and reversing the controls when we lost flying speed at the top of a vertical climb. We were fortunate to be flying Stearman biplanes, a plane so sturdy that it hardly mattered what we did with it or at what speed, it seemed impossible to tear the wings off. For some of us, the sheer exhilaration of flight inspired maneuvers that verged on lunacy, such as flying at each other head-on and breaking right or left or up or down at the last second before impact. Or diving straight down to see how close we could come to the ground and still pull out before we blacked out.

By the time I graduated from advanced flying school, long-range heavy bombers were rolling off U.S. assembly lines in vast numbers. Bomber pilots were in greater demand than fighter pilots. To my dismay, I was sent to bomber school. Perhaps my instructors hadn't spotted the born fighter pilot in me. Whatever the reason, my disappointment at being sent to bomber school ranks with other unrequited loves in my life. Before long, I developed great affection for the heavy bomber and the type of flying Blake Hurlingame does in some of these stories, but of all the world's aircraft, I loved the P-38 fighter the best. In my fantasies, I never stopped flying them. Once in a while, some compassionate crew chief would allow me to climb into the cockpit of a P-38, start it up, and sit for a while listening to the song of the Allison in-line engines on either side of me, feeling the plane tremble like a bird eager to be in flight.

The nearest I ever came to the actual experience of flying a P-38 was a day over the Halmahera Strait, when I was giving a modified B-24 a test flight. My bomb group had an old war-weary B-24 called the Fat Cat, with its gun turrets removed and the bomb bay rebuilt to carry cargo. For a while after I finished my missions and was waiting to go home, a flight engineer, a radio operator, and I flew it to Australia every week for produce, gin, and whatever contraband the three of us could smuggle aboard. It was called the Spam Run. I had finished checking out the plane, and was tooling around at seven or eight thousand feet enjoying the blue sky and the cloud formations, when a P-38 flashed past my side window as if he'd just made a mock attack on my tail. He banked as if he was about to make another run. My body reacted without thought. Simultaneously, I rolled the old bomber over on its side, hauled back on the wheel, fed in some top rudder, dropped a few degrees of flaps, and had the P-38 straight down my nose in the crosshairs of an imaginary gunsight. The P-38 tightened his turn, trying for a shorter radius so my imaginary bullets would miss. I hauled back on the wheel and fed in more top rudder. He rolled over to turn the other way and I almost lost him, then I had the Fat Cat on its other side and the P-38 in the crosshairs again. He tightened his turn; I tightened mine. He tightened more, and as I felt my controls begin to go mushy near stalling speed, the P-38 fell from the sky. Soon he was up at altitude again, trying to get me in his sights from the rear. My radio operator, enjoying the duel as much as I was, yelled that the P-38 had stalled out again.

That evening in the officers' club, a P-38 pilot showed up, looking for me. He'd taken the Fat Cat's ID number from the side of the fuselage. He wanted to know how I'd done it. I reassured him that it had little to do with his skill or mine. On its side, a P-38 has about as much lifting surface as a needle. The B-24 has a deep chested, flat-sided fuselage, and two big tail fins that give as much lift flying on their sides as the wings of a P-38 flying straight and level. This is an exaggeration, but perhaps not much. In a Lufbery circle, without the weight of the gun turrets, the B-24 had the advantage.

As I look back over more than a half century, it seems like kid stuff. Yet that is what we were—kids of nineteen, twenty, twenty-one, piloting the world's top-of-the-line fighters and bombers, full of testosterone, adrenaline, and the irrepressible spirit of youth. All that we were, we still are. What we were then is merely buried underneath all that we've added to ourselves since. I feel as if I never entirely lost contact with the boy who dived at the ground and flew head-on with his buddies, and wanted to be an ace. A few years ago, I decided to get in touch with him again through the alter ego of Steve Larkin in many of these stories, and let him live out his dream of flying a P-38. Naturally, it did not turn out as either of us expected. Steve wasn't thinking much about death or dying in that magic moment when he climbed into the cockpit for his first flight in a P-38. He was thinking only about the privilege of flying that magnificent machine.

THE HURLINGAME TRAINER

It was a clear, windless day in Stevie Larkin's eleventh winter when he stood with his grandparents peeking through the curtains at the three boys racing dirty speed bikes up and down the driveway of the old Paterson place. The boys sprayed gravel when they spun about for another run, and made noises like dive bombers loud enough to be heard across the orchard and through the windowpane. Stevie had already stolen across the leafless orchard to read the exotic syllables stenciled on the yellow pine boxes: PONTCHARTRAIN MOVERS, NEW ORLEANS. It was the time of the Great Depression and many people were moving to California, but not with half a freight car of antique furniture and hired workmen to uncrate it. In the driveway near the boxes stood a shiny Dodge sedan, the model with a little chrome-plated mountain ram leaping forward from the hood. A short, trim man with slick hair, wearing jodhpurs, riding boots, and a neck scarf, strode in and out of the peeling clapboard house, giving directions. He might have stepped from an Indy racing car, a camel caravan, a jungle in Borneo or darkest Africa.

On their bikes, each of the boys held in one hand a model airplane with propeller spinning in the wind. They raced toward each other at breakneck speed, at the last instant snatching the planes from a collision course. Then they turned, got into formation, and made a strafing run at their youngest brother, who dumped his bike, retreated behind a row of rosebushes, and threw clods with great accuracy. The man in jodhpurs did not seem to mind even when the boys roared within inches of him, pedaling like madmen. Stevie's grandfather made a clucking sound.

"We'll want to make sure the buildings are locked up tight tonight."

"Oh, Roy, what are you saying?" his grandmother scolded. "They don't look a bit like that kind of folks."

If Stevie's grandfather said white, his grandmother said black. They'd been this way as long as anyone in the family could remember. Now and then, his grandmother would lean aside or crouch down, the better to see a newly unpacked piece of furniture.

"Roy, will you look at that cut-glass mirror? Why, it looks like it come out of a palace somewhere." Or: "Where on earth did they get all that furniture? Why, the house must be full already, and now they're filling the garage. Do you suppose they plan to start a furniture store?"

"I don't reckon it's any of my business," his grandfather said.

"Is that right? Well, then, why don't you just go on outside and take care of something that is your business?"

His grandparents' argument had subsided to a distant mumble. Stevie could hardly wait to get outside and make his presence known across the orchard.

While Stevie got to know the Hurlingame boys, his grandparents could not seem to keep their minds off the parents. A few days after their arrival, Stevie's grandfather thoughtfully buttered a slab of homemade bread and breathed heavily through his black mustache to preface a major announcement.

"I talked to Paterson at the lumberyard. This man Hurlingame intends to start a chicken farm. He's ordered all-new lumber. Paterson says he plans to build houses and pens for two thousand chickens."

"Mercy," Stevie's grandmother said, spooning a rich lamb stew onto his plate. "It takes me a good part of every day to look after thirty chickens."

His grandfather snorted.

"Paterson says the man wants to hire full-time help. Did you ever hear such tomfoolery, with three able-bodied boys over there?"

"Maybe he wants them to do their studying," his grandmother said.

Long ago, Stevie's grandfather had taken Stevie's father out of high school to help dig wells and plant an orchard. Stevie's grandmother had never forgiven her husband. It was her favorite reproach, a battle she joined at every opportunity. Because of his grandfather's stinginess, she maintained, Stevie was deprived of a proper home. Her reasoning escaped him. His grandparents' little farm seemed to have everything a chubby, solitary boy could want. At one end of the property, his grandfather was building small rental houses. With the scrap wood, Stevie was allowed to construct miniature cities in the orchard. He flew his toy airplanes from water-hardened runways of sifted dirt. His planes flew over the cities and dropped clods of dirt that exploded almost like real bombs. Through the fields was a creek with a dump where Stevie found sheets of rusty tin for sledding down the creek bank. Bordering the creek were tall trees for climbing, and cliffs for digging caves. Within a week, Elwell, the youngest Hurlingame boy, had become Stevie's partner in all his enterprises. As a bonus, Elwell sneaked Stevie into the Hurlingame basement to look at his family's Mardi Gras costumes and the uniform and medals of an uncle who had been an aviator in World War I.

Soon there were daily clouds of dust and the rumble of motors on the other side of the orchard. Stevie's grandfather would stand at the window shaking his head, watching graders, plumbers, cement workers, electricians, carpenters and their supplies arrive by the carload and truckful. He would run his callused fingers through his curly black hair, only then beginning to gray, and stamp into the kitchen with his high, powerful voice rising to an aggrieved pitch.

"Thunderation! That man is spending enough money to build ten chicken farms! Why don't he use secondhand lumber? He could get the old Mendoza barn for the asking. There's perfectly good galvanized pipe down at the dump. That would be the way to do it." His complaints, which seemed perfectly sensible to Stevie, only aggravated his grandmother.

"Quiet down. I don't see why you're so blame worked up over it, Roy Larkin."

The pitch of his grandfather's voice rose another notch.

"People are starving in this country, Gert. This is no time for anybody to be wasting good money!"

"Well, it for sure ain't your money," his grandmother said, thrusting her square chin forward as she stirred a bowl of batter.

The barb fell short. His grandfather's dark, deep-set eyes flickered with foreboding.

"I don't think the man knows what he's doing, Gert."

"Like you said the other day, it's none of your business, so why worry about it."

Stevie's own fascination with the Hurlingames equaled his grandfather's, but for very different reasons. Stevie had learned about the family plantation, now the property of a great-uncle. There was a Confederate general in the family, and a famous pirate, ancestors who went back to England, France, and Spain. Nearly everything about the Hurlingames had made an impression on him, from the aviator's uniform and medals to Mr. Hurlingame's quiet, genteel manner of speaking not only to his sons, but to Stevie also. It made a startling contrast to his grandfather's piercing diatribes on the harsh realities, the unemployed, the hungry millions, the war that was coming. Every two or three days, Mr. Hurlingame stepped out of the house in an elegant double-breasted suit, with Elwell's mother clinging to his arm in one of her flowing, gossamer dresses, exposing slim stockinged legs as she daintily maneuvered herself into the shiny Dodge sedan for a trip to San Francisco, Elwell said, or an afternoon at the Tanforan racetrack.

Elwell's older brothers, Todd and Blake, were even more intriguing. They had claimed an old cabin behind the garage for their clubhouse. On the door they had painted a skull and crossbones, and blood-red lettering: DO NOT ENTER WITHOUT PERMIT! TRESPASSERS WILL BE DECAPITATED! They had explained "decapitated" to Elwell: a body flopping wildly, blood spurting six feet out of the neck, the head rolling like a soccer ball with eyes bugging and mouth open as if trying to speak. Inside the clubhouse, Elwell's brothers built windup World War I Fokkers and Spads and Jennies of balsa ribbing and rice paper that looked like real airplanes as they soared above the trees and fields. After Todd and Blake had flown a plane for a while, they invited Stevie and Elwell to help them "shoot it down" by lobbing clods at it from the plowed field where they flew their planes. They shouted to imitate the thunder of antiaircraft cannons. Elwell's brothers taught Stevie and Elwell how to lead the plane, as if they were shooting birds in flight. After five hits, Stevie and Elwell were given a badge and a title: "Gunner First Class."

. . .

By late spring, six vast pens and buildings stood in two rows be-hind the Hurlingame house and garage. Trucks arrived, and a sea of white Leghorn pullets flooded the pens, squawking and flapping their wings. Chicken feed, laying mash, chick scratch, crushed abalone shells arrived, boxes of empty egg cartons and sacks and crates of things Elwell did not know the names of. Todd and Blake briefly explained some of it to Stevie and Elwell, then returned to their airplanes and other interests. Blake was now on the freshman football team at high school. Every morning, the hired help arrived. Standing at the window, Stevie's grandfather could not contain his annoyance.

"Don't that beat everything," he would say, running a hand through his unruly black curls. "Two husky teenage boys over there and all they do is spend good money and loaf around that shack."

Stevie's grandmother could not resist the opportunity. Her square, impassive face became even more stonelike.

"Maybe if you'd let your own son do a little more of what he wanted, he'd be a different man today."

His grandfather did not even seem to hear her.

"The man is headed straight for ruin. Paterson says one of his checks came back from the bank."

"That could happen to anybody."

Stevie's grandfather shook his head slowly, his bushy black eye-brows drawn down in stubborn foreboding.

"Something ain't right, Gert."

"I'll tell you what ain't right. What ain't right is them boys over there acting like they was trying to kill somebody."

Stevie's world teetered for a moment. His grandmother was a pacifist, but it had not occurred to him that it might apply to his play outdoors.

"It don't mean a thing," his grandfather grumbled. "My brother and I played soldiers. Only difference was, we darn seldom got to do it. In my day, boys had to work."

Stevie knew his grandfather did not expect him to work, or at least not as he'd had to, himself, in those hard frontier days. Stevie glanced gratefully at him, uncertain whether he'd met his eye.

Stevie's grandparents questioned him about the Hurlingames. He told them about the great-uncle, the general, the pirate, the aviator. Some things he kept to himself, uneasy about their reception. There had been money troubles in New Orleans. Mr. Hurlingame had been ordered to leave the state. Elwell told this to Stevie proudly. Whenever any member of the family spoke of another, the information seemed to flow on a current of pride. Elwell, a year younger than Stevie and small for his age, had inherited some mysterious disease from his grandfather. Todd and Blake boasted about it at school: When the doctor examined Elwell's blood under a microscope, it was full of pus. By rights, Elwell should be dead. Their mother, too, had a mysterious ailment, for which she had to soak her feet every night in a hot sulfur bath. The sulfur got absorbed into her body through her pores, Todd and Blake told their impressed audience behind the baseball backstop, and when she had a bowel movement the whole house smelled like rotten eggs.

Todd and Blake were also proud of Elwell for enduring the ingenious tortures they devised for him, such as nailing him in a barrel and rolling him down the creek bank. Once, when their parents were away, they tied him in a chair blindfolded, with his mouth taped shut, and hoisted him twenty feet into a black walnut tree, then rode their bikes to town. By the time Stevie discovered him and got him down, he was paler than usual; his galaxy of freckles stood out with alarming clarity. He hunched over, massaging his wrists and ankles. "In New Orleans," he said, proudly, "they buried me for three hours with only a piece of garden hose to breathe through."

Though Stevie's grandmother ridiculed his grandfather for his snooping, she planted a new garden on the Hurlingame side of the house. Working on hands and knees, she could see under the orchard branches and across to the Hurlingame driveway. His grandfather spent an unusual amount of time now repairing roofs that looked out over the board fence along the back of the Hurlingame property.

One day his grandfather slipped from a ladder and twisted his ankle. He sat in the kitchen soaking his foot while Stevie's grandmother prepared dinner.

"I told you you'd get your nose caught in something, Roy Larkin. Do you think they don't notice you up there snooping all the time?"

His grandfather winced and grunted as he moved his foot.

"And what are you doing all day in that blame garden? You told me it wasn't good dirt on that side of the house."

Privately, Stevie's grandmother would complain to him that Mrs. Hurlingame was never at home. Most of the time she was off somewhere in the car with Mr. Hurlingame, and the rest of the time she was indoors with the blinds drawn like an invalid. What was the matter with her? Did she ever cook or clean house? What did she do with herself all day?

The more time Stevie's grandfather spent on the rooftops, the more aggravated he seemed to be at the dinner table.

"The man *can't* be making money, Gert. You should see the feed they deliver over there. They don't ship enough eggs out to pay for what's coming in."

His grandmother seemed to take it calmly.

"I'll say this for him—he's generous with his wife and children. I even saw him give some money to a tramp the other day."

This was another of his grandparents' favorite skirmishes. Ragged, homeless men came to the kitchen door several times a week. His grandmother usually kept a pot of soup on the back of the wood-stove. She gave everyone a bowl of soup and a thick slice of buttered bread. The men would eat, sitting on the back steps. She did not offer them work. His grandfather refused to pay good money for work he could do himself. Whenever he came into the house, he frowned at the soup pot, and a little burst of air would hiss through his thick mustache. Stevie's grandmother would torque her heavy shoulders from whatever she was doing and beat him to the punch.

"Now, just never mind—I raised them vegetables myself. Besides, if somebody don't eat it, it'll go bad."

His grandfather would ask her why she thought he paid good money for the Frigidaire. She would say she didn't know how he could live with himself, he was so stingy and mean-spirited.

"Yes, and if I wasn't, I might be one of them tramps out there, and where would you be?"

"Maybe married to somebody who wasn't so stingy."

A wall of silence would establish itself around Stevie's grandfather, where it often remained for the better part of a week.

The Great Depression was now in its eighth year, and it was bone-knowledge in boys of eleven and thirteen and fifteen that even greater disasters were fast approaching. The cities Stevie and El-well built in the orchard became walled fortifications with bunkers and underground hangars and munitions dumps. Their allowances went for lead soldiers that shattered when a clod of plowed dirt exploded among the buildings and trenches. Patiently, Stevie and Elwell glued heads and arms and legs back onto the soldiers, repaired cannons and tanks and planes for the next day's battle.

Todd's and Blake's warplanes now carried little black machine guns mounted on the wings or over the engine. Each plane was flown a few times, and then instead of blasting it from the sky with clods of dirt, the brothers ingeniously rigged it with a fuse and a firecracker or a glob of highly inflammable glue, or both. At the height of its climb the plane would begin trailing smoke, then burn or explode and fall from the sky in one of many fascinating ways, in fragments or in nosedives, spins, or crippled erratic death dances. Sometimes a toy pilot would be blown free by the explosion and would fall to earth trailing a tiny, half-opened parachute.

Stevie's grandmother complained about their yelling and screaming, and the "awful things" that went on in the orchard and the field behind the Hurlingame chicken houses. Once in a while his grandfather would stop to watch, and his dark, deep-set eyes would stir in Stevie a strange uneasiness, though he gave no sign of disapproval. Evenings, his grandfather would sit in a blacked-out living room with his head bent low to the art deco table radio and the newscaster's urgent voice nearly inaudible, in the belief that low volume saved electricity. From the morning paper, he would quote John L. Lewis or President Roosevelt, and rant about Hitler or Japanese atrocities in China, or the greed of the very rich. Stevie's grandmother would reply with a shrug, or find some way to oppose him outright, even going so far as to praise Hitler, though Stevie doubted she believed a word of what she was saying. His grandfather went outdoors in the morning with his feelings pent up, unrelieved. If a neighbor stopped for consultation on those worrisome times, his grandfather would stand in the gravel drive with his arm raised skyward like a prophet of old and his sharp, powerful voice cutting through fields and orchards. "That man Hitler is a menace to the world!" Stevie heard him cry, many times.

"Things will get far worse before they get better!" And: "If the rich continue to get richer and the poor, poorer, there will be a revolution in this country, you mark my word!"

One day when Elwell's parents were not at home, a burning model airplane crashed in a pile of debris behind a chicken house. Tarpaper and empty feed sacks ignited swiftly. By the time Todd and Blake found a hose and connected it, the building was ablaze. Someone called a fire engine. It arrived too late, along with neighbors wanting to help. Chickens flapped and squawked and collided with wire fences. Some ran out of the building with feathers afire, some ran in, many escaped into the orchard. "Wow!" Elwell kept saying, running around so as not to miss anything. "Wow!" For weeks, bedraggled chickens could be seen in the fields and orchards and along the creek, returning to the wild.

"I just knew they'd cause some devilment with them airplanes," Stevie's grandmother declared at dinner.

His grandfather was haunted by the destruction of property.

"The loss," he said, hollowly. "Think how much that chicken house cost to build." The boys, he said, needed to be taught a lesson.

"Stevie didn't have anything to do with it," his grandmother said. "He was just watching."

Nevertheless, his grandfather made his way across the orchard to confer with Elwell's father. Tense with anxiety, Stevie hid behind a shed where he could peek through the fence at the men talking in the Hurlingame yard. His grandfather returned, shaking his head.

"That man," he said. "That man."

"That man, what?" his grandmother said.

"He don't intend to do *anything,* that's what! He's letting them boys off scot-free!"

"He probably figures they've learned their lesson."

His grandfather snorted.

"I'd put them to work rebuilding, if they was my boys. Every last board."

"You leave them alone. Stevie says they make top grades in school."

Stevie was forbidden to play with Elwell or to set foot on the Hurlingame property for an indefinite period. After a few days of watching him mope around, his grandmother declared that he'd been punished enough. His grandfather seemed surprisingly easy to convince, perhaps because Stevie's exile had cut off a major source of Hurlingame news. In town, his grandfather had heard that the Hurlingame chickens were dying. Elwell and his brothers invited Stevie to examine chickens with grotesque wartlike growths on their heads. The brothers seemed as proud of the diseased chickens as of everything else connected with their family. Small mountains of dead chickens awaited burial while the workmen dug pits.

One morning, Stevie's grandfather stamped into the house, yelling as if his wife herself were the culprit.

"Gert, it's no wonder them chickens got sick! The tomfool isn't even putting potassium permanganate in their drinking water!"

His grandmother continued placidly peeling an eggplant.

"Now, how on earth would you happen to know that? You been sneaking over there at night to taste the chickens' water?"

His grandfather stamped out, slamming the back door. The house could not contain his anger at such foolishness, much less his wife's posture of indifference.

All the Hurlingame chickens had to be destroyed, and the houses and pens sprayed with a noxious disinfectant. Stevie and his grandparents could smell it even indoors, when the wind was right. After a few weeks, another sea of chickens filled the pens.

In town his grandfather began to hear of more bad checks, large sums involved. Sheriff's cars appeared in the Hurlingame driveway. His grandmother spent longer hours in her garden. Elwell was impressed by all the commotion. The sheriff had delivered subpoenas, he said. His father expected a warrant, might even be arrested and put in jail. Then the storm was over, all bills paid.

"Paterson tells me it was the uncle in New Orleans," Stevie's grandfather said at dinner. "He made good on the checks. That man was headed straight for the penitentiary."

Stevie now reached a high plateau in his friendship with the Hurlingames. Todd and Blake built an airplane—not a model this time, or a real plane, but a trainer with a cockpit big enough for one person to sit in. The joystick and rudder pedals were connected by cables to hinged control surfaces on the wings and tail. The plane stood on two wheels and a tail skid, and was painted blue and yellow, with U.S. stars on the wings and fuselage. With the pilot in the cockpit, the "ground crew" winched the plane up three or four feet under the main branch of the walnut tree. Hanging from the rope, it could be turned and tipped in any direction. The ground crew held the plane by the tail and wingtips and maneuvered it into attitudes of climb, dive, turn, and level flight, depending on how the pilot moved the control surfaces. The longer the ground crew practiced, the more the pilot felt actually airborne, in control. As the plane came in for a landing with the pilot calling out his airspeed, Todd or Blake would yell instructions such as: "You're going too slow, get your nose down! Crab it, crab it, right rudder, you have a crosswind! Get your nose up, more throttle, flare out, flare out, cut!" and the wheels would thump down as someone released the rope. If the pilot did not follow instructions well enough, the ground crew dropped the plane from two or three feet for a hard landing. Sometimes they broke a wing or the undercarriage. This was even more exciting. They suffered minor injuries, which they hid from parents and grandparents, and proudly displayed at school.

One day, Stevie's grandfather took him aside and told him that the rope they used was worn, too thin in the first place, and the pulleys were too small for the weight they carried. (Stevie did not ask how he knew this.) His grandfather was afraid they would have an accident. It was the only rope they could find, Stevie told him. The Hurlingames had no money for new rope, and Stevie knew his grandfather would give them none. He was bracing himself to hear that he could no longer fly in the trainer. Instead, his grandfather took him into his workshop and lifted a block and tackle off the wall, hung it from a rafter, and explained its operation. "If you're going to be a flier," he said, "you'll want to be sure your airplane is in top-notch working order. Your life will depend on it. Understand?" Stevie nodded. "Now," his grandfather said. "No need to tell your grandmother. Take this over there, and don't fly your plane again until it's hooked up the way I showed you."

As if she'd been eavesdropping, Stevie's grandmother launched an attack on the trainer. He heard her voice one night after he'd gone to bed.

"They could be killed!" she cried. "Suppose the rope breaks!"

"It ain't going to break," his grandfather said.

"How do you know? They were way up in that tree today! Twenty feet or more!"

A door slammed, and Stevie could not make out their words. But his grandfather must have held her off, for he was allowed to continue his flying career.

Every afternoon now, there were eight or ten bikes sprawled in the dirt or leaning against the Hurlingame garage. Stevie and Elwell had become instructors, even teaching older boys. Anyone not in the cockpit was required to yell engine sounds, a thundering roar for takeoff and climb, a high-rpm snarl for dives, and a steady drone for level flight. Todd found an electric fan among the furniture in the garage, and mounted it on the nose. An impressive flow of air now blasted the pilot's face. They installed a windshield. Some father or uncle donated a pair of goggles and an old canvas flying helmet. A white scarf appeared, torn from a ruined bedsheet. They trained for loops and rolls, following Todd's and Blake's shouted instructions, though they could not actually tip the trainer over on its back. All spring and summer they flew, getting up early enough for a flight before they raced their bikes to school, and flying until it was too dark to see.

Stevie learned that the Hurlingame chickens were dying again, this time of some other disease. His grandfather was appalled.

"The man's a fool," he declared. "There's no way in the world he could make so many mistakes if he'd read the government manuals."

Then Elwell reported that his father had given up chicken farming.

"How in tarnation do they expect to eat?" Stevie's grandfather cried, startling him with his passion. It seemed to trigger a corresponding reaction in his grandmother.

"Will you leave off and mind your own business!" she blazed. "Go feed them yourself if you're that worried about it."

There followed an argument so acrimonious that Stevie slipped out of the house and ran to find Elwell.

One morning, he entered a silent kitchen to find his grandmother leaning over the sink with her ear turned to the half-open window. Outside, Stevie could hear his grandfather's passionate voice, and through the curtain he could make out his heaven-pointing arm. Elwell's father stood near him, looking aristocratic as usual in his jodhpurs and the pith helmet he wore outdoors.

"Mr. Hurlingame," Stevie's grandfather was shouting, "the world is headed for catastrophes the likes of which the human race has never seen! Mark my word, you and I will see our sons and grandsons marched away to battlefields in foreign lands! Maybe the very ground we stand on will run with the blood of the dead and dying!"

Mr. Hurlingame answered quietly, and the arm on high descended. The men walked farther from the house. When Stevie's grandfather came in the house for dinner, he sat for a while as if in shock. Mr. Hurlingame, he announced, finally, was going into the business of servicing nickel candy and penny gumball machines. It was all the work he could find. He only got that because his uncle knew somebody. Stevie's grandfather slapped the table with a work-thickened hand. "Now, how the Sam Hill does he expect to support his family on that?"

"Did you ask him?" Stevie's grandmother said.

"Ask him?" his grandfather snorted. "It ain't any of my business."

"Seems to me you've made just about everything that goes on over there your business," his grandmother said.

"Well, I suppose you haven't," his grandfather flared, and they were locked in another battle.

Todd and Blake made further improvements on the trainer. They installed a clock and a Boy Scout compass in the cockpit. They had discovered that the airflow from the fan allowed the pilot to turn the plane slowly without help from the ground crew. Now they were hoisted twenty feet up to "cruising altitude" for cross-country navigation. Todd and Blake would yell instructions, such as "Turn to a heading of ninety-seven degrees, fly two minutes, then turn to three hundred twelve degrees." Stevie and Elwell learned to read maps. They descended into Chicago, Lakehurst, Van Nuys airports, learning landing procedures, downwind leg, base leg, final approach, flareout, and touchdown.

The greatest excitement, though, was at lower altitude, where the ground crew could give the airplane sudden, violent changes in attitude. Todd and Blake built black machine guns and mounted them forward of the pilot. They nailed cutouts of "enemy" planes on surrounding trees and buildings. The pilots now dived and twisted and climbed steeply, making machine-gun noises when they got an enemy plane in the ringsight. Todd and Blake were forever yelling, "Look behind you! Look behind you!" and if a pilot flew too long without rubbernecking for enemy fighters, he was dropped to the ground and declared shot down. Todd and Blake decided that Stevie and Elwell and another boy were "qualified aces," and presented them with medals. They were now addressed as "Ace." Boys at school who had never noticed Stevie before soon wanted to be his friend.

Word got around the neighborhood. Sometimes a strange car would pull into the Hurlingame drive. A local farmer and his wife would stand at a respectful distance while two or three small children jumped up and down excitedly. The fliers invited their parents. Stevie begged his grandmother to watch, but she would have nothing to do with it.

"All this talk about war makes me heartsick," she said. "I don't even want to think about it."

"That ain't going to make it go away," his grandfather said, shaking out his newspaper with a loud rattle.

"Them boys should be studying," his grandmother said, squinting at her sewing. "They can't have much time for their books, the way they're carrying on."

"They should be working," his grandfather grumbled. "Learning a trade. If you have a trade, you always have something."

His grandmother sniffed.

"They're smart boys, every one of them. They could be doctors or lawyers or engineers. Stevie, too."

He studied his grandfather. There was more to him than Stevie had realized. His grandfather did not really approve of the trainer, yet he'd given Stevie the block and tackle. It was like an initiation: A powerful tool or weapon had been placed in Stevie's hands, and along with it the right to decide for himself when and how to use it. Even so, his grandfather had come only once or twice to watch them fly, and Mr. Hurlingame only a few times. Stevie read their lack of enthusiasm as fear that the boys might crash and hurt themselves. Somehow this made flying all the more exciting.

One day they discovered an especially snappy maneuver. Elwell took Stevie into the house to find his mother. Stevie followed him through cool, darkened rooms, struck by the soft glints of heavy, carved furniture, ornate rugs, and sensuous fabrics. They found Mrs. Hurlingame on her bed in a silk kimono, with a damp cloth covering her forehead. Exotic scents stirred in the room, vaguely dizzying in the dim light. A large box of chocolates lay open under a lamp on the bedside stand.

"Oh, you dear boys," she said, in a breathy, almost singing voice as she reached for Elwell's hand, then Stevie's. "That was sweet of y'all to invite me. Go have a good time now, and take some chocolates, you hear?" She held Stevie's hand in her soft, cool fingers again, and for a startling second or two he was looking down at the face of his own mother, whom he had not seen for a month and who, like his grandmother, also hated war. In spite of the celestial flavors exploding on his tongue, he left the house strangely disturbed, relieved that Mrs. Hurlingame would not come to see them fly.

Apart from the action around the trainer, Stevie's grandparents could see little sign of enterprise across the orchard. Mr. Hurlingame would sometimes unload a few cartons from his Dodge sedan, or load a few into it, and drive away for the afternoon. Every two or three weeks, he would hitch a small trailer behind his car and drive away with some furniture from the garage. For a while after that, Todd and Blake and Elwell might appear with new shoes, shirts, Levi's, maybe a new bike or an assortment of model airplanes, and Mr. and Mrs. Hurlingame would resume their day-long and evening outings.

"Where on earth do they go, all dressed up like that?" Stevie's grandmother asked him. He shrugged, and kept his nose in the book he was reading.

"Maybe some relatives in San Francisco."

"Well, they're spending the money he got for that furniture, you can bet on that."

His grandfather would sigh and stamp into another room, as if washing his hands of the whole affair.

After several months, no more furniture came from the garage.

"I should think not," his grandmother said. "He even took some out of the house. Those boys'll end up sleeping on the floor."

One day under the elm trees at school, as Stevie happily chewed one of his grandmother's delicious meat-loaf sandwiches, he noticed Elwell doodling with a stick in the dirt.

"Did you forget your lunch?"

Elwell shrugged.

"Here," Stevie said, breaking off half his sandwich. Elwell shook his head at first, then accepted. Stevie watched him eat the sandwich, then gave him a cookie and an apple. "My grandma always gives me too much," Stevie said.

The next day, Elwell removed four lint-covered dried prunes

from his pocket. It was harder to get him to accept the sandwich this time, but Stevie insisted. "I can't eat it all. I'll just have to throw it away."

After a few days, Stevie was beginning to feel hungry in the afternoons. He asked his grandmother if he could have two sandwiches from now on. She agreed, giving him a curious look. When he opened his lunch box the next day, he also found extra fruit and cookies.

The following week, she confronted him. "Stevie, are them boys over there getting enough to eat?"

He shrugged. "I guess not."

When he came home from school, the stew pot was missing from the stove. His grandmother began baking twice as much bread. He understood what was happening, but did not really want to think about it. The fighting between his grandfather and grandmother grew worse. Once, he heard his grandfather's voice behind a closed door at night: "I lived by the sweat of my brow since I was thirteen," he shouted. "I did not work like a horse all my life to support another man's family!" Stevie heard his grandmother stamp her foot. "Did you work hard all your life to eat well while your neighbor's children starved?"

His grandmother's answer must have cut his grandfather deeply. The back door slammed, and his grandfather had not come in yet when Stevie left for school in the morning. Never again did Stevie hear him complain about the food his grandmother carried across the orchard to the Hurlingames.

But his grandfather was not the only one who changed. Todd and Blake stopped flying the trainer, and Elwell would no longer play with Stevie. Even at school, Elwell seemed to avoid him. He avoided his other friends, too. Once, Stevie found him sitting behind the backstop, chucking pebbles into the dust.

"Why don't we fly the trainer anymore?"

Elwell shrugged one shoulder and did not look up.

"I'm starting a new city in the orchard," Stevie said. "My grandpa says I can use water to make a river and a lake. Do you want to help?"

Elwell barely shook his head, negative.

"What's the matter?" Stevie said. "What's eating you?"

His friend refused to speak, but Stevie had a vague understanding. He spent the rest of the school year moping, with nobody to play with. An orphan girl by the name of Florrie came to live with Stevie and his grandparents, but she was three years older than Stevie and she seemed mostly interested in Blake Hurlingame anyway. Stevie's world had fallen apart. It was no longer fun to build things. He read dumb adventure stories. He wandered along the creek. He watched the wind blow blizzards of spring blossoms, and the green grass along the creek banks turn brown with the approach of summer.

At the end of the school year, Stevie was snatched away to San Jose and a new life. His mother had finished business school, found a better job, a larger apartment. In San Jose, he was in junior high school, no longer a pudgy, reclusive boy. Life picked up speed. A year passed. Two. Three. Some weekends he rode the Greyhound bus to visit his grandparents. A few of the Hurlingames were still there. The shiny Dodge with the little chrome-plated ram on the hood was dented now, driven mostly by Blake. Elwell was long dead, and Todd had gone to live with an uncle in Kentfield, north of San Francisco. Their parents were rarely seen; they seemed to have pulled back from the world, hiding in their dark cave of a house with the blinds down. Maybe they only came out at night, Stevie's grandmother said. "I've seen your grandfather out in the orchard a few times with Mr. Hurlingame, but the nuisance only knows what they talk about."

Stevie looked over the fence once, to see if the trainer was still there. The blue and yellow paint was chipped and peeling, the wings were broken, and the fuselage lay half crushed, as if someone had winched the plane up to its ceiling under the branch and let it take its final dive.

The world blundered on toward the inevitable war. Stevie's grandfather's hair grew white, perhaps from fighting with his wife, perhaps from worrying about the family on the other side of the orchard. Maybe it was the grief of seeing his dreadful prophecies come to pass. Hitler attacked Poland, then gobbled up the rest of Europe. The Japanese bombed Pearl Harbor, and Stevie joined the Air Corps. Todd and Blake, he heard, were already flying bombers. Mr. and Mrs. Hurlingame moved back to New Orleans. The rich uncle had died, and had not been good to them, but in times such as these, they told Stevie's grandmother, where could you turn except to family?

By the time Steve got home from the war, his grandfather was dead and his grandmother was bedridden, waiting to die. The acrimony that had held them together was evidently too strong a bond to let her linger long after. Steve talked about the years he'd lived with her, and a little about the war. Her mind was clear; she had the strength to be happy that he'd come home safe, the clarity to understand when he told her that once or twice he'd heard Blake's or Todd's voice in his ear, yelling, "Look behind you! Look behind you!" and it had saved his life. It was then she told him about the brothers and what had become of their parents. She reached for his hand, laboring to breathe.

"Stevie," she said, at length, "do you remember when your grandfather and I were fighting so much because I was taking food over to them?"

"I sure do."

She turned her head toward the bedside table.

"Look in the drawer," she said. "The yellow envelope."

The envelope was filled with canceled checks made out to a bank. His grandfather's signatures.

"I found them when I went through his papers," his grandmother said.

"Stevie, he was making their mortgage payments."

She gripped his hand like a drowning person.

"Why didn't he tell me, Stevie? Why didn't the tomfool tell me?"

DEAD RECKONING

The light of the desert moon gleamed on the engine nacelles and along the top of the mirror-smooth wing. From his window on the right side of the cockpit, Blake could dimly make out the jagged peaks of the Chiricahua Mountains reaching up beneath him. Somewhere down there was a granite fang that topped off at nine thousand eight hundred feet, only two hundred feet lower than the plane. If his navigation was correct, they would pass three or four miles to the east of the peak.

Blake and Messner had been scheduled to fly together on their final cross-country night flight. Blake would navigate from the copilot's seat while Messner did the flying. At briefing before takeoff, the training officer told them that if they disagreed about navigation or anything else on the mission, they had to work it out between themselves. At thirty thousand feet over Germany or Japan, they'd have no instructor to hold their hand. If they came home successfully, they would graduate in a week as pilots and officers of the U.S. Army Air Corps. If they crashed and survived, or landed anyplace other than Douglas Air Force Base, Arizona, they'd end up as foot soldiers in the infantry.

Though they were on course and the plane was functioning nor-

mally, Messner's eyes darted back and forth across the instrument
panel as if he was afraid the gauges and dials in front of him might
leap out of the window unless he kept them pinned down with his
gaze. For the third time since they'd reached cruising altitude and
set the autopilot, Messner asked to see the map. Blake handed him
the clipboard and the E-6B computer and watched patiently as
Messner hunched over with his little flashlight and triple-checked
Blake's navigation. Messner was a small, worried-looking guy you
hardly noticed on the ground. In the canteen, he sat by himself with
his shoulders hunched as if he expected something to fall on his
head, and on weekends you never saw him on the bus to town. Of
all the cadets in the squadron, he was about the last one Blake
would have chosen to fly with.

Blake could not figure what Messner was so nervous about. They
were sitting in an AT-9, a sturdy advanced trainer that could get
them home on one engine as easily as two. They'd already crossed
Lordsburg, their first checkpoint, and had turned to a new heading
almost due north. They were in no danger unless they'd done
something stupid like turning south instead of north, in which case
they'd now be across the border into Mexico. At briefing, the training officer had warned them not to stray across the border. If they
ran out of gas over the Sonoran desert, there was no way they could
land safely at night. If they bailed out, by the time they were found
they could be dead of thirst or massive cactus punctures, or from
shattered bones if they came down among the cliffs and jagged
spires of the mountains.

Blake had been five years old when he announced to his great-
uncle Andrew that he was going to fly an airplane. His uncle had
dropped his newspaper onto his big round belly and adjusted his
spectacles. Why had Blake decided this? he asked. Because then I

can jump into my airplane and fly away from Leander when he's mean to me, Blake said. Leander was Blake's cousin, three years older, and a bully. The two of them were spending the summer on Uncle Andrew's cotton plantation while their parents were in Europe. Blake had found his uncle alone in the library of the big house with the white pillars, and had stoutly boasted, "I'm going to fly a big silver airplane that drops bombs on everybody who's mean, and I'll shoot all the other planes that want to hurt me." His uncle's steel-wool eyebrows had shot up with interest, which was more than Blake ever got from his father, whose name was also Andrew and who didn't seem to be interested in much of anything except getting dressed up in fine shirts with jewels for buttons and going off somewhere with his wife, Blake's mother, to parties and the racetrack. Uncle Andrew squinted at Blake as if he hadn't ever before really looked at his nephew. "How would you like to go for a ride in an airplane?" he asked.

Blake could hardly believe his luck as the pilot stood next to the big yellow plane and swung him up and over onto his uncle's lap. There was a belt around his uncle to keep him from falling out, and then another belt that went around both of them to keep Blake from falling out. The pilot climbed into another cockpit in front of them and yelled something, and a man on the ground reached up and pulled the propeller and the plane roared and there was a great cloud of smoke. Soon they were bumping and thundering across the ground, going faster and faster until they leaped into the air, and went on climbing until they were higher than even birds can fly. The wind whistled past the cockpit, and when Blake stuck his hand out the air tugged as if it wanted to pull him right out into the sky. Suddenly the plane rolled onto its side and Blake looked down over the edge of the cockpit and felt himself floating the way he felt when an elevator started down, and then they dived and soared upward again and over onto their back and down again, with the earth spinning around in front of them until it stopped spinning and they pulled up and were sailing like an eagle high over the bayous. Blake could see toy cars on a road and boats on a bay. His uncle pointed to a great jumble of rooftops that he said was New Orleans, where Blake had been born.

When the plane stopped and Blake climbed out into the big hands of the pilot and was set down with his feet on the ground once more, he was not the same person who'd been lifted up into the cockpit. Ever since, Blake had wanted to be a pilot, and when the war started, he knew that if he died he wanted to breathe his last breath at the controls of an airplane.

After they turned north over Lordsburg, Blake saw below them an occasional light from a mine operation or ranch or ranger station. Some were marked on the map and some were not. Now, precisely forty minutes from Lordsburg, over the nose of the plane, a small cluster of lights was emerging from the blackness of the desert floor. It should be St. Johns, a crossroads town with a few houses and maybe a gas station and store. Here they would turn southwest toward their last checkpoint, not far from the border. There were fewer lights than there had been at Lordsburg, and Blake wondered if this final test had been devised to make each checkpoint harder to find.

Blake was not worried. He'd mastered every navigation problem thrown at him in class. If he ended up as a fighter pilot in the South Pacific, he'd have to fly alone for hundreds of miles by dead reckoning over an ocean without landmarks. If he flew a bomber and his navigator was killed, it might be up to Blake to get them home, and he would have to fly even farther over ocean than he would in a fighter. Of all the subjects he'd studied for the past year, he'd singled out navigation as the one most likely to get him home alive.

Blake was about to tell Messner they were over their checkpoint when he felt a tap on the shoulder. He moved the earphone away from his left ear and heard Messner yelling over the roar of the engines, "Saint Johns! Saint Johns!" Messner was stabbing his forefinger down toward the floor as if he'd discovered a new continent. Blake nodded, and Messner twisted a knob on the autopilot, and the plane banked to the left. Messner's tongue flickered between his lips until the plane leveled off on a new heading. He reminded Blake of his little brother, Elwell, who had been a nervous and sickly kid. Messner and Elwell even had a similar knotted-up look between their eyebrows.

On their new heading it would take them an hour to reach Benson, their last checkpoint, where they would turn toward Douglas. Their course took them once again over craggy mountains topping off not far beneath the plane, high forested canyons, and stretches of desert. Blake refolded the map to display the terrain beneath them. Since they'd hit their first two checkpoints dead-on, Blake was confident that the wind direction they'd been given at takeoff was still accurate. He adjusted the pitch control so the propellers were in perfect sync, then tipped his seat and leaned back to enjoy the thunder and vibration of the twin radial engines, the subtle, almost intelligent corrections of the autopilot, and the rush of air past the cockpit windows. Unlike some pilots, Blake looked forward to night flying, especially on a night like this, with the moon nearly too bright to look at and the great jeweled belt of the Milky Way arching across the sky from horizon to horizon. The cockpit heater put out a pleasant flow of warm air. The needles and dials on the instrument panel glowed with a comforting green light that did not interfere with night vision. Blake usually felt as warm and secure in the cockpit as he'd felt as a child playing on the floor of his Great-Uncle Andrew's study.

. . .

Tonight, though, Blake was beginning to feel uneasy in his paradise of the starlit cockpit. It bothered him that Messner resembled his little brother, Elwell. Blake was often sorry for some of the things he and his other brother, Todd, had done to Elwell. The doctors in New Orleans had predicted that Elwell would die of some congenital disease before he was twelve. But he was a scrappy kid, and he acted almost proud of the torments his brothers devised for him, like nailing him in a barrel and rolling him down a creek bank, or tying him to a walnut tree when their parents weren't home and riding their bikes to town. In New Orleans, before they moved to California, they'd buried him in a box two feet underground and left him all afternoon with only a length of garden hose to breathe through. When they'd pulled him out of the box and dusted him off, Elwell had tried valiantly to act as if he'd merely been awakened from his afternoon nap. Blake was staring into the night sky at Elwell's face fighting back tears when Messner's hand darted to the autopilot and the plane tipped sharply. Startled, Blake looked at his watch.

"What are you doing?" he yelled. "It's too soon to turn!"

"We're off course!" Messner yelled.

"How do you figure that?"

Messner kept his fingers on the autopilot controls as the compass drifted to a more westerly heading, then stopped as the wings leveled. The new heading would take them farther from Douglas than the flight plan they'd been given. Had Messner flipped? He was staring down into the darkness through his side window. Blake tapped him on the shoulder.

"Why do you think we're off course?"

Messner pointed down to the left of the plane. "Those lights. That's Safford. We should be west of Safford."

"What makes you think it's Safford?" Blake yelled. "Why not Thatcher, or Pima, or Fort Thomas? All those whistle stops might have lights."

Messner's tongue flickered between his lips. Did it help him think? Did he use it to sniff danger, like a snake's tongue?

"There shouldn't be any lights!"

"Maybe it's a ranch headquarters!" Blake yelled. "Or a trailer park put in since the map was made. Or maybe the Army set up some lights to test us."

Messner's eyes made a panicky sweep toward Blake, then darted away.

"That's Safford," he repeated. "It's Safford."

Blake looked at the map again, just to be sure, then leaned over. "Messner, this is a test. We're supposed to trust our instruments. I've been checking for drift. I compensated for it. There'd have to be a hell of a big, sudden shift in the wind to blow us that far off course."

Messner made no response.

"We'd be smarter to stay on course," Blake argued, "and fly the elapsed time to Benson, then turn even if we don't see any lights."

Messner's eyes darted back and forth over the gauges and dials in front of him, as if they'd give him the answer.

"Let's get back on course," Blake said, reaching for the autopilot.

"No!" Messner yelled, striking Blake's hand away.

Blake knew he should have gotten Messner's agreement first. "Calm down," Blake yelled. It was a struggle to sound reasonable, shouting above the roar of engines. They should look for Highway 10, he argued. Benson was on Highway 10. Even if they were off course, they'd cross Highway 10 about the same time they should have arrived over Benson. They might also have the glow of Tucson on the horizon as a reference. They could turn toward Douglas then. They'd still have a few gallons of gas in the tank when they landed.

Messner stared out into the blackness of the desert.

"It's Safford."

Once in a while, Elwell, too, would dig his heels in and insist on some preposterous idea, and Blake and Todd would rap his head or poke him in the ribs until he came to his senses. Messner couldn't be more than nineteen or twenty, about the age Elwell would be if he'd lived. Blake took a deep breath and calmed himself. Elwell had always been easier to convince after they'd left him alone for a while. If there were any headlights in the desert at this time of night, he would persuade Messner to do the easiest thing and follow the highway home to Douglas.

When Blake went up in the plane with his Uncle Andrew, he'd somehow got a feel for flying in his bones that had never left him. He always knew the relation of his plane to the air and earth, and what to do about it. One of his instructors had called him a natural. But working the controls was the easy part. The hard part was learning the hazards, the pitfalls, the errors made by the best of pilots, and learning to expect the unexpected.

Somewhere in the jagged peaks of the Chiricahuas, not many miles off Blake's present course, was the wreckage of two AT-9s. Blake suspected there were others, too, that the cadets were not told about. A couple of wrecks in those mountains might keep cadet pilots on their toes. Five or six wrecks might eat away at their self-confidence or their faith in the aircraft. One of the planes had crashed on a night cross-country mission much like the one Blake and Messner were flying. The other had crashed in the daytime, searching for it. The first plane had been on course, but flying a few hundred feet too low. Maybe the pilot had set the altimeter for the wrong barometric pressure. The instruments were so badly smashed that they provided no clue. The search plane had crashed in a box canyon that the pilot had not scouted by flying high enough on the first pass. He might have made it if he'd remembered how wind behaves coming over the top of a ridge and down the canyons. The rangers had used mules to haul the bodies of the pilots out—that is, what was left of them after the buzzards and coyotes had their share. Blake was constantly impressed by all that he had to learn just to become a competent pilot. As a bomber commander, he would be responsible not only for the plane but for the lives of nine or ten other men. The smallest error could kill them all in an eyeblink.

A light had begun to emerge from the darkness over the snub nose of the plane. Blake leaned forward and watched to see if the light was moving. It was hard to tell. He thought it was. He saw another, fainter light. Both lights were on a line that should be Highway 10. Blake tapped Messner on the shoulder and pointed. Messner leaned forward to see. His tongue flickered.

"There it is," Blake yelled. "Time to turn."

Messner shook his head. "It's not Benson."

"Benson is twenty miles east," Blake yelled. "We missed it." He pointed out his side window. "See that glow on the horizon? That's Tucson." He showed Messner his plot on the map. "Look at the angle. Our elapsed time puts us right here on Highway Ten."

Messner's hand darted to the autopilot, as if to keep Blake from interfering.

"There should be more lights! Benson has more lights! A guy told me!"

Blake swore under his breath and rattled the map in front of

Messner's face. "Look, Messner, *some guy* is not navigating this plane. *I* am. In twenty minutes, we'll be over Mexico without enough gas to get home. See for yourself." But Messner refused to look.

Blake checked the fuel gauge. Soon he would have to switch to the twenty-gallon reserve. He tapped the gauge and leaned across to yell in Messner's ear. "If we turn this very minute, we'll land with a gallon or two in the tank."

Messner shook his head. "It's not Benson."

It hadn't occurred to Blake that it might come to this. He sat back in his seat and studied Messner, and considered his options. It was too late for argument. He could try to knock Messner out with his fist and take over. But Messner, though short, looked pretty sturdy, and it might start a fight in the cockpit that would throw the plane out of control and they'd crash on some mountain peak. Blake's hand crept around behind his seat to the fire extinguisher clamped to the wall. He could hit Messner with it. It was a handy size, but solid and heavy, and if Blake didn't hit just right he could crush Messner's skull. And if he accidentally triggered the thing, it would fill the cockpit with poisonous phosgene gas. You weren't even supposed to take it off the wall unless you were on the ground and could fight a fire from outside the cockpit.

Blake thought of waiting until they ran out of fuel and taking his chances with a belly landing. They might get lucky and find a flat stretch of desert. Blake felt his gut contract. Flat on the desert did not mean flat as in hayfield. He could feel the first thumping, cracking sounds of propellers hitting cactus. He could feel the controls go mushy as the plane slowed to stalling speed, then the impact and the sickening crunch and grinding of rocks against the nacelles and the aluminum skin under the gas tank that the pilots sat right on top of. A spark could ignite the fumes in the tank and blow the plane to bits, Blake and Messner with it.

Or, Blake thought, he could pop the door on his side of the cockpit and jump before they crossed the border.

"Is that your final word?" he yelled. Messner's eyes darted in Blake's direction and then returned to the blackness outside the window. Blake recognized the look. It was the panic he'd seen in his little brother's eyes not long before he died.

Blake's hand shook as he removed his earphones and set them on the floor. He tightened the straps of his parachute. Messner's tongue flickered several times as Blake cinched the chin strap on his leather helmet. He reached for the door-release handle.

"Wait! What are you doing?"

"I'm bailing out before we cross the border!" Blake yelled.

"You'll get sent to the infantry!" Messner yelled, with amazing irrelevance.

Blake grinned.

"And in twenty minutes, you'll be dead."

Messner's hands gripped the wheel and throttles as if that might give him control of the situation. Blake leaned forward to pop the door handle.

"Wait!" Messner's voice cracked. "Wait!"

"What for?" Blake yelled. Messner's eyes darted wildly back and forth among the instruments. Blake slid forward on his seat, put both hands on the handle, and yelled over his shoulder.

"Happy landing!"

"All right, I'll turn!" Messner screeched, wrenching the wheel to overpower the autopilot and put the plane in a steep bank toward Douglas.

Blake and Messner were called into the squadron CO's office as soon as they landed. Messner went in first, while Blake waited. Now that they were on the ground and still alive, Blake was beginning to feel sorry for Messner. He thought there was a good chance Messner wouldn't graduate, even though he'd come to his senses and flown home and made a good landing. The ambulance and fire trucks had been out on the field waiting for them. It was not a good sign. Blake wasn't too sure he'd graduate, himself.

Above the sergeant's desk in the outer office was a blown-up photo of a half-dozen sleek AT-9s in echelon formation against a backdrop of snowcapped mountains. Blake had come to love the plane almost as much as he'd loved Florrie, his first girlfriend. Few experiences compared with leaving the ground in an AT-9 at full power, or sliding it onto the runway at 150 miles per hour. He would never fly an AT-9 again. For all he knew, he would never fly a plane of any kind again. Waiting for the ax to fall, he wasn't even sure that it would be a bad thing. He'd heard of bomber squadrons over Germany that lost half their planes on their first mission. At that rate, a whole squadron would be wiped out in two missions. These were things Blake had only begun to think about with graduation day approaching.

A light flashed on the sergeant's desk. Blake could go in now. Messner had apparently left by another door.

Blake and Messner had been the last plane to land, the CO said. There had been less than a gallon of gas in their tank when the crew chief measured it. The CO wanted some answers. Who had navigated? What had happened?

Blake told the story right up to the time he unbuckled his safety belt and reached for the door handle. Would he really have jumped? He didn't know. The CO nodded, seeming to appreciate Blake's answer. The CO was young, probably not much older than Blake. It sounded as if he'd got a similar story from Messner. "You'll graduate," the CO said, and waited for Blake to compose himself enough to speak.

"What about Messner?" Blake said.

The CO shrugged. "Would you fly with him in combat?"

Messner's resemblance to Elwell still haunted Blake—the look on Messner's face when Blake was about to jump.

"He was okay after that," Blake said. "Maybe he deserves a second chance."

The CO shook his head.

"That's not the question, Blake. Would you fly with him in combat?"

The next day, Blake saw Messner for the last time. Blake and another cadet named Hartley were on their way to a fitting for their officer's uniforms. A cold desert wind sent clouds of brown dust whirling between the barracks and down the street. At a corner bus stop, Messner stood in a long GI overcoat with his collar turned up and his cap pulled low on his forehead. A duffel bag and a suitcase sat on the ground beside him. When a cadet washed out, it seemed like he vanished overnight, as if he'd been hauled away to a firing squad. Messner hadn't seen Blake across the street, or maybe he'd turned his head away on purpose.

"Another one off to the foxholes," Hartley said.

Blake wondered if he should go across the street and tell Messner he was sorry. But why? Men's lives were at stake, the CO had said. Would you want him as your copilot or plane commander? Could you trust him to shoot a Zero off your tail? Messner had almost got both of them killed. Still, Blake thought, there was no reason to be hard-nosed about it. As he crossed the street, he could hear the bus grinding around the corner of the next block.

"I'm sorry, Messner," Blake said.

Messner shrugged. "Don't be. I never wanted to fly anyway." His shoulders seemed straighter, but Blake suspected that he was faking it, like his little brother Elwell when they dug him out of the box.

"Flying was my father's idea," Messner said. "He just wanted a hero flyboy to brag about."

Blake and Messner watched a B-24 rumble toward them as it circled the field for a landing. The cockpit window was open and Blake could see the pilot's head. In a few weeks, Blake expected to be sitting at that window himself.

"All I wanted was to be a carpenter," Messner said.

"Why didn't you tell your father to go to hell?" Blake said.

"Hah," Messner said, with a lopsided grin. "You don't know my father."

"How will he take it?" Blake said.

Messner squinted at the big four-engine bomber, now turning onto the landing approach with its wheels and flaps down.

"That's his problem," Messner said.

Maybe Messner wasn't faking it. Maybe he really didn't care. Blake couldn't imagine feeling relieved if he was told he'd never fly a B-24 or leave the ground at full power in the cockpit of a fighter.

The olive-drab bus swerved around the corner and rolled to a stop. Messner picked up his suitcase. "Anyway," he said, "don't sweat it. The foxholes can't be much worse than the sky over Germany right now." He grinned. "Happy landing to you, too." He tossed his suitcase into the bus and his duffel bag after it, and climbed aboard. The door folded shut, and Messner walked toward the rear of the bus, passing each of the windows without looking back. Blake stood watching as the bus grew smaller and smaller down the street, until it disappeared behind a cloud of exhaust and desert dust.

DOC

Doc raced his jeep past the guards and headed for midfield as the first fighter dropped in over the jungle wall at the far end of the runway. The ambulance and the crash and fire trucks were lined up with motors idling, in order to make a break for it if a damaged P-38 skidded off the runway. They would also be able to make a fast start toward a plane if it caught fire. Doc and his medics might have only seconds to get a wounded pilot out of the cockpit before the plane vanished in a fireball.

Doc pulled in between the ambulance and the squadron commander's jeep. Marchetti was adjusting a dial on the receiver under his dashboard. He raised his head and yelled at Doc over the thunder and prop wash of the first plane rolling past. Somewhere between Port Moresby and the Owen Stanley Mountains, Lieutenant Buster Kemp was in trouble. Captain Courtenay had found his wingman, Buster, wobbling off course on the way home and was flying beside him. Buster seemed to be blind. Courtenay was talking him in. The control officer had ordered radio silence so Buster could hear Courtenay's voice through the hiss and crackle of static from local storms. Doc jumped out of his jeep and climbed into the ambulance, where his medic driver also had the receiver tuned to the squadron frequency.

"What do you make of it, Henry?"

Sergeant Klemmer raised his basset-hound eyes from the speaker.

"Hard to tell, Doc. We'll have to wait till they get closer."

The pilots in the returning planes were the age Doc's own sons would be, if he and Lorraine had been able to have children. Doc hoped he would not have to see another of them shot to shreds. Usually they crashed far from base and he never saw them again. That was bad enough. Doc noticed his cheek and arm muscles twitching on the side away from Klemmer. Doc's tics had been diagnosed as Tourette's syndrome when he was five years old. He'd learned to suppress them in public or to twitch on the side of his body another person could not see.

The fighters were descending in a column out of the northern sky. The lower planes shimmered in heat ripples as they approached the end of the runway with flaps and wheels down, giving them the stretch-legged, flared-out silhouette of birds just before touching down. Clouds of blue smoke puffed when tires made contact with the metal mesh surface and were set to spinning. As the wake of each plane's prop wash blew through the ambulance, Doc smelled exhaust, hot oil, burnt rubber, and sometimes leaking coolant from a plane gashed by enemy fire. One plane rumbled past with a dead left engine and a feathered propeller. There were jagged holes in the cowling of the right engine and in the pod behind the pilot. Another plane with half of one rudder gone looked as if it had taken a direct hit from a twenty-millimeter cannon.

"Jesus Christ, what happened over there?" Klemmer said.

Doc watched the column of planes and said nothing. Day after day, sixteen P-38s flew across New Guinea, rendezvoused with the bombers, and drove off fifty to a hundred Japanese fighters. It took a lot of luck, even for aces like John Bixby and Gregory Danovich, to come home alive.

As Courtenay flew closer to the field, his report came in more clearly. Both of Buster's engines were running and the wings and tail booms were intact, but the cockpit pod looked like a sieve. Buster would not turn his head to look at Courtenay. Evidently, Buster could hear, though, and was following Courtenay's directions: "A little more left aileron, Buster. Hold it, you went too far, back off a little. That's good. Bring your nose up, you're letting down too fast. Easy. More throttle now. Good, hold it there."

Doc noted the white knuckles of Marchetti's long, thin fingers wrapped around the steering wheel of the jeep. Marchetti took it hard when he lost a pilot. He'd lost a lot of pilots since their days on Guadalcanal. There was a burst of static, then a new voice crackled in Doc's speaker: "For Christ's sake, what's going on down there? How is he?" Marchetti brought his microphone up to his face. "I ordered radio silence," he barked. "This frequency's only open for Courtenay." Doc had recognized the voice of Steve Larkin, Buster's best friend.

Doc could now see two planes flying side by side about a wingspan apart, descending toward the end of the runway. Buster was in the plane on the right. For a moment, Buster's left wing dipped. He drifted away from Courtenay and lost altitude. Courtenay's voice crackled louder, more urgent. Buster's wing came up; he was better aligned with the runway, not dropping so fast. "That's it," Courtenay was saying. "That's it, Buster, hold it right there. You're doing fine. You'll be on the ground in about ten seconds. Start leveling off."

Buster's wing dropped a second time, almost hit the ground, then came up. As the wheels touched, the plane bounced and was airborne again. Courtenay yelled a steady stream of instructions.

This time the plane settled, touched the runway, lowered its nose and stayed down, with all three wheels on the mesh. A plume of exhaust billowed behind Courtenay's plane as he gunned his engines and pulled up in a climbing turn, back toward the landing column. Marchetti, the ambulance, and the crash trucks were already accelerating out onto the runway as Buster's plane rolled past.

Buster began drifting toward one side of the runway. When Doc and the others caught up, the plane was bumping slowly across rough ground with the engines idling and Buster hunched over the controls. The crash truck drove up to the plane so Buster's crew chief could jump from the hood onto the wing. He reached through the shattered side window of the canopy and switched off the engines. As soon as the plane came to a stop, Doc's medics helped him propel his thick, stumpy body up onto the wing. The crew chief pried open the canopy so Doc could examine Buster. His flight suit was soaked with blood. He sat in a puddle of blood and the walls and floor of the cockpit were spattered. Doc carefully lifted Buster's head. His throat had been shot away. His right arm seemed to be severed at the shoulder. Peeling back Buster's flight suit, Doc could see the sponge of his lung.

The pilots climbed out of muddy olive-drab jeeps and troop trucks and handed their parachutes to the sergeant in front of the parachute tent. Next to it, in front of the briefing tent, Doc poured each of them a shot of whiskey in a paper cup. Their faces showed the red marks from the pressure of goggles and oxygen masks. Courtenay held out his cup for a second shot. With his rumpled black locks and too-perfect face, Courtenay looked like a Hollywood idol. He was not Doc's favorite pilot, yet he'd done a good job talking Buster down.

"Sorry about Buster, Courtenay." Courtenay tossed down his second shot, crumpled the cup, and turned away as if he hadn't heard. Doc shrugged, and caught the eye of the pilot next in line.

The pilots stood around sweating in the shade of two battered palm trees, waiting for debriefing. There was none of the usual joking and horsing around. They'd lost two pilots today out of sixteen. If they lost that many planes on every mission, in eight days the squadron would be effectively wiped out.

Doc watched a jeep come barreling down the squadron street from the direction of the fighter strip. Before the jeep came to a stop, Steve Larkin jumped out with his oxygen mask still dangling from his helmet, yelling something Doc didn't catch. Steve ran toward the other pilots and gave Courtenay a shove that knocked him back a few feet.

"You son of a bitch!" he yelled. "Buster would still be alive if you'd followed orders!"

Courtenay was ducking and holding his arms up to shield his face.

"Hey, what's your problem, lover boy? I got him home, didn't I?"

Steve tried to get his hands on Courtenay, but another pilot grabbed him from the back in a bear hug.

"Easy, Steve," the pilot hissed. "He could have you court-martialed."

Doc was more concerned about injuries. Steve had been a light-heavyweight boxer in college. Doc might end up with two grounded pilots—one with a busted jaw and the other with a broken hand. A quarter of the pilots were down with malaria as it was.

Doc poured whiskey into the paper cup.

"Drink this, Steve." The pilot holding Steve let go. Steve knocked the cup aside and spilled the whiskey.

"He killed Buster, Doc! As sure as if he'd pushed the trigger!"

Doc was a head shorter than Steve, but his oil-drum body had a lower center of gravity. He stood in front of Steve, blocking the way to Courtenay. Doc refilled the cup.

"Calm down. You won't bring Buster back this way." Doc held the cup high. "Here." Steve tipped his head back and Doc poured. Doc filled the cup again and handed it to Steve. Steve drank, threw the cup down, and walked away toward the parachute tent.

Courtenay touched his lip gingerly.

"Jeez, I need another one, too, after that."

"Beat it, hotshot," Doc said. "You're lucky to be alive."

During debriefing, Steve stared numbly at the floor. Doc was glad Steve hadn't landed yet when the medics pulled Buster's remains out of the cockpit. The pilots gave details of the mission—losses, damage to planes, the size and nature of the opposition, kills and probable kills. General Laird sat in front next to Marchetti, dragging thoughtfully on a cigarette. Laird divided his time between wing headquarters and his fighter bases. Every week or so, he landed in his red-nosed P-38 and stayed a few days. He'd commanded this squadron on Guadalcanal. It was because of the tactics he'd taught them that they were able to survive the odds of three or four to one against them. Laird whacked his aluminum foot with his cane once in a while as the Intelligence officer asked questions and made notes. By the time the debriefing was over in the hot tent, the pilots' flight suits were black with sweat. Finally, Laird ran a hand through his thatch of grizzled hair and cleared his throat.

"Doc, how did Buster manage to live long enough to get that plane home?"

By Doc's estimate, Buster couldn't have had enough blood left in him to run a medium-size cat. Had some supernatural force done the flying? Did it have anything to do with Buster's feeling for his airplane? Doc had seen pilots run their hands over the skin of a P-38 the way they might stroke a woman.

"I couldn't tell you, Sir. I've heard of such things. You saw one yourself. Laney, down on Guadalcanal."

Like Buster, Laney should have crashed in his riddled P-40 before he reached home. He'd lived long enough for Doc and Laird and Laney's crew chief to get the canopy open. He'd wanted to die among friends, Laney said. Laney had always been a joker. Doc had heard of another pilot somewhere in the South Pacific who had landed with his intestines on the floor of the cockpit, tangled in the control column. He'd lived long enough to say the squadron needed the plane. He was sorry about the mess in the cockpit. Laird whacked his foot. There was a stir of recognition among the pilots. Probably most of these lunatics, Doc thought, would fly home with half their blood on the floor of the cockpit, and maybe their intestines, too, in order to save an airplane.

At his desk in the dispensary tent, Doc poured two fingers of medicinal brandy into a beaker and tossed it down. He stared through the screen door at a bomb-splintered palm tree across the squadron street. He hadn't seen a pilot torn up like Buster since Guadalcanal, where they'd sometimes been shot to pieces while they were trying to land their planes. Buster's body now lay on a cot in the back room of the tent, behind Doc's office. Tomorrow, Buster would be taken to Port Moresby and buried under a white wooden cross. Roger, the chaplain, might read a few words. Maybe some of the pilots would be there. Steve, if he wasn't flying a mission. In general, young pilots acted as if they didn't believe in death. Once their wheels left the ground, they were gods. Their clever machines defied rules by which humans had been bound for millennia. Pilots did not even use the words *death* and *die.* They said a pilot *augured in,* or *bought the farm,* or *ate it.* They masked mortality in language, booze, sex, religious belief, anger. But there were injuries nothing could mask or repair.

The screen door opened and Steve stepped into the dispensary. He'd showered and changed his clothes and combed his yellow hair. There was a haunted look in his eyes.

"Can I see him, Doc?"

"I don't recommend it, Steve."

"I want to."

In the back room, Doc folded a sheet down to expose Buster's face. Steve stared.

"Buster always said if he got shot all to hell, he'd just roll over and augur in."

"But he didn't," Doc said.

After a moment, Steve stepped closer.

"I want to see where he was hit."

"Are you sure?"

"Yes."

Doc shrugged and folded the sheet down to Buster's waist. Steve recoiled. His face contorted and tears flooded his eyes. He sat down hard on a folding steel chair, put his face in his hands, and leaned on his knees with his shoulders shaking. "That son of a bitch," he sobbed. "That son of a bitch."

Doc had often seen grief turn to anger. In order to deal with their feelings, some men even blamed the pilot for his own death, accusing him of stupidity or incompetence. But it was Courtenay whom Steve blamed instead. In his greed for a kill, Courtenay had turned, with Buster covering his back. You never turned with a Zero, you fired and flew straight through at high speed. It was a wonder Courtenay hadn't been killed, too.

After a moment, Steve stopped crying, wiped his eyes on his arm, and stood up. Doc rummaged for medical criteria to give

Steve a few days' reprieve from flying. Doc and Marchetti watched their pilots the way a trainer watches his racehorses. Pilots had different tolerances. They got in moods, they got the twitches and the shakes. They did not see as well or react as fast or shoot as accurately. Sometimes they needed to be grounded and sent home for good. Steve looked as solid as any man in the squadron, but a pilot often knew his limits better than Doc did.

"How would you like to take a few days off?" Doc said. "I'll write a release."

"I'd rather fly, Doc. Thanks anyway."

It was the answer Doc had expected. When the screen door closed, Doc turned and watched to make sure Steve was headed for the old plantation house that served as the officers' club. The sagging tin-roofed building was the social center for the pilots, the place where they went to drink and gamble and talk about everything except death. Doc envied the speed at which young pilots bounced back from their losses. Sometimes when they climbed out of their cockpits, they looked as if they'd aged ten years. Within a couple of hours, they were showered and fresh-faced in clean white T-shirts with emblems of rank like fraternity pins at the middle of their chests, cutting up like college drunks.

Unlike the pilots, Doc could not forget fallen comrades. Forgetting somehow seemed to diminish not only the dead, but Doc himself. Soon after they moved up from Guadalcanal, Doc had begun printing the names of dead pilots on little crosses and setting them in rows in a forest clearing. He'd been careful to keep his behavior secret. Certain men in the squadron already considered him odd. Courtenay publicly imitated Doc's tics and twitches.

Doc unlocked a metal filing cabinet and removed three wooden crosses about ten inches long. He slipped the crosses into a manila envelope and closed and locked the file. From the top drawer of his desk, he took a wooden flute and slid it also into the envelope. Outside, he climbed into his jeep.

The Aussies had cut roads into the jungle a few months earlier, when the Japanese were thirty miles from Port Moresby. On one of the roads, at a place where the jeep could go no farther, Doc got out and squeezed through the brush toward a giant banyan tree. On the far side of the tree was a trail he'd found one day as he explored the fantastic pattern of roots buttressing the trunk. After a mile or so, Doc stepped into a clearing surrounded by forest giants soaring two hundred feet overhead. Creepers and air roots hung down everywhere. From a break in the dome of leaves, a column of sunlight fell into a patch of wildflowers. Iridescent butterflies danced in and out of the light. Doc had the feeling of being in a cathedral whenever he came here.

Near a patch of wildflowers stood thirty-one small crosses. Doc sat down on a rotting log and removed the three new crosses from the manila envelope. With a soft pencil, he scratched the name *Buster Kemp* on one cross, *Benjamin Marsh* on another, and *Tim Hansen* on the third. He broke off a piece of the log and pounded the crosses into the ground. Then he sat again and surveyed the graveyard. Doc had placed the crosses in perfect rows like the ones he'd seen in the vast military cemeteries in the States. He counted the crosses again. Thirty-four now, just since they'd moved up from Guadalcanal. Every time a pilot was lost or came home wounded, Doc wondered if he'd failed to see some warning sign—a tic, a mood, an obsessive behavior. The crosses did not account for all the pilots they'd lost, either. Doc made a cross for a pilot only if someone had seen him crash or explode in the air. A pilot who simply vanished sometimes reappeared after days on a life raft or weeks in the jungle.

Doc removed his wooden flute from the envelope and placed it to his lips. He began to blow, no recognizable melody, just what came to him, what sounded right. After a while, he stopped and looked at Buster's cross, remembering the reason Buster had once given for enlisting. Japanese soldiers were in the Aleutian Islands, halfway to the farm in Oregon. There was not a gun or bullet left in the hardware stores from Seattle to Portland. He'd helped his father stockpile bottles, rags, and kerosene for Molotov cocktails. Farmers were getting ready to dynamite the passes and burn their farms the way the Russians were doing as the Germans advanced. Buster's mother and sister had talked of committing suicide before they'd let themselves be captured by the Japanese.

Doc recalled his own feelings when he'd volunteered for combat. He had no mother and sister and children to protect, and his wife lived in the relative safety of their home three thousand miles from any shore where the Japanese might rape and pillage as they had in China. But he was a physician by temperament and training, a man whose life was dedicated to healing, and he saw the greatest need for his abilities on the front lines. Once the call for doctors went out, there had been no question about what he had to do.

Often when Doc came to visit his little graveyard, he found it hard to get to his feet and leave. There was another reason for his being here—maybe the reason underneath the reason. Sometimes Doc felt as if a graveyard was his true home. His mother had died giving birth to him, her only child. He'd been cared for by a neighbor woman, Mrs. Kraus, while his father worked in the steel mill. It was Mrs. Kraus who showed him where his mother's grave was. Mrs. Kraus who told him, as kindly as she knew how, what had happened. He understood instantly. He'd killed his mother. That was why his father had always seemed so distant, so hard to talk to, beyond reach. When Doc was old enough, he started riding his bike to the graveyard and sitting by his mother's grave. For a long time, he said nothing, then one day he found himself chanting, "I'm sorry, I'm sorry, I'm sorry . . ." He could not even say "mother," for the unfamiliarity of the word in his mouth.

Doc felt as if his mother's grave was the single speck of the world that belonged to him, a place more solid than the house where he slept and ate and hung his clothes. This graveyard felt like that. These had been his children to defend, more real than any he would ever have by his wife Lorraine or the body and spirit of any other woman. It was here that he came every few days to speak the litany of their names and to tell each one, "I'm sorry, I'm sorry," and to make a solemn promise to those still living that if he were called upon to do it, he would willingly lay down his own existence to save the life of any one of them.

FAMOUS ACES

Steve was Bongo Two, flying behind and to the right of Bix in a loose formation of sixteen P-38 Lightnings cruising east across the Owen Stanley Mountains. Their mission was to rendezvous with the bombers south of Lae, New Guinea, and fly cover. Bix led the fighters over snow-dusted peaks, zigzagging through a forest of towering cumulus until they broke out into clear blue sky. Three miles below lay a featureless gray-green rug of jungle all the way to the Solomon Sea. Danovich's flight of eight planes began to climb. They would fly top cover and dive out of the sun as the Japanese fighters closed on the lower flight or on the bombers.

They intercepted a formation of four-engine Liberators coming up the coast. They buzzed the bombers. The pilots and gunners were waving and grinning and giving the victory sign. The day before, they'd been jumped by ninety Japanese fighters. The odds were usually three or four to one against the P-38s. Plane for plane, they had the firepower and the Japanese had the maneuverability. Except for aces like John Bixby and Greg Danovich, the best tactic was to shoot and run. If they ran too far, though, the bombers were sitting ducks.

As they crossed a wide blue bay, Steve heard Bix's matter-of-fact drawl in his earphones.

"This is Bongo Leader. Snappers at two o'clock high."

Bix led them in a climbing sweep over the bombers. In the sky ahead, a cloud of black specks blossomed and grew darker by the second. Holding formation on Bix's wing, Steve checked his fuel, oxygen flow, safety belt, gun sight, gun heater, switches. Eight belly tanks dropped away.

"Bongo flight, this is Bongo Leader. Stay together as long as you can."

In Brisbane, the place to go to drink beer and talk flying and meet girls was the Lufbery Circle. Wooden propellers hung over the bar. Photographs of famous fliers lined the walls: Lindbergh, Chamberlin, Amelia Earhart. Aces of World War I and the heroic motorized kites that made the first ocean crossings. There were many other places to drink and meet girls, but the girls at the Lufbery Circle came there expressly to meet fliers. Bix said he felt as if he was coming home when he came to the Circle. Some of the girls had theories to explain their preference for fliers. Addie said it was because she and everybody she knew might be Japanese slaves today if it hadn't been for the fighter pilots at Port Darwin.

Bix and Danovich and Steve had staked out a corner full of overstuffed chairs and couches. Above them hung the largest picture of all—the World War I ace Raoul Lufbery, for whom the fighter tactic known as the Lufbery circle was named. Addie had invited three girls. Steve was still trying to sort them out by name. Addie lounged on the arm of Bix's chair with her body draped over his shoulders like a boa. Her half-lidded, humorous eyes watched Steve studying the girls. Addie's photo sat on the ammunition box next to Bix's cot in the tent he shared with Steve in the jungle up at Port Moresby. Her small, off-center mouth always seemed on the verge of some canny, maybe embarrassing observation of the sort Steve might get from an older sister.

In the crowd standing at the bar were uniformed American and Australian men talking flying. Their hands swooped and danced in the air and froze at critical angles to demonstrate punishing turns, deflection shots, maneuvers by which fighter pilots lived and died. Or they told jokes and roared with laughter, and the women with them laughed with embarrassed shrieks or hands over their mouths, and sometimes kicked a man in the shins.

A tall Australian with pilot's wings on his shirt walked toward Bix and Dan none too steadily, holding a glass in one hand.

"Captain Bixby and Captain Danovich," he enunciated carefully, "you blokes are all right." Bix and Danovich gave a friendly salute.

"Thank you, Lieutenant," Bix said.

"Sir," the pilot said, as an apparent afterthought, caught his balance, and returned to the crowd at the bar, where he stood looking back at Bix and Danovich with several others.

"You've been discovered," Addie said, stroking the back of Bix's neck with long, fine-boned fingers.

The Japanese opened fire before they were in range, so the P-38s seemed to be flying into a wall of tracer bullets. Bix and Steve fired at the same instant, a Zero exploded as they passed under it, and the first wave of fighters flashed by with red suns gleaming on their wings and fuselages. Steve heard someone yelling, "I'm hit, I'm hit! Somebody get this bastard off my tail!" Then Bix and Steve had their hands full, diving and twisting to get a half-dozen Zeros off their own tails. Steve heard a few thuds, knew he'd been hit, did a quick assessment, holes in the right wing, no streak of leaking fuel, the self-sealing tanks were doing their job. Then Bix growled, "Turn, baby." Steve dropped his flaps, hauled back on the yoke, and went into a shuddering, bone-crushing turn alongside Bix, with one wing pointed straight down at the ocean. It was a live-or-die maneuver, but the aces who had lived long enough were perfecting it, and Bix had been teaching it to Steve, and suddenly they were on the tail of three Zeros who were evidently so startled that they delayed a fatal millisecond. A wing and assorted pieces of junk separated from a Zero as Bix and Steve fired, the plane in Steve's gun sight flipped over and exploded, Bix swung toward the third and raked him as he turned away, the Zero began trailing smoke, the canopy opened, and the pilot jumped. This time, Steve and Bix were the ones who had delayed a millisecond too long. The sky swarmed with Japanese fighters getting lined up on them. Steve and Bix rolled into a dive and abruptly discovered P-38s all around. Danovich had come down out of the sun with his eight planes. There were burning Zeros falling out of the sky behind him. Bix and Steve joined Danovich's squadron in a climbing turn and they dived back into the main swarm.

They were keeping the Zeros busy. The contrails of fighters flying at full power streaked the sky like chalk scribbles of an angry child. Steve had a glimpse of the bombers flying north unopposed. Bix fired, and a Zero blew up ahead of him so close that Bix seemed to fly right into the explosion. Steve lost him. There were fighters on Steve's tail and coming at him from the sides and above. He had no time to look for Bix; he made every evasive maneuver he knew, scissor turns, sudden deceleration, found himself on the tail of a Zero, pushed the button, and missed. At the same instant, he glimpsed a Zero in his rearview mirror, broke sharply to the right, and everything in his cockpit seemed to explode. His face had been hit; instinctively he rammed the yoke forward and dived. He could not see. He tasted blood. He grabbed his scarf, tried to wipe his eyes, and discovered that his goggles had been knocked around to the side of his head. He could see a little better now, his forehead ached, he heard air screaming, his speed was getting critical. He throttled back, held the scarf to his forehead half-blind, trying to find the horizon and pull out before he hit the sound barrier or the ocean.

He leveled off a few hundred feet above the water. He saw no planes after him; the fight had gone elsewhere. He assessed the damage. His helmet was torn, his forehead cut, one lens of his goggles was cracked. His flight instruments were wrecked, compasses shattered, radio dead, oxygen hose cut in half. A bullet had gone through one fuel gauge and the other was unreadable, but he thought he had enough gas to get home. The controls responded as they should, and his engines thundered sweetly on either side of him. There was a tremendous draft blowing through the shattered side of the canopy, and through holes beside him where bullets had torn the radio off the cabin wall. He tied the scarf around his head to stop the bleeding, and finished cleaning his goggles. He made a cautious turn toward the coastline and began to climb, looking for enemy fighters or someone to fly home with.

The three girls were named Polly, Francine, and Rachael. Steve was beginning to make small talk with them. Polly was tall and self-contained. Francine was skinny, pretty, and a bit simple. Rachael appealed to Steve most. She had a mischievous look in her eye. She had grown up in the outback with Addie. She gave the overall impression of roundness—round eyes, round breasts, round hips, round high cheeks with a tapering heart-shaped face narrowing to a dimpled chin.

"What part of the outback are you from?" Steve asked.

"Rum Jungle."

He glanced at Addie to see if he was being teased.

"That's right," Addie said. "Near Birdum."

A group of men and women had come over from the bar and crowded around Bix and Danovich. A short major not much taller than Bix and Danovich introduced himself. Aide to General Kenney, he said. He clapped Danovich on the shoulder and grinned at Bix. "I read the reports every day," the major said. "What's the score now, boys?" He winked at Steve to let him know he knew of the rivalry between Bix and Danovich.

Bix's eyes were hidden under his bushy eyebrows while he filled his glass from a quart bottle.

"It's hard to say, Major. We haven't seen the newspapers yet."

The major laughed generously and clapped Danovich's shoulder again. Danovich's big soft-looking jaw made ruminant motions around his unlit cigar.

"Well, that's all right," the major said. "I'll get the score through official channels. The main thing is, Bong and Boyington and Lynch had better look to their laurels, eh? The way you boys are going. How do you do it?" He looked at his friends. "That's what I want to know. How do you do it?"

Danovich wrapped his stubby fingers around the cigar and removed it from his teeth, grinning.

"I use the aim-and-shoot method, myself."

When the laughter died down, he turned his slightly bulging eyes toward the three girls.

"Now, Bix here," Danovich said, "he uses psychokinesis."

The girls looked at each other, unsure who was being stared at, or why. The major grinned, uncertainly.

"What's psychokinesis?" Polly said.

"You know what mental telepathy is?" Danovich raised his hands, and his fingers became vibrating electrodes zapping his brain. "You send your thoughts into another person's mind. Right? Well, when

Bix uses psychokinesis, it's like sending his *hands* out." Danovich's eyes bulged whitely at the girls and his arm seemed to stretch like rubber across the table toward them. "He makes bullets go where he wants them to go," he said, hoarsely. "He takes the controls of an enemy plane and makes it dive into the ocean." Danovich's voice deepened to an ominous rasp. "He *touches* things, he *grabs* things, *he does exactly as he pleases!*"

The girls looked at Bix. Under his bushy eyebrows, Bix's eyes burned with lunatic fervor. The eyes of the girls darted back and forth from Bix to Danovich to Bix.

"Eeeeeeek!" Rachael cried out in mock fear, flinging her hip against Francine next to her on the couch. Francine gasped, and jumped, with her eyes locked on Bix's.

"What are you . . . ?" she cried, moving her hands first as if to shield her crotch, then her breasts.

"See?" Danovich said, hoarsely.

"Stop! What are you doing?" Francine cried, then screamed: *"Stop it!"*

A very large soldier in an Anzac hat plowed through the crowd and stood over Bix and Danovich, dwarfing them.

"'Ere now," he demanded, "what are you blokes up to?"

Steve stood up slowly. He'd done some boxing in college and didn't mind flexing a bit in front of Rachael.

"It's quite all right, Sergeant," he said. "They were demonstrating psychokinesis."

"You don't say. What's that?"

"They were touching things with their minds."

"Their minds, is it? What things?"

Polly giggled. The Anzac sergeant turned his attention to the girls.

"What things?" he demanded.

Francine cringed, as if she would like to disappear.

"Us," Rachael said.

The Anzac blinked, stepped back unsteadily, stared down at Bix and Danovich for a moment, then slapped his thigh.

"The Devil!" he roared. "Say, mates, do you think you could teach me to do that?"

Bix was staring at the girls. The afternoon light slanting through the window onto his shaggy eyebrows and sunburned high cheekbones made his eyes seem deeper than usual, sunk in shadow. He looked stricken.

"What is it?" Addie said, quietly.

"I humiliated her," he said.

"It was only a joke."

"Jesus. I need to apologize."

He got up and went around the low table and sat on it in front of the girls and spoke to them. All of them put their hands on him, on his hands or his arm or his knee. Francine put her hands on his face.

Steve was following a chain of small jungle-covered islands toward the mainland. Under his wing drifted turquoise lagoons surrounded by breakers and white sand reefs. He spotted a formation of two planes emerging from jungle background over water. There was something odd about them. Edging closer, he made out the twin booms of a P-38 flying wingtip to wingtip with a Zeke—a late-model Zero. What was going on? Steve shoved the throttles forward, wondered if his guns still worked, and pushed the button. There was a familiar roar and shudder, a burst of tracers out the nose, and a whiff of gun smoke. He was closing behind the Zeke. The P-38 should not be flying alongside it. The Zeke could maneuver faster in the first few degrees of turn.

As Steve got in gun range, he saw a flash of metal high and to the right. He was a second or two away from finishing off the Zeke and turning to meet this new threat when the flash became another fork tail, streaked past him, past the Zeke, pulled up overhead, and circled upside down for a better look. It reminded Steve of Buster, as much at home upside down as right side up. The P-38 descended, rolled out, and Steve saw Danovich's markings on the nose. By now, Steve could see Bix's markings on the P-38 flying alongside the Zeke. Bix was looking over at the Zeke. What was going on?

There were now three P-38s bracketing a Zeke. There was no way the Zeke could escape, but he was still dangerous. He could ram Bix. The pilot did not even have to be a kamikaze. A P-38 pilot had once rammed a Zeke after running out of bullets. Why was Bix so close? Without a radio, Steve had no way of finding out. It seemed crazy. He kept the Zeke centered in his gun sight, his thumb tensed on the button. The Zeke's wing dipped away from Bix and recovered. It fishtailed a little and began to drift, lost altitude, and recovered again. The Zeke was like a man staggering. Bix raised his hand. Was he saluting? The Zeke abruptly rolled over and dropped like a stone. Steve's training said go after it, but Bix waved him back and led him in a shallow dive, banking to watch. The Zeke flew straight down, shrinking to a dot in seconds. There was a tiny flash of white spray on the vast sheet of blue-black water, then nothing.

Steve turned toward the coast again. Danovich climbed away once more. Danovich never quit. He'd be hunting the enemy until his wheels touched down on the metal mesh at Port Moresby. Bix flew up alongside and examined the holes in Steve's plane, the shattered canopy, his bloody scarf. He dropped down and flew under Steve's plane to inspect it. When he came alongside again, he gave Steve the thumbs-up sign. No leaks or critical damage. Steve kept trying to catch Bix's eye behind the goggles. Steve held up the wreck of his radio like a trophy, stuck his tongue out, and dangled the end of his ribbed oxygen hose like a severed trachea, hoping to

get a laugh. No reaction. Bix throttled back and took up position behind and to the right, on Steve's wing. Something strange had happened with the Zeke. Danovich must be chewing on something,
too, apart from an unlit cigar stub. Maybe Bix was still ahead of him
in the ace race. Maybe that explained Danovich, prowling up there
on the edge of the stratosphere. He'd left without so much as a nod
at Steve's damaged plane.

Steve felt better with Bix flying near him. If Steve's plane fell
apart, Bix would have an idea where Steve had bailed out, or as
good an idea as anybody could have over this featureless gray jungle. If Steve bailed out near either coast, there was a fair chance he'd
be rescued. The Americans and the Dutch and Australians paid the
natives to bring fliers safely to places on the coast where they could
be picked up. If Steve had to bail out over the coastal enclaves occupied by the Japanese or over the cannibal and headhunter country inland, though, his chances were not good. It seemed like hours
before the sawtooth peaks of the Owen Stanleys began to emerge
from the haze along the horizon. The plane felt and sounded
healthy. Once in a while, to reassure himself, Steve rocked the
wings, fishtailed, and bucked the plane just enough to feel it.

Steve's head began throbbing. He wanted to loosen his scarf and
helmet, but he was afraid he'd start bleeding again. He wondered
how badly he was injured. He tried to remember the symptoms of
a fractured skull. Bleeding from the ears, he thought. Gingerly, he
slid his fingers inside the canvas helmet and moved an earphone
away from his ear. His fingers came out wet with blood. But the
blood could have come from his cut scalp; it proved nothing. His
arms and legs and senses all seemed to be working, so he probably
did not have a fragment of something in his brain. You never knew,
though. He'd heard of symptoms not appearing until later. He
probably wouldn't know anything for sure until he got home and
Doc had a look at him.

. . .

Addie had squeezed herself down in the big leather chair alongside Bix and was pensively twisting a short lock of his wiry brown
hair. "I took statistics at the university," she said. "I've made a
study of fighter pilots. Would you like to know your chances of living till the end of the war?"

"No," Bix said.

"It might help you understand why I won't marry a fighter pilot.
At least not until the war ends."

Bix did not answer.

"I don't want any other kind of man, you know. My husband was
killed at Darwin only a year ago. I'm just beginning to live again, Bix."

Steve knew Bix wanted to marry her. Steve wondered if he
should pretend not to hear. It seemed like such intimate stuff. An
audience did not seem to bother Addie, though. Maybe this was the
kind of girl they raised in the outback. In spite of her words, it was
hard to understand why she would not marry Bix. She sat on him,
around him, under him, seemingly so merged that when one of
them stood up, it was sometimes startling to remember that they
consisted of two bodies after all. One of her hands always seemed
to be inside Bix's hair, in his shirt or a pocket, and one of Bix's
hands always rested lightly on the little rise of her belly or her thigh
or neck or ribs, a part of her costume. She seemed on the verge of
tears, or anger.

"Because you've lived long enough to become aces doesn't mean
a bloody thing," she said. "I know you hero types. You get a few
victories and you start thinking you're immortal. You fly differently. I saw it. It happened to Decker. Hazelton, Rauch, LeFevre.
They got cocky. They got too big for their boots."

She sounded like a combat pilot with a thousand missions. She had known all of them at Port Darwin. She'd kept in touch with the few who were still alive. Pilots came down from the islands and told her the latest stories.

"I'm safe," Steve said. "I'll never be an ace."

"You're doing fine, Steve. Lyska flew forty-seven missions before he had a victory." She knew her facts. The pilots couldn't argue with her.

"I guess you heard about McGuire," Danovich said.

Even pilots who didn't like McGuire felt his loss. He'd wrecked a few P-38s turning too hard, pulling out of dives too fast. He'd come home in P-38s that flew so cockeyed they were good for nothing except salvage, but he'd been a scourge of the Japanese air force. The more of them he knocked down, the fewer Americans and Aussies were lost.

"He's another," Addie said.

Bix patted her on the hip.

"Let's talk about something else, Addie."

"I'm done," she said brightly, bouncing her leg over Bix's knee to the beat of a tune on the jukebox. She had her own knack of sudden turns.

Steve had been catching Rachael's eye a bit. He thought he'd try his luck again.

"Did you say you're from Rum Jungle or Birdum?"

"Birdum."

"I could have sworn you said Rum Jungle."

"Well, they're not far apart."

She was definitely twisting his tail.

Danovich was chewing his cigar, studying Polly and Francine.

"Where are you from?"

"Humpty Doo," said Polly.

"Mistake Creek," said Francine.

• • •

When Steve left the infirmary tent, Major Marchetti, the squadron CO, was waiting in a battered jeep in his pith helmet, with his long legs crooked up on either side of the steering wheel.

"How do you feel?"

Steve climbed into the jeep. "A few stitches. Doc says I can fly to-morrow."

Marchetti eyed Steve's bandaged head skeptically.

"It's only a scratch," Steve said. "Flying glass or something."

Marchetti nodded. "We lost Marsh."

"I thought so." It had sounded like Marsh on the radio. Steve would miss his belly laugh, his mangled quotations from Shake-speare, even the garbage dump in the corner of his tent that he cleaned out only when General Laird flew in to give them a little encouragement.

"What happened to Bix?" Bix hadn't turned up at debriefing. Steve told Marchetti what he knew. Marchetti was a good com-mander. He watched his pilots as closely as Doc did. He sometimes knew before Doc did that a pilot needed an unscheduled rest leave. The jeep bounced along a dirt road through a splintered coconut plantation toward the jungle canopy that hid the squadron's tents from the Japanese bombers.

Bix was lying on his cot in his shorts, half hidden behind the mosquito net. They were all sweating. Marchetti pulled up an am-munition box and sat down.

"How you doing, Ace?"

"Okay."

Marchetti rubbed his big forehead for a while. Sitting on the low box, he looked like a giant grasshopper grooming himself. Steve sometimes wondered how he got those legs inside the cockpit of a fighter.

"Bix," Marchetti said, "I hear you were flying formation with a Zeke."

There was a long silence.

"He didn't have any face, Bob."

"No face?"

"There wasn't anything left below his nose. Stuff hanging. Blood squirting out."

"It's a wonder he was conscious."

"Yeah."

"Why didn't you finish him off?"

"I saw it hit him, Bob. I could swear I saw the bullet hit him. His face exploded. I was so close I almost rammed him. I came around to have a look. He wasn't going to fight any more. I tried to finish him off. . . ." Bix stopped. Marchetti waited.

"He looked at me."

"Looked at you?"

"Like he wanted to tell me something. Then he rolled over and went in."

Marchetti stared at the canvas floor for a while. He did not say it was bad tactics. They all knew it was bad tactics. They also knew there were times when the rules did not apply. They knew Bix's intuitions, they flew by them, even Marchetti sometimes.

"Bix," Marchetti said, "half my pilots are down with malaria. If you don't want to fly tomorrow, it's okay."

"I'll fly."

"You don't have to."

"I'll fly."

At the tent flap, Marchetti stopped and looked back.

"You're still ahead."

"Shit," Bix said.

When Bix was ahead, Danovich worked his jaw muscles a lot, scolded junior officers, and became an obnoxious poker player.

They could already hear his bullhorn voice two tents away, ordering somebody to deal cards and stop wasting time swatting mosquitoes. Danovich knew the score of all the major aces in the Pacific, and most in Europe. Bix couldn't care less. If you wanted Bix's score, you had to ask his crew chief. In the air, Bix and Danovich had saved each other's life, and Steve's, too. Their teamwork was silken, professional, deadly. But on the ground, there was this tension. Now there was tension in the air, too.

"Maybe you should play poker with him," Marchetti said. "Try to lose."

As the sound of Marchetti's jeep faded in the jungle, Steve watched Bix wrestle with whatever was haunting him.

"Maybe we should, Bix."

He swung his feet off the cot.

"Let's do it."

Steve marveled at how fast he pulled it together. Steve couldn't have.

Danovich paid no attention to them for the first few hands. The pilots sat on ammunition boxes and dealt cards on a cable drum somebody had scrounged from the Corps of Engineers. Mosquitoes whined around the naked lightbulb like a cloud of tiny fighters. Every so often, one would hit the hot bulb and fall out of the swarm like a stricken plane. Danovich was losing. He threw his tattered cigar stub out the door of the tent and fished in his shirt pocket for the other half while Steve raked in a pot. Danovich rolled the cigar on his tongue and stared at Bix.

"Who was your buddy in the Zeke?"

"I couldn't tell," Bix said. "His face was blown off."

"Poor boy. Good thing it wasn't your face."

"You can say that again."

They picked up their new cards and arranged them.

"Exactly what maneuver was that you were using?" Danovich said. "I don't remember it from fighter school."

"PK," Bix said. "Psychokinesis."

"I know what PK is. What I want to know is, how reliable is it?"

"Get off his back, Dan. He's made a full report to Marchetti." Steve was startled by his own voice. He'd never stood up to Danovich except in training, in the air. There was a murmur of agreement around the table. Danovich's eyes bulged at Steve, at Bix, and at the circle of pilots. He discarded, and took an extra-long time arranging his new cards.

"Well, just tell me one thing, Bix. How did you know that meatball wouldn't ram you?"

"Telepathy."

Danovich shook his head slowly and gave a deep sigh.

"Telepathy. May the Lord help us and preserve us."

When Rachael came back from the loo, Danovich grabbed her hand and guided her to a chair next to him. Steve had the sinking feeling he got when he heard bullets thumping into his plane. Danovich clenched his cigar in his teeth, grinning.

"Would I like Humpty Doo?" he said.

"Not Humpty Doo," she said. "Birdum."

"Birdum, then."

"Let me see your teeth."

"Why my teeth?"

"Come along. Let me see your teeth."

Danovich removed his cigar and opened his mouth.

"You'll need big strong teeth," Rachael said. "We eat eucalyptus bark and raw lizards in the outback. Open wide." She recoiled. "Poo. You have swamp breath." She rummaged in her purse. She handed him a small packet of mints. "Here, chew these. And throw that cigar away."

"I didn't know you had swamps in the outback."

"We have everything in the outback. Don't we, Francine?"

"I don't know. I've never been there."

"Well, you live in Australia. Addie knows. Don't you, Addie?"

"If I had any sense," Addie said, "I'd fall in love with bomber pilots. They're more like family men. Their crews are their family. They can't go around getting themselves killed, competing with each other."

"Who's competing?" Bix said.

"You blokes don't even talk to each other."

"We talk to each other all the time."

"Yes. Bongo One, this is Stogie One, do you read me?"

"We play poker every day."

Addie bounced her leg over Bix's knee, looking at Danovich.

"What about the hard feelings when you lose?"

"Me?" Danovich said. "I don't have any hard feelings. Do you, Bix?"

"Hard feelings? What for?"

"That's what I say."

"We came down from Moresby together," Bix said. "Here we are. Right, Steve?"

Steve didn't feel like covering for anybody, not even Bix. He'd been thinking of things to say that might amuse Rachael when she came back from the loo.

"Right," he said.

He'd always been mixed up about Danovich. When Steve first joined the squadron, Danovich insisted on being called Captain Danovich. He reprimanded Steve for not saluting him. He ordered Steve around like a servant. Then, late one night, Steve heard someone out in the jungle playing "Ave Maria" on a harmonica. He found himself all choked up. Later he discovered that the musician was Danovich. Even so, Steve could not like him the way he liked Bix. One of the first things Bix ever told him was "Call me Bix. When you need me to come shoot a Zero off your tail, you won't have time to say Captain Bixby." Addie was right, Steve thought he was immortal, but his immortality had a lot to do with what these two old men of twenty-five were teaching him about flying.

Addie's eyes had fixed on Steve. There was an ironic curlicue in one corner of her mouth.

"Sometimes I think we should call this place Klein's bottle," she said.

"What's that?" Polly said.

"It's a model of the Einsteinian universe," Danovich said.

"There are no straight lines in the universe," Bix said. "If you go far enough, you'll meet yourself going."

"I always thought," Rachael said, "that if you could see far enough, you'd be looking at your own bum."

"I like to think if you go far enough, you come face-to-face with yourself," Addie said.

"Think of it as a Lufbery circle," Danovich said. "You'd end up shooting yourself down."

"You blokes scare me," Francine said.

"Humpty Doo," said a tall, wobbly beanpole figure topped by an Anzac hat over Rachael's shoulder. She turned to look.

"Birdum," she fired back.

"Banka Banka," the beanpole said in a loud, shrill voice, followed by a sound of strangulation evidently intended as laughter.

"Pandie Pandie," Polly offered, catching on.

"Pigeon Hole," Addie said.

"Bushy Park!" the beanpole cried, nearly falling as one leg collapsed and recovered, righting himself without spilling his beer. "Beetaloo!" he challenged. "Rumbum!" Strangled laughter, followed by a sip of beer as the girls applauded.

"Bumpalong!" Francine offered, getting in the spirit.

"Kittakittaooloo!" Rachael said.

The beanpole looked pregnant with inspiration, gathering himself up precariously to full height.

"Cadibarrawirricanna!" he yelled, triumphantly lost his balance, nearly fell, recovered in a rubbery spasm that started at his feet and traveled up his body until it snapped his head sideways, nearly launching his hat across the room. Strangled laugh, sip of beer, as they all cheered and raised their glasses high.

The mission started out as a rerun of the day before. The wall of backlit towering cumulus stood along the crest of the Owen Stanley Range. In all other directions, crystal blue sky filled the bowl of the world. On this morning, as on others, Steve was half drunk with the sizzle of takeoff, the privilege and power of climbing into the cool sweet air high above the jungle where ordinary mortals dripped with sweat and moved at a snail's pace. At cruising altitude, the sun was warm and comforting on his head and shoulders. He had slit his khaki helmet to take the pressure off the bandages. His Allison engines thundered tirelessly on either side of him. The flow of air through the spinning propellers, around the pod and across the airfoils of a P-38, sang a song, pilots said, more beautiful than the song of any other aircraft.

They crossed the mountains in two flights of eight again, with Danovich's flight climbing to fly high cover. They met the bombers, buzzed them, crisscrossed the sky until they unloaded their bombs. Steve wondered if his childhood friend Blake Hurlingame was piloting one of the bombers. He knew Blake was based somewhere in the islands around New Guinea. No Japanese fighters appeared. Sometimes this happened. Sometimes it was a ruse. Bix led them far south until the bombers were safe. Then they headed for the mainland with plenty of fuel to get home. They loosened the formation, keeping within a few hundred feet of each other. Steve could not have asked for a better way to fly home, with a sky full of friends in the world's most beautiful aircraft, and no losses. He trimmed the controls and kicked back to enjoy the scenery. They crossed the coastline south of Tufi with Bix navigating, and vectored toward Port Moresby. On the horizon ahead was the sawtooth line of white-tipped peaks.

"Bongo flight," Bix said, "let's climb to fourteen thousand."

Another voice crackled in Steve's ears.

"Why don't you just give the snappers our coordinates while you're at it?"

It was silly of Danovich to scold about radio silence this late in the mission. By now, they were out of range of the Japanese bases.

"Not a bad idea, Stogie," Bix drawled. "I wouldn't mind a little action."

Steve advanced throttles, trimmed for a leisurely climb, and was getting his engines in sync when two things seemed to happen instantaneously. There was a flash in the corner of his eye, and he registered the image of a P-38, bottom view, standing on its nose where Bix should be. By the time Steve turned his head, that volume of sky was empty. He flipped over and saw two P-38s disappearing straight down. He hauled back on the yoke and went after them. There was a chance the Japanese had captured a P-38. He pressed his radio button.

"This is Bongo Two," he said. "What's going on?"

"Bongo, this is Stogie Two. Stogie One just buzzed you. We're coming down."

By the time Steve matched speed, the two planes were pulling out of the dive into a turn. A row of silver needles streamed down on his left, flashing as they turned to get lined up on the duelists. Steve was ahead of them with the wheel practically in his lap, hoping Bix was on Danovich's tail. He was. Steve shoved the throttle full forward, trying to take up his position on Bix's wing. Suddenly, the duelists flipped over and dived again, leaving Steve standing. When he spotted them, they were climbing straight up. Planes with more altitude circled, watching. Danovich barrel-rolled going straight up and pulled out in an Immelman, still rolling. Bix was a few yards behind, still on his tail. Danovich flipped over and went straight down, zigzagging. Bix followed. Steve dived after them, matched speed, watched his airspeed needle move into the red zone, and hauled back on the yoke as they began their pullout. His plane began to shudder, he began to black out, he could break apart under these stresses, he eased up on the yoke and immediately lost the duelists. When he pulled out, they were miles away in a series of turning, twisting maneuvers that allowed him to catch up.

Steve joined the rest of the planes, circling and trying to keep the duel in sight. The sky was full of flashing and sparkling as planes kept changing their angles to the sun. Sometimes Bix was on Danovich's tail, sometimes Danovich on Bix's. They pulled out of dives and went into high-speed turns so savagely that Steve half expected to see wings or tails fly off. Danovich dropped his flaps and seemed to stop in midair, trying to make Bix overshoot him. Bix was too quick. Bix tried the same maneuver. Danovich was too quick. Several times, one tried to turn tighter than the other in a Lufbery circle, and one or both spun out. A few times, Steve slid in close to his wing position near Bix, only to be flung off in a maneuver so violent that he could not see risking his ship and his life for a flying lesson. He felt himself slammed around the sky by forces he had only trifled with. It made him think of McGuire. Was this what it took to be an ace?

The battle went on until Steve remembered that they'd been using up fuel at a prodigious rate. He pressed his radio button.

"Bongo leader," he said. "Check your fuel gauge. We better head for home if we want dinner tonight."

All planes in the sky abruptly aligned themselves in the same direction like a school of fish. They throttled down to cruising speed, gradually moving in closer to keep an eye on the duelists. Even at a distance, Steve could see the cockeyed angles of their tails, the bent booms. Nobody said anything on the way home.

Addie had bought a superb white silk scarf for Bix. They passed it around to feel how smooth it was. The girls at the Lufbery Circle were the first Steve had met who knew why fighter pilots wore silk scarves. Most people thought it was vanity. Without the scarves, they would chafe their necks raw on their collars, rubbernecking for enemy fighters. Addie draped it around Bix's neck and smoothed it down, leaning away to admire it.

"So what brings you to Brisbane again so soon?" Addie said. "Did somebody get the shakes?"

"You could say that," Bix said.

Addie sized Steve up.

"What's the real story, Steve?"

"Well, things got a little hairy for a while there."

"I'll bet." She was waiting. It was hard to resist that curlicue at the corner of her mouth.

"We decided, the hell with it. Let Bong and Boyington win the war."

"Right." She wasn't buying it, but Bix liked it. Danovich winked at Steve. He was groping around for something at least halfway truthful when a waiter arrived with a fresh armload of frosty Australian beer bottles, followed by three American pilots and a couple of fliers wearing navigator's wings. One of the pilots said, "We hear you're the guys who've been flying cover for us over Lae. We wanted to buy you a drink."

"To you, too, gentlemen," Bix said, raising his glass.

One of the pilots stood near Bix.

"I always wanted to wear a silk scarf."

"It's a great life if you don't weaken," Danovich said.

"We do get to fly upside down a bit," Bix said.

It was one of their favorite recreations, trying every known maneuver inverted. It was also frowned on by Fighter Command. One of the pilots laughed.

"We had a whole squadron escorting us upside down the other day. Was that you guys?"

Danovich grinned.

"You see funny things in the air. I know a transport pilot who swears a Buck Rogers rocket ship escorted him from Christmas Island halfway to Fiji."

The pilots laughed.

"We haven't been able to do that stuff since we were in Primary," one said.

"We'd spill our coffee," another said.

"I'd swear those guys were upside down for ten minutes."

"Nah, more like three."

"At least eight."

"You can't be upside down more than five minutes without passing out."

"I can do fifteen," Addie said.

"Impossible."

"Really?"

"Absolutely."

"Would you like to bet?"

"How much?"

Addie looked at Bix.

"Five pounds?"

Bix put a five-pound note on the table.

"How are you going to prove it?"

Addie extracted herself from the chair beside Bix and stood up. She pulled her dress up and began tucking it into her panties, exposing her stockinged legs and garters. The men began cheering. Rachael jumped up and began tucking her dress in also. The men cheered louder.

"Place your bets!" Danovich yelled. "Step right up, folks!"

Men, and some of the women, too, threw bills on the table. Others covered them. Addie and Rachael kneeled on the large, low table and tipped themselves up into a headstand. The uproar increased. The betting accelerated. Francine screamed with excitement, tucked up her skirt, and joined Addie and Rachael on the table. Steve was struck by Francine's lovely legs. She was not skinny at all. She was slim. The cheers were deafening. The entire crowd at the bar surged over to their corner. People came in off the street. The rubber beanpole in the Anzac hat gave a prolonged and agonized strangle of joy, fell down, and had to be set upright again, his hat restored and a new glass of beer poured for him.

For the condition of their planes, Bix and Danovich made remarkably smooth landings. As Steve rolled down the runway working his brakes behind Bix, he spotted a red-nosed P-38 parked next to the control tower. Maybe Laird was getting ready to fly back to headquarters. A small group of men stood near the plane, watching the landings. As Steve taxied past them toward the revetments, he recognized Doc, and General Laird leaning on his cane next to Marchetti. Laird was the youngest general Steve had ever seen, one of the first aces in the Pacific. The crashes he'd survived had left him with prematurely grizzled hair.

In the briefing tent, Laird sat looking at the pilots as they made their reports. He knew them all by first names, even second lieutenants. The glint in his eye was hard to read. When they were through, he stood up and congratulated them, an undermanned squadron always hurting for operational aircraft, he said, turning the tide of war in the Pacific. When he got back from headquarters, he'd be handing out medals. Meanwhile, he'd like Bix and Dan and Steve to stay for a little chat. As the last of the pilots filed out, Doc and Marchetti, too, remained in their seats. Laird shook his head slowly, side to side.

"When I saw that first plane landing, I thought, my God, Tom McGuire has come back from the dead."

Laird lit a cigarette, dragged on it, and blew smoke. When he looked up, Steve felt as if he were flying broadside at the *Yamato*.

"What the hell do you think this is," Laird said, "a sandbox?"

"I guess we got a bit carried away, Sir," Danovich said.

"Don't give me that 'Sir' crap. We flew together on Guadalcanal. You used to have some sense. What happened to it?"

The *Yamato*'s guns converged on Steve.

"Where were you when all this was going on?"

"I was trying to figure it out, Sir."

"Did you figure it out?"

"I thought at first the Japs might have captured a P-38. I called Stogie Two and found out it was a duel. We do that sometimes to keep on our toes."

"Have you done it?"

"Yes, Sir."

"Did you destroy your aircraft?"

"No, Sir. But I don't have twenty-three victories, either."

Steve had no idea where that came from, the logic of panic. Laird had the mercy to laugh. In fact, it seemed as if he had to force himself to stop laughing.

"So you don't have twenty-three victories," he said. "Well, you have three, and you're still alive. That's something I'm personally grateful for. I hope you are, too."

"Yes, Sir."

"Steve wasn't in it, Sir," Bix said. "It was just Dan and me."

"Don't tell me how to do my job, Bix. Steve is here in case he decides to get the Famous Ace itch like the rest of us idiots. Do you read me, Steve?"

"Yes, Sir."

Probably no other man on the planet could get to them the way Laird could. He'd flown with Chennault in China, then in Burma. He'd had his foot blown off dive-bombing a Japanese cruiser. In the first days on Guadalcanal, he'd taken off in a war-weary P-40 to battle alone with a dozen Japanese fighters and bombers so his returning pilots would have a runway to land on.

Bix and Danovich were sort of shrinking under his gaze.

"You could be tried for committing an act of sabotage in wartime. Do you know the penalty for that?"

"Yessir."

Laird blew smoke, letting it sink in.

"This may be hard for you to believe, but there actually are things even famous aces can't get away with."

"Yessir."

Bix and Danovich were as still as birds in the tall grass. Laird whacked his cane against the side of his artificial foot.

"All right. I've been in a few Lufbery circles myself. I know how it gets. You know damn well I can't court-martial you—you're the best I've got. I'll cover your ass if you'll do me a personal favor."

They waited while he studied their faces.

"Decide which war you want to fight—against the Japanese or against yourselves. Okay?"

"Yessir."

Laird whacked the side of his foot again.

"You might need a little time to make a big decision like that. There are three new P-38s waiting on the ramp at Brisbane. I don't want to see you back here for two weeks." His eyes checked out Steve's bandages. "You, too, Steve. Go make sure these guys eat their cereal."

CEILING ZERO

Every morning at dawn, weather permitting, the P-38s of Doc's squadron took off from Port Moresby and crossed the Owen Stanley Mountains to fly cover for the bombers. The Japanese fighters that came up to meet them outnumbered the P-38s three or four to one. The squadron lost one or two planes every week, and recently, three. It might have been only one, or even none, if Bix and Danovich had been flying. But Doc the flight surgeon had seen the signs of combat fatigue in his top aces, and General Laird had agreed to pack them off to Australia, along with Bix's wingman, Steve. Their orders were to indulge in the pleasures of Brisbane for two weeks and then fly three new P-38s back to Port Moresby.

The aces had no sooner returned home than Doc began to wonder if rest leave had restored Bix's cool, steady judgment or only made matters worse. One morning, Doc sat in his jeep next to the control tower and watched Bix make an especially foolhardy takeoff. When his plane reached flying speed on the runway, instead of pulling his nose up, he retracted his wheels and allowed the plane to accelerate with the propellers almost clipping the ground. Just as Bix seemed about to hit the jungle wall, he pulled up into a nearly vertical climb and vanished into the overcast.

The next day, Bix and Danovich and several other pilots shot down Zeros. Doc usually learned of these when returning planes flew low over the field doing victory rolls. It was dangerous to roll at low altitude, and Marchetti, the squadron commander, had talked of forbidding it. One plane came across the field rolling not much more than a wingspan above the runway. As it flew past the control tower upside down, Doc saw the name of Bix's Australian girlfriend, Addie, in big orange cursive letters on the nose. Bix had never bothered with a victory roll in Doc's memory, let alone a roll anywhere near the ground.

After debriefing, Doc went looking for Bix. Somebody had seen him in a truck headed for the repair tents. As Doc passed the field, a C-47 transport drifted over the road with its engines throttled back, letting down toward the runway. Doc recognized the plane that flew men back and forth on rest leave. There might be mail from the squadron box at the Lufbery Circle, their favorite pub in Brisbane. Private mail delivery was against regulations, but a man could be long dead before a letter from his Aussie girlfriend arrived by military post. The pilot handed Doc a packet of letters. In his jeep, Doc idly thumbed through them, reading names. There was one to Bix from Addie, addressed in a handwriting of fine, well-formed letters. There was a thick envelope with Doc's name on it in the same handwriting.

On leave from Guadalcanal, Doc had spent some time with Bix and Addie in Brisbane, envying the way they twined around each other like two vines in the big leather chairs at the Lufbery Circle, and the way their faces glowed in each other's presence. Addie had asked Doc if she could write to him, but he hadn't really expected her to. For several weeks, the memory of her big, intelligent hazel eyes and the touch of her hand in his had triggered an episode of combat tics and twitches. Doc opened the thick envelope with an uncomfortable mixture of happiness and apprehension.

"Dear Doc," Addie began. "How I wish I could see you in person again. With my aunt in England for the duration, you are the only other being I know who might help me understand the events of the past week. You will have seen Bix by now, back in the squadron. I've given him such a shock that I wonder if I know who I am, and I worry terribly how he's taken it."

There's your answer, Doc grumbled to himself. Woman trouble can kill a pilot as surely as combat fatigue.

It had all started, Addie wrote, one evening at her aunt's beach house in the dunes north of Brisbane. They'd driven up in two cars—she and Bix, Dan and Rachael, Steve and Francine—loaded down with cases of beer, a box of records for the hand-crank phonograph, and a football Dan had carried with him from America. They'd been sitting on the veranda, listening to the soft rumble of surf and watching a red sun sink above the western hills, when the lads began talking about Steve's friend Buster. How he'd flown almost all the way across New Guinea with his throat shot out, his shoulder gone, and his lung exposed. It didn't seem possible, yet there it was.

Strange things happened in the air, Danovich had said. PK. Telepathy. You heard voices. Something told you which way to turn to escape the bullets. Once, he said, he'd felt something grab the controls and turn the plane *for* him.

Addie said Kevin had told her something like that, once. Rachael and Francine had looked at her, surprised. She was surprised, herself. She hardly ever spoke her dead husband's name, even to her best friends.

The Japanese fleet had been offshore, over the horizon, Addie told them. Carrier planes had been bombing Port Darwin around the clock. The invasion of Australia was expected any day. Most of the pilots' wives had left. Kevin wanted Addie to go, too. She refused. He said do you know what the Japanese do to the women they capture? She said she knew. In a week, the Australians had lost most of their planes and pilots. They had only a half dozen left. A few replacements flew in, but they seemed to arrive just in time to get shot down. The odds were terrible. One day they sent up three war-weary P-40s and a damaged Spitfire against seventy or eighty Japanese fighters. Kevin told her he thought the only reason he was still alive was that she was there. Addie had asked why that was so. He said sometimes he heard her tell him to look behind him, and sometimes it was as if she had pushed the stick or kicked his rudder pedal just in time to escape the bullets. He'd been quiet for a while, holding her, then he said he didn't see, though, how even she could help him fight much longer against such odds. The next day, he was killed.

Addie wrote that she might not have told the story if they hadn't been drinking strong Australian beer all afternoon. It had loosened everybody's tongue. Danovich laughed about the planes he and Bix had ruined, dueling with each other. Danovich confessed that he'd turned with a Zero a few times, trying to get a kill when Bix had pulled ahead of him in total victories. The barest flicker of a smile had appeared on Bix's thin lips, and Addie knew instantly that Bix had done the same thing trying to get ahead of Dan.

She'd said wonderful, why didn't Bix and Dan simply take their forty-fives out in the dunes and decide who was the best once and for all? Bix said they weren't shooting at each other. They'd pushed their planes to the limit and found out how much they could take. It was useful information. Addie said she wasn't talking about information, she was talking about turning with the Japs. Steve had to stay on Bix's wing to cover him. Wasn't that how Courtenay got Buster killed? Bix said he'd never done it with Steve on his wing.

Addie had felt herself begin to panic. Did he mean that he did it with nobody to cover him? Bix said sometimes they couldn't help it. To save a friend's life.

Addie wrote that something had snapped inside her. Oh God, she'd cried, that's what Kevin said. She ran into the house with her hand over her mouth. She'd never spoken to Bix in anger, and it shocked her as much as hearing that Bix took the same risks Kevin had, and for the same reasons.

The following morning, Addie said, she felt more like herself again. She'd apologized to Bix for snapping at him. The trouble was that she loved him too much. The fear of losing him made her a little crazy. He told her that in spite of how it seemed, he actually took fewer chances because of her.

After breakfast they'd gone down through the dunes for their morning swim. They'd just come out of the water and were spreading out towels to lie in the sun when the wind brought a familiar thunder to their ears. A P-38 was cruising along the shoreline toward them, a hundred feet above the water. They jumped to their feet, cheering and waving towels and beer bottles. The pilot gave them the V-sign. The plane shot past with the whistling, singing sound a P-38 makes even with the engines at full throttle, and began a climbing turn out to sea. For a few minutes, it gave them a dazzling display of aerobatics, diving, looping, rolling, then it leveled off high up, sparkled once in the sun, and continued on its way.

I've always wanted to do that, Addie had said. Me, too, Rachael said, with her pale oval face still turned toward the sky. Francine said, did she mean fly a fighter? No, just ride in one, Addie said. Just once in her life. To see what it was like.

The men stared at each other. Danovich said, were they thinking what he was thinking? Bix squinted at the long, flat stretch of wet beach. There was nobody in sight for miles. Actually, he said, they *were* supposed to give the birds a test flight before they took them home. Steve said, but not with the girls. They could be court-martialed. Danovich said, who was going to find out.

It had taken them no time to work out the details. They walked the hard, wet sand to make sure it would hold. Planes as big as a B-24 had landed on wet sand and taken off, Danovich said. They would not be able to fit a passenger behind the seat without removing radio equipment, but they'd heard a story about a P-38 pilot in occupied France who had made a forced landing in a field. Rather than let him be captured, his flight leader landed alongside, sat the pilot in his lap, and flew him out. It was a squeeze, but they got home. It would be a piece of cake, Bix said, especially if they didn't take parachutes.

Doc lowered Addie's letter to the steering wheel and stared across the landing strip at the jungle wall. There were certain pilots for whom war did not seem dangerous enough. They had to up the ante. Were they trying to distract themselves from war, or from something worse than war?

Addie wrote that she could hardly believe what she was doing as she climbed into the cockpit. She was still trying to understand what happened to her, sitting on Bix's lap, feeling as if they were one body, so tightly held against him was she by the safety belt. First there had been the takeoff, the long surge of power until the wings gripped the air, then the earth and sea fell away underneath, a thrill she'd only half imagined from Kevin's descriptions.

They'd flown out over the ocean so as not to attract attention. The other planes flew alongside for a while before swooping off by themselves. Reaching around her waist, Bix had experimented with the controls, then told her to hold tight. The sky and ocean whirled around her several times and stopped with the ocean underneath. They turned on their side and fell weightless and rose again, turning the other way as she'd seen hawks do, hanging lazily on the wind over the dunes. Then Bix shoved the throttles and the wheel forward, and her body lifted up, pulling against the safety straps. They headed straight down, the engines roared as the plane went faster, Bix brought the wheel back against her stomach, the nose came up, and she was crushed down against him, beginning to black out, then the pressure stopped and they were climbing straight up, as if they would leave the planet. Soon she was weightless at the top of a loop with the ocean above her head, and then they were diving again, she saw pale green needles spinning on the dial faces in front of her, the air was clawing at the canopy like a wild beast inches from her face, and as their speed built up she felt a burst of fear, then a stronger burst as gravity hit her, crushing her, the world disappeared around her and suddenly she was somebody else, she was Kevin, all she knew of Kevin was still inside her, it burst out of hiding, she felt his last dive, everything he'd felt, the bullets shredding his body, her body, the explosion, the broken wings, the torn limbs, her limbs, everything spinning, tumbling, bleeding, burning, falling toward the ocean.

Doc had to stop the tics and twitches in his arms and face and remind himself to breathe. Doc had his own problems with combat fatigue.

Addie had hidden her feelings as she climbed from the plane and waved to Bix taking off. That night, Bix had held her, trying to calm her while she explained, but she kept finding herself in the fighter cockpit with Kevin's broken body, sobbing, for all of them of course, but mostly for Kevin, who'd suffered the worst of it.

Doc could not finish reading. He drove back to the tents. He left Bix's letter on the ammunition box next to Addie's picture, and distributed the others. In his office, Doc poured himself a double shot of brandy and stared at Addie's letter on the desk in front of him. He was not sure he wanted to read it to the end. He had a bad feeling about it.

Addie said that ever since their plane ride, Rachael and Francine had been giggling and whispering like schoolgirls. Addie had only recently discovered the reason. Over the ocean, sitting on Dan's lap, Rachael had joined the mile-high club. She and Dan had enjoyed it so much that they'd done it twice, and had been the last plane to land. Addie said she envied Rachael and Francine, who could live with a man for two weeks, hear that he'd been killed, shed a few tears, and go live with another. They were not hard hearted, they were simply women adapted for war. If only she could adapt, too, Addie said, but there was something in her that made her more vulnerable than most. She allowed men to reach so deeply into her that when they died, she died with them. She'd told Bix she thought she should stop seeing him until the war was over.

That night the weather closed in solid, and the next morning the planes were grounded. The clouds were so low that the tops of the palm trees vanished in mist. After sick call, Doc went looking for Bix again. With no mission to fly and the tents nearly as damp inside as outside, the pilots showed up early at the old plantation house that served as an officers' club. The poker and crap tables were already manned. Bix should not be hard to find, Doc thought, as he scraped the mud off his boots, but Bix was not at poker nor at any of the other tables.

Doc ordered a gin and juice and stood at the bar, wondering what to do next. He spotted Dan at the crap table chewing his cold cigar stub and shoving bets and yelling at the dice. Addie's description of Rachael and Francine seemed to fit Dan as well. Doc had never known him to show much grief, neither about women nor about dead buddies. He was adapted for war. Doc was not. Maybe this was why Addie could bare her soul to Doc. The two of them were much alike. When one of his pilots died, a part of Doc died also, as if he were Doc's own son. He had his favorites, of course, and they made him especially vulnerable. If anything happened to Bix or Steve, there might not be enough force left in him to move a pencil or get himself from his tent to the mess hall. There was one thing, though, that he would have to find the strength for. Addie had ended her letter with a plea. If Bix was ever killed, it was Doc she wanted to hear it from. He was wondering what he could possibly say that would make it any easier for her, when the door opened and Steve came in from the veranda with water dripping off his hooded raincoat.

"Where's Bix?" Steve said, scanning the room.

"I don't know. Why?"

"A plane just took off."

"In this soup? Bix wouldn't do that." His eyes met Steve's. "Or would he?"

Steve had been in the operations office when the line chief called from the repair tents back in the jungle. He thought he'd heard a plane take off, but he wasn't sure. Steve wanted to go check the revetments. Would Doc give him a ride? They should tell Danovich, too.

Doc stopped the ambulance in front of the parachute tent. Danovich rolled down the side window and yelled through the rain. The sergeant packing parachutes assured him that nobody had taken one out.

"It doesn't prove anything," Doc said, while Danovich cranked the window up. "If he's crazy enough to fly in this stuff, he's crazy enough to fly without a chute."

Red-brown water sprayed from the tires on either side as they drove. Small lakes lay across the road in places, hiding mud holes that could swallow a wheel at a gulp. Several times, the tires spun before getting traction. Twice they thought they heard a plane, and Doc stopped and switched off the engine and they poked their heads out with an ear tilted to the sky.

In the repair tents, the mechanics and machinists were using the lull in fighting to put the planes in top condition. They were even restoring a plane they'd intended to cannibalize. One plane with empty engine cowlings looked like a sad, dismembered creature with its severed veins and nerve bundles dangling in the air.

The line chief was a bulky career sergeant who knew nearly everything there was to know about the workings of an airplane. He stood sweating in greasy fatigues under a wing, wiping black oil off his sausage fingers, looking worried as the ambulance rolled to a stop inside the tent.

"I thought it was kinda weird," he said. "But I thought I oughta report it. Course, with the rain coming down like this you can imagine damn near anything. Mickey Spottorno used to say he heard all kinds of music and shit in the rain. He said if he could put the stuff down on paper, he'd be famous."

"You were right to report it," Danovich said. "Get in the front seat so you can check off the planes." Dan climbed into the back of the ambulance and sat on the bench across from Steve.

All the planes were in their revetments, including Bix's. The revetments of planes recently lost stood empty.

"Wait a minute," the chief said, flipping a page on his clipboard. "Where's Shirley?" Shirley was the name of a pilot's wife painted on the nose of a newly overhauled plane. The plane had been gassed up and readied for a test flight just before the storm set in. "Did Bix know about it?" Dan said. The line chief nodded. "Captain Bixby knows the disposition of all the planes, the same as you, Sir."

"What now?" Doc said.

Dan's eyes looked as if they might pop out of his skull.

"Wake this place up," he said. "That's what."

They drove back to the repair tents. While Danovich was making phone calls, Steve sat in the back of the ambulance, cracking his knuckles.

"Stop it," Doc said, over his shoulder. "When you're an old man, you won't be able to bend your fingers."

On Guadalcanal, Doc had got into the habit of saying goodbye to a pilot when his wheels left the ground. But Bix and Danovich and a few others had seemed to live charmed lives. Doc had grown lax in his leave-takings. He did not see how Bix could get back on the ground alive. There would be another cross in the cemetery soon. Doc did not know which was harder—expecting them back or saying goodbye. When you gave up on them, you gave up something of yourself. Life seemed safer but poorer. With his right hand on the wheel, Doc's twitches had moved over to his left cheek and arm and were pulsing furiously on the side hidden from Dan and Steve and the chief.

Within a quarter of an hour, the field had come alive. Generators were producing power, the runway lights were on, the radio operators were trying to contact Bix. Doc drove Danovich and Steve to one end of the runway and then the other to make sure the searchlights in the jungle were on and manned. The heat of the giant beams evaporated the mist directly overhead, but Doc knew they would cause no more than a pale glow a few hundred feet into the overcast. The crash and fire trucks waited near the ambulance next to the control tower. Henry, Doc's medic with the sad, basset-hound eyes, had brought Doc's jeep with some of the pilots and jugs of coffee from the mess tent. The men crowded into the downstairs room of the control tower, not talking much. A few of the pilots speculated about what they would do to get down out of this weather alive. Once in a while, Doc stepped outside and stood under the thatched overhang, listening.

When the rain lightened a bit, Doc could see the trunks and lower branches of trees behind the radio shack, but no higher. For all practical purposes, it was ceiling zero. With luck, Bix might fly close enough to the searchlights to locate the runway, but by the time he broke through the overcast his wings would be mowing the treetops. Steve came out and stood beside Doc with his hands sunk in the pockets of his raincoat.

"How is he going to find the field, Doc?"

Doc grunted. "And if he does find it, what then?"

Doc stared at a new wall of rain sweeping in from the jungle. What could he have done to prevent this? Bix and Addie had seemed so perfect for each other. Sometimes it was the supremely happy ones who were in the greatest jeopardy.

"How much time does he have?" Doc said.

"They hadn't put the belly tank back on," Steve said. "I'd guess he has another twenty minutes."

The men in the tower smoked and drank coffee and grew quieter as the minutes passed. Stubbed-out cigarettes piled up in the coffee can on the cable spool near the wall. Somebody was always looking at a watch. Doc walked over to the radio shack. The sergeant in charge wore earphones and the hunched, glazed look of a radio operator listening for a weak signal. He was getting only static. He looked up with a worried frown.

"What's he doing up there, Doc?"

"I think he's trying to escape," Doc said. "Maybe permanently. Sort of an experiment, you might say."

The sergeant nodded as if it made perfect sense, though the frown remained.

"Keep trying," Doc said, and walked back to the control tower, thinking Bix had not planned this, it had to be the result of an impulse. Doc remembered the story of another impulse. Six young people were driving in a car at night. There was a collision. One girl in the backseat survived long enough to tell Doc the story. The driver had grown increasingly angry at oncoming cars that would not dim their headlights. Finally, with a curse, he had wrenched the steering wheel and crashed head-on into a car with bright lights. How many times, Doc wondered, had the lives of families and whole nations been torn from their moorings and even extinguished by an impulsive word, a single bullet, a reflex of wrist or finger?

More pilots and crew chiefs crowded into the ready room. Ten minutes passed. Fifteen. A jeep stopped outside, and Marchetti and the operations officer ran inside with water streaming off their hooded raincoats.

"He should be down by now," Marchetti said, looking from face to face, as if hoping somebody would contradict him.

"Don't write him off yet," Danovich said, and told them what he knew. But Doc knew a few things, too, and in a part of his mind the sorrowful, grieving words were already lining up into sentences for the letter he would have to write to Addie.

"Who gave him clearance?" Marchetti asked, as if he didn't really expect an answer.

Another five minutes went by.

"Jesus," Steve muttered, cracking his knuckles. He had opened his mouth, apparently to add something, when they heard the sound. Then Doc was trying to get past bodies blocking the narrow doorway. Over the drumming of rain came a soft, muffled rumble too steady for thunder. It faded as the men lined up outside to listen, then reappeared. It seemed to come first from the direction of Port Moresby, then from some other direction, then maybe overhead, but Doc knew it could be the trickery of wind or cloud and the plane might be even farther away or higher than it seemed. Now it grew louder again and appeared to be coming from one side of the field, now from over the jungle beyond the end of the field, now from the other side, as if Bix was circling, trying to catch a glimpse of the little cut-out slot in the jungle that held the runway. It seemed a miracle that Bix had got even this close to the field without a radio compass like the ones the bombers carried. Doc, who thought prayer was nonsense, found his lips moving: *Let him make it, let him make it, let him live.* The motors of the crash and fire trucks came to life.

Doc stood with the pilots under the overhang. The searchlight beams beyond each end of the runway were hidden by rain and cloud. The rumbling seemed lower now, then it grew powerful and passed overhead close enough for Doc to recognize the roar of Allison engines. The sound faded, changed angle, then quality from the direction of one of the invisible searchlights. This is the moment, Doc thought. He tensed and heard his heart pound, thinking he saw a flash of light, but it had to be an illusion—the plane was too far away in this murk, Doc would not be able to see the flash of an explosion unless the plane had already dropped in over the jungle wall. The rumbling ceased. Doc's breath stopped with it. Then it resumed, softer, with the addition of a hissing sound as the landing lights of a plane emerged from the rain and the dim outline of a P-38 slid past on the runway, caught in the headlights of the vehicles lined up next to the tower.

FIRST LOVE

The sky was turning pink over the jungle island of Morotai as Blake coaxed the heavily loaded four-engine bomber out of the revetment onto the taxi strip. There he steered the plane into the line of B-24s slowly moving forward for takeoff at one-minute intervals. Blake's copilot, Darrell, sat with the plastic-coated checklist on his knee, scanning the engine instruments and watching the bombers as they thundered past on the runway. It was the seventh mission for Blake and his crew. Today they were headed for the Japanese oil refineries near Surabaja on the north coast of Java.

At briefing, the bomber crews had been told to expect fighters and heavy antiaircraft fire. No Allied fighters would be there to fly cover for them, because Surabaja was beyond their range. The bombers would be in the air fourteen hours. The more experienced crews had flown other missions without fighter protection. Blake and his crew had heard the stories. This morning in the truck on the way to the planes there was none of the usual banter and horsing around. Even Darrell, whose twenty-year-old exuberance sometimes made Blake feel like an old man at twenty-four, stared silently into the dark wall of jungle alongside the road.

Next to the bomber runway was a shorter landing strip used mostly by C-47 transports carrying men to Australia on rest leave or to Brisbane or Sydney where they boarded troopships for the States. The men on those transports were the envy of the men in the bombers who still had many missions to fly before they would be sent home or on leave. The window next to Blake and the one on the other side next to Darrell were open to prevent a buildup of carbon monoxide in the cockpit before takeoff. Down at the end of the C-47 runway Blake could see landing lights flare brilliantly as the plane swung around and lined up for takeoff. Over the soft rumble of many idling B-24 engines Blake and Darrell could hear the rising pitch of the transport's engines as it started down the runway, gathered speed, and rose from the ground with its wheels retracting.

"Lucky bastards!" Darrell yelled, and gave them a snappy salute.

Blake and Darrell watched the plane climb toward them. Blake figured it would be nine months before he and his crew would be on that plane or one like it on their way home.

When the C-47 was about fifty feet off the ground and almost parallel with Blake and Darrell, they heard the unmistakable snarl of a runaway propeller, the sign of a broken hydraulic line that had caused the propeller blades to go flat and lose their thrust. "Ah, no, Jesus Christ, no, no, no!" Darrell wailed, clapping his hands to his head. Blake felt his body react as if he were himself the pilot of the transport, fighting to keep it in the air. Blake and Darrell watched helplessly as the good engine pulled the left wing straight up and the plane veered off toward the trees. There was a sickening crunch of cracking branches and tearing metal and the transport vanished in a fireball that went rolling back into the jungle, breaking into smaller pieces. At that moment, Blake got radio clearance from the tower. They were next in line for takeoff.

Blake had set the autopilot for a slow climb over the Molucca Sea. On the other side of the cockpit, Darrell was not looking so cheerful anymore. He had pulled a small gold ring on a chain from under his shirt and slipped it over the tip of one forefinger. He stared absently through the windshield at the horizon and rubbed his thumb around and around the red stone set in the ring. Blake turned his head so he would not see the incessant motion of Darrell's thumb. Many fliers carried mementos for good luck. They had always seemed a bit silly to Blake, but lately he'd found himself wishing he had one. He'd want something from his first love, Florrie. He hadn't seen her since she was almost sixteen and he was seventeen. She'd been an orphan girl who lived with Stevie Larkin's grandparents on the little farm next door in California. One night in the orchard, she'd announced that she was in love with him and he could do whatever he wanted with her. Since that day, Blake had not met a woman as honest and uncomplicated as Florrie.

Whenever he turned to look at the instrument panel, Blake could see Darrell's thumb going back and forth over the ring. Blake did not enjoy feeling irritated toward his copilot. He leaned across the cockpit and tapped Darrell's shoulder.

"Is that Arlene's ring?"

Darrell roused himself and leaned closer so they would not have to yell so loud.

"She gave it to me the last time I saw her." He stared at Blake, as if wondering why he asked. "Do you have a good-luck piece?"

Blake shook his head and made a minute adjustment on the propeller pitch controls.

"Sometimes I wish I had one," he said.

"Hey," Darrell said. "I carried an 1880 silver dollar before Arlene gave me the ring. I still have it. It belonged to my grandfather. It's yours if you want it."

Blake studied Darrell's round, snub-nosed face to make sure he really meant it. Blake liked his copilot, but he hadn't realized how much. He nodded.

"I'll give it back after the war."

"It's a deal," Darrell said.

On her sixteenth birthday, after Blake had left for college, Florrie had been taken away by the county and sent out in the world on her own. Blake had tried to find her when he came home that summer. When he got his first job after graduation he'd even hired a detective. Blake had known many girls since then, but it was Florrie's slender arms he dreamed of even as he lay beside another girl, and it was Florrie's honest cloud-gray eyes he'd begun to see more often on these long journeys across the alien oceans and enemy-held islands of Indonesia.

After they leveled off at cruising altitude, the crew test-fired the machine guns and made sure all equipment was battle-ready. Blake was relieved to hear that the gunners and his bombardier, O'Bannon, had settled down to the running poker game on the waist deck. Darrell had gone remote again, staring at the ocean and rubbing the ring. Blake tapped him on the shoulder.

"Hey, Darrell, why don't you go on back and play a few hands?" It would take his mind off things.

"Don't you want to go check the plane over?" Darrell said.

"I can do it later," Blake said. "Go ahead. Clean those guys out."

After Darrell left, Blake scanned the instruments and listened for the wa-wa beat, however gradual, of a propeller out of sync. He switched off the autopilot and adjusted trim tabs so the plane would fly itself, then switched the autopilot on again. For a while, he watched the planes scattered about the sky a few hundred yards apart. The big round tail fins were the most visible feature of the bombers farthest away in the morning sky. Blake called his navigator for a position check. Even though the whole formation followed the mission leader, every crew had its own navigator in case they had to fly home alone. Blake kept his receiver tuned to the formation frequency in case the leader broke radio silence. In his earphones came the faint crashing of far-off lightning strikes.

They'd been in the air for a couple of hours when a line of thunderheads began to edge their glowing anvil tops above the horizon. As the clouds rose higher above the rim of the earth, Blake searched for open spaces between the mountainous pillars. But in a half-hour, he was looking at a gray wall too solid to slip through and too high to fly over.

"Nice of them to tell us!" Darrell yelled, climbing back into his seat. They had not been warned of a storm in briefing. In this part of the world, weather reports were sketchy at best, usually from a surfaced submarine.

The steady explosions of static in Blake's earphones told him what to expect inside the clouds. He clicked his intercom button and ordered the crew to secure everything not already stowed or tied down, and return to their safety belts. Maybe they'd be lucky and miss the worst of the storm. The B-24 had strong, flexible wings that could flap ten or fifteen feet in such weather, but it was also true that once in a while a B-24 flew into a thunderhead and did not come out the other side.

The sea below them became a churning mass of whitecaps. The planes of the lead squadron winked out of sight one by one as they entered the cloud, and a few seconds later Blake and Darrell were riding a bucking, rocking plane with their hands and feet on the controls in case the turbulence overpowered the autopilot. Rain and hail hammered the windshield, lightning flashed around them, and blue Saint Elmo's fire streamed from the propellers and wingtips. Blake and Darrell kept their eyes trained on the flight instruments. Without them, they would not know if their plane was turning off course or going into a spin. The gunners in the turrets were their outside eyes now, watching for other planes in the dense gray soup that hid them from each other.

The light abruptly brightened and the plane burst out into blue sky, clear all the way to the horizon except for widely scattered popcorn puffs of cumulus. The ominous wall of cloud had merely been a squall line. Hap, the flight engineer, climbed down out of the top turret and stood between the pilots, his narrow, bony face grinning with relief.

"Nice flying!" he yelled to Blake and Darrell. "I didn't even spill my coffee!" Hap was a little guy who could crawl into difficult places in the bomber to work on it. Something was always malfunctioning on a plane as complex as the B-24, and so far Hap had never failed to fix it or figure out how to get them home safely in spite of it.

The squadrons scattered about the sky now turned onto a heading that would take them across a narrow arm of the Celebes mainland and then out over the Makassar Strait. If they were spotted by a ground observer or a Japanese ship, they would appear to be headed for docks and refineries along the east coast of Borneo. But out toward the middle of the Strait, they would turn south toward the Java Sea and remain out of sight of land until they were a half-hour from Surabaja. They still had hours to go in a clear sky. Blake tapped Darrell's arm. "She's all yours," he yelled, and tilted his seat back and closed his eyes.

Two or three nights a week, Florrie had sneaked out of the house to meet Blake. Stevie, who was too young to really know what they did in the orchard, still thought it a big adventure to carry coded messages between Blake and Florrie. When Blake came home from college and found Florrie gone, he did not know if he was more angry at the county, himself, or his parents. He already carried a mountain of anger toward his father for gambling on the horses, losing their home in New Orleans, and failing at everything he tried. And toward his mother for lying around all day with a wet towel on her forehead, though she was always ready to dress and go to a party in San Francisco with Blake's father. Blake suspected their mortgage payments were made each month by their uncle in New Orleans.

Blake's father merely shrugged about Florrie. "You don't want to marry an orphan girl anyway. You should marry your cousin, Belinda May."

"What for?" Blake had snapped. "So you can lose her money on the horses, too?" Marrying Belinda May would have guaranteed them an easy life, but the thought of it made him squirm. He wasn't going to marry anybody unless he had the feelings he'd had with Florrie. Sometimes he wished he'd got her pregnant on one of those moonlit nights in the orchard. Maybe they would have made him marry her. Maybe it would have been the best thing.

Once, when she'd missed her period, they'd talked about it. What would they do if she was pregnant? "I'd run away," she said.

"No," he said, scared by the certainty in her voice. "Why?"

"I'd ruin your life," she said. "You have to go to college."

"I could work my way," Blake said. "You told me Stevie's uncle worked his way, with a wife and two kids. Anyway, Uncle Andrew says he'll put me through college."

"Not if you're married to me. I'd never fit into your family. I wouldn't even know what to do at the table."

"You can learn that stuff," Blake said.

"I'm nobody. I don't even know who my parents are." She sounded resentful that he would try to persuade her.

"That's crazy," Blake said. "We're nobody, too. Look at the dump we live in. My father has to sell the furniture to feed us."

Florrie's voice rose, almost a cry.

"At least he has furniture to sell!"

"Hush," Blake said, and held her close until her anger seemed to subside and her body softened.

"I could be a carpenter," he said. "Like Stevie's grandfather."

"And not go to college?"

"Why not?" he said. "The point is, I could make a living and support us." It was not just a wild idea. It had crossed his mind already. His admiration for Stevie's grandfather grew every day. Blake spied on him from the big walnut tree in the backyard, watching him build a new rental house single-handed. Every last shovelful of dirt and concrete, every nail and pipe and wire and beam and shingle, passed through his able hands. He built with the meticulous care that Blake put into the building of his model airplanes. Blake felt some kind of kinship with the old man. A few times when Stevie's grandparents had gone to town, Blake had sneaked across the orchard and examined the half-built house. Beams and studs fitted so seamlessly that they might have grown out of each other. There was not a nail split to be found. The spikes in the floorboards had been driven so artfully that Blake could rarely find the mark of a hammer head. The further miracle was that the house was made of lumber Stevie's grandfather had got for nothing by tearing down an old house in town.

But Florrie shook her head against his chest. "You'd still be a Hurlingame," she said, and at that moment he hated his family. Blake wanted a grandfather who could hammer nails flush without leaving a mark. A man clever enough to build a house of free used lumber and good galvanized pipe salvaged from the dump that other men had stupidly thrown away in a depression year. A man as solid as oak in all the ways Blake's father was a wet noodle.

The planes thundered steadily southward in a clear blue sky, holding their distance from each other like a school of fish. A few diehards in Blake's crew kept the poker game going on the waist deck. Others were able to sleep. Blake took control of the plane to let Darrell doze off before the battle. Below the plane, the ocean lay dark and mirror smooth in places, miles deep. It made Blake uneasy, thinking of its depth. He felt safer flying high above it than he would in a boat or swimming in it, though he wasn't sure why. The chief danger was drowning, and he'd be just as dead whether he drowned in ten feet of water or ten thousand.

As they crossed the Java Sea, the planes began to draw closer. A hundred miles from the coast, they sighted a small island that had been chosen as their rendezvous point. Blake ordered his crew to battle stations. He and Darrell strapped on their flak suits and Blake ordered the crew to do the same. The armor plate and steel helmets were heavy and unwieldy, and sometimes a gunner with more courage than sense would decide to tempt fate without armor. Blake switched off the autopilot and adjusted the trim tabs for manual control. He worked the plane into a mile-wide circle, where the squadrons gradually assembled in the massed herringbone formation that was most dangerous to the attacking fighters and most vulnerable to antiaircraft fire from the ground. He now focused all his attention on keeping the wingtip of the plane tucked in just behind the wingtip of the squadron leader, and on matching the speed and direction and tilt of the other plane as the whole formation leveled off and headed south toward Surabaja. As they approached the shoreline, Blake's earphones crackled: "Bogies at twelve o'clock!"

This was about the time Blake would have enjoyed looking up and seeing a squadron or two of P-38s in the sky above him, maybe one of them flown by Stevie Larkin. Steve was out there somewhere, Blake had heard, busy becoming an ace.

Soon a cloud of black specks appeared, growing larger, spreading across the sky. Then the first wave of fighters streaked through the formation. The bomber shuddered steadily from its ten fifty-caliber machine guns. A pungent haze of gun smoke drifted back from the nose turret into the cockpit. Blake could not risk taking his eyes off the plane next to him, but in the corner of his vision he could see white streaks of tracer bullets crisscrossing the sky from every direction. A Zero came straight at him with little red snake tongues flickering along the wings. A favorite tactic of the Japanese was to try to kill the bomber pilots by firing into the windshield. Fortunately, few of them had the stomach for flying straight into all the forward-firing guns. Sometimes a cone of bullets from many bombers would converge on a Zero and practically blow it out of the sky. If Blake switched over from radio frequency to intercom, his ears would ring with the cheers of the gunners.

On radio, Blake heard that some of the Zeros had broken off and were going after two bombers that had been hit and were losing altitude. The lead plane began a shallow turn, and the formation followed, leveling off on the bomb run. The plane rumbled as the bombardier opened the bomb-bay doors. The fighters pulled away to avoid being hit by their own antiaircraft fire. The bombers were now sitting ducks, flying straight and level while the gunners on the ground improved their aim. As the planes approached the bomb-release point, the sky thickened with red flashes and brown puffs of smoke. A shell went off directly in front of Blake's nose, and the plane bucked as it hit the turbulence. Blake pushed the intercom button. "O'Bannon, Cone, are you guys okay?" The intercom clicked. "Okay here," the bombardier reported. "Okay here, boss," the nose gunner said. "Damned if I know why." The wings rocked from another burst, then another. It seemed to take forever to get to the target.

At last a string of bombs fell from the lead plane, and in the following instant from all the other planes. Blake's plane jumped from the sudden loss of weight. The whole formation went into a diving turn to make a more difficult target. As soon as they were out of range of the ground guns, the Zeros moved in again like sharks for the kill. Blake turned the controls over to Darrell and flexed the weariness out of his arms and legs. The plane began to vibrate once more with gunfire. A Zero, maybe a kamikaze, came toward them head-on with its tracers streaking past Blake's window so close that it might have flown into the cockpit if Darrell hadn't dumped the nose and immediately pulled back up into formation as the Zero passed overhead. At the far left of the formation, a bomber was smoking. A burst of flame appeared behind one engine, the wing broke off, and the remainder of the plane rolled over in a crazy death spin and fell toward the ocean. Blake heard the cries of a trapped pilot who must have thought he was on intercom, ordering his men to bail out. At that instant, the plane exploded like a seed-pod, scattering little black specks of bodies into the sky, some on fire, one trailing a half-opened parachute. Then the scene was hidden by a white lacework of tracer streaks, as ball turret and tail gunners began firing at a Zero coming straight up under the formation.

In another ten minutes, the Zeros left them. The bombers stayed in tight formation for a while to make sure it was not a ruse. Blake looked back at the target to see clouds of black smoke billowing fifteen or twenty thousand feet in the sky. The bombardier in the lead plane had aimed well, but the bombers had paid a price. Blake could see most of the planes off to the left from his side window. It looked as if only three out of six planes remained of the far squadron. Two planes from another squadron were missing. Blake's tail gunner reported one still in sight, losing altitude. The pilot reported two engines out. He was trying to restart one of them. The group commander ordered a plane to fly cover for the crippled bomber and report his position if he made a water landing.

As they climbed slowly back to cruising altitude, Blake stared at a few puffy clouds on the distant horizon. When he'd thought the

Zero was going to fly right into his cockpit, Blake had heard a cry in his mind: "Oh, Florrie, I'm sorry!" Where had it come from? He hadn't seen Florrie in seven years. It felt as if he thought that in dying he would abandon her. If anything, he'd deserted her long ago, and he hadn't felt good about himself since. He'd left for college in New Orleans shortly before she'd turned sixteen, and he'd known the county was going to stop supporting her.

"I'll never see you again," she told Blake.

"You will," he said. "We'll keep in touch. Someday I'll send for you."

"No, you won't," she said. "You'll forget all about me. You'll marry your rich cousin."

He wanted to see her until the last day, the last minute before he left, but she refused to meet him in the orchard again. He'd climbed the walnut tree in his yard and tried to see across the orchard, but Florrie managed to keep out of his sight so that he never actually laid eyes on her again. Blake wrote a few times from New Orleans, but his letters were returned, marked "No Forwarding Address." Stevie Larkin's grandfather once answered Blake's query in a work-stiffened but legible hand, to let Blake know that they'd lost track of her and they missed her, too.

In some ways, it had been a relief. Florrie had a somber side, often brooding about something. It got worse as the time approached for Blake to leave. "The man always dies before the woman" was her theme one week. "The woman gets left all alone." And another week it was, "Even if we got married, you could be dead soon. Stevie's grandfather says there's a war coming." After Blake went away to college, he didn't think of Florrie for a while. There were so many new things to experience—girls, parties, ideas, people from all over the country and from other countries. But he found that he wanted somebody to share it with. There was something lacking in college girls. He missed Florrie's savvy that must have come from being kicked around, seeing life raw in orphanages and foster homes. More and more, he was merely bored by college girls from good homes with their expensive frocks and French perfumes and summers in Europe.

Blake shook his head to clear it of regrets. He had a plane to fly. He took off his flak suit and helmet and unbuckled his safety belt, and got up to check on his ship and crew. Before he left the cockpit, he leaned over with his hand on Darrell's shoulder.

"I owe you one," he said.

Darrell looked quizzical.

"That kamikaze," Blake said. "We all owe you one."

Darrell's round face beamed, and he tossed his head in dismissal.

"Luck of the draw," he yelled. "What if that guy had dived when we did?"

Blake patted Darrell's shoulder.

"Hey, in this business you get medals for luck, too."

Blake went through the plane talking to everybody. His navigator and bombardier. His flight engineer, radio operator, gunners. Miraculously, nobody was hurt. The crew hadn't even found a bullet hole or flak hole. Maybe the wings would tell a different story when they landed. Blake and his engineer stood at the waist windows and watched the trailing edge of the wings for an oil leak from the engines or a thread of mist that would indicate a fuel leak. Blake wasn't sure he could believe their luck. The flak had looked thick enough to walk on.

As the bomber droned steadily homeward over the Molucca Sea, a hundred-mile streamer of cloud above the horizon flamed orange in the sunset. Soon the light faded and the first stars began to sprinkle the sky. The rows of gauges and dials on the panel in front of Blake and Darrell glowed with a soft green luminescence. For some reason, Blake felt more secure in the cockpit at night than he did during the day. He even preferred night landings. Maybe it was some age-old feeling that the night kept you safe by hiding you from the enemy.

Blake's earphones clicked and his navigator gave him a change of heading. Somewhere over the Molucca Passage, the radio compass needle swung to a vertical position, indicating that they were headed straight for home. Soon after, Darrell cranked the radio dial and began tapping his foot to music from the shipboard station in Morotai harbor. In half an hour, a faint glow appeared on the horizon from the air base and ships at anchor. In the sky around the plane, Blake could see landing lights and the red-and-green running lights of the bombers slowly drifting into line as they approached the field. Badly damaged planes and those with wounded were calling for clearance to land first.

Over the straits, Blake switched off the autopilot and took the controls, while Darrell called out the checklist and prepared the ship for landing. Blake throttled back and dropped a few degrees of flaps. "Gear down!" Darrell yelled, shoving the landing gear lever. The plane rumbled as the nose wheel compartment dropped open and the main gear descended. A warning light came on, indicating trouble with the right wheel. Blake looked out his window to make sure his own wheel was down. He turned to Darrell, who pointed to the right side. "It's not down!" Darrell pulled the lever and Blake watched the wheel on his side come up and disappear under the wing. When the lights on the panel indicated wheels up and locked, Darrell pushed the lever again with the same result. Blake's wheel was down. Darrell's was not.

"Try it once more!" Hap yelled. Their engineer stood behind Darrell's seat, studying the right wing through the side window. Still no wheel appeared.

"I'll get the crank!" Hap yelled.

"Get Cazzazza to help you!" Blake yelled over his shoulder. Cazzazza was one of the waist gunners. He had the strength of a bull. If anybody could crank the wheel down, it was Cazzazza.

As Hap disappeared through the bomb-bay door, Blake turned the ship out of the landing column and called the tower. They would fly a holding pattern over the ocean until they got the wheel down. From the fuel gauges, Blake estimated they had a half-hour of flying time left.

But the wheel would not come down. After twenty minutes of sweating, hammering, and wrestling with the crank, Hap stood between Blake and Darrell again. The plane must have taken some damage over the target, he said. One of those bursts under the wing might have done it. From inside the plane, there was no way they could check it out. This was one of those situations pilots rehearsed many times in their minds, but there was no way to practice it. Blake turned to Darrell.

"What'll it be? Belly landing or one wheel down?"

"Belly might be safer," Darrell said. Blake nodded, glad to have his copilot's confidence. Belly would be safer only if Blake could slide it onto the runway so skillfully they'd hardly know they were on the surface except for the noise and the slowing down.

The chatter on intercom ceased as the crew buckled safety belts and Blake turned the plane onto the landing approach and lowered the nose toward the lighted runway. The squadron radio frequency was silent, too, so Blake could keep in touch with the tower. He brought the plane in as low as possible over the end of the runway to give himself the entire stretch of coral ahead. That way he could keep his engines powered up and take his time. He leveled off with the coral surface streaking three or four feet under the plane's exposed belly, then two feet, then one, then inches, where it seemed to remain stuck for an interminable time as the plane glided on a pressure cushion. Then so softly that you could not be sure at what split second the belly made contact, the screech of assaulted metal began and quickly became a tormented roar, and Blake and Darrell were thrown forward in their safety straps. At that instant, Blake chopped the throttles, and his hands and Darrell's flew about the panels, closing switches to prevent sparks. Then there was not much Blake could do except to hold the wheel back in his lap for whatever small effect it might have in keeping the nose high, and except for hoping that the plane kept sliding straight down the runway with wings level, and that no bump in the runway jogged them off course or threw them sideways and broke off a wing or made them flip over and explode. He could feel as well as hear the roar of grinding metal under him, and he chilled and his stomach tightened almost as if the coral were tearing at his own belly.

The plane held steady, slowing with its wings level, until the last moment when it veered to the left, the right wing came down, and the tip crumpled on the runway and the plane started to swing to the right, then came to a full stop. Fire trucks and ambulances pulled alongside, as Hap and Darrell and then Blake scrambled up the ladder and out through the hatch in the roof of the flight deck and slid off the nose onto the ground, while the rest of the crew jumped out of the waist windows. Within seconds, the crew had pulled each other into a troop truck that nearly threw them out again, racing away from the plane in case it was about to explode. The crew crowded around Blake, pounding him on the back.

"Great landing!" Cazzazza the waist gunner yelled. "I couldn't have done better myself!"

"Fantastic landing," O'Bannon said. "Better than some you've made with wheels down."

Blake felt as if he hadn't laughed in a year. Then the crew fell silent. They were driving past the hole in the jungle where the transport had crashed. There were lights among the trees, and men moving about, searching, perhaps—for what? Blake had once seen medics walking alongside a runway carrying buckets, picking up pieces of a dead Spitfire pilot.

"Poor bastards," Darrell said, but nobody answered, and nobody spoke as the truck turned onto the road and sped through the dark jungle toward their tents.

In the headlights of a truck following them, Blake saw Darrell again rubbing his wife's ring. Blake wondered what Florrie might have given him if he'd thought to ask. A lock of hair? A photo? He recalled a strange thing that had happened as the plane descended toward the runway. He could swear he'd seen Florrie's thin blond face at his shoulder, but when he turned she was gone. Then he'd been too busy easing the plane down the last few feet, then the last few inches. As soon as the plane stopped sliding, Blake had unbuckled to climb out the hatch. As he jumped up and turned toward the ladder, he'd seen Florrie step out of his way. He guessed he'd been hallucinating from all those hours in the air. But maybe, too, he was carrying something of Florrie's after all, something he couldn't just take out of his shirt or his pocket and rub with his thumb. Maybe she was thinking of him even now and could half guess what was happening to him. It brought to mind a time when he'd forgotten to send her a message to meet him, and he'd missed her so much that he'd left his bed in the middle of a windy night and had gone down to the orchard anyway to sit under the tree where they usually met, and to think of her, and she'd been there waiting for him.

TRAITOR

Sometimes Doc wondered if he was coming unglued, but he couldn't help himself. He was responsible for hundreds of men besides the pilots on the fighter base outside Port Moresby. In addition to his official duties as a flight surgeon, he took it upon himself to check roads and buildings, electrical systems, swamp drainage. He made sure enough lime was being used in the latrine trenches. On Guadalcanal, he'd begun inspecting the P-38s for bullet holes the mechanics might have missed. One night, Marchetti the squadron CO had found him walking the runway with a flashlight, looking for broken joints in the metal mesh. Marchetti had leaned out of his jeep to see better.

"We have technicians to do this, Doc. Are you drunk?" Lately, Doc had been running a projector half the night, studying film taken by the wing cameras each time a pilot pushed the gun button.

From the day Courtenay had talked his dying wingman down to a safe landing, Doc had been suspicious. Doc was half convinced that on the way home from a mission Courtenay had started a mock dogfight, had forgotten to turn off his gun switches, and had shot his own wingman. The film from Courtenay's plane would have provided proof, but when Doc went looking, it was nowhere to be found. According to the photo technicians, film was often lost. Doc dug into the files and found that film from Courtenay's plane turned up missing more often than film from other pilots. On two more missions for which Courtenay's film was missing, the squadron had lost a senior pilot who would have stood in the way of Courtenay's advancement to squadron commander. Doc was so shaken by the implications that he tried to shut them out of his mind for a while. He drank too much and used morphine to get to sleep, but to no avail. The idea grew like a cancer in his mind.

Doc knew that if he went to Marchetti or an Intelligence officer, they would say there was not a shred of solid evidence. Doc was accusing Courtenay of an act that would send him to the firing squad. Doc's own mental stability might come under scrutiny. What Doc needed was a new approach, a bolder plan than burrowing like a mole for data. He would get close to Courtenay, take notes, keep a record, find the flaw in Courtenay's strategy. From the day of his arrival in the squadron, Courtenay's arrogance and vulgarity had offended Doc. He'd tried to ignore everything about the pretty-boy captain that did not appear in his military records. Now Doc began to infiltrate Courtenay's small crowd of sycophants in the old plantation house that served as the officers' club. Doc was soon learning more than he bargained for.

He heard about family scandal. Courtenay's alcoholic mother. His sadistic father. Courtenay had been expelled from six universities. His father had threatened to have both of Courtenay's legs broken if he didn't graduate. Courtenay knew the dirt on President Roosevelt. Eleanor was screwing the Secretary of the Treasury. Courtenay let it be known that women fell over backward for him. He spoke of women as broads, cunts, meat; of their gender parts as apples, headlights, pussy, gash. Courtenay complained that his father had pulled strings in Washington to keep him in the States the first year of the war. Otherwise, he'd be the top Pacific ace by now, running his own squadron. Courtenay said he'd hollered and kicked ass and tried to pull strings, himself. He'd finally had to fuck a general's wife to get sent to combat.

Once in a while, Doc scribbled in his notebook. One evening, Courtenay yelled the length of a table full of pilots.

"Hey, Gramps, I hear you're writing my biography! Did I ever tell you about the time I fucked a cow?" Courtenay gaped, looking around with wide-eyed innocence to others at the table. "That oughta sell books, huh?"

The men around him laughed.

"Sure," Doc said. "Maybe you could give instructions. Like E. E. Cummings."

"E. E. Cummings?" Courtenay said. "Who's he?"

"A poet. He wrote a poem about it." Doc quoted: "'The way to hump a cow is not to elevate your tool, but drop a penny in the slot and bellow like a bool.'"

"That's it?"

"There's more."

Courtenay leaned on his elbows and studied his drink, evidently trying to turn inside this one. It did not take long.

"Hey, Doc, how about movie rights? You think we could get cow-fucking on the screen? Maybe I'd get to be a big movie star!"

He seemed to be looking for Doc's shock threshold.

"Why not?" Doc said. "If that's the kind of work you like."

Courtenay threw back his head and guffawed. There was no limit to the man's insolence.

"Hey," Courtenay said, with an aggrieved tone, "you think I'd kid my biographer? Why, if you left anything out, Doc, they'd say we didn't tell the whole story. They'd say you left out the part about cow-fucking. Bad reviews! No, sir! The whole truth, Doc! The whole man! Nothing less! Right?" His handsome black eyebrows arched high with expectation.

Now that Doc had attracted Courtenay's attention, he found himself regularly in the line of fire. When Courtenay could not seem to get under Doc's skin he began to ridicule the medical profession. If Doc passed somewhere near Courtenay, expressions such as "pill dispenser," "sawbones," and "dick inspector" would emerge from the hubbub just loud enough for Doc to hear.

Doc decided he was getting nowhere. He needed to see more of Courtenay than his usual charade, but Doc could think of only one way to do it. He had to get Courtenay off by himself where he couldn't stir up so much commotion to hide behind. The Tourette's tics and twitches that lived like a separate being in Doc's body convulsed at the thought of it.

One clear day when Courtenay was not scheduled to fly, he was complaining in the mess tent about being stuck on the ground with nothing to do but beat everybody at poker and read dirty books. Gritting his teeth, Doc invited Courtenay to go to the lagoon with him after sick call. He half expected Courtenay to offer some new vulgarity and refuse outright.

"What's there?" Courtenay said, with a skeptical twist to his full pink lips.

Doc shrugged. "You wanted something to do. Find out for yourself."

Up the coast was a long stretch of white sand with a coral reef a half mile offshore. The seafloor was no more than ten or twelve feet deep as far out as the reef. The green, crystal-clear water was teeming with brilliantly striped and spotted fish in all colors, in addition to squid, gigantic serrated pearl clams, coral formations, and otherworldly plants and creatures waving a few feet below the surface. One of the crew chiefs had been cutting and sealing glass bottoms on two-pound coffee cans for peering at the life underwater. Doc and Steve and a couple of other off-duty pilots sometimes took their air mattresses to the beach, blew them up, and floated out, lying on their stomachs and studying the seafloor. Doc could spend hours drifting, covered with suntan oil to keep from burning. It was like floating in the atmosphere, looking down at the fantastic life of another planet.

Ten or fifteen minutes after getting launched in the lagoon, Doc heard Courtenay splashing toward him. A school of fluorescent green and lavender fish with extravagant flaglike fins that Doc had been watching whipped about in formation and fled into a forest of seaweed. Courtenay stopped his rubber mattress a few feet from Doc, with his head raised and the expression of a fretful baby.

"What the hell do you do here, Doc? What is there to do? Shit, you can't just float around all the time with your head stuck in a coffee can!"

Doc controlled himself.

"You can go lie on the beach if you want to."

"A beach bunny? Hey, not without babes, Doc. Not me. Come up with another plan."

"You could try looking at the underwater life. You said you wanted to see it."

"I just did." Facing Doc on his belly, Courtenay spread his arms out like wings and splashed peevishly.

"You can't see much in ten minutes," Doc explained as he would to a seven-year-old. "They're wild creatures. It takes a while for them to come out of hiding after you've disturbed them. Sometimes even the pearl clams close up until you're quiet around them for a while."

Courtenay's interest seemed to perk up.

"Do those clams really have pearls in them?"

"That's right. The natives dive for them. Don't get close to one, though. They're big and powerful. If one of them closes on your hand or foot, it's all over." It made Doc queasy. He felt as if he was betraying the underwater life just by drawing Courtenay's attention to it.

Courtenay splashed away, whether more interested in the promise of danger or in a source of wealth, Doc could not imagine. His interest was certainly not in the beauty of that fantastic bivalve with the glassy pink-white interior and the sine-wave serrations that fitted perfectly together when the shell closed. At any rate, Doc had a half-hour of quiet, bobbing gently on the low swells, easing an arm or leg into the water to keep himself cool, watching the rich and varied life come out of hiding once more beneath him. Only gradually did he become aware of loud splashing a hundred yards away. Doc looked up. Courtenay was surfacing for the second or third time, blowing like a whale.

"Clam!" he yelled excitedly at Doc, pointing down. "Clam!"

Doc waved, and went back to observing the life beneath his air mattress. If Courtenay was getting too close to the clam underwater, it was not Doc's fault. Courtenay had been warned. If the clam caught Courtenay in its serrated jaws and held him until he drowned, for all Doc knew the world might be a better place. In spite of himself, Doc looked up when Courtenay yelled again and began splashing toward shore. Before long he was back, circling over the area where he'd seen the clam. Doc raised his head and squinted, trying to see past the sparkle of sun on water. Courtenay seemed to be carrying something clenched in his teeth. "My God," Doc said, and began stroking toward Courtenay, but Doc still had thirty yards to go when Courtenay sat up on his mattress and waved, with an eight-inch trench knife in his teeth.

"Don't, Courtenay!" Doc yelled. "Wait, don't do it!"

Courtenay jerked the knife from his teeth.

"It's all right!" he yelled, as he raised a sturdy stick, a small log really, in his other hand. "I've got a stick!"

"No!" Doc yelled, paddling. "Courtenay, wait! You don't know what you're doing!"

But the trench knife was back in Courtenay's teeth and he went off the side of the air mattress and disappeared underwater, just like a real pearl diver. Just like in the movies.

There was nothing Doc could do except wait. He could dive with Courtenay, but that would only add to the commotion and make it more likely that Courtenay would do something foolish. Doc paddled close to Courtenay's air mattress and peered down into his coffee can. He located Courtenay next to a clam that might have been four feet long, end to end. Courtenay was kicking to keep himself underwater, inserting the stick between the open jaws. He appeared to jiggle the stick a bit, to excite the clam into closing tight against the ends of the stick. It seemed to work. The stick stayed in place. Next, Courtenay poked his arm down inside the clam. Doc watched with a deepening sense of doom. Courtenay could bump the stick loose. The clam could open slightly to release the stick, and then close its jaws. Or both. Doc had a vision of himself having to dive down and cut off Courtenay's arm in order to keep him from drowning. Then he realized that Courtenay's knife would be unreachable inside the closed clam. Doc would have to swim to shore and get the trench knife out of his own pack, and by the time he returned, Courtenay would be dead. Doc shook this scenario out of his head and watched with horrified fascination. As it became more likely that Courtenay was going to survive this adventure, what he was doing to the clam began to register more clearly in Doc's mind.

"My God," Doc said. He had only himself to blame.

Courtenay was coming up. He burst to the surface with the knife in his teeth, holding a gobbet of torn guts and bleeding pink flesh triumphantly over his head. He blew like a whale and tossed his wet hair aside as he gasped for air.

"Hey, Doc!" he yelled. "Look!"

As accustomed as he was to looking at torn flesh, Doc felt sick to his stomach. Courtenay threw the whole mess onto his air mattress and began stabbing at it with his trench knife.

"Where's the pearl, Doc? Where do I look for it?"

The damage was done before Doc could stop him. Air bubbled and hissed from a puncture in the mattress.

"Shit!" Courtenay yelled. "*Shit!*" He looked desperately at Doc. "What'll I do?"

"Put it on my mattress," Doc said, quietly. "Push it to shore. I'll swim."

Doc took his time, glad for the soothing tepid water flowing over his skin. This was the man, Doc thought, who wanted to command a squadron. Yet Courtenay had been a flight instructor. He had talked Buster Kemp's corpse safely down out of the sky, maybe after fatally wounding him. How could you predict when Courtenay was going to behave competently, and when like a psychopath or a brain-damaged five-year-old? Doc watched Courtenay reach shallow water and begin wading with the air mattress cradled like a large platter in front of him. Suddenly, Courtenay yelled and began limping.

"Ow!" he yelled again, and threw the mattress and its cargo of clam innards onto the sand. Courtenay thumped his butt down on the sand and turned up the bottom of his foot to examine it.

"Ow!" he snarled. "Aw, *shit!*"

On the beach, Doc stood looking down at the pink and white mess that only a few minutes before had been one of the wonders of nature. Doc shook his head sadly.

"Why did you do that? They're getting hunted out, you know. Someday there won't be any pearl clams."

"I cut my foot!" Courtenay wailed.

"To hell with your foot. Look what you did to the clam."

Courtenay looked up from his rueful examination of his foot.

"The damn thing would have killed me, Doc!"

"Only because you attacked it, Courtenay."

"I wanted the pearl!" Courtenay exclaimed, as if this was all the excuse he needed. "See if there's a pearl in there, Doc, will you?" Courtenay returned to a pouting examination of the coral cut in his foot. "Shit," he mumbled as the guts and fluids of the forgotten clam slowly oozed out along the ridges of Doc's air mattress.

The next day when the planes returned, Courtenay flew over the field doing a victory roll. Doc had never allowed for the possibility that a demented child might start shooting down Zeros. The situation was getting desperate. One of these days the squadron would return with another senior pilot missing, and Courtenay's gun film nowhere to be found. Doc would then have more evidence, but he would also have another dead pilot—maybe even one of the pilots like Bix or Steve who were like sons to him. Maybe it was time to trust Marchetti with his suspicions. What could Marchetti say, after all, except that Doc needed more evidence? That night, Doc opened another ampoule of morphine and injected himself in order to sleep.

The next morning, Doc missed briefing and got to the landing strip when the last plane was climbing into the northern sky. Marchetti pulled up alongside Doc's jeep and yelled over the noise of his idling engine.

"Where were you, Doc? What's going on?" The set of Marchetti's small jaw could be as intimidating as that of General Laird's large one.

"I need to talk to you, Bob," Doc said.

"Good. I need to talk to you, too," Marchetti said. "Come over to the office."

Marchetti sat as expressionless as a telephone pole while Doc closed the screen door behind him and sat down. It was clear that he wanted some answers. Doc tore a page from his notebook and dropped it on the desk in front of Marchetti. It was a record of the two missions on which senior pilots had disappeared and on which Courtenay's film was missing.

"Just the way it was on Buster's last mission," Doc said. "No film."

Marchetti's face said Doc had finally gone over the edge.

"Are you saying what I think you're saying?"

"He's a lunatic, Bob."

"We're all lunatics, Doc. Would sane men volunteer to do what we do?"

"It's more than that," Doc said. "I'm saying he has a plan."

"I know what you're saying. Can you imagine what would happen to morale in this squadron if a rumor like this got started?"

"I haven't told anyone. I . . ."

"You didn't have to. The technicians are already onto you. They haven't caught up exactly, but they're not far behind. I'm going to shut you down, Doc. Stay away from Courtenay. Get off his back. Stay out of the photo tent. The mission files are off-limits. Closed."

"Bob, I know the evidence isn't enough, but suppose I'm right. . . ."

"You let me worry about that. If you touch those files or the film canisters or you're late one more time, I'm going to pack you off on rest leave. Maybe I'll send you back to the States."

Doc felt panic rising, his twitches taking over. If he was sent away, who would protect the pilots?

He heard his voice grow shrill. "Bob, listen to me. There's a madman—"

Marchetti's voice rose also. "You listen to me, Oscar. This is for your own good. You're cracking up."

. . .

Doc sat in his office tent, staring through a window screen at bomb-splintered palm trees across the squadron street. For every four beats of eye blinking, his arm and leg pulsed twice. Doc, the man to whom others brought their troubles, needed somebody to talk to, himself. The only other person in the squadron whom Doc trusted as much as he'd once trusted Marchetti was a sergeant radio operator by the name of Arthur, whose tentmates called him the Mad Monk. The Monk had lived in a French monastery for ten years before the war. His broad face and high, pronounced cheekbones suggested American Indian or Siberian ancestry. Their conversation had begun on Guadalcanal when the Monk came to Doc with a minor jungle infection. A chance remark had caught Doc's ear.

"You're a man of the cloth," Doc had said. "Why are you not a chaplain?"

Leathery skin crinkled at the corners of the Monk's charcoal eyes. He was a slight man, nearly a decade younger than Doc.

"Because I have no faith in answers. Only in questions."

Doc was surprised at so scientific a reply from a monk. There were no others awaiting treatment in Doc's dispensary tent, and he'd opened a bottle of sake the Japanese had left behind.

"What do you have faith in?" Doc had asked.

"In ignorance. In how we live with the impossibility of knowing."

Doc had some thoughts about this, himself. There followed a discourse on quantum mechanics, the Upanishads, metaphysics. The Monk wove an intriguing tapestry. He'd been expelled from a monastic order for his heresies. Like Doc, he had only his speculations for company in the abyss of unknowing.

After his conversation with Marchetti, Doc found the Monk in the thatch-roofed radio shack, monitoring the squadron frequencies, even though the planes were now out of range over the Owen Stanley Mountains. Sometimes a plane turned back with mechanical trouble. The Monk lowered the volume of static on the speakers and turned his metal chair around to greet Doc.

"Well, Oscar, this is a pleasure." They'd been on a first-name basis since Guadalcanal.

"I need your help, Arthur," Doc said. The Monk spread his hands in a gesture Doc understood to mean that considering the impossibility of controlling anything, he'd do what he could.

Doc sat down as the Monk poured a cup of tea from his thermos and handed it to him. Doc wasted no time in preliminaries.

"There's a murderer in this squadron, Arthur. He's shooting down our own planes." While Doc talked, the Monk frowned at a gable he'd made with his long fingers. When Doc had finished, the Monk's head bobbed up and down as if he was not surprised. What he said, though, was, "Oscar, the first thing to consider is that nothing is ever exactly the way we think it is."

Doc was startled.

"Are you saying I could be wrong about Courtenay?"

"No, I'm not saying that," the Monk said.

"Then what exactly are you saying?" Doc was suddenly angry. "I might as well be talking to Marchetti." He'd never been angry at the Monk before. The Monk looked as if he was not surprised at this, either.

"You have to admit, though, that it's one possibility. Isn't it?"

Doc steadied himself. "I admit, I don't have enough data to prove it in court, but I know it in my bones."

The Monk nodded, judicially.

"That is one way of knowing."

"I should be allowed to do my research, Arthur. I'm responsible for their lives."

"You can't do it all, Doc. Let Marchetti take over."

"Marchetti won't take over," Doc said. He heard the sharpness in his voice. "He's like you. He doesn't believe me."

The Monk raised his hand as if to calm the waters. "I didn't say I don't believe you. There may be a grave danger here, as you say, Oscar. But it's you I'm worried about. You've always worked enough for three men. Your tics and twitches look as if they might tear you to pieces. Give yourself a break. You don't have to do it all. What is it? What are you trying to atone for? You act as if you're apologizing for your very existence."

"Give myself a break, is it?" Doc heard himself shouting. "While I'm giving myself a break, that madman could kill another of my pilots!"

The Monk gazed quietly, as if inviting Doc to calm himself.

"It's the old problem, Doc. You still think we control our destiny."

Doc jumped to his feet and headed for the door.

"Gah!" he yelled. "Arthur, I don't have time for philosophy. You're not listening to me either." His anger frightened him, and he wanted to go back, but it was like his Tourette's tics and twitches, as if somebody else had grabbed the controls. As he raced his jeep along the red gravel roads back to the tents, the Monk's words burned in his mind. So the Monk thought he was apologizing. What was so surprising about that? After Guadalcanal, when Doc had been sent on rest leave in Brisbane, he'd run into Abe Markowitz, a friend from medical school. Abe had invited him aboard his hospital ship. They were about to sail for the States with twelve hundred wounded soldiers. Part of Abe's staff were on shore leave; the ship was shorthanded. Doc moved aboard the ship and spent his entire rest leave tending the wounded. On one deck were padded steel cells for soldiers who had gone insane. Sometimes Doc heard their babbling and screaming echo down a passageway before a steel door clanged shut. Most of the soldiers were in casts encasing arms, legs, sometimes whole bodies. Underneath the casts, swarms of sterile maggots ate dead flesh to prevent infections. The sickly sweet stench of rotting flesh permeated every part of the ship, even the mess halls.

If Doc was apologizing, it must be to those he could not help. Why would he not apologize? He was still in possession of his arms and legs and face and genitals. He was a walking affront to the men in the hospital beds. He was a walking affront to the pilots he hadn't been able to protect, and to the ones he would now not be allowed to protect. How could he ever apologize enough?

THE JUNGLE—PART I

The parachute rattled and popped as it opened. Steve slammed into the straps, bounced, and sat swinging gently in a hot blue sky. He looked up to see if the silk had tangled or torn, but the white dome billowed in the sunlight, taut as a full sail. He looked below him. By pulling the ripcord soon enough, he'd allowed himself a few minutes to study the hazy, gray-green rug of jungle as he fell toward it.

Except for the current of air flowing across his hands and face, he might have been suspended motionless above the planet. He'd lost his sense of direction as he tumbled from the plane. He gripped the straps above him and twisted to scan the horizon. Over his shoulder he spotted distant thunderheads and beneath them the white fangs of the Bismarck Range. That way was Port Moresby, where he'd taken off only a few hours earlier. Many nights he'd lain awake rehearsing this moment, hoping it would never happen. He spied his plane, a dark speck unfurling a long ribbon of black smoke as it plunged toward a ridgetop. He flinched as the speck vanished in a rosette of flame that itself winked out, inconsequential on the face of the jungle that reached as far as Steve could see in all directions.

A shadowy lacework of ridges and canyons began to emerge

from the haze below him. Steve knew the country from maps, brief-
ings, stories he'd heard from Philpotts, the barkeeper in Port Moresby.
He was falling into the foothills of the Bismarcks sixty or seventy
miles from the coast. His crippled P-38 had lasted long enough to
carry him beyond the swamps around Wewak. In the crocodile-in-
fested swamps, Philpotts had told him, the life expectancy of an inexperienced European was about six hours if he sat still, less if he
stood up, and even less if he took a step. In the foothills, there were
other problems. If Steve went uphill toward the highlands, he
could be captured by cannibals and headhunters. The cannibals,
Philpotts had said, would keep a captive tied spread-eagle around
a large tree, and slice pieces off his legs and butt whenever they
wanted fresh meat. Over the wound, they slapped a broad leaf that
stopped the bleeding. A captive could live as long as two weeks.
Steve's best chance was downhill. Along the coast, the Allies gave
native tribes a reward for the safe return of a downed airman.
Along the coast, though, Steve might be caught by a Japanese patrol. Another problem was that some of the natives hated people
who looked like Europeans as much as they hated the Japanese.
They would sell an airman to the side they thought was winning
the war that day.

The jungle canopy was coming up fast. Steve had been looking
for a clearing that he might sideslip into, but he saw only a solid
layer of vegetation coating a jumble of razorback ridges and canyons.
He was falling onto a steep slope. Clutching the straps overhead, he
held his elbows in front of his face and his legs tight together as he
crashed into the trees. Branches cracked and scraped against his
legs and ribs. He slammed to a stop, hanging sideways. When his
eyes adjusted to the dim light, he saw that he was dangling forty or
fifty feet above a clifflike tangle of roots and scrubby undergrowth.
If he jumped free of the chute, he would be sure to break bones. Because of the steep slope, the canyon wall was only twenty feet or so

from him. Maybe if he started swinging he could build up enough momentum to carry him to the wall. He bounced a bit to see how firmly the chute was attached to the trees above him. A limb snapped and he dropped a yard closer to the ground. He decided against swinging.

Steve studied the parachute above him. One edge sagged, bringing strands of cord within reach. He could make a rope. He took off his flying gloves and stuffed them in a pocket. He drew his bayonet knife carefully from its scabbard, thinking if he dropped the knife, he might never find it on the forest floor. He cut a length of cord and tied one end to his wrist and the other end to the knife. Then he began cutting lengths of cord and tying the ends together. Twice he dropped the knife and retrieved it by the cord. He made a rope with many knots in it so the thin cord would be easier to grip. He made it long enough to loop through his harness with both ends touching the ground. He put his gloves on and wound the double length of rope once around his leg. He unbuckled his harness and let himself down toward the ground, hand over hand, reminded of things he had done with the neighbor kids on his grandfather's farm. On the ground, he tried to tug the parachute loose from the branches, thinking it might be useful as a blanket or shelter, maybe even for trading with the natives. But it held fast. He pulled the rope free of the harness and tied it to his belt.

He was dripping with sweat. The air was like a steam bath, not a breath moving in any direction. He took off his jacket, rolled it, and tied it around his waist. Swatting mosquitoes, wiping his face on the sleeve of his flight suit, he began picking his way down the steep slope. In the shade of the forest, the undergrowth was sparse, but tree roots seemed to gully, ridge, and furrow every square foot of surface. Each step was a balancing act. His foot sometimes slipped into pockets among the roots filled with black, oily-looking water that stank of rotting vegetation. Once, he fell on his side in a large puddle, and climbed out covered with an obscene slime. A cloud of mosquitoes whined around him. He found his insect repellent and rubbed it on his hands and face, but it was soon washed away by sweat. He had lost his khaki helmet when he bailed out. Mosquitoes worked their way down through his hair and bit his scalp. As he wiped his face, his sleeves were soon black with a mash of mosquitoes, sweat, blood, repellent, and slime.

Steve tried to travel as quietly as possible. Even this far from the coast, a patrol might have seen his parachute. He'd been walking for two or three hours when a faint hooting echoed through the canyon. He stood still and listened. Was it a signal? He did not know the sounds of the animals on this island. He realized for the first time how silent the forest was. Even in the jungle around Port Moresby, he sometimes heard hooting and screeching and birdsong. Was there a reason for the silence? Was there danger? Philpotts had said there wasn't enough animal life in the jungle to keep a hunter alive. In forty thousand years of continuous occupation, the natives had killed most of it. What little there was would poison you or kill you outright. Crocodiles. Vipers. Ten-foot monitor lizards. A one-hundred-ten-pound cassowary that could disembowel a man with a single kick. A bird of paradise with a lethal glue on its feathers. Steve unsnapped the holster under his arm and drew his forty-five automatic to make sure it was dry and loaded. He checked his pocket for extra clips, returned the pistol, and shifted the holster forward for an easier draw. Then he remembered Philpotts's warnings about roots, leaves, bark, tubers, flowers, seeds, and fungi as well. Philpotts knew of some that hadn't been mentioned in Steve's jungle survival training. The best bloody thing, Philpotts said, was not to touch any bloody thing at all. But with nearly every step, leaves brushed against Steve's face or he found himself hugging a mossy tree for balance or clinging to creepers or small branches to keep from slipping as he let himself downhill. He kept his gloves on, hot and sweaty as they were, to protect his hands from acid sap or other poisons.

Steve had not eaten since breakfast before takeoff that morning. He found a thick root to sit on, where he could rest his back against a tree. He removed his gloves and wiped his face and unzipped a pocket of his flight suit to examine his K rations. While he was chewing a piece of rubbery flavorless cheese, the shade in the forest deepened and a rumble of thunder rolled through the canyons. It was the season of afternoon thunderstorms. Missions were timed so the squadron could strike and get home before the weather closed in. Steve looked at his watch. The planes had landed by now. He wondered how many had made it home. He'd seen one plane going down on fire and heard another reported on the radio. It was stupid to use P-38s for strafing. The liquid-cooled engines were too vulnerable to ground fire. MacArthur's orders, Marchetti had said. Steve had argued, but the squadron commander brushed it aside. "MacArthur says if you don't meet the fighters in the air, hit them on the ground. They're there somewhere. Find them." MacArthur could add this to his other disastrous decisions. The trouble with having High Command practically next door was that you heard more than you wanted to hear. Like the slaughter at Buna and Gona on the north coast, and the rumor that MacArthur had refused to send reinforcements because he couldn't admit he'd underestimated the strength of the Japanese.

The rain hit the jungle like a falling cliff. Water poured off Steve's head and down inside his shirt and pants. Within a minute or two, it was running into his boots. There was no shelter anywhere, so he stood and began to pick his way downhill again. He had not included a waterproof poncho in his survival gear. Philpotts said it would be about as useful as a paper umbrella in a monsoon. Once in a while, it seemed as if a small dam broke among the high branches and a bucket or two of water crashed down on Steve's head and shoulders. In compensation, the rain washed away the sweat and slime and blood and dead bugs, and the steady downpour seemed to beat the mosquitoes out of the air around him. He resigned himself to living in a liquid medium. Lightning flashed above the treetops and the thunder left his ears ringing. He twisted his ankle several times among the slippery, moss-covered roots and rotten leaves, and began limping.

As it grew dark, the rain stopped. Steve stood at the lower end of the ridge he'd been descending. In the dim light, he could see water on either side and hear the rumble of streams merging below him. He was on the point of the ridge, trapped between two muddy torrents. There was no way to cross. If the water did not subside by morning he would have to go back up the ridge and around the head of the canyon to find another way down. He looked for a place to spend the night and found a cup-shaped depression on the uphill side of a tree trunk. With his machete, he cut brush and ferns and made a platform above the pocket of water and rotting leaves. He removed his shoes and poured the water from them. He took off his flying suit and his shirt and pants and wrung them out. He dressed, flailing at the cloud of mosquitoes that had found him again as soon as the rain stopped. Sitting on his bed against the tree trunk, he ate a cracker and a chunk of chocolate. He had four packets of K rations. Each packet was food enough for one day. He decided he would try to make each packet last three days. If he hadn't found a friendly tribe in nine days, he would try to make the remaining packet last longer. He drank the rest of the water in his canteen. Tomorrow he would get water from a stream and begin using iodine pills to purify it.

Steve pulled his jacket over his head and closed his eyes, but he was too angry to sleep. It was no use blaming MacArthur. It was his own fault for following a stupid command. By the time the squadron had completed the second pass, the Japanese had had time to man their guns and improve their aim. The white streams of incendiary bullets had laced the air so thickly around his plane that he could hardly see the sky. On the radio, Steve had heard Courtenay, the flight leader, yelling, "I know the bastards are there! Follow me!" Steve had followed in disbelief when Courtenay pulled up over the trees and banked for a third pass at the field. "Get 'em yourself," another voice had growled, "I'm low on gas." Then in the laconic Bayou accent of Steve's friend, Gumbo: "Me, too. Have fun, y'all." Two planes peeled away toward the south. Technically, it was desertion, but nobody would be able to prove it. Gumbo and his buddy would burn a fuel-rich mixture all the way home and arrive with tanks nearly empty to prove they'd been low on fuel. Steve had almost followed the deserters. Courtenay was a fool. Steve had stayed in formation alongside him and aimed at gun emplacements, while Courtenay roared across the field blasting shadows under the trees. Nothing on the ground exploded, nothing smoked, the decoy planes didn't even burn. By the time they pulled away for the last time, there was a trail of coolant pouring from Steve's left engine and holes in his right nacelle. He knew he was not going to get home. He'd be lucky to make it across the swamps.

Steve awoke in total darkness, thinking he'd heard crashing sounds. Was it a tree falling in the rain-softened earth? A ten-foot lizard looking for a meal? The luminescent hands on his watch said three-twenty. He was wet, cold, stiff. He felt filthy, as if things were crawling on his skin, but he did not dare use his flashlight to look. He slept fitfully, trying to ignore crawling sensations under his clothes. At daybreak, he took off his trousers and found slimy slug-like creatures stuck to his legs. He tore them loose and flung them away. Blood spattered from the squashed bodies. Philpotts had told him about the leeches. All you had to do was get wet. Steve cut lengths of parachute cord and tied them around his pants at the ankles. He took off his shirt and removed a few leeches that had somehow found their way under his belt. He knew he should eat before starting out, but he felt like vomiting instead.

It looked as if one of the streams had shrunk in volume. The water was still a muddy yellow, though, with invisible footing. He found a place where he might be able to cross. He walked upstream and looped his rope around a tree near the bank, then paid it out and walked downstream again. He tied the ends of the rope together and stepped into the water, using the rope to steady himself in the current. When he was halfway across, his foot slipped and he fell underwater. He hung onto the rope and remembered to keep his mouth shut. He found his footing and climbed up the opposite bank, where he untied the ends of the rope and pulled it from the tree. He felt crawling, wriggling sensations and tore his clothes off again. His shirt had acted like a fishnet, capturing the leeches that poured in under his collar. Their sucker mouths were already fastening onto his skin. He clawed them off, inspected his clothes, wrung them out, poured water from his boots a second time. The scratches he'd accumulated when he crashed through the treetops stung when he touched them. He found iodine in his first-aid kit and painted the scratches and also some of the nastier welts made by the leeches. After he dressed, he dried his pistol and knives as well as he could. He decided he would force himself to eat. It seemed as if everything that crawled, swam, or flew in the jungle wanted his blood. He'd better keep busy making blood if there was going to be enough for his own use. A cracker he had unwrapped the day before was soggy with stream water. He threw it away in disgust. There might be native villages upstream. The creeks and rivers were their toilets. He tried not to dwell on the knowledge that the streams were now his only source of water.

He wished he had gone with Gumbo and let Courtenay take his chances. Steve had already told Marchetti that Courtenay was an egotistical lunatic. "You're all lunatics," Marchetti had said. "Look, you're only a second lieutenant. Courtenay's a captain. He's new on the block, but he's not stupid. I can't hold him back because he doesn't talk nice." The crowning insult was that Steve had to fly as Courtenay's wingman because Steve had more experience in combat. Marchetti had promised it would only be for a mission or two. If Steve hadn't been so busy firing at gun emplacements to protect Courtenay, maybe Steve would be home getting loaded on gin and juice right now, and Courtenay would be the one sitting in the slime chewing pemmican and picking leeches out of his crotch. Steve spat the pemmican onto the rotten leaves of the jungle floor.

The ridge was much the same as the one he'd landed on, though not as steep. His sore ankle had not improved overnight. Since it appeared that his feet were going to be wet all the time anyway, he began setting them down in pockets of black water and rotting leaves. Sometimes he found a flat surface under the water that allowed him to step forward without slipping. Among the roots, it was like walking on broken bricks and boards sitting on edge. He twisted his ankle again, worse than the other times. He laced his boot tighter and cut a crude cane from a bush. His limp slowed him down, but during the day he crossed two small streams, then found fairly even footing on a ridge with less slope. For a while, he heard rustling sounds in the branches overhead and saw little monkey-like creatures that had to be the tree-climbing kangaroos Philpotts had once mentioned. In some tribes, Philpotts said, raw kangaroo brains were a great delicacy, like raw monkey brains in Borneo and the Philippines. Once Steve heard planes that might have been P-38s, but he could not see through the leaves overhead. Even if he'd been able to get their attention, they probably could have done nothing about it except mark his grave on the map. At least he'd had the foresight to bring extra food and a machete, in spite of teasing from the other pilots. Now and then, he saw brilliant berries or strange green swellings on branches and vines that might have been edible, but he did not recognize any of it from survival train-ing. Bugger survival training, Philpotts had said. "If you haven't eaten it once and survived, don't touch it."

By the end of the third day, Steve's feet were raw in patches and his ankle was swollen. Before sleeping, he painted the raw patches with iodine, wrung out his socks, and put them back on. In the morning, his ankle was still swollen. He was not able to walk fast anyway, because the tall forest was being replaced by shorter trees, ferns, creepers, and brush. Steve heard exotic birdcalls and some-times a flapping of wings, but he could see only the press of foliage around his face. It was beginning to seem like the impenetrable scrub described by Philpotts. In places, Steve could barely squeeze through the undergrowth. By the end of the fourth day, the brush was so thick he had to use his machete. He worried about the noise. He hacked and sweated and went to sleep that night with blistered hands.

In the morning, Steve came to the understanding that, without some miracle, he was not going to reach the coast. He could not have traveled more than ten or fifteen miles. He had forty or fifty to go. As far as he knew, the scrub continued all the way to the coast. He might never encounter a native tribe, friendly or unfriendly. That day, he hacked and slashed at the brush like a swordsman dismembering the hated enemy. About midmorning, he cut into what looked like a nar-row trail through the undergrowth. After his initial elation he re-flected that he now had a new set of problems. Who used the trail? Natives? Friendly or unfriendly? Animals? What kind of animals? He stopped often to watch and listen. Once, he heard a spine-chilling scream not far away. He froze, and heard crashing and thudding sounds that might have been dinosaurs in mortal combat. When all was silent for a while, he edged cautiously forward. He studied the ground for footprints or tire tracks. The Japanese used bicycles to move troops fast even on crude, bumpy trails, a trick the Aussies and Americans had not yet learned. Steve found no tracks of any kind. As the rain began to thin toward dark, he left the trail and squeezed through ferns and trees and creepers until he found a small, flat clearing that seemed a good place to spend the night. He put more iodine on his cuts and bites and blisters and went to sleep aching, he thought, in every muscle and trying to ignore his empty stomach. He dreamed of hacking brush that sprang up twice as thick as fast as he cut it, and of telling General MacArthur he didn't know which end of an airplane the propeller was attached to.

Steve awoke in the morning with his jacket being slowly lifted from his head and shoulders. His arms were wrapped around his chest, and he carefully unsnapped his holster and loosened his pistol. The jacket pulled free of his face and rose skyward on the tip of a long black spear. All around him, spear points bristled inches from his skin. Farther back, a fence of legs supported potbellied bodies smeared in gray mud and decorated with shell beads, armbands, and colorful feathers. One of the mud men held Steve's parachute rolled in a loose bundle. The fence opened. An elder with hair matching the gray, dried mud on his face stepped through and motioned with his hand that he wanted Steve to stand up. When Steve uncoiled to his full height, he towered over the mud men. There were exclamations of surprise, and the war party fell back a step or two with spears held ready to thrust. One muddy savage with the beetle-brow of a Neanderthal and half his teeth missing noticed the machete hanging in its scabbard at Steve's side. Beetle-brow grunted and grimaced and poked at the machete with the point of his spear until the elder barked at him. The whole group began clacking and clicking and grunting in a speech unlike any Steve had heard. With their spears, they pointed to various parts of his body and uniform, apparently trying to decide who or what he was. The elder waved at Steve's eyes. A jabber of interest and what sounded like argument swept through the party. Perhaps they had never seen or heard of gray-blue eyes. Maybe they were comparing him to the Japanese. Then again, maybe he reminded them of some German or Dutchman or Englishman who had shot their fathers and raped their women not so long ago.

The leader babbled what sounded like a command and started back toward the trail. With their spears, the mud men prodded Steve to follow their leader. When Steve tried to step forward, he stumbled and fell on his knee. As he reached for his cane, the spears ringed him again and there was more clicking and clacking. The leader returned, there was more jabbering, and the spears withdrew. Steve stood and began to hobble forward with his cane. The mud men doubled over, howling with laughter. One mimicked Steve, stumbling, falling, hobbling with his stick, then threw his head back, cackling and slapping himself. When he had himself under control, he repeated the act several times, as if his companions were none too swift in getting the idea. Soon most of the mud men were doing the imitation, rearing back or doubling over to cackle or howl, showing the others their own rendition. Some were quite good at it. Even Steve found himself chuckling. The mud men laughed even harder when they saw this, and repeated the imitations for Steve's benefit.

Beetle-brow had been watching with an evil glitter in his eyes, unamused. He now snarled an order that put a stop to the entertainment. He thrust his spear menacingly at Steve, and the whole group moved forward out of the clearing. Steve stumbled along, afraid to draw any more attention to himself by stopping to tie his shoes. The comic who had started the mimicry still giggled furtively on the trail behind Steve and carried on an ill-concealed imitation like a schoolboy unable to contain his mischief. Any tension that might have been relaxed by the imitations, though, now returned under Beetle-brow's influence. The mud men seemed to compete among themselves, yelling at Steve and feinting at him with their spears. Twice, Steve felt a spear point cut through his clothes and puncture his skin. The second time he recoiled and yelled and drew his pistol. All spears went up into position just as the leader turned on the trail and barked a command. The mud men froze while the leader clicked and clacked. There was an argument in which Beetle-brow seemed to give the leader some back talk. Leader and Beetle-brow snarled and yelled and waved their spears until Steve could not tell who had the authority. It sounded like the bare-fanged show-down of a dog pack. At the end of an especially vicious snarl by the leader, Beetle-brow subsided and Steve returned his pistol to its holster, with his heart pounding. He'd made a risky move. Still, Phil-potts had said you might as well follow your instincts in dealing with these bloody savages. You never know what they're going to do anyway. Nothing means the same to them as it does to you or me.

The mud men walked barefoot on cracked calluses so thick that their feet might have been soled in slabs of truck tire. They had walked most of the day without stopping. Steve's ankle nearly gave out a few times, but he was able to keep up because of his longer legs. The trail was now a flat surface sloping gradually downhill. Steve was hungry, but he did not eat for fear of causing more ruckus. When he unclipped his canteen and drank a few swallows, the mud men in front and behind him clicked and clacked and Beetle-brow hefted his spear as if he could hardly wait for the pleasure of running Steve through. By midafternoon, the patches of sky showing among the treetops began to cloud over, and soon it began to rain. The feathers in the mud men's headdresses and arm-bands drooped and the clay that covered their faces and bodies streaked and ran. Beetle-brow turned out to have reddish-black skin so deeply pockmarked that his face looked like lumps of stale hamburger. Steve began to notice rows of bean-size swellings on their backs and chests, curving and coiling in geometric patterns.

Philpotts had said the mud men shoved pebbles under their skin to make the bumps. Many died of infection. Some had hundreds of these scars. Steve wondered what kind of idiot would be willing to submit to such punishment. Maybe the same kind who would make a third pass at a heavily defended Japanese air base.

Beetle-brow had emerged as a first-class troublemaker. He followed close on Steve's heels, and while he no longer prodded Steve with his spear, he now slid his spearhead deftly under the machete scabbard and lifted it out to the side. The chattering behind Steve ceased as among a group of small children up to some mischief. Beetle-brow let the machete fall back against Steve's leg. He repeated this several times, as if trying to get a reaction. Then Steve discovered the spear blade sawing back and forth as Beetle-brow tried to cut the machete loose. Steve twisted the machete forward on his belt, away from the spear. There was a pause. Beetle-brow appeared at Steve's side and looked up into Steve's face while he grabbed the machete and yanked hard, evidently hoping to break it loose. Steve jerked it out of his hands. There was a murmur behind Steve as the mud men raised their spears again. Beetle-brow grabbed the machete again with both hands and appeared ready to wrestle.

When Steve was a boy on his grandfather's farm in California, he and his friend Todd Hurlingame had practiced roaring like a lion. Steve had developed an impressive volume. After his voice changed, he had roared on the football field in high school, and by popular demand at drunken fraternity brawls. On impulse, he roared now. Beetle-brow recoiled, the natives fell back, the war party came to a halt. Steve roared again. The natives fell back farther, spears raised, but they seemed unsure, some of them looking down the trail in the direction of their leader. Presently, the leader strode toward them, eyes glittering. The talk quickly grew excited. Beetle-brow pointed to the machete, yelling, and raised his spear as if to run it through Steve's chest.

Steve would probably never fully understand why he did so, but he unbuckled his belt, slid the scabbard off, and extended it to the leader. *Take,* his gesture said. *Take.* Brandishing the machete, the leader seemed once again solidly in command. He clicked and clacked what seemed a statement or two, and the mud men resumed marching without a murmur. More important to Steve, they no longer menaced him with their spears. Beetle-brow fell to the end of the column, where he leered murderously if Steve glanced behind him.

The trail continued downhill at a shallow slope. In places it seemed to end, but the natives knew exactly where to turn sideways and slip through seemingly solid walls of leaf and branch. Rain fell until the light began to fade. Steve's feet sloshed in his boots, and his clothes were so saturated that he could sometimes suck a drink from a waterlogged sleeve. After their feathers wilted and the mud ran off their skins, the natives seemed to be bothered not at all by the rain. It ran in rivulets down their faces and dripped off their oily skin and matted kinky hair. At dusk, when Steve's feet felt like vast boils and his legs were beginning to wobble, he smelled wet wood smoke. Shortly after, the trail ended in a muddy clearing by the bank of a stream. A circle of thirty or forty thatched huts stood around the clearing, with several larger huts in the middle. One large roof stood on posts, open around the sides. Under it, people clustered at small fires, maybe cooking. Men, women, and children splashed toward the war party, yelling and clicking and clacking. The mud men who had been most skillful at mimicking Steve began performing for their new audience. Villagers doubled over and shrieked with laughter at Steve stumbling and struggling to his feet and hobbling like a crippled old man. The mud men who were not such gifted mimics strutted about and poked Steve with the butt ends of their spears until the leader yelled at them again.

Suddenly the crowd parted and grew quiet. Spear points once more ringed Steve. A small native with a gleaming ebony belly strode toward Steve. The bellies are the chiefs, Philpotts had said. The chief's white hair rode like a cloud around his head. Among the beads on his neck hung what appeared to be a human jaw-bone. The chief stopped and waved his hand. The spear points with-drew and the spears once more stood on their butt ends. At a command from the chief, three men stepped forward. One was the leader of the war party, another carried Steve's parachute, and the third his jacket. The three men jabbered and gestured while the chief hefted the machete, fingered the parachute silk, and studied the insignia on Steve's jacket. Then the chief pointed at Steve's chest. As the leader of the war party reached for the pistol, Steve in-stinctively turned away. The spear points appeared again. One point rested solidly under Steve's chin so he could not look down. He felt the holster straps being cut, and the weight of the gun leave his shoulder. The mud men seemed to know nothing about straps and buckles. A bad sign. They handled the gun gingerly, though, as if they had just been told of its power.

There was more jabbering and clacking, then Steve felt his bayo-net knife removed from its holster. He was now without a weapon except for a pocketknife in his flight suit. The chief gave another command and the spear points withdrew. Beetle-brow stepped out of the war party and started across the clearing. Spears prodded Steve until he followed. He felt the urge to take out three or four mud men with their own spears before they finished him off. He was prodded toward a sagging thatched hut at one side of the clearing. As he ducked into the doorway, he felt a spear point jab one buttock and he recognized Beetle-brow's moronic cackle.

Steve sat down holding his buttock, trying to stay calm. Two na-tives, evidently his guards, took positions outside the doorway. Some unnamable stench filled the hut. Gagging, Steve explored the floor around him with one hand. The floor was damp but not muddy, and seemed free of any recognizable filth. He could not decide which hurt most, his buttock, the raw itchy patches in his crotch and armpits and under his beltline, or his feet. He examined the spear wound in his buttock. It was the deepest of the three he'd suffered so far. The mud men seemed to have a fiendish ability to puncture just enough to torment but not cause serious damage. Forty thousand years of practice, he could hear Philpotts saying. Steve stuck a bandanna in his pants to soak up the blood, and turned his attention to his feet. He had hardly been able to walk the last few yards on the trail, but he'd refused to let the mud men see. He removed his boots and poured water from them at the edge of the hut. When he removed his socks, it felt as if his skin were peeling off. His feet were too sore to touch in some places. He wanted to examine them by flashlight, but he was afraid his guards would notice and take the flashlight, too. He painted the sorest spots on his feet with iodine, then loosened his clothes and painted the spear punctures in his belly and buttock. He made bandages and taped them over the wounds. In the first-aid kit was a powder for the raw, itchy patches. It was effective against some kinds of jungle rot, but not against others. He would use it when he had dried out a bit. His clothes were going through a transition from sodden to merely wet. He decided to let them dry on his body. If he undressed, the mud men might decide he didn't need his clothes either. Or if they came to get him again, Beetle-brow might spear him because he couldn't dress fast enough.

Now that his injuries were more or less attended to, Steve began to speculate about his situation. He was somewhat reassured by the fact that the mud men had not taken his clothes. If they were going to eat him or take his head, why would they let him keep his pants and shirt and flight suit with its bulging pockets? It was Steve's impression that the thinking of the chief and the war-party leader, at any rate, extended beyond mere meat or a trophy head. Steve hoped it extended to reward money. Of course, maybe the Japanese would pay them more. And maybe they were so far back in the jungle that reward money meant nothing to them, in which case he would be more valuable as meat. He wondered how many other unlucky captives had sat contemplating their fate in this stinking hut. He held his breath as long as he could, then breathed through the fabric of his sleeve. If prisoners had used the hut as a toilet, they'd probably used the floor close to the wall. Steve would not be able to examine the floor until daylight. Meanwhile, he tried to avoid contact with the ground outside the area he'd already touched. He wiped the sweat and mosquitoes from his face and reached for his canteen, then realized that the natives had taken it. This could be a disaster. He was now dependent on their polluted water. He was devising a strategy for getting an iodine pill into whatever water they might give him when he heard a commotion outside.

A group of mud men were approaching the hut. Beetle-brow snarled in the doorway and made gestures commanding Steve to come outside. Steve towered above Beetle-brow, ready to punt him across the clearing, but the spears immobilized Steve again, one of them under his chin. Beetle-brow stepped close and began tugging at Steve's flight suit, evidently trying to pull it off. Clearly he knew nothing about zippers, and as if he did not want to display his ignorance, he stepped back and yelled a command. Steve found himself flat on his back with spear points bristling around his face. The one under his chin made a slight puncture. Beetle-brow's gestures explained what he wanted. Keeping an eye on the spear points, Steve unzipped the front of the suit, then carefully rolled from side to side to pull the sleeves off. He drew his knees up and unzipped the legs and pulled the suit off over his feet, thinking of his precious K rations, his pocketknife, his compass, and other survival equipment in the pockets. One of the mud men grabbed the suit away as soon as it was off, and an argument started, with much pointing at the shirt and trousers Steve still wore. Steve decided it would be better to die on the spot than be tied to a large tree and kept for live meat. If they demanded the rest of his clothes, he would grab a spear and do the best he could to finish off a few of the runts before they turned him into a pincushion. The mud men, however, had become distracted, groping at objects inside the zippered pockets, and the argument shifted to the flight suit once more. Presently, the spears lifted away and Steve was poked into the hut again, while the mud men moved across the clearing, jabbering and pointing and feeling the suit.

Inside the hut, Steve tried to take stock. His chances seemed to be getting slimmer, though as long as he wore his shirt and pants he felt some hope. He still had his boots. He realized with a small surge of elation that he had left his first-aid kit in the hut. For the moment, at any rate, he could tend to his injuries. His food was gone, but if the mud men planned to collect their reward, they would probably feed him, and if they were going to keep him for meat, what did it matter whether he ate or not? Maybe he would find out more about this soon. He noticed that the fires were burning higher and more people seemed to be crowded under the big thatched roof on posts. In the dim light, he thought he could see some of the people eating. There was an aroma in the air that was not familiar, but it identified itself as food of some kind. In spite of his worries, it made Steve hungry. He was thinking about what Philpotts had told him of native food, such as raw white grubs and uncooked kangaroo brains, when a scream echoed from the jungle at the other side of the clearing. The people at the fires seemed to go about their business unconcerned. There was another, prolonged scream of such a character that Steve lost all interest in food. There were two more screams, then silence. There seemed to be more activity around the fires. Not long after, Steve could have sworn he smelled the aroma of meat cooking.

THE JUNGLE—PART II

All night in the fetid hut where he was being held in the village of the mud men, Steve listened to the booming of drums in the jungle. Philpotts had told Steve about the big hollowed-out logs carved like crocodiles and mythical monsters that the natives could hear in villages miles away. The intricate patterns in the still air shifted and changed, near and far off, sometimes faint as a heartbeat. Were the mud men calling their relatives to the feast? Was he the feast?

At Philpotts's waterfront bar in Port Moresby, Steve had learned more about jungle survival than in any training class. Philpotts had told him of plants he could eat and plants that would kill him. A medicinal leaf to cover wounds. How to protect himself against leeches. But there seemed to be no preventive or cure for cannibals and headhunters.

As night came on, Steve tried to stay awake in case the savages came to prepare him for the fire, but he dozed in spite of himself. He would wake with a start, and shift position to minimize the pain of his wounds, trying to stay inside the small area of the filthy floor he'd already touched. He heard the rustling of creatures in the thatched walls of the hut and the coughing and spitting of the guards standing outside. Through the stupor of fatigue, he listened for a code or pattern in the drumming, but he could make no more sense of it than he could of the clicking and clacking of tongues he'd heard on the trail after his capture. Through the open doorway of the hut, he at least saw no activity in the village, no fires or torches in the darkness. He'd once poked his head out to see farther, only to hear a snarl and catch the glint of a swordlike spear tip that might have sliced off his nose if he hadn't jerked his head back inside.

Steve had first visited Philpotts's bar on a trip to town with Gumbo and another pilot from the squadron. Gumbo had been born in the bayou. Philpotts and Gumbo took to each other right away. Evidently, swamp spoke to swamp.

"Not much diff between a bloody croc and a bloody gator with yer bloody leg in his mouth, right, mates?" Philpotts yelled across the bar, his beefy face aflame with broken capillaries and alcoholic cheer. He reached into his cash drawer and extracted a head the size of a small apple. With bright blue pebbles for eyes, it bore an uncanny resemblance to Philpotts. It was the head of his fraternal twin, who had disappeared in the jungle up near the Bismarck Mountains. Philpotts had searched for him for five years. One day he'd encountered a native wearing the head on a thong around his neck. Philpotts had traded it for a new hunting knife. "And losing your 'ead ain't the worst of it, lads," he said. If they ever had to bail out, they'd be better off coming down in Japanese-held territory. At least they wouldn't be tied spread-eagle to a tree and have pieces sliced off their legs and butt for the chief's breakfast every day until they died.

But Steve hadn't bailed out over Japanese territory. He'd come down in the slopes of the mountains where Philpotts had found the head. Since his capture, he'd been treated like meat on the hoof. The foul-smelling hut he sat in reminded him of the holding pens he'd seen in the States, full of pigs or cattle waiting to be slaughtered.

Steve resolved on a plan. If the mud men approached him with ropes or ringed him with spears and tried to herd him toward a large tree, he'd pick up the nearest midget and throw him at the rest of the spears. He'd fight as long as his arms and legs functioned, and try to get himself killed outright. He even rehearsed in his mind pulling a spear from his own gut, spinning it end to end like a baton and running it through a mud man. He rehearsed many possible maneuvers so he would not have to think or plan what he was doing while he was doing it. The whole repertory would be there as a reflex, like pushing the gun button the instant a Zero entered the ring of his gun sight. He was glad his grandfather and grandmother did not know what was happening to him. If his head ended up hanging from a thong on the belly of a fat chief, at least they would never have to see it.

Steve opened his eyes and saw the gray light of early morning in the low doorway. It took him a few seconds to recall where he was. A fire flickered and smoked in the open-sided cooking hut across the clearing, and shadowy figures moved about. Presently, a group of figures detached itself and approached his hut. He braced himself, ready, reviewing his plan. His guards stepped away from the door and a bushy-haired mud man crouched to peer into the hut. The bush clicked and clacked and set two coconut half-shells down on the floor inside the doorway. One shell held water and the other was almost full of a mushy substance that resembled cream of wheat. The mud man stood up and walked away. Steve's guards followed the bringer of food while two new guards took their places on either side of the door.

When his hands stopped shaking, Steve groped for the bottle of iodine pills in his pocket. He dropped a pill into the water bowl. He spat on a filthy finger and wiped it on the inside of his shirt, then stirred the water with his finger while the pill dissolved. He drank.

Even with the iodine, the water tasted good. With the same finger, he sampled the pasty substance in the other bowl. It had a faintly woody flavor and went down easily. He speculated about the meaning of the food and water. Maybe the mud men planned to fatten him up like beef cattle were fattened at home. Or maybe the relatives and friends of the mud men in distant villages couldn't get to the party for a few days. He began to watch for any signs that the villagers were preparing for a feast: The piling up of food in the communal cookhouse. The gathering of fuel and digging of pits that Philpotts had told Steve about, for the roasting of large animals whole.

It was possible, of course, that the mud men were keeping him until a coastwatcher or the coastal natives or the Japanese came for him. That, too, would explain the drumming. Several days passed, and Steve began to feel a return of hope that he would not be converted to meat after all. Then one day Beetle-brow came by the hut. As Beetle-brow passed the doorway, his eyes met Steve's with an evil leer. He grabbed his bushy hair and yanked upward as he drew his other hand like a blade across his throat. He doubled over, cackling, then he was out of sight.

From the very first, Steve could not get outside or make his guards understand that he had to relieve himself. If he tried to poke his head through the doorway, he found spear points bristling a few inches from his face. He decided that adding to the stench in the hut was less inconvenient than getting an eye speared out. With a boot heel, he shoved his own filth and whatever else he could find into a corner of the hut and managed to scrape a little dirt over it. The stench built up, though, especially after rain or on sticky, airless nights. Breathing through his sleeve no longer helped. He discovered a trick of breathing in through his mouth and out through his nose after his lungs had processed the foulness from the air.

One day there was a commotion in the jungle at the other side of the village. Shouting and clicking and clacking grew louder as mud

men and bare-breasted women in grass skirts ran from huts, followed by children of all sizes. Soon a party of warriors with spears
marched out of the jungle into the open space at the center of the
village. Their bodies were smeared with gray-white mud, evidently
the standard traveling costume. The white-haired village chief
waddled out of his hut behind his shiny ebony belly. The men from
the village gathered around him, spears in hand, and began a parley. Among the visitors, Steve saw feathers tied to a cap of the kind
worn by Japanese infantrymen. Another visitor carried a steel machete in his belt and wore a pair of high-topped tennis shoes with
his toes sticking out. These were not good signs. The mud men
might have taken these things from dead Japanese soldiers, but
they might also trade with the Japanese.

Steve took the precaution of tying his bootlaces. It was not long
before his guards motioned him out of the hut and prodded him
toward the new group of mud men, who nodded and jabbered and
seemed to recognize what Steve was and then ignored him. The
parley did not take long. The new mud men placed an open basket
on the ground. The contents rattled softly as the chief and his second in command pawed around, clacking and clicking, letting
handfuls of cowry shells pour through their fingers. The chief barked
a command, apparently satisfied, and his warriors picked the basket up and carried it toward his hut. Steve's guards left him and the
new mud men gathered around. "*Coom*," one of them said. "*Coom.*"
It sounded like a word learned from a German or Dutchman. They
motioned with their spears toward the jungle. Steve now seemed to
be their property. Evidently, lunch was not part of the deal.

These mud men treated Steve differently. They were not especially
friendly, but they were not threatening either. They did not poke
and prod him with spears or try to touch him. Of course, he was no

longer carrying interesting things like knives and guns and bulging pockets. There was less talking among these warriors, and no quarreling. The trail they followed led gradually downhill toward the coast. The mud men seemed eager to get out of the high country as quickly as possible. For the first time a mud man smiled at Steve, who tried to smile back. Don't be deceived, he heard Philpotts saying. Those bloody savages can run a spear through your gut and laugh while they're doing it. These mud men, like the others, had swirling patterns of bean-sized stones under the skin of their chests and backs, as well as slivers and blades of bone skewering the cartilage between their nostrils. Pain means something else to these people, not what it means to us, Philpotts had said.

The village of the mud men was farther than Steve expected. They drank water from streams and marched until it was too dark to see. When Steve drank, he held an iodine pill in the water in his cupped hands and hoped it dissolved enough to sterilize. He felt dizzy once in a while from hunger. Toward the end of the second day, the mud men seemed to relax. They stopped, and some of them fanned out into the jungle. Presently, there was a shout and the rest of the mud men pushed a few yards through dense foliage to a fallen tree where others were chopping at pithy, rotten wood. They were pulling four-inch white grubs from the wood and popping them happily into their mouths. They held the larger grubs in their thick lips for a second or two and let them wriggle as if it improved the taste, then bit them in half and palmed the outer half into their mouths. One warrior offered Steve a handful. Steve was revolted but half starved. He took one, tried to make his mind blank, and threw the squirming creature into his mouth and bit down. It was rubbery and tender. He swallowed as quickly as he could, almost gagging, and only afterward tasted a mild nutty flavor. But his stomach was doing flip-flops and he could not bring himself to eat another.

In two days on the trail, the jungle floor had gradually flattened out, and Steve guessed they were not far from the coast. On the afternoon of the third day, the mud men picked up the pace and soon popped out of the jungle into a clearing around a village much like the first one. Here, though, were all the signs of preparation for a feast that Steve had watched for—stacks of firewood, a roasting pit, piles of coconuts and fruit, and what looked like yams in the shade around the cookhouse. The villagers had apparently been expecting him.

Steve prepared himself for attack. He gauged the distance between himself and the nearest mud men, much as he would take an instantaneous mental picture as he dived into a dogfight, registering the positions of the nearest fighters. He watched for any sign of a mud man pointing a spear at him or any attempt to surround him. Someone in the village gave a yell, and naked children and bare-breasted women in skimpy grass skirts began piling out of the thatch huts and the cookhouse, as they had in the last village. The women and children soon surrounded Steve, all mixed up with the men. The clicking and clacking was not as pronounced here. In this language, there seemed to be more grunting and hooting and hissing. The black shining bodies did not smell as bad as they had in the last village. In fact, as they crowded closer, Steve smelled rather pleasant herbal odors. The stink seemed to be coming mostly from himself.

He tried not to cringe as the villagers reached out to touch him. Were they testing to see how much meat he had on him? To make an estimate of roasting time? But the spears and shields and bows and arrows seemed to be moving farther away. The crowd parted and two girls with attractive, pointed bare breasts held up necklaces of lavender and orange flowers and put them around his neck, Hawaiian-style. Steve had heard of peoples in different parts of the world who decorated the animal they were about to kill.

Events moved swiftly. An enormous chief's belly appeared, festooned with necklaces of cowry shells, fangs, feathers, and carved bones. Supporting himself with a decorated staff, the chief stood in a half-circle of less resplendent dignitaries and warriors and gave a speech that seemed addressed to Steve. Every so often, a ripple of clicking and cooing ran through the crowd. When the speech ended, the chief waved his staff. Among the beads and feathers flying around the top end of the staff were what appeared to be several shrunken heads on thongs. The crowd parted and Steve could see women in the cookhouse dipping some kind of fluid out of a carved hollow log into coconut half-shells. A warrior brought a shell to Steve. When the men all had shells in their hands, the chief barked a command and the men drank. To Steve, the drink had a sweetish coconut flavor, slightly alcoholic. The women in the cookhouse threw fuel on the fires and began preparing food. As the crowd milled and thinned, Steve could see smoke rising from the cook pit. Philpotts had said the natives wrap the carcass in leaves, lay it on the coals, and cover it with earth for a few hours. Whatever they were roasting was already in the pit. Apparently Steve was not going to be the meat course, at least not today.

The girls who had put the flowers around Steve's neck flitted about, clicking and cooing and touching his cup, urging him to drink. Their little bare breasts bounced and pointed this way and that. The girls giggled and seemed to know the effect they had on him. As soon as he finished his drink, they took his coconut shell and placed a full one in his hands. He was torn between wanting to stay alert and clearheaded enough to fight, and not wanting to offend by refusing. He was already beginning to notice the village warp and fade and spin around him when warriors appeared, carrying a board with a hole in it. They set the board on two logs. Another warrior clutched what seemed to be a small kangaroo in his hands. With its tan fur and long nose, it reminded Steve of a fawn he'd taken care of one summer on his grandfather's farm. The kangaroo struggled soundlessly, twisting its head about like a pilot with a Zero on his tail. The mud man squatted and shoved the kangaroo's head up from underneath so the shallow bulge of its cranium rose through the hole in the board. Another mud man placed a steel machete flat on the board and with a flick of the blade separated the shallow skull plate from the rest of the head. Someone flipped the plate over, jabbed a forklike utensil into the brains, and handed it to the chief. The chief scooped out the warm brains in one piece and smacked his wet lips while the natives debrained another kangaroo and handed the skull plate to Steve. The two girls cooed and clicked and made enthusiastic eating motions. The village turned over sideways and disappeared in a burst of stars as Steve's head collided with some hard surface.

Steve awoke in cool water. Several mud men and women appeared to be washing him in a shallow stream. He was naked. In a panic, he struggled to stand, looking for spears, rehearsing his last-resort scenarios. The mud men and women fell back, cooing and clacking, letting him stand. He saw his clothes spread out on bushes as if they had been washed. They appeared almost dry. He must have been unconscious for a while. The mud men and women were looking him over and waving their hands and talking. An older woman with breasts like hoses hanging down to her waist pointed at his crotch. *"Hoo,"* she said. *"Hoo. Click clack."* The two girls giggled and peeked from behind a couple of older women. A mud man brought Steve's clothes to him and gestured that he should put them on. The natives clicked and hooed as he dressed. They pointed and exclaimed as he buttoned and zipped. Each item seemed to inspire a separate discussion.

One of the girls placed new flowers around his neck, and a mud man gestured. *"Coom,"* he said, using what appeared to be his tribe's only European word. Steve followed the men, with the women taking up the rear. Steve heard the beating of drums as they neared the village. In the open space at the center of the village, warriors were dancing, decorated with feathers and beads. There were drums large and small, a wooden flute, sticks and gourds for percussion. Hooting and howling from the crowd. Steve was urged to sit on a mat near a coconut tree where he could see the dancers. He seemed to be the guest of honor. One of the girls shoved another shell into his hand. It appeared to be more of the drink that had knocked him out. She squatted in front of him so that her skirt fell away on either side of her legs and only a few strands of grass covered her dark crotch. He could smell her, sweet and swampy. She cupped her hands under his and gave the coconut shell a little lift toward his mouth. She chirped as if she might be encouraging a baby. Steve laughed in spite of himself, and drank. The girls giggled. Women began setting baskets of fruit along a flattened log outside the cookhouse. Steve noticed men digging dirt out of the roasting pit by the side of the cookhouse. Presently with much yelling and tugging and blowing on fingers, they wrestled the steaming carcass of a pig out of the pit, laid it on a mat of green leaves, and unwrapped it. Other mud men dug with sticks in the pit and threw leaf-wrapped objects onto another mat of leaves. A kneeling woman gingerly unwrapped them, blowing often on her singed fingers. The chief appeared and sat down next to Steve under the coconut tree. The musicians set aside their instruments and the feast began.

That night, Steve lay on a woven mat in a clean hut, beginning to hope that he might be rescued after all. At the same time, he remembered Philpotts's warning not to assume anything. It could still turn out to be his last supper. He looked out at the village. A point of fire flickered in the cookhouse, almost gone. There was the faint sound of a voice from the far side of the clearing, then silence. The opening of sky above the clearing was inky black, like the village and the surrounding jungle. It looked like a treetop overcast, a blanket of fog spreading inland from the coast. Steve could see and hear nothing, yet it felt as if the volume of space around him was awash in waves of color and sound. He shook his head, but the impression remained. He had been very drunk a few times and fairly drunk a lot of times, but he could remember nothing like this. Maybe it was the stuff they'd given him in the coconut shells.

Steve floated, not sure of his contact with the mat under him. He did not know how long he'd been asleep when he heard a familiar soft giggle and felt a flutter of little hands unbuttoning his shirt, and other hands working at his belt buckle. He lay still, uncertain what to do. He decided that the mud men would not bother sending two nubile girls as assassins. What worried him now was some jealous brother or father or suitor. Maybe what these girls were doing was taboo. The two girls eased Steve's clothes off like little Houdinis. They had evidently paid close attention while he dressed at the side of the creek. By the time they got his shorts off, he was in a state of nearly painful excitement.

Every time he tried to take charge, they pushed him softly away, whispering and chirping until he understood that he was supposed to lie still on his back and let them entertain. As one of the girls slid onto his belly and worked him into her, her breathing quickened. Her body was so small he was astonished that she could find room for him. It was soon over for both of them and she slid off, giggling as the other girl took her place. The second girl lay on his belly for a while, quivering. He wondered if she was afraid. Then he began to realize that this one was different, more skilled maybe, for something unusual was happening to him. Slowly she spread her legs while she held her hands up under his shoulders and her cheek on his chest so he could inhale the strange but not unpleasant odor of her fuzzy hair mingled with the odors of sex that were beginning to fill the hut. She would not let him move. When he tried, she clamped down on him in a way that told him to be still. Then she lay motionless, barely breathing.

Prevented from touching her with his hands, Steve felt as if his mind was sprouting fingers. He could feel her body without touching. He was not sure when he was fully inside her, but he thought he must be inside by the sensation that he was rising off the surface of the planet. He could swear she was doing something more than having sex with him. She was loving him. He wondered if he was drunk or drugged or maybe something else. He remembered Philpotts saying you can find any bloody thing you can possibly imagine somewhere on this bloody island. When a faint flush of light in the sky silhouetted the doorway of Steve's hut, the girls slipped away with tiny chirping sounds. Sleep fell on him like a mountain. When he awoke, the sun blazed down into the jungle clearing. His body still tingled. He looked cautiously outside his hut. Nobody seemed to be looking his way or paying the slightest attention to him.

Steve bathed in the creek every day. His spear injuries healed. His beard grew out gold and curly. The mud men and women and children reached up to touch it, oohing and hissing and clicking. Now and then, he would notice a sparkle in the eyes of a girl and he knew she was the one who'd been the tenderest with him in the hut, and he longed for the night to come. One day a mud man pointed at Steve, then at the sky, and began running around with his arms spread in imitation of an airplane. Steve nodded and ran around roaring and turning and diving, and fell to the ground to show himself crashing. Other mud men jabbered excitedly and joined in, chasing each other with arms spread, roaring, until they ended up in a big Lufbery circle around the clearing at the center of the village. Every so often, one of them crashed and played dead. The whole village came to watch and laugh and yell. The children shrieked and jumped up and down and presently formed their own circle.

That night after he lay down, Steve thought about combat. He hadn't flown for at least ten days. The war seemed a million miles away, another planet. It was strange, but he felt as if the native girl lying on his belly at night had softened something in him that might spoil him for combat. Then again, maybe she'd joined with him in some feeling that was already there. Only a week before he was shot down, Steve had found himself with a Zero in his gun sight and realized he was about to kill a green pilot. Steve had stayed on his tail long enough to find out how green. The Jap pilot made every mistake in the book. He flew as if he was just out of training school. He might have been younger than Steve. A Japanese pilot had been captured recently who was only a teenager. Steve could feel what the kid was going through. In a Zero, there was no armor at a pilot's back as there was in American planes, and no parachute. His efforts to shake Steve off grew more frantic, which only made him more vulnerable, and finally it felt as if he no longer had any idea what he was doing. In the end, the kid seemed to give up and fly listlessly, as if he was merely waiting for the bullets that would end his torment. He reminded Steve of an exhausted deer his uncle's dogs had once cornered in a box canyon. Steve had rammed his throttles to the firewall and climbed away, unable to shoot.

One morning when Steve awoke, he saw mud men running across the clearing toward three undecorated natives carrying rifles, and a tall, bearded European in fatigue clothes with a backpack and a Thompson machine gun. Steve knew he was on his way home. He dressed quickly. The European was an Australian coastwatcher named Malcomb. He wanted to leave right away, without ceremony, because of the timing of the Japanese patrols. The chief appeared with a few of his warriors. Malcomb clicked and hooted, evidently proficient in the language. He handed the chief several silver coins. The chief seemed pleased, and pointed at Steve with his staff. The village was gathering, maybe to see another white man, maybe to say goodbye to Steve. *"Coom,"* a mud man said, *"coom,"* and made pushing motions, as if urging Steve to go with Malcomb. Maybe mud man language had only one word for both come and go, and the distinction between the two was supplied by gesture. Steve looked for the two girls, but did not see them. He hoped they were not in trouble because of him. As Malcomb threw the carrying strap of his machine gun over his shoulder and adjusted his pack, the girls came running from the direction of the creek. Beads of water sparkled on their hair and skin. Steve tried not to give them away by staring, but it was hard to keep his eyes off them. As he caught the eyes of the slightly taller one, a shock passed through his body. He felt as if he'd been made love to one last time.

It took two days to get to Malcomb's hideout. Steve could see no signs of a trail under his feet. Their path twisted and doubled back and seemed to consist only of places where Malcomb and the natives knew to slip through the foliage. Fronds and branches and creepers closed in place behind them like water behind a swimmer. When they heard shrieking in the jungle, they crouched and listened. "Birds?" Steve whispered to Malcomb. "Could be Japs," Malcomb replied with one ear cocked. After a while, a native signaled and they continued on their way. When it rained, Malcomb untied waterproof ponchos from his pack for himself and Steve. The natives did not seem to notice the rain. Their black skin shone with oil or grease that shed both water and mosquitoes. They stopped at dusk and Malcomb handed out K rations for everybody. They talked in lowered voices and pinched up the smallest crumb that fell to the ground.

Malcomb's base was a well-camouflaged shack on a rise overlooking a small bay. Between the rise and the bay was a mile of jungle and a gravel road. Malcomb showed Steve a tree where he sat on a hidden platform each day watching the road through binoculars. If he saw troops or armor, aircraft overhead or ships offshore, he sent coded messages. The Japs knew he was working along this coast, he said, but so far they'd been unable to find him. Whenever he thought they were getting close, he packed up and moved. Steve wanted to know more, but Malcomb would not give his real name or any personal information. As far as Malcomb knew, his wife and children were prisoners. They would be killed or tortured if the Japanese learned what he was doing. In the shack, Malcomb switched on his shortwave radio. He listened in the earphones for a while, turning dials, then began keying Morse code. In the morning, Malcomb woke Steve before daylight. In the faint light of dawn, Steve followed one of the natives across the road and into the jungle that sloped down to the bay. Near the beach, they hid in thick foliage where they could peek out across a strip of white sand. Shortly after the sun slid out of the ocean in the east, Steve heard the muffled sound of aircraft engines. Low on the horizon, safely beneath the beams of Japanese coastal radar, a pale blue and white Catalina flying boat was emerging from the haze and settling slowly toward the water. Considering all he'd been through, Steve thought, it was odd that he didn't feel more enthusiastic about being rescued.

FLYING WITH ANGELS

An hour from the Borneo coast, the weather began to change. Tropical thunderheads stood here and there, some with anvil tops as high as Everest. Their black shadows on the ocean surface drifted slowly under the wing. Blake adjusted his cap against the brilliant sunlight in the cabin and slid his armored seat closer to the controls. He and Willy were about to take the plane down from cruising altitude and fly across Borneo above the trees. If there was a storm ahead, they would have to fly higher and risk detection by radar. The Japanese fighters might have time to get off the ground.

In the copilot's seat, Willy gazed in silent worship as they flew past the giant clouds. Sometimes Willy quoted the Upanishads. He'd carried a volume with him since his days at the University of Chicago. He waved at the clouds, taking in the whole sky. "Everything is inside us," he shouted at Blake over the thunder of engines and the rush of air past the cabin windows. "The clouds. The sea. The mountains and lakes and rivers, all the creatures of the earth. The entire universe. The universe is God," he said. "We are all God."

Blake winked at O'Maera, their crew chief, studying the engine instruments over Willy's shoulder. O'Maera was so short he barely had to duck his narrow, curly head to stand between the pilots' seats. It was O'Maera's favorite spot on the plane, listening to cockpit talk.

"What about the Japanese?" Blake said. "Are they God, too?"

"Everything," Willy said. "The Japanese, too."

Blake made a small adjustment on the autopilot controls.

"Let's try to make sure God doesn't shoot us down, today. Okay?"

Willy threw his head back and gave a gleeful screech that sounded something like a train with locked brakes. Willy lived at full throttle. On the five-hour flight across the Celebes Sea, he'd half filled a notebook with sketches and poems for his girlfriend Michelle in Sydney, and had topped it off with a few pages of calculus. On one mission, he'd written a quartet for strings. At night on his cot, he slept three or four hours and spent the rest of the time reading or working by flashlight under a blanket.

The intercom clicked in Blake's ear. From the navigator's console on the flight deck, Dermott called a course correction. Blake turned a knob, watched the compass swing a few degrees, then stop. Along the horizon, a dark line was emerging from the haze. Blake pointed to it. O'Maera gave a thumbs-up, went back to the flight deck, and opened the hatch to the top turret. Blake pushed the intercom button on the wheel, held his throat mike tight against his larynx, and ordered the crew to battle stations. Then he began their descent to the enemy coast.

Blake had flown only a few missions when he met Willy. Blake was flying with another crew then, before the Borneo strikes. The officers of the squadron lived along a beach in framed tents open around the sides and mounted on empty oil drums to catch the sea breeze. Tall coconut palms rustled above the tents. Blake lay in his cot after breakfast, drifting off to sleep. A Japanese bomber had kept him crouched on the cold coral floor of a dugout half the night.

A loud voice outside the tent awakened him. A stocky officer with captain's bars pinned to the middle of his T-shirt ran past, waving his arms. At the water's edge, a bony, white-haired native in ragged shorts stood next to a beached outrigger. A few men had come out of their tents. The captain was yelling at them to run, hit the deck, how the hell did they know the gook didn't have a grenade in his hand or a machine gun strapped to his back that triggered when he bent over? A loose-limbed blond lieutenant was waving at him to stop. As the captain reached the scene, Blake heard for the first time the manic screech that served Willy for laughter. "Relax, Captain," Willy said. "He's come to trade. First, he wants a gift. Then he'll give us one." With that, Willy slipped his Air Corps–issue wrist-watch off and handed it to the native, who looped it over his brown thumb, placed his palms together in front of his chest, and bowed his head. The captain gave a howl and lunged for the watch. Willy became a windmill of knees and elbows, blocking the captain long enough to let the native launch his canoe. For a while, there was talk of charges against Willy, a court-martial, but nothing came of it.

Blake had never met anyone less impressed by authority. In fact, the bigger the authority, the greater Willy's contempt for its failings. When the commanding general ordered officers to stop fraternizing with enlisted personnel, including their own flight crews, Willy ripped the order from the bulletin board. "Bullshit!" he yelled. "Fascist bullshit!" Laughing, Blake and the others tried to quiet him. Back at the tent, Willy scribbled in a notebook with enough pressure to tear the paper. Every so often, he would snap his head up and snarl, "Fascist pig!" between clenched teeth, then resume writing.

"The general can't hear you," Blake said. "He's three miles away."

Willy's chair crashed to the floor as he jumped up, threw the tent flap aside, and let loose with his three-mile scream: *"Now can you hear me, you Fascist pig?"* He ran back to his chair with a prolonged screech and picked up his notebook. *"Heeeeeeeeeeee!* Now where was I?"

This mission, like the others, had begun with a predawn takeoff. Blake and the crew were briefed the night before, and got to bed early. At midnight, the air-raid siren sounded. A Japanese bomber was prowling somewhere nearby. Running to the bomb shelter with his flak helmet, Blake heard a snarl of rage. Willy had stubbed his toe in the dark. Someone laughed.

"Hush, Willy, they'll hear you."

"I hope you do, you Fascist bastards!" Willy screamed at the sky. A scream was usually sufficient release for Willy. By the time he dived into the shelter, his good humor was restored. Not so for the other officers crouched between the palm-log roof and the lumpy coral floor.

"Buggers," someone growled. "Why don't the nightfighters ever get those guys?"

"It's not easy," Blake said. "It's like pinning the tail on the donkey."

"A live donkey," Willy said. A few men chuckled, grudgingly.

Finally, the bomber began its run. Antiaircraft cannons thudded around the island. Anyone who looked outside would see high in the sky a fragile-looking white cross caught in the cone of search-light beams, and surrounding it a swarm of white sparkles where the shells were exploding. Presently, there were muffled detonations from the direction of the oil-storage tanks. When the all-clear sounded and the men walked back to their tents, the northern sky and the crowns of the palm trees overhead glowed softly in the orange light of fires. As Blake was getting to sleep again, the sirens began to howl once more.

In the predawn darkness, the fires were still burning. There was little of the usual banter as the crew climbed into the truck with parachutes and flight gear. Blake was grouchy, looking forward to an hour or two of sleep over the ocean. He was just getting settled when Willy vaulted the tailgate like an Olympic high hurdle. Somebody groaned.

"Jesus, Willy, how do you do it?"

Willy screeched.

"I think it's something they put in the food."

As their plane lifted off, sluggish and heavy-laden with fuel and bombs, Blake could see under his wing the trucks and ground crews readying other B-24s for the day's mission. The squadrons had been bombing docks and airfields in the Philippines lately, even Japanese battleships. Almost every day, fliers Blake knew did not come home. Above the other bombers, Willy slid his side window back and screamed out, *"Give my regards to Hirohito!"*, then slammed the window shut, grinning hugely. Willy's voice had such carrying power that Blake could imagine the crews on the ground recognizing it through the thunder of engines, raising their fists and cheering as Willy passed over.

One night in the dirt-floored, tin-roofed officers' club, while Blake was slowly losing his Dutch East Indies currency at the crap table, Willy's laughter sliced through the clink of glasses and the half-drunk uproar.

"Willy's crazy," the shooter said, rattling the dice. "Doc should have sent him home long ago."

A captain across the table reached for his winnings.

"I don't know. Willy got the formation lined up over Balikpapan after that dumb-ass colonel from Wing HQ couldn't do it."

"Bennettini knew Willy in college," Dermott said. "He was the same back then."

Anyway, Blake thought, all of them had a screw loose somewhere. Alone in his tent one sweltering, windless day, he'd held his loaded forty-five to his head with the safety off and his finger lightly squeezing the trigger. Recently his bombardier, McClatchy, an otherwise sensible man, had been using a pocket compass to align his cot exactly north-south before he went to bed. Blake's crew chief, O'Maera, took his teddy bear with him on every mission.

Sometimes Willy seemed saner than any of them. After every mission, flying officers were given a two-ounce whiskey ration. Enlisted men were given two cans of beer. Flying officers were billeted four to a tent, enlisted men six to a tent the same size farther back from the beach, where there was no breeze. Willy gave his whiskey to his enlisted men. He wrote a letter to the squadron commander, Major Neal. "Are six members of my crew second-class citizens?" Willy said. "Are we Nazis?" The major had called Willy in, explained privilege of rank, and apologized for it. "He gave me the runaround," Willy grumbled later, but he did not call the major a fascist pig. That was for people Willy hadn't met. Once Willy looked a person in the face, his antagonism seemed to collapse. Willy's worst-kept secret was that he liked everybody, even those he hated, even Fascists, even the people he helped to kill.

Over Borneo, the thunderheads had not thickened into a storm front after all. Giant cumuli glowed here and there in the sky, with gray curtains of rain hanging under them. At the radar screen, Dermott plotted headings to help Blake navigate around the weather. While they wrestled the lumbering bomber up the eastern slope of jungle and across the central highlands, Blake and Willy had little time for cockpit talk. This close to the treetops, a small mistake in altitude, attitude, airspeed could turn them into a fireball before they noticed the error.

They were following a river valley that snaked its way down

through the mountains toward Jesselton Harbor. A month earlier, it would have been suicide to fly a single four-engine bomber over Borneo. Lately the Japanese had been pulling their fighters back to defend the Philippines. On the first two missions, Blake and the crew had sunk a total of three armed cargo ships. They had come home with only a few bullet holes. Then, on the third mission, a ship blew up under them. This was not supposed to happen. Their bomb carried a delay fuse, but it had punched through the hull into the ship's magazine. The explosion split the ship in half and blew a hail of wreckage up around the plane. As they bucked in the shock wave and Blake and Willy regained control, Blake could hardly believe the plane was in one piece, responding to the wheel and rudder pedals. Among the junk flying around them, Blake could swear he'd seen an open-mouthed, brown-skinned sailor poised at apogee outside the cockpit window.

According to Dermott's map, the bay they were looking for lay on the other side of some forested hills ahead. Blake was about to alert the crew when the intercom clicked, and O'Maera in the top turret and Raskowsky in the tail began yelling at the same time. Two Japanese fighters were closing on them, one from each side.

Blake shoved the throttles full forward. With one reflex he and Willy hauled the plane over into a steep, climbing turn to face the closest fighter head-on before the other could catch up. Blake could see the red snake tongues flickering along the Zero's wings as it came toward them, an inexperienced pilot firing too soon. Then the bomber shuddered and the smell of gun smoke filled the cabin as the forward-firing turrets opened up. The fighter disappeared in a cone of tracer bullets. The gunners began cheering on intercom. Blake and Willy stood the bomber on one wing, nearly stalling as they wrestled it around to face the other fighter. In the corner of his eye, Blake saw a fireball in the jungle below. The second fighter banked sharply away, with the red sun insignia gleaming under its wings. Blake pushed the intercom button.

"I don't know what that other snapper wants to do, guys, but we're ten miles from Jesselton. What do you say?"

The cheering increased. Willy stared ahead, his eyes hidden by his goggles, but he gave Blake a thumbs-up. Across the harbor sat the gray silhouette of a medium-sized cargo ship low in the water. As Willy opened the bomb-bay doors, the fighter closed on them, firing, flew through their tracer cone and climbed for another pass. Fire from the harbor guns laced the air ahead of them, falling short. The ship's guns began flashing as the bomber approached. The plane shuddered as its own guns raked the ship. Blake had a glimpse of half-naked gunners jumping overboard, then the plane was above the ship at mast height, the bomb was gone, and someone on intercom was yelling "Bull's-eye!" A second later, someone yelled, "Snapper at four o'clock high and closing!" and a second after that, another voice, "We're hit! We're hit! Number three engine's on fire!"

Everything was happening at once. Blake was pulling up for altitude, trying not to stall while he turned the big, slow bomber to make it a more difficult target from the ground. Number three engine was on Willy's side. Willy seemed to be doing everything he should, feathering the prop, punching buttons, closing switches, starting the fire extinguisher. At this altitude, there would be no hope of diving to put out the fire. If the extinguisher didn't work, they would have to ditch right here in Jesselton Harbor before they exploded or a wing fell off.

"I think it's out!" Willy yelled, looking back at the engine.

"It's out!" one of the gunners yelled from the waist window. "There's a fuel leak!"

Then the fighter was closing again, its tracers streaking around the cabin. If a tracer ignited the fuel leak, it was all over. The bomber was vibrating steadily. Blake could feel his gunners on the edge of panic; there was hardly a pause between long, savage bursts.

"Fascist bastard!" Willy screamed as the Zero flashed by, so close that it changed the intensity of light in the cabin. Blake could see the pilot's high, broad cheekbones, the slit eyes behind the goggles, the raffish white silk scarf.

Raskowsky in the tail turret reported the fighter climbing again, and turning. Blake struggled for altitude with three hot, straining engines. If they could pop this fighter, he would get O'Maera down out of the upper turret to transfer fuel to the good tanks. Blake braced himself for the next attack, but it did not come. Raskowsky reported the Zero going home. Blake eased the throttles back a bit. "Don't break for lunch yet," he told the crew. Maybe the fighter was hit, or out of ammunition or running low on fuel. And maybe it was a trick. But the fighter was soon out of sight. Blake was about to call O'Maera when Dermott began yelling from his navigator's table, pointing at blood dripping out of the top turret onto the floor of the flight deck.

"Oh, Jesus," Willy said, looking back. "Oh, Jesus."

Blake called McClatchy away from his bombsight in the nose. By the time Dermott and McClatchy got O'Maera down from the turret, they were covered with blood. The flight deck was awash. It was hard to believe O'Maera had any blood left. As they were laying him on the deck, something fell out of the turret onto McClatchy's head, spattering more blood, and rolled on the floor. It was O'Maera's teddy bear. Blake ordered Willy to fly the plane so he could go transfer fuel. But Willy was already half out of his seat.

"Blake, I know anatomy, I know where the arteries are!"

"It won't make a damn bit of difference if we don't get home!"

"Blake!"

"Sit down, Willy! I only need to turn two valves. They have to be the right ones." He slipped in blood as he climbed over O'Maera and the others. Willy was yelling back at Dermott, telling him what to do. As Blake got back in his seat, Willy crowded past. Soon Willy had tourniquets and pressure bandages on O'Maera's head, arms, chest. He administered morphine from the first-aid kit. He wrapped O'Maera in flight jackets and held O'Maera's head in his lap. Whenever Blake looked back, Willy was testing for a pulse, loosening or retying knots, or sitting with his head bowed as if communing with O'Maera's small, shattered body.

Blake was sure O'Maera was dying. He would have to think about it later—he had things to do, damage to assess, a plane to fly. They might not have enough fuel to get home. He set the autopilot for a barely perceptible rate of climb. He ordered the gunners to drop the side guns and any nonessential equipment out the waist windows. He redistributed bodies in the plane for the most efficient flight angle. He was ready to chop the belly turret free, but delayed because if they had to ditch, the plane might break in half or fill with water too fast. He used all the tricks he knew, spent two hours descending, leaning the fuel mix until it was barely combustible, finessing gravity to give them forward momentum. An hour from Morotai, Blake got clearance for a straight-in approach. Soon after, a PBY rescue amphibian appeared alongside in case they went down in the water. Blake called Willy to help him land. As they rumbled low across the lagoon with wheels and flaps down, one engine began coughing, then another. All the fuel gauges read zero. Blake could see the fire trucks and ambulances and jeeps waiting with motors on, ready to make a run for it in case the plane went out of control and skidded toward them. As the wheels touched down, number four engine quit. While the last propeller was still spinning, the medics were through the open bomb bay and on the flight deck around O'Maera. Blake unbuckled, threw his helmet on the seat, and went back to them. The flight surgeon looked up and shook his head slowly. Willy stared out the windshield with his hands still gripping the wheel. Blake went forward and put his hand on Willy's shoulder.

"Willy?" No answer. "Listen, you did everything possible, Willy. Doc says he couldn't have done more, himself."

Willy stopped his production of sonnets, sonatas, and mathematical theories, and began drawing angels. He drew them on everything within reach—the tent, his sheets, his clothes. Pages in most of his books soon contained beautiful angels with Botticelli faces, wings folded or in flight, superimposed on the text. Some of the faces resembled O'Maera's. A protective phalanx formed around Willy. Dermott and McClatchy and some of the fliers in nearby tents kept undecorated T-shirts and khaki shorts for Willy to wear when they took him to the mess hall or the officers' club.

Three days after O'Maera died, Dermott noticed Willy had stopped eating. Dermott came to Blake's tent one morning. Willy, he said, was awake almost all night now, under his blanket with a flashlight. At lunchtime, Blake went to see for himself. Willy's crew-cut blond head popped up from the sketch pad.

"Eat?" he yelled, incredulous. "I just ate, yesterday!" He said it half laughing, as he said most things when he was not in a rage.

"You have to eat every day if you want to fly," Blake said.

"What is this, the German army?"

"I'm going to ask for another copilot if you don't eat."

"All right, then, I'll eat." Willy scribbled. "See, I've written it right here in my notebook."

"I don't care about your notebook. I want to see you in the mess hall in about five minutes. Tonight, too."

While he ate with one hand, Willy drew angels with the other.

His pen moved so swiftly that he hardly seemed to plan or think about where the line was going.

"I have to draw fast," he told Blake. "If I don't, they're gone."

"Where are they?" Blake said, glancing around. "I can't see them."

"Don't look right at them," Willy said, sketching while his eyes darted about the mess hall. "Look a little to one side."

Fitch maintained that all Willy needed was to get laid. Blake wasn't so sure. He'd been with Willy in Sydney. He'd danced with Michelle first. But it was Willy she'd gone home with. A few days later, Willy showed up at the hotel.

"Michelle wants you to come for the weekend," he said. "She wants you to meet the family. They're all freethinkers." Willy threw his head back and screeched as if he'd discovered the long-lost continent of Atlantis.

So Blake met Michelle's freethinker parents and grandmother in a tattered Victorian mansion full of books and well-worn comfortable furniture on the outskirts of Sydney. Her parents treated Blake and Willy like sons, gave them their dented Hillman sedan and their gas coupons, introduced Blake to Lisa, a beautiful cousin who promptly moved in with him. Blake's room was in an upstairs wing near Michelle's and Willy's rooms. The parents and grandmother slept in another part of the house. There appeared to be no rules. They were freethinkers to the core, Lisa among them.

"I don't want to be a wife," Lisa said. "At least not now. I just want to be myself." She was tall and fine-boned, with wavy, chestnut hair that smelled of springtime. Blake thought of her as a woman he might meet in a novel. "I don't believe everything I was taught in school," she said. "Do you?"

Even so, it was Michelle who held Blake's attention as they drove about town partying, being treated like family by Australians wherever they went. Blake noted Michelle's wide-set gray eyes that seemed to take in so much, her quick smile, her legs and hips a little too heavy for conventional beauty. He watched her whenever he could do so without offending Lisa, noted the way Michelle stood close to Willy and made sure he had a drink, enough to eat, a good place to sit. Now and then, Blake noticed their heads together over some weighty-looking book. Evidently, Michelle and Willy had devoured the same libraries. Blake had many sweet and exciting moments with Lisa, and regretted parting, but it was Michelle on his mind as he sat next to Willy on the transport plane, flying back to the islands.

"You scored big there, my friend," Blake said.

Willy threw his head back and screeched.

"How did you do it?" Blake said. "I couldn't figure it out. You didn't do anything I wouldn't have done. Except, of course, the seven pen-and-ink portraits, the watercolors, the Italian sonnets, the relativistic calculus, the design for the Sydney opera house, and the sonata for piano and strings you dashed off one afternoon. When did you have time to make love?"

Willy slapped his head as if he'd forgotten the most important thing.

"Don't joke," Blake said. "It's no joking matter. Don't tell me you didn't get in her pants?"

Willy stared with a corrugated forehead at the back of the seat in front of him.

"I don't believe it," Blake said.

"To tell you the truth," Willy said, "I didn't think we were ready."

"What does it take, for God's sake? How do you know when you're ready?"

"I guess when you know each other well enough. When things seem just right. How do *you* know when you're ready?"

"When I've got an erection."

. . .

After O'Maera died, Blake and the crew deliberated talking to the flight surgeon. Doc Hugo was a gruff, relaxed tank of a man who defied regulations in his own way by flying a combat mission now and then. But what would they tell him? That Willy was drawing angels? The last time they checked, artists had a right to draw what they wanted. That Willy didn't sleep? Willy had never slept much. Willy was still Willy, only a little more so. He still screeched, and raged at discrimination. He still gave his whiskey ration to his enlisted men. "Don't they take the same risks we do?" He was still writing letters to the White House calling President Roosevelt and J. Edgar Hoover Fascist pigs for imprisoning Japanese-American citizens in concentration camps.

Sometimes Blake wondered how Willy had managed to get into the Air Corps in the first place. Maybe it was his perfect health and his intelligence. Bennettini had found out about his genius IQ. Maybe it was his coordination, too. Blake had seen Willy walk on his hands past Wing Headquarters after a night of drinking, singing "The Star-Spangled Banner" in a vibrant, on-key falsetto. What kind of brain was required for such control? At the officers' club, Willy had won a sizable bet by drinking a glass of water through his nose. Yogis do this every morning, he said. That's why they never get colds.

They spent five days on the ground before the next mission. Bomber Command wanted to keep the Japanese guessing. The waiting made Blake jumpy. They'd been assigned a crew chief named Messinger to replace O'Maera. Blake and Dermott and Mc-Clatchy kept an eye on Willy, tried to keep him from being too conspicuous. One night the air-raid sirens went off again. The men tumbled out of their cots, cursing, groping for clothes and shoes and flak helmets. The Japanese bombers were not inflicting much damage on the base; they were a form of psychological warfare, intended to keep American fliers on edge and degrade their performance the next day. A gunner might miss a critical shot, a bombardier push a button a second too early or late, a pilot misjudge distance by a few feet.

On this night the bomber was overhead longer than usual. Maybe there were two bombers. An oil tank was burning, shedding its faint orange light over the island. The all-clear did not sound. Tension mounted in the shelter. Someone stuck his head out the door. "What the hell's going on up there?"

An authoritative voice rang out: "Get in here! We have strict orders!"

"That meatball's trying to make us nervous."

"Get in here, Nash!"

Willy's screech was almost earsplitting in the cramped shelter: "Come on, you fascist bastard! Get it over with!"

As if in answer, the guns began firing. Through chinks in the top logs, Blake could see the lower segments of the searchlight beams.

"Hey, this guy's coming in low and fast!" the voice in the doorway yelled, as ships in the harbor opened up with a steady roar.

"Nash, Goddammit!" Nash ducked inside. A murderous crossfire of tracers filled a slice of sky visible through the opening of the shelter. A bomb landed so close that Blake could feel the concussion through the coral floor. Then another bomb, loosing a dribble of sand through the logs overhead onto Blake's shoulders. Willy screamed.

"Come and get me, you fascist pig!" he yelled, and dived for the door. He was outside, pulling free of hands that tried to hold him back, before Blake could reach him.

"Willy!"

Blake struggled over bodies and out the door.

"Willy, dammit, come back here!"

Willy was outside, waving his flak helmet overhead, dancing down the squadron street in the orange light, screaming.

"Bomb me, you fascist bastards! Look, here I am, right here, right here! Bomb me, you bastards! Here I am! Come and get me, I dare you!"

Blake sprinted, but Willy dodged among the tents, screamed, disappeared, then screamed again farther away. Another bomb landed among the tents, inland from the beach. Thousands of tracers laced the sky in a low arch over the harbor. Antiaircraft cannons thudded everywhere. There must be two bombers, Blake thought, one high, one low. What might have been a spent bullet or shell fragment smacked into a tent near him. Blake ran back to the shelter, cursing.

"Looks like Willy's finally gone around the bend," someone said.

There was no laughter. From time to time, they could hear Willy outside, hurling challenges at the sky.

"Yay, Willy," someone else muttered. "Let's all get out there."

"Stay here, if you know what's good for you."

The guns stopped firing. There was an eerie silence. They heard distant cheering. Somebody poked his head out.

"They got him! They got him!"

Blake tumbled out with the others. The men began waving their arms and cheering. High in the sky was a yellow-white flame like a very bright star. It seemed stationary, like a star, then it grew brighter and began to fall, gyrating like a plane in a spin. There was a terrific explosion. The flame vanished. There was more cheering, all along the shore. Cheering echoed across the water from ships in the harbor. The searchlights went off and the all-clear sirens sounded. Blake and Dermott and McClatchy found Willy in the tent under a blanket with his flashlight. He was writing a song. It was called "Star of Morotai." He would sing it for them, he said, as soon as he finished it.

Major Neal got interested this time. Blake sat with Dermott and McClatchy in front of the olive-drab metal desk. Blake studied Neal's face, noticing a slight resemblance to Charles Lindbergh. Neal was waiting for an answer. Was Willy crazy, or just eccentric?

"Eccentric," Blake said.

"He doesn't follow orders," Neal said.

"He follows them fine in the air."

"He draws angels on everything. What's that all about?"

"No law against it," Dermott said. The major studied Dermott's stubborn, long-jawed face, and scratched his ear.

"I have to make a decision here, fellas. Calling in the psychologist is a serious matter."

"Why?" McClatchy said. "What will happen?"

Neal deliberated.

"Well, at worst, they could give him electroshock. You know what that is?"

They had talked about it.

"They'd cook his brains."

Neal nodded. "That's what some people say." He gestured at the three of them. "You fly with him. Should he be grounded, for your safety?"

"No." It was unanimous.

"Should he be grounded for *his* safety?"

There was the briefest pause, but this, too, was unanimous. Blake hoped they had done the right thing. Anyway, they were almost finished with Borneo. He'd heard the next mission might be the last. He hoped so. He was ready for regular missions with a P-38 escort. He'd like to see his childhood friend Stevie Larkin flying alongside him one day. He'd had news of Stevie, out here in the jungle somewhere, getting to be a top gun in his squadron.

From the start, the mission was different. A submarine had reported an unseasonal storm over the South China Sea, moving toward Borneo. The plane had barely crossed the Molucca Passage when thunderheads began to appear like gigantic columns holding up the sky. The sea below was foam-flecked, gray as steel. Three hours out, Dermott's radar screen showed a solid wall a hundred miles ahead. Blake shrugged. You didn't fly into a front if you didn't have to, but it was no cause for alarm. You hunted for gaps and trusted your instruments and strong wings. Blake pushed the intercom button and told the crew to tie down everything loose, buckle in, put on oxygen masks. He eased the throttles forward and set the autopilot for climb.

It took ten or fifteen minutes to get through the front. The plane bucked and shuddered, plowed through rain and hail. The cockpit smelled of wet metal. An hour later, they flew into the second front. This one was stronger and wider. Lightning cracked around them. Blue Saint Elmo's fire streamed off the antennas, the wings and propellers. The long wings flexed like a bird's, flapping ten or fifteen feet up and down at the tips. Blake knew they were through the front when the violent buffeting stopped. But they found themselves flying in a world of uniform gray, caught in a slab of cloud that might be hundreds of miles wide and a thousand feet thick. They would cross the Borneo coast soon. If it was clear beneath the cloud, they might still be able to fly at treetop level. Blake descended to five thousand feet, then three, then two. Jungle appeared below, through rain. Blake could barely make out the silver thread of a river. But where were they? Dermott could give them only an approximate location.

The central highlands lay somewhere ahead. Blake climbed to a safe altitude. A hundred-mile corridor cleared between two walls of cloud. Off the wing, a peak poked above lower clouds.

"Looks like Mount Obong," said Dermott over Blake's shoulder. "If it is, we're too far south." He went to his desk and brought back a course correction. Blake turned them onto a new heading. They entered clouds again, a world of flickering lightning, blue electrostatic streams. Rain and hail smashed against the nose and windshield. The plane bucked, yawed, and shuddered as fists of turbulence hit it from different directions.

Dermott studied the flight instruments over Blake's shoulder.

"Are we going in high?"

"The way I figure it," Blake said, "the radar won't even see us in this shit. There's probably another front ahead. We'll decide what to do when we get over the coast." He turned to Willy. "What do you think, Willy? Shall we go in high?"

Willy gave the barest flicker of recognition. He seemed to be looking at the sky, around the plane, everywhere. His expression was strange. Blake's and Dermott's eyes met.

"Willy?"

The plane hit a wall of hail and extreme turbulence. Willy's hands and feet were on the controls, helping Blake back up the autopilot in case the weather overpowered it. The turbulence was the worst yet. For a while, Blake's world consisted of airspeed needle, flight indicator, altimeter, compass. Another slab of cloud extended all the way to the far coast. They could not find Brunei Bay. Blake turned north, still on instruments. The clouds broke enough to show a cape they recognized, a harbor north of Jesselton. They descended, guns ready, bomb-bay doors open. There was no ship, no gunfire, no fighter. They flew up the coast as the weather closed in again, zero visibility. It was time to think about fuel consumption. Blake leaned toward Willy and tapped his arm.

"Let's go over Sandakan. If we don't find a ship, we'll unload our bombs on the docks and go home. What do you say?"

Willy grimaced. It could have been agreement. He was squinting, twisting his head, trying to see the sky in every direction. On regular missions, Willy was often the first in the squadron to spot approaching fighters. He was not likely to see any in this soup.

Soon after they turned toward Sandakan, they plowed into turbulence again. Blake's muscles were beginning to cramp. The right wing felt heavy.

"Willy," Blake called. "See if the de-icer's working over there."

No response. Willy was staring at the sky above. It was getting weird.

"Willy!" Blake took his hand from the wheel to tap Willy's shoulder, but the ship hit turbulence that seemed to be trying to throw them over on their back. At least Willy's hands were still on the controls. Blake pressed the intercom button and called Messinger in the top turret. Could he see ice on the wings? Negative. The plane felt better, more balanced. Sometimes a pilot hallucinated, flying on instruments. What was going on with Willy? He was staring overhead, mouth open. His even white teeth were bared in a beatific smile at the sky. What was it?

Blake was suddenly slammed upward, checked only by his seat belt. The ship was dropping out from under him. The altimeter needle was spinning downward, passing hundreds, more hundreds. In seconds, they had lost a thousand feet, then two thousand. Blake struggled to keep the plane in level flight. He shoved the throttles forward, trying to climb. In sixty seconds, they lost five thousand feet, a mile. Then the ship hit bottom and a giant fist punched them skyward again. In a minute, they had regained all five thousand feet and were shooting still higher. There was a moment of calm. The light brightened, the plane burst free into an open space a few miles across. From a brilliant blue sky, the sun poured in, the upper billows of clouds seemed afire, lined with golden flame, reaching higher than they could fly. Willy cried out.

"Oh!" Then louder. *"Oh!"*

Blake grinned.

"Really something, isn't it?"

Willy cried out again, looking above, below, all around. Blake saw nothing more unusual than the clouds.

"Oh, my God!" Willy yelled. His head seemed to be turning everywhere at once. "Oh! Oh, my God!"

Blake looked again. Were there fighters?

"Willy," he yelled, "what is it? What do you see?"

"My God!" Willy shouted as if his vocal cords would split. "The angels! They're all around us! They're everywhere!" He lunged from his seat, but was checked by straps, wires, cables, his umbilicals to the ship. He lunged again, grabbed, seemed to find a safety catch, tore other connections loose as he struggled out of his seat toward the flight deck, dragging equipment behind him. Blake grabbed his arm.

"Willy, what the hell's going on? Get back in your seat!"

Willy tore loose as if Blake's fingers were butter. Blake grabbed again.

"Willy!"

"No! They want me to go with them! Wait! Don't go!" he screamed as he dived through the bulkhead door and onto the catwalk through the bomb bays. "Wait! Wait! I'm coming!"

Dermott had been watching from the navigator's desk. His eyes met Blake's. He dived after Willy. Blake called McClatchy up from his station at the bombsight.

"What about Sandakan?" McClatchy asked.

"The hell with Sandakan. We'll dump the bombs in the water."

The intercom came alive with yelling, garbled words, the crackle of loose and broken connections, two or three voices at once from the rear of the plane.

"Calm down," Blake ordered. "Keep to your stations. We're still over Borneo. Somebody tell me what's happening."

Blake recognized one of the waist gunners. He could hear the hysteria.

"Willy's trying to jump out the waist window, Blake! He's scream-ing about angels! There are four of us! We can hardly hold him!"

Blake turned to McClatchy.

"Take my chest chute back there and pop it. Use the cords. Tie him up."

There was more confusion, broken sentences, broken connec-tions. For a while, it sounded as if Willy was half out of the plane. Blake changed course for the nearest clouds. It was no time to get jumped by a fighter. Inside the clouds, he wrestled the plane alone. Dermott came to tell him that Willy was tied up, still screaming that the angels needed him. He wanted to see Blake. Blake would let him go, Willy said.

Dermott had sat in Willy's seat a few times.

"Do you think you could fly this plane?" Blake said.

"In this weather?"

Blake knew it was a stupid idea, even in good weather.

"Go back and talk to him. Tell him I'll see him when we land. Tell him everything is going to be all right. And keep an eye on him—he's a regular Houdini."

As Blake cut the engines and set the brakes, silence fell around him like a tomb. After so many hours of thunder and vibration, there was always a moment of discontinuity before his body fully recognized the solid world. Unbuckling, he could see Doc lumbering like a tank toward the plane. Major Neal was with him. The psychologist. Shit. A flock of medics, an ambulance backing under the wing. Blake left the rest of the procedures to Messinger and tried to get to Willy ahead of the mob. Doc Hugo stopped him in the bomb bay.

"Let the medics get him out, Blake."

Blake jumped off the catwalk and ducked under the fuselage. A gale wind caught him and tried to spin him around. He vaguely remembered a crosswind during landing. The medics eased Willy out of the waist section, down through the bomb bay onto a stretcher. The crew had used so much parachute cord that Willy appeared to be wrapped in a white cocoon. He was not moving. Blake elbowed forward. There was a cut on the bridge of Willy's nose. His eyes were locked open to the sky overhead.

"Willy," Blake said, leaning over. "Willy, can you hear me?"

Willy might as well have been flying with the angels. Blake reached for his pocketknife. "Let's get these ropes off him."

"We'll do it later, Blake," Doc said.

"We'll do it now."

Doc held Blake's arm.

"Blake, he might hurt himself."

Everybody was watching. Willy's lips began moving.

"He's talking," Blake said.

"He's hallucinating," Doc said. The medics began moving Willy toward the ambulance. Blake pulled his arm free and ran alongside.

"Wait a minute, for Christ's sake. Let me talk to him." He grabbed the stretcher and made it stop. The medics waited. Doc and Neal and the psychologist waited.

"Willy," Blake said. "Willy."

The wind blew his words aside and flattened Willy's short blond hair against his forehead. Blake leaned closer.

"Willy, I saw them."

Willy twisted, searching Blake's face, his eyes dancing like Saint Elmo's fire.

"The angels, Willy. I saw them, all around us. The sky was full of them."

Willy gave an agonized screech.

"They wanted me to fly with them, Blake! Why didn't you let me?"

"I couldn't, Willy. You forgot your wings."

"No!" Willy protested, trying to show his back. "They're right here, see?"

Blake felt Doc's hand on his shoulder.

"Why don't you ride in the ambulance with him?" Doc said. "I think he'd like that."

THE JAPANESE ACE

One rainy day when the fighters couldn't get off the ground, Steve went to visit the Monk. There were men in the squadron who said if you have trouble in your mind, the Monk is the man to talk to. The Monk had a theory that the pilots who stayed alive longest were the ones with a wife or girlfriend waiting for them back home. At any rate, the pilots seemed to think so, for notice, the Monk said, how many of them had a woman's name or picture painted on the nose of their plane, or carried a photo or a ring, or a single earring in their pocket they'd promised to bring home so the pair could be reunited.

Steve had been in the squadron seven months, and nearly half the pilots he'd arrived in New Guinea with were dead. His odds didn't seem too good. He wondered if the Monk was right and his chances would be better if he had a girlfriend. The last had been a girl in California whose house he'd buzzed regularly in his Stearman trainer. Then he'd been transferred to another flying school and he figured somebody else had started buzzing her. The Monk said that didn't count. It had to be a woman you longed for and thought about all the time. The Monk knew a few things. He'd spent ten years in a French monastery before being kicked out, he said, for asking too many questions. He spent every day in the radio shack monitoring the squadron frequencies. After takeoff, the planes were soon out of range and the only sounds coming from the ear-phones and speakers were the crashes of static from distant lightning and the steady whisper and crackle of mysterious origin that the Monk called the music of the universe. He could have listened to Tommy Dorsey or Glenn Miller from the Port Moresby station all day on at least one speaker, but he preferred the music of the universe.

The Monk's theory about fighter pilots and their women wasn't the most radical thing Steve had heard from him. Steve was even skeptical of it, but it stuck with him nevertheless. He thought of it in the C-47 transport on his way to Australia for a two-week leave that Doc and Marchetti made him take after he was rescued from the headhunters. He sat in a bucket seat with his back against the wall of the plane and his head twisted to see out a window. An atoll with a jade-green lagoon was creeping under the wing. In the seas north of Australia, there were thousands of little coral islands like the one below, with a few coconut palms and a sheltered lagoon where a castaway might survive like Robinson Crusoe. Steve would want a girl with him, though. It was remarkable even to him how much time he spent thinking about women, though not seeing one for months at a time certainly must be part of the reason. He daydreamed about their bodies, what it felt like to touch them, what they smelled like. He thought of their faces, particular expres-sions, the sounds of their voices and the things that made them laugh. Some he thought about all the time, and others had made so little impression on him that he remembered them hardly at all.

As the transport descended along the coast of Queensland, Steve thought of Addie's friend, Francine, the girl he'd taken for a ride in his P-38 the last time he was on leave. She'd been a pleasant com-panion for two weeks, but since that time he'd hardly thought of her. This time, he resolved, he would not get tied up with the first girl he met. This time he'd like to meet a girl whose name he might want to paint on his plane.

In front of the Brisbane Hotel, Steve sat gazing out through the rain until most of the men had left the bus lugging their bulky B-4 bags. Some of the men horsed around in high spirits with two weeks of leave ahead. One of them goosed another with his cane, souvenir of a recent crash landing. Most of the pilots still wore the forty-five automatics they carried over enemy territory. Steve was watching a girl with a black umbrella who stood just outside the glass doors of the hotel. She wore a tan belted raincoat, heels and stockings, and a scarf around her neck that was more colorful than Steve expected to see on an Australian woman. There was a regal quality in the way she stood. Sometimes she would nod and smile when a man passed by, as if he had spoken to her. Several times she did not smile, and finally she turned her head away and would not look at the men at all. Steve felt a flash of anger. There were men on the bus who had not seen a woman for a year, but that was no excuse for raw remarks. The girl did not look easy at all, but even if she was, the men had no right.

As Steve made his way down the narrow aisle, he noticed that his B-4 bag was unzipped. He had stepped in a puddle at the airport and had changed his socks. He reached down and zipped the bag as well as he could while walking. A few feet from the bus, he tripped on an untied shoelace and swore under his breath. He was aware of the girl watching him. He tried to keep his bag off the wet sidewalk as he bent over to tie his shoelaces. It was impossible. He stuffed the laces in alongside his ankles, then stood up and started for the hotel entrance.

"You're about to lose a sock," the girl said.

Steve looked down at his feet.

"Your bag," the girl said, pointing. Three-quarters of an army-green sock dragged along the sidewalk, soaking up water. Steve mumbled thanks and felt the cold rain hit his back as he squatted down to stuff the sock in. The zipper was jammed on the sock. Steve was about to give up when the rain stopped. The girl stood beside him holding her umbrella over both of them, so close that he could feel the heat from her legs. He looked up, and they both laughed.

"I hope you don't think I'm being forward," she said, though she did not sound at all apologetic.

Her name was Jennifer. She had elusive green eyes and a quality of reserve that made her seem imperious. At dinner, they talked about their families. Jennifer had lost a brother in Burma and an uncle in New Guinea. Her father had been gassed in World War I and had died when Jennifer was a child. Sometimes when they were talking, Steve saw a look in her face that made him reach out and touch her hand. Usually she withdrew her hand quickly, as if she did not want to trouble him with her feelings. She had freckles on her nose and thick waves of reddish-blond hair. Later in the evening, Steve discovered to his delight that it matched the hair elsewhere on her body. He found himself more excited than he really wanted to be. He was doing exactly what he had resolved not to do.

Jennifer found someone at work to replace her for a few days so she would have time, as she put it, "to see what Steve had to offer." Jennifer had opinions. She started right off arguing with him about almost everything. For a while, Steve found it attractive. She argued about where to have dinner, why he cut his hair so short, the existence of the Devil, who started the war. His head looked like a bullet, she said. The Devil had been invented by the Pope to control the people. The war had been a business deal cooked up by Krupp and Rockefeller and the British bankers to get the world out of the Depression. She'd read it. There were people who knew about these things.

Steve liked it that she read about things and thought about them.

It was more than Francine did. But if Steve laughed at something she said, she grew cold and silent. He would make faces at her. He would cross his eyes and hook his forefingers in the corners of his mouth to pull it wide. He would push his nose up with one finger and pull his lower eyelids down. People in a restaurant or on the bus would laugh and Jennifer would be forced to smile. One day they argued on a boat ride in the bay. Another day they went to the horse races and Steve won fifty pounds. He tried to give it to Jennifer, but she refused it. He slipped it into her coat pocket and she threw it on the sidewalk. She said men still bought women, like slaves. He dashed about picking up ten-pound notes and ran to catch up with her. She reminded him of his Irish grandmother who'd shocked the family by getting a job in an office even though her husband made a perfectly good income. When they went to bed at night, Steve placed three or four quarts of Australian lager by the side of the bed and opened the hotel window to let the cool night air flow down over the bottles. In the morning while the room was warming, Steve and Jennifer drank cold beer and argued and made love.

One night, Steve was awakened by a nightmare, trapped in the cockpit with his plane on fire, about to explode. Another night, he woke up screaming with a half-dozen spear handles sticking out of his body. "What's the matter with me?" he said, still shivering. "I don't have nightmares."

"You've had too much war," Jennifer said, and made no move to comfort him. He wondered sometimes if she disliked him. But she showed no signs of wanting to leave.

In the lobby of the hotel, Steve and Jennifer ran into a pilot from the squadron. More pilots were expected from Port Moresby the next day. There would be a party at the Lufbery Circle. Why didn't Steve and Jennifer join them?

"Let's do it," Jennifer said. "I've heard so much about the Circle."

Steve was noncommittal. He hadn't told her about Addie, the

Aussie girl his friend Bix had planned to marry. Steve thought Bix might still be alive if it weren't for Addie. Steve wasn't sure he wanted to run into her. The next morning, Jennifer reminded him they'd been invited to the Circle. Her damp legs were intertwined with Steve's. He tried to explain his feelings about Addie. Her husband had been shot down at Port Darwin. She'd told Bix that if she lost him, too, it would kill her, and she didn't want to see him until the war was over. "After that," Steve said, "Bix flew different. He acted as if he was trying to get himself killed."

The bell of a trolley car clanged on the street. A man in a nearby window shouted at somebody below. Jennifer seemed to withdraw. She slid her leg off Steve's and the hand that had rested on his belly now lay on her own.

"So why don't you want to see Addie?"

"I thought when you love somebody you stick with them."

"Maybe you just stick with them until you can't."

Steve reached down beside the bed for the open quart of beer. He took a long pull and held it for Jennifer to drink, but she shook her head. He placed the bottle carefully on the floor against the wall.

"Well," he said, "Bix was risking his life every day for her and her country."

"And she wasn't, for him?"

"Not in the same way."

"Certainly not in the same way," Jennifer said. Steve could feel her green eyes heating the side of his face. "Why didn't your flight surgeon ground him when he started flying like that?"

Steve reached for the bottle again and sat it on his chest.

"Doc's losing it, too. He's a great guy, but he's been in combat too long."

"Why don't they send him home?"

"Unless you do the actual fighting," Steve said, "they keep you out here forever. It's the same in the infantry."

Jennifer was silent, lying stiffly beside him.

"Yes?" Steve said, sniffing an argument.

"What's wrong with men?"

"Men?" Steve said. "Which men?"

"They run the world. Look at the hell they've made of it. They have a disease called war. It gets passed on from father to son."

"I don't know," Steve said. "Don't you think mothers might have something to do with it, too?"

He felt her bristling.

"Such as?"

"Such as the way they brought up the men?"

"I had three brothers," Jennifer said. "Have you ever known a boy past the age of eleven who listened to his mother?"

"A few."

"And what kind of men were they?"

Steve chuckled.

"About what you'd expect."

She pulled away from him abruptly.

"You're like all the others, aren't you?"

"What others?" Steve saw real anger in her face. "Hey, I was only kidding, Jenny."

She jumped out of bed and began dressing.

"So you're not sure you want to see Addie, are you? Who do you think you are, to judge Addie?"

Steve sat up on the edge of the bed.

"Wait a minute, Jenny. What's the matter? Do you know Addie?"

"I don't have to know Addie. You Yanks think you're God's gift to Australian women because you defended us from the Japs. You think every girl in Australia is only too glad to spread her legs for you if you feed her for a week and leave her with a ten-pound note. Then you go back to the islands and tell your mates about the trollop you slept with and forget all about her."

"Jennifer, that's not true," Steve protested. "I've been thinking how much I'd like to come back to see you and maybe . . ." He tried to touch her, but she flung his arm away. She seemed in a regular rage. "Jenny," he pleaded, "how did we get into this? We were talking about mothers and fathers. What does this have to do with anything?"

"If you don't know," she said, pulling her slip down over her head, "I can't tell you."

"But I *like* you, Jenny. Don't do this!" She was a different person from the one he'd made love to and argued with all week. He had thought he knew something about her. She was a regular Jekyll and Hyde. He reached out to her again. She twisted away.

"Don't touch me!" she cried. "You make me sick, all of you! I'm sick of your slime, too!" She grabbed a towel from the back of a chair and pulled up her dress and wiped herself and flung the towel at Steve. He ducked.

"Jennifer!" he wailed. "Stop! Wait! I don't understand! We were having such a good time!"

"Oh, yes, you were having a very good time, weren't you?" she said, working her feet into her shoes.

"I thought you were, too!"

"Did you, now? Well, think again, hotshot!"

Jennifer slammed the door and was gone.

Steve was dumbfounded. What had he done? He couldn't chase after her. She'd be blocks away by the time he dressed. He threw on a shirt and raised the big sash window and watched for her on the street below but couldn't see her. He did not even have her address or phone number. He'd kept intending to ask and hadn't got around to it. Maybe she was right and she was just a convenience for him. But he'd really liked her. Would he have come back to see her? He'd thought of it, but to be honest, he wasn't sure. Maybe he had been exploiting her. But she'd started it, hadn't she, with that umbrella?

Should he have ignored her? He was getting angry. He pulled his shirt off and threw it across the room. He hadn't caused the damned war, either. He was just as mad as she was at the men who'd caused it, whoever they were. They were trying to kill him. They'd killed a lot of his friends. And that thing about the slime. Women had left him before, but not feeling dirty. It was his own fault for not taking his time, as he'd promised himself. He saw something glittering on the floor and bent over to pick it up. It was one of Jennifer's earrings. He hauled his arm back to throw it out the window after her, but something stopped him. He hefted the earring, felt another urge to throw it, then dropped it in his pocket instead.

For the next week, Steve could not keep his eyes off the girls of Brisbane. The glossy bouncing curls of one, the hips of another, flutelike laughter and the white stem of a throat, their perfumes and odors. Blue eyes, amber, brown meeting his with little flickers of lightning. But that was as far as it went. He kept remembering how Jennifer held the umbrella over him, and the green fires of her eyes when she was angry. He'd even enjoyed the arguments. He guessed she had a right to be angry. War had taken all the men she loved most.

Steve was sorry he hadn't gone looking for Addie. He guessed a woman could lose only so many of the men she loved, before it started killing something inside her.

The day after Steve returned to the squadron, no mission roster was posted. Mechanics and crew chiefs worked overtime to service every available plane. Rumors flew. Pilots who second-guessed the High Command said with Rabaul nearly neutralized, MacArthur was ready to break out of the Solomons and head for the Philippines. The squadron hadn't met Japanese fighters in the air for a while. Danovich said the Japs could be hiding planes in the jungle, waiting for the next Allied landing. Nobody asked Intelligence. Pilots were told only what they needed to know for the day's mission.

If a pilot was captured and tortured, the Japanese would learn nothing of strategic value.

After lunch, Marchetti, the squadron commander, called Steve into his office. Marchetti wanted Steve to know that the mission tomorrow would be at the extreme range of the P-38. Intelligence reported a Jap fleet approaching Hollandia from the north. Steve should pay special attention to fuel consumption. They might have only enough fuel for fifteen or twenty minutes of combat at full throttle, then they would have to cut and run. Steve would lead a flight of eight planes. Marchetti would lead another flight of eight and command the mission. All through briefing, Marchetti sat behind his desk flipping and catching an 1890 silver dollar, his good-luck piece. Steve had never carried a good-luck piece. In his tent, as he was getting his gear ready for the mission, he remembered Jennifer's earring. He found it in his wrinkled khakis in the laundry bag. He held it in his hand, remembering how it had looked on Jennifer's ear, then a lot of memories came flooding back and he felt the tightening in his chest that he felt when he missed someone badly. He placed the earring by itself in a chest pocket of his flight suit and zipped it in.

Steve was cruising just beneath a stratus layer that covered the entire sky overhead. The planes of his flight were spread out in loose formation around him. Now and then, his plane would buck as it passed through a downward-reaching rag of cloud. The silver needles of Marchetti's planes traveled a mile below. Two miles farther down lay an iron-gray floor of ocean that faded into haze toward the horizon. In a half hour, the squadron would rendezvous with the bombers and head north over the Pacific Ocean to hunt for the Japanese fleet. Steve kept looking for the end of the overcast so he could take his flight higher. If they flew up into the overcast, they would not be able to see either the bombers or the approaching enemy.

Except for the slow drift of planes in his flight a few feet up, down, away, then closer, in slight but constantly changing relation to each other, time seemed to pass with no sense of motion across the earth. They had maintained radio silence since shortly after takeoff. Hour by hour, the only sound had been the soft drumming of the engines and the rush of air past the cockpit. It was spooky. Steve tried to peer up into the overcast. It could be hiding an armada of Japanese fighters. Once in a while, a plane would move close to another, as if looking for company. Steve's wingman, Waller, flew in alongside Steve, raised his goggles, and, with a worried grimace, pointed to the overcast. Steve nodded, checked his instruments, then bucked his plane. When all his fighters had responded to the signal, he began a climb into the overcast.

They broke through into brilliant sunlight and blue sky above a floor of blinding white cloud that stretched to the edge of the world. There were no Zeros, not a black speck to be seen in any direction. Steve descended through the cloud again and the flight resumed positions in loose formation just under the overcast. It was still spooky. The Japanese could be hiding in the cloud. They would risk midair collisions that way, but they were a mysterious enemy, you could not always predict what they would do. Steve adjusted his goggles and oxygen mask. He rechecked his fuel gauges, oxygen flow, safety belt, gun sight, gun heater, switches. He fingered the handle of his parachute rip cord. Fliers had been known to panic, bailing out, and to claw the flesh off their chest trying to find the handle on the wrong side.

From the beginning, there was no hope of fighting an organized battle. Zeros poured out of the overcast like rain. Steve remembered

at least two P-38s going down right away, one burning and then exploding. A voice still rang in his ears: "I'm on fire! I'm on fire! Oh God!" Then silence. Steve missed a deflection shot, then looked for another target. The Zeros now seemed to be streaking back up into the cloud. Steve climbed after the nearest, hunted briefly in the blind whiteness of the overcast, then dived out of the cloud in case the Japs had come out again. When he broke into the clear, there was no other P-38 in sight and there was a Zero on his tail.

The pilot was good. Steve was soon sweating, trying to stay alive. He was using every maneuver he knew, everything his mentor Bix had taught him, and still it was not enough. They had crossed a large island and were headed out to sea. Steve had a vague impression that the Zero was forcing him farther from land, herding him like a cowboy would herd a steer on his uncle's ranch. The main battle had gone elsewhere, fast. Steve could hardly hear voices in his earphones now. They never had found the bombers and turned toward their target.

The Zero maneuvered Steve out beyond the edge of the overcast so he could not escape into the cloud. Looking back, Steve could just make out the dark line of the island on the horizon. The chalky scribble of fighter contrails that defaced the sky of every dogfight had disappeared. Whenever Steve tried to turn back toward land, the Zero got closer. If Steve flew much farther from land, he would not have enough fuel to get home. The pilot of the Zero surely knew this. Steve's engines were running hot, almost at redline. His only consolation was that the Zero must be near redline, too, and the Zero had only one engine to burn up.

Steve managed to get on the Zero's tail once and he nearly tore his wings off doing it. The instant Steve fired, the Zero flipped over and performed as neat a split-S as any Steve had seen. Many times Steve nearly blacked out turning or pulling out of a dive, only to find the Zero still behind him, a few feet farther back, maybe, but

still dangerously close. Steve was not allowed to rest his tired muscles, even for a few seconds. This had to be a new, late-model plane flown by one of their best pilots. Why me? Steve asked, shoving his sweat-fogged goggles up onto his forehead. He was beginning to feel like the green Jap pilot he'd once taken pity on and allowed to get away. He did not think this pilot would return the favor. He risked a split-second glance at his fuel gauges. In a minute or so, he would not have enough fuel to get home even if he could avoid getting shot. He rolled the plane over on its back, pulled the nose straight down, and deployed the dive brakes as he felt the plane shudder past redline. The controls got erratic, but still functioned, as he began his pullout in the opposite direction, playing the edge between blackout and hitting the water as he leveled off above the waves. He'd broken the third commandment of fighters: Do not sacrifice altitude. But he'd gained on the Zero and he was headed for the coast.

Steve had just begun to make out the dark line of the island on the horizon ahead when he noticed the Zero gaining on him. He cursed. How could that happen? His engine temperature was creeping above redline on both engines. The black disk of the Zero's engine cowling slowly expanded in the rearview mirror. Steve's throttles were as far forward as they could go. Still the Zero gained. It would soon be in firing range.

Steve was not a natural killer, but he was a natural flier. In primary training school, he'd almost been washed out for flying under telephone wires, coming home with grass in his wheels and leaves in his wingtip. There was a rumor that he'd taken his girlfriend's brassiere off her carousel clothesline with his wingtip. Actually, Steve had only imagined it and talked about it. He'd discovered, though, that if he could imagine a maneuver that was physically possible, he could sometimes perform it on the first try.

The waves beneath him rode high, with deep troughs between. With the Zero almost in firing range, Steve imagined turning so close above the water that he would have to tap the top rudder pedal and make a minute adjustment of ailerons a fraction of a second before his wingtip clipped the whitecap cresting a swell, then another adjustment to dip his wing down between the swells, then up again, tightening the turn as he got into the rhythm of it. The pilot of the Zero would have to fly and aim, while Steve only had to think about flying.

As the Zero began firing, Steve banked and felt a tiny lurch as his wingtip nicked the top half inch or so of the swell. Too close. He would have to refine it next time. Tracers streamed past underneath him, his wing dipped between swells, more tracers streamed past, it seemed like a river of bullets. Steve was turning so tight he could feel blackout beginning. If his plane stalled now or even dropped a few inches, it was all over.

His wingtip crossed the third swell, dipped, the bullets were still missing him by a few feet, the Zero was not quite close enough to the water, not turning quite tightly enough, the pilot was trying to do too many things at once. Evidently this super-ace had never imagined taking his girlfriend's brassiere off her clothesline with his wingtip. Steve was resisting blackout and wondering what to do next, when there was a flutter of light in the cockpit and the tracers stopped. Steve gave the top rudder a tap and looked around in time to see white spray shooting skyward behind him. The Zero was cartwheeling. Steve could hardly believe it. He pulled up as the Zero plunged into the water and vanished, leaving a geyser falling back into the sea.

Steve was alone in the sky. There were only the glassy blue-black swells of the heaving sea beneath him. He throttled back and began climbing slowly toward the coastline. His flight suit was heavy with sweat. He became aware of his hands and arms and legs again. It was as if somebody else had been flying the plane. He studied the fuel gauges, computing his chances of getting home.

He did not see how he could make it. He crossed the Bismarcks twenty feet above a glacier, held a few degrees of flaps for lift, descended in a power glide a steady two or three feet per mile all the way down the southern slope to the gulf at Kerema. With Port Moresby visible on the horizon, Steve's gas gauges read near zero. He would soon be too low to bail out. Over the water the red-nosed P-38 of their wing commander made a wide sweep above Steve and came down alongside. General Laird raised his goggles as if to get a better look.

"Good to see you, Ace. What are you using for fuel?"

"Damned if I know."

"Keep your altitude. If she conks out, bail out. The boat's waiting."

"I think I can make it, General."

"Keep your altitude, Steve."

"Thanks for your concern, Sir. I'll need this plane tomorrow."

The general glared, replaced his goggles, and pulled a hundred yards off to the side. Steve maintained his steady, slow descent. He could see the whitecaps, individual waves, and the rescue boat turning to follow underneath him. The men in the boat were looking up, shading their eyes with their hands. He crossed the shoreline. He was now too low to bail out. His body would hit the jungle before his parachute opened. His engines continued their soft, smooth thunder. The strip of gray metal mesh slowly widening just above the nose seemed a hundred miles away. Before he reached the mesh, one engine quit. He lowered the other wing to compensate for torque and shoved the throttle forward only to hear his good engine cough and quit. He eased back on the yoke to stretch his glide and felt the controls go soggy, ready to stall. The wings lost lift, the plane dropped, and the wheels hit hard. The plane did not flip over, disintegrate, or explode. He was safely on the runway.

They'd been cut to ribbons, Marchetti said at debriefing. He gave statistics. They'd lost three out of sixteen planes and brought home six more damaged. The Japanese had lost twice that number, but it was small consolation. There were two wounded pilots, one badly. He might not live, according to the flight surgeon. The bombers had also taken a beating. Marchetti said the pilots who'd flown to-day did not have to fly tomorrow. There was little talk. The poker game died early that night. Nobody even got very drunk.

The next morning, Steve slept through breakfast. In the after-noon, he took a trail into the jungle. A few hundred yards from the tents was a clearing in the process of recovery from a bulldozing operation. Creepers hung from branches and the jungle canopy was open to the sky overhead. Now and then, some exotic bird screeched or warbled in the forest. Steve thought it was a good place to think about the narrowest escape of his life. It was there that his friend Gumbo found him. General Laird and two Intelli-gence officers wanted to talk to Steve in the briefing tent.

The Intelligence officers had a transcript of Steve's debriefing. They asked about Steve's duel over the ocean. The Zero's markings, the pilot's ability, his style of fighting, details Steve would not have thought Intelligence officers paid much attention to. Did Steve be-lieve he'd been cut out of the battle and herded out to sea? Steve was sure of it. The Intelligence officers nodded at Laird.

"What's all this about?" Steve said.

"We're ninety percent sure you downed Ishigawa, one of their top aces," Laird said. Ishigawa had made his reputation in China. He came from a long line of samurai. It was his habit to pick out a flight leader for single combat. It was all over Radio Japan, Laird said. Their great ace had died heroically, dueling with one of America's most vicious killers. Tokyo Rose was threatening to have Steve's balls for breakfast. Laird was giving Steve credit for Ishigawa. He was writing Steve up for a Distinguished Flying Cross.

Steve lay on his cot inside the mosquito net and tried to remember the details of the battle. He could still see the perfect split-S. He remembered a storm of tracer bullets streaking past on all sides, and flying flat-out with the black disk of the Zero relentlessly growing larger behind him. He saw again the split-second image in the corner of his eye, the feather of spray fanning out behind Ishigawa's caught wingtip. Steve began to shiver. His teeth chattered. It couldn't be malaria—he took his Atabrine every day. Maybe he had the combat shakes. Was he getting to be like their flight surgeon, who'd been in combat too long? Steve couldn't stop shivering. He was beginning to realize what a dangerous business he was in. You'd think he'd know it by now, after all that had happened. Flying itself was a distraction, shoving the throttles forward and roaring down the runway and rising into the sky, godlike. You forgot that inside your powerful machine you were only a sack of protoplasm that could be rendered lifeless, inert matter in an eyeblink by a small sliver of metal. It could just as easily be Steve's bones instead of Ishigawa's rolling with the tides at the bottom of the Pacific Ocean.

Steve thought of Jennifer's earring. He got up and found it, still in a pocket of his sweaty flight suit. He sat down again on his cot and looked at the little gold-plated trinket, wondering if there was anything to the Monk's theory. Could a woman somehow protect you, thousands of miles away? According to the Monk, it had to be a woman you thought about all the time and longed for. Jennifer hadn't even liked him. But for some reason he liked her more all the time. Maybe he should write to her and thank her, just in case. Then he remembered that he'd never bothered to get her address.

ADDIE

After Bix disappeared, Addie vowed that she would have nothing further to do with men until the war was over. By day she managed her aunt's dress shop in Brisbane, and at night she went home to her flat and locked the door, and tried to understand her life. She especially did not want to meet fighter pilots. In the year since the Japanese had attacked Port Darwin, she'd lost her husband, Kevin, and now Bix. Sometimes she thought the men had the advantage. For them, when they were gone, that was the end of it. She felt a man's death like her own. She had to struggle to walk, to breathe, to wash herself, to eat. How many lives did she have? How many deaths could she endure before she stayed dead?

If she had kept her promise to herself, the encounter with Courtenay would not have happened. Her girlfriends had been begging her to go out: She'd been a recluse long enough, she couldn't mourn forever, Francine said. There's a war on, the men are still fighting, Rachael said, they need us. Besides, they'd heard there were friends of Bix's in town, pilots from his squadron. Maybe Steve would be there. Steve had been Bix's wingman. Addie loved Steve like a little brother. She'd heard he'd been shot down and rescued. If Steve was lost, too, Addie thought, she might never come out of her flat again.

After three months of seclusion, she'd forgotten the din at the Lufbery Circle. American and Aussie fliers drank and yelled and danced with local girls, and did their best to work off the shakes and jitters of combat. There was always a wait for the comfortable leather chairs and couches where Addie used to snuggle down with Bix for an afternoon or evening under the big oil portrait of the World War I ace Raoul Lufbery. She was relieved that the press of the crowd kept her from seeing that part of the room from the bar. While she stood with Rachael and Francine, waiting for their drinks, Addie saw no male face she recognized, though all else was familiar—the raucous laughter, the American dance music from the jukebox, the uniforms, the odors of spilled beer and men and their perfumed girlfriends. In the mural that covered the wall over the bar, World War I fighter planes wheeled in a great circle trying to shoot each other down. Spads and Fokkers and Sopwith Camels fell from the sky or lay crumpled, burning. Baron von Richtofen streaked earthward at the controls of a red Fokker triplane on his last dive, trailing a column of flame and smoke. There was not a parachute in the sky, as there would be in a mural of a World War II dogfight. Those pilots had flown before parachutes were invented. Dead or alive, they fell with their planes. The pilots in the room around Addie flew with parachutes, but she knew them, they were the same breed. They, too, would fly without parachutes if necessary.

It was not long before Rachael and Francine and Addie were surrounded by Americans in uniform. They brought news of the squadron: who was dead, promoted, or gone home to the States. Miraculous crash landings, rescues at sea. A young lieutenant introduced himself to Addie as Howard, a friend of Bix's. He was a small, wiry pilot who reminded Addie of Bix himself as he might have appeared at twenty or twenty-one. Like Steve, Howard claimed he was still alive because of what he had learned from Bix. He recognized Addie, he said, from the photo in the silver frame that had sat on the ammunition box next to Bix's cot up at Port Moresby. Addie leaned close to hear him through the noise. Nobody had actually seen Bix crash, he said. There was still hope that Bix had been captured. Addie touched his arm to stop him. His impulse was kind, but she had steeled herself against hope. The coastwatchers had seen what the Japanese did to captured American pilots.

The noise around Addie suddenly increased, if that were possible. A voice like a Mitchell bomber on takeoff was yelling, "Fire! Fire! Bail out! Every man for himself!" Then the men in the circle with Addie were bowled aside and a large creature on all fours was barking at her feet, snorting and growling and chewing her ankle, trying to sniff her all over, then Francine, giving Rachael a nip on an ample buttock as she fled behind one of the men. While the women screamed and dodged, the men yelled, "Down, boy! Bad dog!" and pretended to kick the beast aside. Then it rose up on its hind legs and metamorphosed into a tall pilot with captain's bars on his collar and deadpan features who began a rapid shuffle side to side, pointing and protesting in two voices, each aimed at the other: "He did it. No, he did it! I did not, he did! He's lying, he did it! I did not, he's the liar! Ridiculous! He did it! I did not!" till the illusion was created of two men pointing at each other accusingly, about to start punching. When everybody stopped laughing, one of the pilots introduced Courtenay. Addie had heard of him. Nobody ever called him by his first name. It was always Courtenay. Somebody shoved a glass of beer into his hand, which he half emptied at a gulp. His right shoulder jumped and twitched forward as he spoke.

"For a minute, I thought you guys were going to blow yourselves new assholes." His eyes focused across the room at a grazing angle that would allow him an impression of the girls' reactions.

Addie had forgotten most of what she'd heard about Courtenay. She vaguely remembered a picture so appalling as to be almost interesting. She saw before her more of an adolescent clown than the bully Steve had told her about, or the self-serving egotist described by Doc. Courtenay raised his glass and yelled, "To rape, riot, and revolution!" Adolescence had not been a time of misery for Addie as it had been for many of her friends. Actually, she had fond memories. It was a time when her friends had seemed sillier and freer and larger than the people they became later. Courtenay's shoulder twitched every few seconds. A new pilot joined the group, and Howard introduced him as Larch MacGinnis.

Courtenay turned his head toward the girls for a *sotto voce* aside.

"Yes, but is he larch enough?" He imitated protruding buck teeth. "Hyuck, hyuck."

"How old are you, Courtenay?" somebody asked.

"Twenty-four. Why, do I seem older?" He snorted and ducked his head, then charged into the crowd, yelling and waving at somebody across the room. He was back shortly with news of old comrades. Bostick was shacked up with a girl who ate apples in bed while they were doing it. Higgins over there was limping around with his foreskin shot off. "Can you imagine that? Only his foreskin!" Courtenay made a nipple-like appendage with his fingers for all to see. "A piece of flak came through his seat and took it off." He stared with blank amazement into Addie's eyes.

"What was he doing with a foreskin in the first place?"

Addie returned an equally blank look.

"I'm sure I couldn't tell you."

She was certain that Courtenay had made up the story. Yet strange things happened in combat. At Darwin, a pilot had had his oxygen mask torn off his face by a Japanese bullet, without injury. Another had had his shoelace severed. And anyway, what did it matter? It felt good to laugh. Courtenay's shoulder twitched, and he was gone again.

Soon after, a pilot from the squadron beckoned to those around Addie to come and take the comfortable chairs and couches they were about to vacate. Addie had no sooner found a place to sit than Courtenay vaulted the back of the couch and crashed into place beside her.

"How would you like to go to a party?"

"We're at a party," she said.

He leaned closer and spoke confidentially. He had some business at the consulate. He could bring a guest. They had a great dance band.

"I'll think about it," Addie said. Courtenay bounced his knee, twitched his shoulder, drained his glass, and launched himself into the crowd again.

It felt strange to Addie, being here where she had spent so much time with Bix. She wished she had gone somewhere else. While she thought about Courtenay's invitation, she danced with Howard, then with another pilot, and went to the loo. She decided she could not get in too much trouble at the American consulate, even with Courtenay behaving like a jumping jack. He did belong to Bix's squadron, after all. It would be a bit like going with a member of the family.

Outside, it had been raining. Queensland had had unusual storms lately. Puddles glittered; the streetlamps were on; the blackout sirens had not sounded for several weeks. In the cab, Addie noticed that she had pressed herself against the window as far from Courtenay as possible. She tried to relax, and for a while could think of nothing to say. She felt virginal, as if she'd never before sat in a taxicab alone with a man. In the light from a streetlamp she noticed Courtenay's hand doing a playful two-finger walk across the seat toward her. She tried to ignore it. She shifted her body, and the hand retreated. In the corner of her eye, she saw it advancing again. She did not mind Courtenay's silliness so much as her own cringing. It was as if her body had a mind of its own. As the hand approached her leg, she turned and looked at Courtenay full in the face. The two-fingered creature beat a panicky retreat and Courtenay made a great show of studying the city outside his window.

"Courtenay."

He presented a face of bland innocence.

"Addie."

"I should probably go home, Courtenay. I'm not ready for this."

"Go home?" he wailed.

"I'm sorry."

They were paused at an intersection with the rain drumming lightly on the roof. The driver seemed to delay longer than necessary, as if awaiting her decision.

"I lost Bix only three months ago, Courtenay."

"He could still be alive."

Addie's face pleaded with him not to offer false hope.

"You promised to go to a party with me, Addie!"

There was no question in Addie's mind that Bix would want her to go on living her life. He would not want to impede her in any way. It was one of the reasons she'd allowed Rachael and Francine to persuade her to come out tonight. In a way, it would seem disloyal to Bix to run home now. Once you're committed, she'd heard Bix tell another pilot, you're better off flying right through it.

"All right," she said, and the cab moved ahead once more across the intersection. She lowered her voice. "But that's all I promised."

Courtenay's hands flew up in startled innocence, his voice falsetto.

"Whatever do you mean?"

At the consulate, Courtenay abandoned Addie almost immediately, returned with a glass of champagne for her, and was off again. She was content being left alone to look at the crowd and sort through her thoughts and impressions. The musicians in the next room were as good as advertised, Americans in uniform. She could not resist letting her body respond to the rhythms. Courtenay appeared at her side again, said there was someone else he had to see, then they could dance. She watched him make his way across the room a head above the crowd with his shoulder twitching, grinning and making faces. He gave a sedate old gentleman a broad wink, and leered cross-eyed at a sausage-like woman in a magenta dress. He stopped long enough to grab a glass of champagne from a tray, drain it, and return the glass. Addie wondered how a combination of beer, champagne, and gin would affect him. He seemed rather drunk already.

An American major asked her to dance, then an Aussie paratrooper who did not want to let her go. When she stood once more where Courtenay had left her, she began to feel abandoned. Why had he asked her to come if he was going to ignore her? Was he looking for a woman who could offer more than Addie could? She had not seen him talking to women, though. Once or twice, when she had spotted him in earnest conversation, he was talking to senior officers. Addie had heard that Courtenay was ambitious. But he seemed such a child. How had he managed to become a captain in the first place? There were special circumstances, of course. At Darwin, with the Japanese fleet standing offshore, squadron leaders were lucky to live a week. As fast as one was shot down, somebody was promoted to take his place. Before the Japanese turned back, Addie had seen a twenty-five-year-old American pilot wearing the insignia of a full colonel. But times had changed; the skies over the Indies were not quite so deadly now. Maybe influence was Courtenay's game. As Addie pondered these things, a young man dressed like a British diplomat appeared at her elbow.

"Mrs. Courtenay?"

Addie started.

"I beg your pardon?"

"Oh, dear. The captain told me . . . How odd. Well, there must be some mistake." He excused himself and fled, looking back once with a perplexed expression.

Addie decided she'd better find Courtenay. She looked for a head of wavy black hair as she edged her way about the room. She nearly stumbled over him squatting on the floor in front of two small children. They shrieked as he plucked a rabbit's foot from the girl's hair, and gaped in wonder as he stuffed a white handkerchief into one of his ears, then unfurled it slowly from the other.

"Courtenay," Addie said.

"There you are!" he cried, as if he'd been hunting everywhere. As he climbed unsteadily to his feet, Addie was struck again by how tall he was. Bix had been perfect, just above her height.

"Did you tell someone I was your wife?"

He crossed his eyes and staggered as if struck.

"Courtenay, I live in this city."

He slumped, a parody of dejection.

"You're ashamed of me."

"Oh, stop it."

He brightened.

"I'll make a public apology."

"Courtenay, you're a lunatic."

His shoulder twitched.

"Enough of this lovemaking," he said. "Let's dance." He grabbed another glass from a passing tray, drained it, and pulled Addie toward the dance floor.

Courtenay was very drunk. Addie felt like a rag doll flung about the dance floor. She was about to suggest that they quit, when he tripped and fell down. Others helped him up. "Man the lifeboats!" he yelled, as he was being lifted to his feet. "Damn the torpedoes!"

"I think I'd better go home, Courtenay."

"Right-o," he cried, stumbling after her to the checkroom, glassy-eyed.

When Addie awoke in the morning, she lay for a moment assessing the mild pounding in her temples. She must have drunk more champagne than she realized. She had not drunk as much, though, as the curious man she'd been out with the night before. An assortment of memories flickered in review: Courtenay, chewing her ankle, pulling a handkerchief out of his ear, falling down on the dance floor, stumbling in and out of the taxi in the rain, looking for his hotel. Suddenly, Addie sat bolt upright. Oh good Lord, she whispered, swinging her legs out of bed and reaching for her robe.

Courtenay was lying on his back on the davenport, snoring gently. The blanket she remembered throwing over him lay on the floor. She was sure she had not made love with him. Even so, it was reassuring to find him fully clothed. It was completely unlike her to bring home a man she had just met. But there had not been an empty hotel room anywhere at that hour. What could she have done—allow him to continue stumbling around in the rain, maybe to pass out on the sidewalk somewhere?

Addie tiptoed into her kitchen and put water on the stove. She wondered if she'd been tricked or if Courtenay really had forgotten the name of his hotel. Doc had told her that Courtenay was a dangerous man. Addie was inclined to see in Courtenay an innocence that men do not in general appreciate in other men. The evening had amused her more than it had offended. Courtenay was not the only falling-down drunk she'd known. Besides, since she'd been a small child, she'd been taking in helpless creatures. On her father's sheep station, she'd had a regular zoo: parrots with crippled wings, a blind dingo, a young wallaby with half its tail torn off.

Addie would have liked a bath, but she felt too exposed with

Courtenay in the flat. She dressed quickly and brushed her hair. She carried a cup of tea into the sitting room and eased herself into a cushioned chair, trying not to wake him just yet. He would have to leave, of course, as soon as she could get some hot tea and a scone into him. She studied the straight, strong nose, the flawless white skin with pink rosettes on the cheekbones almost like rouge, the crisp black hair. Traveling in Europe with her aunt before the war, Addie had occasionally found herself in a village where everybody resembled each other, and all of them looked like some person she knew in Australia. She had seen a village of Courtenay's face somewhere in Normandy. Addie did not remember the color of Courtenay's eyes, but she knew they must be blue. He lay with legs bent, reminding Addie again how tall he was. Bix had been able to lie on the davenport with his legs stretched out and room to spare. Courtenay must be miserable on the five- and six-hour missions she'd heard they were flying now, cramped in a P-38 cockpit with no room to stretch. She knew of tall pilots who had to be pulled out of their planes and held up until they could walk again. Courtenay would also make a big target for an enemy plane behind him, trying to shoot around the armor plate protecting his back. A tall friend of Bix's had had the top of his head creased by a Japanese bullet. Another had lost a shoulder joint.

Addie noted the rise and fall of Courtenay's chest, his partly open mouth, the peacefulness of his body in sleep without the shoulder twitch, the explosive sentences and departures and arrivals. She could not imagine doing what fighter pilots did, though Bix had once told her she had the nerves of a fighter pilot. Watching Kevin take off day after day at Port Darwin to face the planes of the Japanese fleet practically single-handed, she thought she understood even less. The more of their old, outclassed fighters they lost, and the more hopeless the odds against them, the calmer Kevin seemed to become. It was as if he accepted his death in advance. As if, when he left her that last morning, his spirit had already entered some other realm. Clearly, Courtenay had not reached that place yet, and maybe never would. Most pilots she'd met or heard of seemed to believe in their personal immortality. The day Kevin and two other pilots took off to face the whole Japanese fleet by themselves, she knew that Kevin no longer believed.

Addie had been gazing at a few tea leaves in her empty cup, as if the mysterious runes might render some meaning to the agonies of her time. She looked up to confront two intense blue eyes. The mouth began to smile, the head moved, the perfect Norman face winced, two long-fingered hands raised up to clutch the head.

"Don't move," Addie said, and went into the kitchen for aspirin and a glass of water.

Addie wanted to dress and go to work, but Courtenay seemed determined to reward her with the story of his life. His full name was Gilliam Lafayette Courtenay the Third. He could trace his family back to the Crusades. His mother was dead. His father was an unmitigated jerk, but a political power in the States. Courtenay had a near-genius IQ. He'd graduated from college at nineteen. The next time he came to Australia, he'd be an ace, maybe a double ace. He had fantastic reflexes. He'd got some of the highest scores ever recorded on the psychomotor machines at Santa Ana. She'd be amazed at what he could do with his body. He could simultaneously cross his eyes, flutter his nostrils, wriggle his chin, and move one ear forward while the other moved backward, in addition to farting "Dixie" if given a moment to prepare.

"Do you have any beer?" he said.

"No. I have to go to work."

"Nonsense, it's Saturday."

"Women shop on Saturday."

"Take the day off. It's your store."

"All the more reason for me to be there."

"Do you have a razor? I need to shave."

"You need to find your hotel."

"Tell you what," he said. "I'll stay here till you get home and then I'll take you to dinner. Any place you want to go."

"I'm engaged this evening."

"Can't you break it?"

"Courtenay."

He sighed. His shoulder twitched. He looked depressed and angry.

"I need to pee."

"Go pee, then. While you do that, I'll ring for a cab."

The sound of his stream hitting the water resonated down the hall. Some men peed secretly, hitting the side of the bowl instead of the water. Others, by hitting the water, made themselves sound like a horse, as if volume were a measure of manhood. Maybe, Addie thought, it was a way of making sure everybody knew they were there, and male, the impulse of a dog leaving his presence on a tree trunk. The men she'd loved had peed silently except when they thought they were alone. They'd had other ways of marking their territory.

What Addie had not told Courtenay was that she was going to drive to her aunt's beach house on the coast north of Brisbane as soon as she closed the shop. Bix and Doc and Steve had all given her their unused petrol ration stamps, so she could afford the luxury of driving alone. The next morning, Rachael and Francine and another of Addie's girlfriends would drive in a separate car. Addie did not want to go to the country with a man, but neither did she want to be alone. She had not stayed at the beach house overnight since Bix's last leave. She had been there once for a few hours since then, and had found it more than she could cope with. She wanted to feel at home again in this house where she had spent happy childhood vacations. With her girlfriends she would have company to distract her, yet be free to walk on the beach and be alone when she wished.

The light was beginning to fade when she passed the last village and turned onto the narrow road that ran toward the coast. Tatters of gray cloud hung from a low overcast, and the giant stringybarks along the road swayed and thrashed in the wind. Inside the house, Addie soon had water on the stove for tea and an electric heater warming the sitting room. In the last light she went out and stood on the veranda, looking seaward, inhaling the salt wind and listening to the thunder of waves breaking on the beach. A heavy storm was on the way. When she began to shiver, she went into the house and carried her suitcase down the hall to her room.

As she was unpacking, Addie happened to open the drawer of her bedside stand. In it lay a blue-black forty-five automatic pistol that Bix had left because of her habit of staying in the house alone. She had protested: People on this coast did not even lock their doors. Besides, it was illegal for a civilian to have a pistol. If anyone asks, Bix had said, tell them it's mine and I forgot it. She'd probably never need it, but he'd sleep better knowing she had it. One bullet from this gun would take the fight out of the biggest man. It was the very pistol Bix had carried under his shoulder on seventy missions. To please him, she had learned to use it on a deserted stretch of beach, shooting at sea shells propped on the dunes. She had actually become a rather good shot. But the weight and violence of the gun appalled her. She had not thought about the pistol since the day she and Bix had driven back to Brisbane together for the last time.

Addie fixed a cup of tea and a snack and sat in her grandfather's old wicker chair in front of the heater. Lamplight glowed softly on the wainscoting and the polished wooden floors where they were not covered by rugs her grandmother had plaited before Addie was born. The storm was arriving. In Addie's memory, nobody had ever pulled the blinds in this house either. Through the windows, she could see the inky blackness of the night and the occasional glitter of rain slanting through the cone of light from a window. The old wooden walls stood solid, but doors and windows rattled, and rain drummed distantly on the tin roof. Addie felt warm and safe, not as haunted as last time, more her old self. She loved being in this house during a storm; it kept her company as she sat near the heater or snuggled under her blankets. The wind itself was exciting. Maybe before she went to bed she would take a torch and walk down to the ocean.

But she continued sitting, staring at the red glow of the heater. She thought of the time she had been here with Bix and Steve and Danovich and her girlfriends. The time Bix had landed on the beach in a new P-38 he was ferrying back to Port Moresby. He could have been court-martialed for it. Of qualities that fighter pilots had in common, Addie thought it must be their daring that most endeared them to her.

It was getting late when a flicker of light in one of the front windows caught her attention. A car was approaching the house on the long driveway. Had Rachael and Francine decided to come early? Was it a neighbor coming to make sure she was all right in the storm? Presently the light resolved itself into two headlamps stopped in the yard. Addie went out and stood on the veranda. After a few moments the lights turned away from the house and two red taillights rapidly shrank in the darkness. Somebody had made a wrong turn, Addie surmised, and had seen the wrong house in the headlamps. It seemed odd, though, that they did not ask for directions. Maybe they did not want to get out in the pouring rain or had recognized the house and got their bearings. Addie was about to go back inside when a bulky figure emerged from the dark in a military trench coat. Light from a window fell on a beaming Norman face topped by a dripping officer's cap. Addie recoiled in surprise.

"Courtenay! What are you doing here?"

"I was just driving by and I thought I'd stop and say hello."

Addie did not know what to make of it. She felt forced, resentful, imposed upon. She did not want him to set foot on her veranda. But she could not very well let him continue standing in the rain.

"Come in. How did you find me?"

"I asked your landlady."

"I told you I was engaged."

"It turned out you weren't. She said you were coming here alone. And here I am!" He displayed his perfect white teeth, and flung his arms wide as if to celebrate their great good luck.

"Yes," Addie said. "Evidently."

Inside, Courtenay removed his hat and sailed it across the room onto a chair. He plunged an arm into his trench coat and produced a bottle of liquor with a magician's flourish.

"Presto!" he cried. He placed the bottle on a table and reached again. He materialized another bottle with a triumphant cry, then more, until a row of bottles stood like a rank of soldiers, glistening in the lamplight. Courtenay seemed to be enjoying himself hugely. Beefeater's gin, Chivas Regal scotch, Irish whiskey, rare items in wartime Australia. He had obviously drunk quite a bit already. As he struggled out of his trench coat he announced that he had come all the way from Brisbane by cab. He'd been lost for a while in the ink soup out there. His driver had had to go pry some farmer off his wife to get directions. It had cost him a damn fortune to get here. He hoped Addie appreciated it. He stood back, surveyed the row of bottles with a satisfied smirk, and hitched up his beltline.

"Now," he said, "let's get down to some serious drinking." He pronounced it "drankin," in an accent Addie had heard American soldiers affect when they wished to project one of the grosser forms of masculinity. Addie could see that she was trapped unless she wanted to drive Courtenay back to Brisbane tonight.

"I'm exhausted, Courtenay. You can have the room at the end of the hall." She pointed to a hall that ran toward the end of the house farthest from her own room. "I'll have one drink with you, then I'll say goodnight."

"So be it," he declared, holding a bottle in the air. "All we need is some glasses and fixins. Ditch water is fine for me." He collapsed into a chair and began to bite the tin off the cork stopper. His necktie was askew, and locks of his wavy black hair had fallen over his forehead to make him look both boyish and dissolute.

Courtenay half emptied his first glass at a gulp, leaned back, smacked his lips, and waved at the row of bottles.

"You reckon we can drink all those tonight?"

"I'd imagine you'd want to recover from last night."

"Recover!" He looked insulted. "Hell, this is my natural state. I never pass out. I never barf. I shot down a Jap after drinking all night. I get it from my old man. He can put anybody in Washington under the table. One of my great-great-granddaddies invented sour mash whiskey. Know what sour mash is?"

Addie did not. Courtenay drained his glass, refilled it, and proceeded to describe a brewing process in detail. He had got as far as the technology of aging whiskey in charred oak casks when his head wobbled and he glared at Addie cross-eyed.

"Damn!" he said, with passion. "This is *boring!* Why are we talking about this?"

"You are," Addie said. "I'm not."

"Hey, that's right!" he yelled, waving his glass as if to celebrate her brilliant perception. "Let's take off our clothes and run in the rain."

Courtenay slapped himself in the face.

"Behave yourself, Lafayette!" he said, in an angry basso.

"Yessir, I will," he said in a tiny falsetto.

"See that you do."

"I will, I promise." Then to Addie, in the voice of Courtenay: "Let's dance. Do you have any music?"

"Just an old hand-crank gramophone. My friends are bringing a record player tomorrow."

He looked surprised.

"Your friends?"

"You might know them. They'll be here in the morning."

"Damn," he said, and grabbed a bottle by the neck. "We better make whoopee while we have the chance." He filled Addie's glass with whiskey. "Drink up!"

Addie stood, ignoring the glass.

"I'll say goodnight now, Courtenay."

"Aw, no!" He looked devastated.

"I'm afraid so." As she turned toward the stairs, he leaped to his feet and grabbed her arm.

"You can't go now!" he protested. "I just got here. Come on. One more drink."

The instant he touched her, she froze, as she had done once at a sheep station in the outback when a snarling dog rushed out of a shearing shed and clamped its jaws on her wrist. The dog had frozen also, released her, and backed away. It had the same effect on Courtenay. For a moment, he stood as if puzzled by what had just happened.

"Jesus Christ, you're no fun," he said. He waved his arm and stumbled back toward the bottles. "Be that way. See if I care. I'll party by myself."

While she prepared for bed, Addie heard Courtenay thumping about, muttering to himself. She heard him drop or knock something over, a bottle perhaps, or a chair. Addie tiptoed along the hall between bathroom and bedroom. She turned lights on only after closing doors behind her. It annoyed her to be creeping like a fugitive in her own house. She wished she could lock her room, but the doors inside the house were fitted with old-fashioned locks that could be opened from either side with a skeleton key. She remembered seeing such a key in a drawer somewhere when she was a child. She could not remember anyone locking a door inside the house, either. But she was too nervous to go to bed without a measure of security. In a picture show she had seen someone prop a straight-back chair at an angle under the doorknob. The only straight-back chairs in the house were in the kitchen. The best she could do was to tilt a wicker armchair at a precarious angle so it would tip and fall if the door was opened. That would wake her. Then she went to the bedside stand and removed Bix's pistol from the drawer. The weight and feel of it frightened her but also gave reassurance. She arranged herself in bed with an arm outside the blankets, holding the pistol pointed toward the door. She remembered Bix's warnings about keeping a shell in the chamber. If the chair fell and awakened her, she would have time to cock the gun.

As she lay in the dark, she grew angry. Were it not for the storm, she would have driven Courtenay back to Brisbane. But in such weather, creeks might overflow, bridges wash out, roads disappear under water. She listened to the rain and wind, and could not get to sleep. After a while, she got up and stealthily moved the chair. She opened the door partway and listened. Courtenay was singing drunkenly off-key, not the ribald songs that soldiers sing when they march or get drunk together, but a sad lullaby that Addie half remembered from her own childhood. For a moment, she felt stupid taking such elaborate precautions. Courtenay was a lonely, confused soldier half the planet away from home and his nerves shattered. He and his kind were a major reason why her own country was still free and she was not a slave of the Japanese. She should probably be in the sitting room with him. But her instinct told her she was in danger. She closed the door and replaced the chair. She climbed back into bed, listening to the storm for a while longer, and slept.

She awoke to violence, as if a mountain had fallen on her. Her legs were being forced apart, her wrists were gathered together in spite of her struggle and locked above her head. She did not waste her breath screaming. She grew icy calm the way they said Bix did, entering combat. Where was the pistol? She felt something solid against her hip. She tried to stay in contact with it. If she could get an arm loose, she would try to reach it. As her legs were forced farther apart, she noted that Courtenay was hard in spite of all he'd had to drink. It must excite him terrifically to take a woman by force. She had a mad, momentary impulse to surrender, but her instincts revolted. She did not want this. She was enraged. He had trapped her in her own house. As he was about to enter her, she turned her head and sank her teeth into his ear. She heard cartilage crunch, tasted blood, heard him scream, and felt herself flung out of bed, tangled in blankets that padded her fall as she hit the floor. She had landed on some solid object; it might have fallen with her. While Courtenay was screaming, Addie groped among the blankets and found the pistol. She stood, straightening her nightgown with an outraged swipe, and felt along the wall to the light switch. When the light went on, Courtenay was standing on the other side of the bed, holding his ear. A rivulet of blood ran down his arm. His erection was gone. He stared at the blood on his hand, then at Addie. He looked as if he could hardly believe the evidence of his senses.

"You bit me! You bitch! You bit me!"

"Get out of my room."

He made a motion toward her. She grabbed the barrel, pulled it

back, and released it. The crash of the action ramming a shell into
the chamber stopped him. She held the gun in both hands. She
hoped he could not see how frightened she was.

"You wouldn't," he said.

"Don't count on it." She waved the gun toward the door, as she'd
seen tough characters do it in American picture shows. "Out," she
said, swinging the gun back to point at his chest. "Now."

Courtenay raised his free hand defensively.

"All right, for God's sake," he said with an injured air. "You
don't have to point that thing at me." As he backed toward the
door, he looked at the blood on his hand again. "Christ," he wailed,
"I'm bleeding to death! I need medical attention."

"Out!" she said, and followed him into the hallway. "You'll find
everything you need in the bathroom cabinet."

"You're not going to help me?"

"I'm not coming anywhere near you. I'll give you a few minutes
to bandage your ear, then you're going to put your clothes on and
get out of my house. If you don't, I'm going to shoot you."

He glared at her as if he thought she'd gone insane. But he
turned and stumbled down the hall. At the bathroom door, he
stopped and looked at her reproachfully. She started toward him
with the gun aimed. He retreated into the bathroom. Addie drew a
chair to a position where she could look down the hallway to the
bathroom and also see into the sitting room where Courtenay's
clothes lay scattered on the floor and furniture. Her heart was still
pounding. She had not felt so alone since Kevin died. She must
calm herself. Bix had told her he did not notice fear until the battle
was over. Her battle was not yet over. If the house had a telephone,
she would call the police. What would Bix advise her to do? Or
Steve, or Doc? Steve would say don't negotiate; shoot the bugger.
Steve hated Courtenay. Was it worth killing a man to avoid being
raped? Bix would have defended her, no matter what she did. Doc

was the person she'd most like to talk to, but she was not sure even Doc would have the answer. Doc saw God in stones, trees, animals, people. She was God. But so was Courtenay. Doc had not been able to be a surgeon because he could not cut people. He had the hands for it, the dexterity, the mind, but not the heart. Addie thought she knew what he would tell her: "Philosophy is mostly the rationalizations of men. What can I say? I am not a woman."

Addie's mind raced ahead as in a chess game, imagining ways Courtenay could still trick her. She was cold; Courtenay must be colder still with no clothes on. That would get him out of the bathroom sooner. She needed to make sure he came directly into the sitting room. She would not feel safe if she had to go into the hallway after him.

"Courtenay," she called. "Look out here for a moment."

"I can't!" he yelled, as if he thought he was dying. "I'm bandaging my ear!"

"You'd better look. It's for your own safety."

He poked his head out, and recoiled, screeching at the sight of the pistol.

"Stop pointing that thing at me!" He peeked out again. "Christ, I'm freezing!"

"Good. In case you get any clever ideas about barricading yourself in there and staying the night in a tub of warm water, you may have noticed that the boiler isn't on yet. And in case you come out of the bathroom and try to go back into your room or anywhere else except out here to your clothes, I'll shoot."

His head vanished from the doorway with a snarl.

"Ow!" he screamed a moment later, but made no further sound until he staggered out of the bathroom, clutching his bandaged ear and glaring resentfully while Addie tracked him in the sights of the pistol. She did not look directly at his body while he was dressing. Some distant portion of her mind had registered that it was a beautiful body, but she could feel only loathing. While he was pulling his shoes on, Courtenay seemed to hear the storm for the first time. He looked up at her with his mouth agape.

"You expect me to go out in *that*?"

"Yes."

"Where will I sleep?"

While he stared at her, he reached for an open bottle on the table, upended it, and took a long pull.

"You're crazy," he said, and coughed, and put the bottle back.

"Tie your shoelaces."

He obeyed, with his good ear cocked at the sounds of the storm.

"It's pitch black out there. I don't even know where the road is. I could drown!" Addie said nothing. "Don't you even *care*?"

Addie almost laughed. She waved the gun.

"Put your hat and coat on."

Instead, Courtenay leaned forward, buried his face in his hands, and began to cry.

"Everything I've ever done has turned to shit!" he sobbed.

"Get out, Courtenay."

"You don't understand! I can't even remember what my mother looked like!" Words tumbled from him while Addie tried to think what to do. He seemed so distraught, she was afraid he'd force her to shoot him. He told her that his father had killed his mother. It was supposed to be an accident, but nobody in the family would talk about it. They were all afraid of his father. Courtenay had been expelled from three universities. He'd graduated only because his father had threatened to have Courtenay's legs broken if he did not graduate, and Courtenay was afraid his father was crazy enough to do it. While he was hiding from his father, he'd got drunk and set fire to his best friend's house with a cigarette. The only girl he'd ever been in love with had been killed in a car wreck, with Courtenay at the wheel.

Addie stood up. Every word could be true, but she was too exhausted to care. She was utterly sick of him. If he forced her to shoot, so be it.

"Put your hat and coat on." She moved farther from the front door to give him a wide berth.

"Addie!" he wailed. She could see that he still did not quite believe her, or was pretending not to. She waved the pistol toward the door.

"I'm good with this gun, Courtenay. Bix taught me. I'll aim for your leg first. If I hit an artery, though, you'll be dead in ten minutes."

As he went toward the door, Addie realized that at this moment above all others she must be prepared for anything. She released the safety. Courtenay yanked the door open savagely and recoiled in a blast of wind. He stood in the open doorway, pointing.

"Good God, you can't send me out in *that*!"

Addie aimed the gun at the darkness past his head and pulled the trigger. The explosion in the enclosed space of the room deafened and terrified her. But it had got rid of Courtenay, who stood outside in the yard screaming that she was a crazy bitch and it was too bad he hadn't let the Japs come and take her fucking country and turn her into one of their whore slaves, and much else that Addie was too shaken to hear.

COURTENAY

When Steve got back to the squadron, he found that Courtenay had gone to Australia. For ten days, Steve enjoyed the absence of Courtenay's arrogant bleat in the officers' club, the mess hall, and in his earphones during flight. Then one day, Steve returned from a mission to find Courtenay moving into the tent next door.

"Just to be near you, Stevie," Courtenay warbled, giving Steve a lascivious wink. Courtenay wore a white bandage over one side of his head. He'd split his ear, he said, when he tripped over a curb trying to keep a world-class ass in his ring sight.

With the side flaps of the tent up for air circulation, only the mosquito net walls and fifteen feet of steam-bath jungle atmosphere now separated Steve's cot from Courtenay's. Steve's tent became a torture chamber where he had to hear every fart, belch, and fatuous insult from Courtenay, in addition to the screeching of his alcoholic parrot, Wellington. Courtenay had bought the garrulous bird from a trader in Port Moresby. Wellington had mastered the trader's waterfront vocabulary plus Courtenay's malicious cackle. "Motherfucker!" Wellington would screech whenever he heard a loud noise, day or night. It could be a pilot calling to another outside on the squadron street, or snoring in a nearby tent. "Motherfucker!" Wellington would scream. "Cackle cackle! Bugger the Japs!"

Since Bix had disappeared over New Britain, Courtenay had become even more obnoxious. Bix had been the squadron's top gun, and the man everybody wanted to fly with. Only General Laird commanded more respect. Steve had been Bix's wingman ever since he'd joined the squadron, and with Bix's help he'd become an ace, himself, with more Zeros to his credit than Courtenay. It was as if Courtenay now felt free to throw all the pent-up, scurrilous insult at Steve that he hadn't dared to aim at Bix, or at Steve as long as Bix was around.

Another person Courtenay had singled out for persecution was Doc, the flight surgeon. Doc advised Steve to keep cool. Courtenay had no control, Doc said. If Steve let it bother him, Courtenay would go for blood like chickens pecking each other to death. As a tournament college boxer, Steve could make a mess of Courtenay's pretty face, but as a captain, Courtenay could have Steve court-martialed. Once, before Doc had started going goofy with combat fatigue and maybe Courtenay's abuse, he'd promoted a more charitable view. Remember, Doc had said, this is a guy whose mother died when he was seven, and whose father threatened to have his legs broken if he didn't graduate from college, and probably would have done it.

But the advice was of no use to Steve. Courtenay had a genius for getting under his skin. Courtenay taught Wellington to warble, "Stevieeeeee!" whenever Steve entered or left his tent, followed by, "Cackle cackle!" Courtenay respected no quality or accomplishment. After Steve shot down the Japanese ace, Courtenay referred to it so often that his very mention of it became ridicule. Steve was already avoiding Courtenay whenever he could. Now he tried even harder. He sat as far as possible from Courtenay in the briefing room or mess tent and left a poker game if Courtenay joined it.

"Aw, Stevie, you're leaving?" Courtenay would say, looking devastated, then winking at the others as Steve got up. Or when Steve found Courtenay already at a table and did not sit down, Courtenay would pat the bench next to him and pout: "Aren't you going to join us, Stevie? Here's a place, right here. Come and tell us all about how you shot down Ishigawa."

One night in the old plantation house that served as the officers' club, Steve was placing a bet at the crowded crap table when Courtenay shouted from the other end, "Hey, Stevie, I met that broad who was after your body in Brisbane." Courtenay winked at the men around the table. "What was her name? Francine! That's it!" Courtenay threw the dice and yelled when his number came up.

Steve picked up a few chips, disgusted at winning on Courtenay's roll.

"Man, you're sneaky, lover boy," Courtenay yelled, raking in his own winnings. "I couldn't lay a hand on her. Old Lafayette went down in flames." Courtenay rattled the dice and yelled at the crowd around the table. "I couldn't believe those knockers!" He wrinkled his forehead at Steve. "Right, lover boy? Let me guess—chocolate-brown nipples, right? About this big when excited?" He stared, openmouthed. "No? Pink?" He frowned in disappointment. "Guess again, Lafayette!" He fired the dice against the far wall of the table and called out his number, which did not come up. He had bet a large sum. He seemed indifferent as others collected their bets from him. He often made it clear that he was not dependent on his paltry captain's income.

Courtenay reminded Steve of Bully Bob, the nightmare of Steve's paper route days. Bully Bob had been bigger, two years older. In the paper shack, he bumped into Steve when nobody was looking, pinched him, tripped him, stole papers from Steve's bag so he'd run short at the end of his route. When Steve accused him, Bully

Bob pretended to be outraged and shoved Steve around. Bully Bob taunted Steve with names that made the other paper boys laugh. He knocked Steve off his bike, poured Coca-Cola into his paper bags, and stole Steve's bike seat so he'd have to ride his route sitting on the bar or standing on the pedals. Like Courtenay, Bully Bob had a rich, influential father. Courtenay and Bully Bob even had similar abrasive, high-pitched voices. They had the same pink and white complexion, black wavy hair, and the smug bearing of a rich man's son. Courtenay and Bully Bob were beginning to merge in Steve's mind, becoming one person.

One day when they were not flying, Steve and a few of the other pilots drove to a stretch of white coral beach up the coast from Port Moresby. They took air mattresses and glass-bottomed coffee cans and floated on the lagoon, looking down at the exotic plants and creatures under the clear green water. After a while, the other pilots splashed ashore to lie in the sand, leaving Steve alone in the lagoon. He took off his shorts to get some sun on the whitest part of his anatomy. Presently, he heard a muffled thunder and looked up in time to see a P-38 headed straight at him with its propeller tips nearly churning the water. Steve rolled off his mattress and dived, trying to hang on to his coffee can. Even under water, he could hear the roar of engines. When Steve surfaced, the plane was climbing, doing a victory roll out over the gulf. In the mess tent that night, Courtenay peered around and between heads a few tables away. Every time he caught Steve's eye, he would cackle or wink, or throw his head back in silent laughter. After dinner in the plantation house he stood at the bar with a few other pilots, when Steve walked in.

"Hey, Stevie, come over here!" Courtenay yelled. "Let me buy you a drink! That wasn't you out there, was it? Damn!" He cackled, gleefully. "I just flew over because I thought maybe some jigaboo had stolen an air mattress and then I saw your white ass going overboard like a big snowball. Blinding! Blinding!" Courtenay shielded his eyes. "Whoooeee! You should have seen yourself, Stevie. I thought maybe you'd shit while you were at it!" He waited, wide-eyed and openmouthed, for Steve to react. When Steve did not, Courtenay said, "Oh, hey, we're buddies, aren't we? Didn't old Lafayette get a bogey off your white ass just the other day? Didn't he?"

Like Bully Bob, Courtenay seemed to have an inexhaustible repertory of insult. On Steve's last rest leave, the C-47 transport carrying him home to Port Moresby had run into rough weather. The pilots in the cockpit took the plane higher, then lower, then climbed again above a solid layer of stratus, hunting for openings between thunderheads. The men began taking bets on their altitude. After the bets were placed, someone would open the door to the cockpit and read the altimeter. Steve had learned a trick early in his flight training: With his lips and the back of his tongue sealed, he sucked to make a vacuum between his tongue and the roof of his mouth. From the size of the cavity he could determine altitude to within five hundred feet. By the time they were letting down over Port Moresby, Steve's pockets were bulging with Australian and U.S. currency, and he explained the trick.

The next day, Courtenay yelled across the mess hall, "Hey, lover boy, I hear you made a lot of money on the way home from Brisbane. Let me know when I can come over and get a sucking lesson!" Courtenay made a lewd sucking motion with his lips and threw his head back, cackling. That night shortly after Steve's tentmate had turned out the light, Courtenay began singing in a falsetto voice, just loud enough so the words reached across the space that separated his tent from Steve's.

"Oh, a very hot pilot named Steve-o
Was diddling a dolly on leave-o.
She said, Now be nice,
And stick it in twice,
Or I'll give you the jolly old heave-ho."

Courtenay cackled softly, then crooned like a lullaby, *"Snowballl! Snowballl!"* His voice faded away at the end, as if the name itself had sent him off to dreamland.

The next day over the Bismarck Mountains, Courtenay pulled alongside with his wingtip nearly touching Steve's, unfastened his oxygen mask, made sucking motions, winked grossly, and winged over to resume position in loose formation.

When Courtenay had been home a couple of weeks, a rumor followed him that he'd cornered Addie somewhere and had tried to rape her, and she'd nearly bitten his ear off. One of the pilots had heard it from Addie's friend Rachael. As vicious as Courtenay could be, it was hard for anyone to believe he would go that far. They could imagine him raping another woman. Not Addie. Not Bix's fiancée. But it did explain the bandage that nearly covered one side of his head. Nobody believed his story anyway, about tripping over a curb. Doc had seen the ear, but would say nothing. Courtenay was still his patient, no matter what Doc's personal opinion of him might be. One pilot suggested putting a bullet through Courtenay's head.

"Gone take more than a bullet to fix what's wrong with that guy," Gumbo said, in his bayou accent.

Steve was in shock. He found Marchetti, the squadron commander, in his office. Before he took matters into his own hands, Steve said, he wanted Marchetti to start an investigation.

Marchetti leaned back in his battered oak swivel chair, as always looking too tall for his desk and especially too tall for a P-38 cockpit.

"An investigation." He blinked. "Now, how am I supposed to do that? If it happened at all, it happened two thousand miles away on another continent."

"Bob, he's a fucking maniac. If Addie said he did it, then he did it."

Marchetti threw himself forward, as he did when he was annoyed.

"Look, Steve, commanders hear all kinds of shit. They get letters accusing men of everything you can think of. Rape, robbery, paternity, kidnapping, even murder. You name it. We can't even begin to do anything unless Addie files charges."

"You could interrogate Courtenay."

Marchetti's expression said, *Do you really think Courtenay would incriminate himself?*

"Send me to Brisbane," Steve said. "I'll get the story straight from Addie."

Marchetti looked sympathetic, but shook his head. "You know I can't do that, Steve. You just came back ten days ago. You're needed here."

"I'm needed there, too. I have to go see if she's okay."

Marchetti shook his head.

"Sorry, Steve. We've got a war to fight. I understand your feelings."

Steve stood up, thinking at least he'd tried. He'd settle it with Courtenay himself. Marchetti called as he opened the screen door.

"A word of advice, Steve. Don't take matters into your own hands."

But Steve could not resist stopping Courtenay in the squadron street.

"Tell me about Addie," Steve said, feeling his body tense up, ready to launch a doomsday punch.

Courtenay's mouth and eyes opened wide in a mockery of innocence.

"About Addie? Why," he declared, "I hardly know the lady!"

"The whole squadron knows the story, Courtenay."

"A story? Oh, goody, I love stories!"

Steve realized it was useless. Only a bullet could get around Courtenay's defenses. He should have listened to Marchetti. Soon after, Courtenay began mentioning Addie's name where Steve could overhear. Courtenay even got a story started insinuating that Addie had made a pass at him.

There were rumors of an invasion farther up the north coast. The squadron would probably fly to targets beyond Hollandia, drop their spent belly tanks, defend the bombers, return to refuel at Lae, and then fly home. The pilots would find out for sure in the morning at briefing.

When the mission roster was posted, Steve discovered that he was leading the second element in Courtenay's flight of four. Marchetti was leading the squadron. Steve once more confronted Marchetti in his office.

"Give me a break, Bob. I may not be able to control myself if I find myself on his tail."

Marchetti leaned back and wiped the sweat off his domed forehead.

"I know you have some personal problems with him, Ace. I'm not asking you to kiss him."

"Personal problems? Is that what you call it?" They'd talked about Addie only a few days before.

Marchetti growled.

"Look, Steve, it's not a permanent assignment. As a personal favor to you, I did ask Milton before he made up the roster, but I guess he forgot. Besides, what the hell, you won't know where he is after a pass or two anyway. Do the best you can. The Japs are going to throw everything they've got at us."

Steve had been given a new P-38. He loved the feel of a new plane, the controls smooth and precise, the engines at peak performance. The paint inside and out was not yet chipped and the cockpit smelled of new enamel, freshly tooled metal, machine oil, and plastic. It was reassuring to fly a plane that hadn't yet been punctured by too many bullets or landed hard or pushed past redline. It almost compensated for having to fly in the same sky with Courtenay.

As they scissored back and forth over the bombers, Steve could see explosions along the coast. Out at sea the dark gray silhouettes of Navy ships sat low in the water. Once in a while, their guns flashed, followed shortly by sudden pink blossoms ashore that vanished in clouds of dust. Columns of black smoke stood high around Hollandia and up the coast. There was an occasional explosion in the water among the ships. Above the ships, black dots circled like a swarm of gnats. There was at least one U.S. carrier farther offshore. There were Navy Hellcats and gull-wing Corsairs in the air today, formidable allies. They would stay above the ships, away from the bombers and P-38s. The Hellcat and Corsair each had a large, round radial engine cowling in front. Head-on or tail-on, they could be mistaken for a Zero. You had to look a fraction of a second longer to make sure you were not firing at one of your own planes.

Marchetti's voice crackled in Steve's ears.

"This is Red Leader. Bogies at ten o'clock high. Let's give these meatballs something to think about."

Steve checked his fuel gauge, oxygen flow, safety belt, gun sight, gun heater, switches. He touched the handle on his chest and reminded himself for the thousandth time: If you have to bail out, don't pull the ripcord until you're only a few hundred feet from the ground, unless you want a Japanese fighter to finish you off as you sit helpless in the harness. There had even been reports of a Zero cutting a flier's legs off with its propeller.

A cloud of black dots ahead and to the left expanded quickly. Belly tanks dropped away from the P-38s like a cluster of bombs. Steve cinched his safety straps tighter, made a last-second check of the cockpit, and noted the positions of his wingman and the other planes. The P-38s flying top cover were diving on the Japanese formation. There were silver flashes as planes changed angles to the sun, white contrails streaking down the sky, a ribbon of smoke, then another, an explosion, then Steve and the P-38s around him were firing. They flashed through the main swarm too fast to see if they'd done any damage and instantly looked for new targets, beginning to turn, twist, zigzag, dive, and climb to get Zeros off their tail, while trying at the same time to get lined up on others. Once or twice, Steve could see the bright red disk on the wing or fuselage of a Zero as it streaked past. Courtenay's flight was getting scattered as they tried to stay between the bombers and the Japanese fighters. One of the B-24s exploded in formation. In the corner of his eye, Steve saw another go down in a long, shallow dive, trailing smoke. Every time a bomber went down, Steve thought of his childhood friend Blake Hurlingame, who was out here somewhere, flying B-24s, and his brother Todd, in Europe. They could both be dead, and Steve wouldn't hear about it for months.

Steve could not find his wingman. He saw a Zero going after a lone P-38 and took off after it, caught up and chased it away with a short burst. By the nose markings on the other P-38, he discovered he'd rescued Courtenay. There were no other P-38s nearby, so Steve pulled in on Courtenay's wing. As a two-plane element, they were harder to attack than they would be alone. Other Zeros found them.

Courtenay made bone-crushing maneuvers, like Bix and Danovich. Steve nearly tore his wings off keeping up. Courtenay was no coward; he would continue firing at a Zero with tracers streaming past his cockpit from another on his own tail. Once in a while when he fired his guns, Courtenay would push his radio button and scream as if he thought the Jap pilot could hear him: "Take it, you cocksucker!" Or: "Up your ass, motherfucker!" When a fighter blew up in front of him, he cackled madly and crooned, "One meatballll! One meatballll!" There were other voices on the radio, pilots giving terse directions, calling warnings, calling for help. Marchetti's voice cut through the noise, commanding One Meatball to stop the radio chatter. There were planes flying in every direction. A distant voice was screaming, "Kamikaze! Kamikaze!" One of the ships offshore vanished in an enormous explosion.

Steve had a sure victory, a Zero breaking up in view of the gun cameras, and he thought Courtenay had at least one. They might have more, but when a Zero went down, they had no time to follow and confirm it. The bombers were fighting, too. In tight formation, they threw out a dense white net of tracers and Steve saw a Zero fall away smoking after flying through it. The slow bombers seemed to take forever getting to Hollandia. Steve was sweating. His muscles ached and did not react as swiftly. Often by now, in a melee this size, an element leader would be flying without his wingman. Steve stayed with Courtenay. Just to show the son of a bitch, Steve thought. It was exhausting flying with Courtenay. It was not like flying with Bix, whose style was lightning quick but somehow fluid, with one maneuver flowing into the next. Courtenay jerked his plane around the sky as if it, too, were the enemy, a mean horse that understood only kicking, beating, breaking. Steve would never treat a plane like that. If he hadn't already hated Courtenay, he would hate him for the way he treated a plane.

The Liberators unloaded their bombs and went into a diving

turn away from the antiaircraft fire, toward home. The cloud of fighters had thinned and spread out into smaller battles. The chalky scribbles of contrails littered the sky. In the effort to get a Zero off his own tail, Steve finally got separated from Courtenay. As usual, Courtenay was nowhere to be seen when he was needed most. Luckily the pilot of the Zero was not good. Steve maneuvered to get a deflection shot. The Zero went straight down and began to burn. Steve was having a record day. Two kills, maybe three. He looked around. He seemed to be in a volume of sky empty of fighters. Where was Courtenay? Had he been hit? Had he gone off on a chase? Steve could see only a few distant streaks in the sky. He circled, looking up at the sky with one eye closed, keeping his thumb between his open eye and the sun. It was a trick his friend Blake Hurlingame had told him about when he was eleven years old. If there was an enemy fighter above, he would try to attack out of the sun. Suddenly a river of tracers streamed past Steve's wingtip. Steve threw the plane into a turning, twisting dive at full throttle and began a pullout, trying to see his attacker. A P-38 streaked past as Courtenay's voice cackled in Steve's earphones: "One snow-ballll! One snowballll!"

Steve continued to scan the sky. There was no doubt of it, Courtenay had fired. Doc, the flight surgeon, believed that Courtenay was shooting down his own planes. But Doc was going mad with combat fatigue. This was merely more of Courtenay's shit, the impeccable tradition of Bully Bob. Courtenay leveled off alongside Steve with his goggles up on his forehead and his shoulders jumping as if with laughter. Steve unsnapped his oxygen mask and pulled it aside. *You son of a bitch,* he mouthed. *You son of a bitch.* Courtenay peeled off his own mask and made sucking motions with his mouth. Steve flew straight and level, watching. Courtenay gave an exaggerated wink involving one whole side of his face, then held his mask to his face and whispered on the radio, "Hey, Snowball! Addie baddy! Addie baddy! Right?" His heavy black eyebrows jiggled up and down.

A storm of tracer bullets poured down around them. Steve shoved the yoke forward and dived, twisting, turning, swearing, trying to see his attacker and refasten his oxygen mask all at once. There had to be at least two planes to fire that many bullets. They, too, had come out of the sun. That son of a bitch, Courtenay. A Zero popped into Steve's rearview mirror in perfect position to fire. Bullets thudded into Steve's wing before he could react, then quit. The Zero went straight down as if hit. Why? Once again, Courtenay was not in sight. Maybe the Zero had run out of ammunition. Steve figured he was almost out of bullets himself. Steve held his altitude and located Courtenay below him chasing a Zero but being overtaken by another. Steve dived, closing fast. He thought the Zero hadn't seen him, but he was not sure he'd get there before it fired on Courtenay. He pushed his radio button. "Blue Leader, break off, break off, there's a bogie on your tail!" Courtenay's voice crooned sarcastically, "Well, get him off it, asshole." Then Courtenay began singing softly as he maneuvered closer to the Zero ahead of him: "One meatballll! One meatballll!"

Everything seemed to happen at once. Courtenay began firing. Just as the Zero behind Courtenay appeared dead center in Steve's gun sight, Courtenay started babbling: "Addie baddy! Addie baddy! Oh my goodness, we forget so fast, don't we, that sweet little bad little end-of-the-world pussy." The Zero behind Courtenay began firing. Courtenay screeched, "Get this meatball off my ass, Stevie!"

Steve delayed a second or two. The face of Bully Bob swam before his eyes. "Sweat a little, you son of a bitch," Steve whispered. Then he fired. Pieces of the Zero's tail broke off and flew past Steve. The Zero rotated once and fell off in a wild tumble, end over end. But a cloud of black smoke was pouring from Courtenay's right engine. Flames. Courtenay rolled over, popped his canopy, and fell out into the sky. The plane exploded.

Courtenay's parachute opened almost immediately. Steve began screaming, throttling back as if he could stop and help: "No, no, no, you stupid son of a bitch!" Courtenay had panicked and forgotten the first rule of bailing out in combat. Steve went after the Zero that had got away from Courtenay, before it could return and shoot Courtenay in his harness, but it fled. Steve turned back, hoping he had enough ammunition to defend Courtenay if another Zero approached. He spotted a white parachute below, but there was a Zero already streaking toward it like a shark moving in for the kill. Had the one without ammunition returned? Steve began firing in a dive before he was in range, hoping to scare the pilot. Just as he came in range, Steve's guns quit. The Zero pulled away, turning, but did not seem in any hurry to leave. Steve throttled back and flew past Courtenay at stalling speed. Courtenay had lost his helmet and goggles and oxygen mask. He sat in his harness, making sucking motions at Steve. The Zero was making a wide turn. Steve went after it, hoping to bluff the pilot. The Zero continued turning, not running. The pilot was sizing up the situation. Steve wondered if he could ram the Zero and survive. A P-38 had once rammed a Zero, destroyed its tail, and flown home on one engine. Japanese pilots, of course, rammed regularly and died for the glory of the emperor.

If the Zero could get lined up on Courtenay, Steve wondered, what was he going to do? Maybe this was not the one that had run out of ammunition. The Zero suddenly turned toward Courtenay and accelerated. Steve banked and tried to bluff a deflection shot, but the Zero flashed past him. It was not firing; it must be the one without ammunition. Steve's gut tightened as he brought his plane around, nearly stalling, and saw the Zero fly just under Courtenay, then bank, make a quarter turn, and depart in a long, shallow dive. Steve deployed his flaps, throttled back, and drifted past Courtenay close to stalling speed. Courtenay was making no more sucking motions. He was looking thoughtfully at his feet, only there were no feet. Instead, there was a river of blood pulsing down into the sky. Courtenay looked up, his mouth a round, black hole, his eyes disbelieving. The next time Steve flew past, the blood had stopped. Courtenay slumped motionless in his harness, with his head hanging to one side.

THE EMISSARY

Doc, the flight surgeon, had been in combat since the squadron landed on Guadalcanal. He'd seen half his pilots die. By the time the squadron moved up to New Guinea, his Tourette's tics and twitches were so bad that Marchetti, the squadron commander, offered to send him back to the States. Doc refused. Even Doc knew he'd been in combat too long, but his life was here, taking care of his pilots. Too many of them were being shot down. Marchetti said it was normal attrition, but Doc knew better. Something was going on. He'd already seen the signs, heard the Voice. The Voice had addressed him as the Emissary. He'd been chosen for a task that could alter the course of history. To start, he must make a secret investigation.

It was not long before Marchetti called Doc into his office and ordered him to stay out of the mission files and stop viewing gun camera film. The men said Doc acted like he was suspicious of something. It was getting to be a morale problem. Doc had found enough evidence anyway. Captain Courtenay, their arrogant movie-star look-alike, was ambushing and shooting down his own men in order to advance himself in rank. Doc had compiled a list of the pilots who'd disappeared on missions with Courtenay. The gun camera film from Courtenay's plane was nowhere to be found. Doc was sure the film would have shown a stream of tracer bullets converging on a P-38. The Voice said Courtenay had plans that went far beyond command of the squadron. If somebody had stopped Hitler before he really got started, millions of people would still be alive.

When Marchetti ordered Doc to stay away from the files and the film, Doc merely shifted the focus of his investigation to Courtenay's everyday habits. Doc kept meticulous notes in a code of his own invention. He recorded especially Courtenay's attempts to undermine confidence and self-respect, a demagogue's first stratagem. Courtenay referred to General Laird, who'd earned an aluminum foot dive-bombing a Japanese cruiser, as Peg-Leg Pete. Courtenay imitated his limp. Doc was Gramps, or the Pill Dispenser, or the Dick Inspector. Courtenay mimicked Doc's tics and twitches. Marchetti was the Cranium, and Courtenay contrived to imitate his undershot jaw and bulging eyes. Meanwhile, to their faces, Courtenay ingratiated himself. He flew cases of booze from Australia in the ammunition compartment of a new P-38 and threw a party. On leave in Brisbane, he bought timber leases and practically gave away stock to the pilots. Even Marchetti had shares. Doc was biding his time. He stopped using morphine to get to sleep. He needed a clear head. Sooner or later, Courtenay would make a fatal misstep.

One day, Milton, the operations officer, who stood directly in line for command of the squadron, nearly became Courtenay's next victim. Milton had come down with a head cold the night before takeoff. Doc grounded him. The fast changes in air pressure could rupture a pilot's eardrums. In Milton's place, Marchetti assigned a pilot by the name of Thorpe, who had nearly finished his missions and was about to go home. Thorpe's plane was in the repair tents, so he took Milton's plane. At takeoff, Doc watched Thorpe accelerate past him down the runway. As Thorpe approached the point where the heavily loaded planes ahead of him had lifted off the runway, Doc thought he saw something happen to Thorpe's right wheel. A split second later, the landing gear collapsed, the right wing dropped, the belly tank scraped the metal mesh, and the plane vanished in an orange fireball and a cloud of debris that hid the whole far end of the runway. Doc and his medic, Klemmer, raced in the ambulance along with the fire and crash trucks, but they could not get near the fire. In the flames, Doc could see something writhing and flopping on the ground. Then it was still. Doc leaned over and vomited beside the jeep. He held himself together long enough to talk to Milton's crew chief.

"It looked like he blew a tire," Doc said.

"I saw it blow," the chief said. "Those were new tires. I make sure the tires are okay after every mission. There wasn't hardly any wear at all on those tires. They'd only been flown a couple of times."

The Voice rang loud and clear in Doc's ears. It was time to take action.

The next morning after takeoff, Doc caught up with Milton in front of his office.

"Milton, I've got to talk to you."

Milton squinted, baring his snaggle teeth.

"Right now?"

"Right now. Alone."

Milton looked up and down the squadron street. Nobody was nearby. He stepped into the shade of a palm tree with half its fronds blasted off.

"Heck, Doc, my ears are fine now. I could have flown yesterday."

"Milt, your life is in danger."

Milton looked scared.

"What have I got?"

"I mean, in the air."

Milton grinned.

"No shit."

"I have proof, Milton."

Milton seemed confused.

"Proof of what?"

"I don't have it all, Milton. But you could be dead before I do have it." Doc explained about Courtenay and the lost pilots, the missing film, the tire on Milton's plane. Milton stared at Doc as if seeing him for the first time.

"You say he sabotaged my tire?"

"Your crew chief says those tires were like new. Put it together with the information I've dug up," Doc said. He tapped his notebook. "It's all right here, Milt. In code. In case it falls into the wrong hands."

Milton shuffled his feet, sucked air through his clenched teeth, and scratched his head.

"Jeez, I don't know, Doc. Don't you think this is a job for Intelligence?"

Doc gripped Milton's arm.

"You're not listening to me! You could be dead before Intelligence finds out anything! And after he gets rid of you, he'll go after Marchetti."

Milton was looking down at the fingers digging into his arm. Doc let go. He realized he'd been yelling.

"Just be careful," he said. "Look behind you all the time and don't get caught alone behind a cloud somewhere. Don't relax for a minute. And order security doubled on the planes. Do you hear?"

Milton was backing out of the shade into the hot sun.

"I'll do that, Doc, sure thing. Thanks for the warning. I'll do that. Remember, keep this stuff to yourself until you crack that code, okay?"

"What code?" Doc said. "I made the code. I don't have to crack it."

"Sure thing, Doc. I'll remember what you said."

. . .

That afternoon, Marchetti asked Doc to come by his office. When Doc got there, the CO was sitting sideways at his desk, whacking his foot with a yardstick the way General Laird used his cane.

As Doc sat down, Marchetti put the stick on his desk and spun around in his squeaky chair.

"How are you feeling, Doc?"

Doc knew he had not been asked here to exchange pleasantries.

"He was after Milton, Bob. That was no accident—"

Marchetti raised his hand.

"Doc . . . listen . . . tires fail, even new ones. Machines break. Planes crash. It's not anybody's fault. Do you understand?"

"Maybe if I'd told somebody sooner," Doc said, "Thorpe would still be alive."

"You also told the crew chief just enough to get him worried. The trouble is, out there in the repair tents they don't know who's under suspicion, so everybody is. Now I've got a morale problem."

"Listen to me!" Doc said. "You're next on the list after Milton! What am I supposed to do, wait till he slashes your tire and turns you into a streak of grease on the runway?"

The look on Marchetti's face stopped him. Doc discovered himself standing up, leaning over Marchetti's desk. He'd been yelling again. Doc sat down in his chair and took a few deep breaths. He made his face stop twitching.

"Doc," Marchetti said. "Get hold of yourself. Your nerves are shot. You're leaving tomorrow for Australia. Two weeks. If good flight surgeons weren't so damned scarce, I'd send you home to the States." He shoved a manila envelope across the desk. "Here are your orders."

As Marchetti shoved the envelope across the desk toward him, the Voice spoke again. It gave Doc a plan that could not be executed in the setting of the squadron. Doc needed the privacy of a Brisbane hotel room to set up his operation. Marchetti had given it to him almost as if the Voice had ordered it.

When he got out of the airport bus in Brisbane, Doc hailed a taxi and asked the driver to take him to some small out-of-the-way hotel. The manager was a potato-shaped woman with frizzy blond hair by the name of Mrs. Bedford, who explained proudly that the red brick hotel was an old mansion that had once been occupied by the governor of Queensland. Mrs. Bedford led him to a dark paneled room on the third floor overlooking a rear garden. She pulled a curtain aside to show him the flowers, a gazebo, and a patch of lawn. "We takes pride in our garden, luv. Nice place to sit and chat of an afternoon."

But Doc had no time to sit and chat of an afternoon. As soon as he could get Mrs. Bedford out of the room, he opened his notebook. He'd made a list of what he needed: a typewriter, letter paper, envelopes, erasers, stamps. Tomorrow he would go to a library for the addresses. His letters would go to all U.S. Senators and at least two Representatives from each state. It would also go to the President and Vice President of the United States, the members of the Presidential cabinet, the Joint Chiefs of Staff, all commanding generals and admirals in the Pacific theater of operations, and to Winston Churchill, General Charles de Gaulle, Joseph Stalin, and Generalissimo Chiang Kai-shek. This meant that Doc would have to type seventeen or eighteen letters per day for two weeks. He had a moment of panic, wondering if he could keep up with this schedule. He must. He was still shaken by a new discovery. Weeks earlier, Doc had added the digits of Hitler's and Courtenay's birth dates and displayed his finding in the following way:

Hitler's birth date: 4/20/1889 $(4 + 2 + 0 + 1 + 8 + 8 + 9 = 32)$
Courtenay's birth date: 2/29/1918 $(2 + 2 + 9 + 1 + 9 + 1 + 8 = 32)$

The night before he left for Brisbane, Doc had found the numerical value of each letter in the word *traitor*, given $A = 1$ and $Z = 26$. He had multiplied these values by each other and arrived at the number 17,496,000. Doc had then divided this number by 32, the sum of the numbers in Hitler's birth date and also in Courtenay's birth date. This yielded 546750, which was Courtenay's Army Officer serial number, the number stamped on his dog tags and all his official records.

As the transport set its wheels down at Port Moresby, Doc saw General Laird's red-nosed P-38 parked alongside the control tower. Next to the P-38 was a jeep with two men sitting in it. The transport taxied to the tower and the pilot swung the plane around to park and cut the engines, and Doc saw that the two men were Marchetti and General Laird. When Doc stepped off the ladder with his B-4 bag, the jeep pulled in close to the plane. Marchetti waved. "Over here, Doc!" Doc could not read the expression in either face. While they drove, Laird chatted over his shoulder about the invasions. Hollandia and Aitape had fallen. Everybody was going to move soon, maybe to Aitape and even farther north, within reach of the Philippines. Doc only half listened. He'd more or less expected the greeting committee. When they stopped in front of Marchetti's office, Doc guessed he would soon learn the effect of his letters. Maybe Courtenay had already been arrested.

"How was your leave?" Marchetti said, leaning back in his squeaky desk chair. "Did you have a good time?"

"You could say that."

Laird sat facing Doc, tapping his cane against the shoe on his aluminum foot.

"Did you hear about Courtenay?" Laird said.

Doc's heart accelerated.

"What about him?"

"He's dead."

Laird had the usual blue-sky look in his eyes, but Doc was not fooled. Doc would soon find where Courtenay was hiding. Steve and Gumbo heard things. Steve would be very interested to learn what was in the letters. Marchetti was talking.

"Courtenay bailed out and popped his chute too soon. A Zero cut his feet off with the propeller."

For a second or two, Doc was horrified, then he caught himself. It was incredible, the lengths they would go to, the lies.

"How do you know Courtenay's dead?"

"Steve saw it. He tried to stop it. He ran out of ammo."

Was Steve lying, too? Had Courtenay's corruption of the squadron reached that far? Laird was talking.

"Doc," Laird said. "I'm afraid we'll have to send you back to the States."

Doc sat very still, suppressing an avalanche of tics and twitches.

"Why?" Doc was tempted to believe the concern in Laird's face, but he reminded himself that Laird was clever, they were all clever.

"You've been under a hell of a strain for a long time, Doc," Laird said. "It's for your own good. You're to report to the field hospital at one o'clock tomorrow for a checkup."

"A checkup for what?"

But Doc knew what it meant. Depending on the results of the "checkup," he would be sent home either by air transport or in a padded cell on a hospital ship. Doc told them what it meant. Laird and Marchetti both looked unhappy. Laird whacked his foot and cleared his throat.

"Our thinking hadn't gone quite that far, Doc. I wouldn't like to see you in a padded cell."

"No? Why not?" Doc knew his face was twitching, but he couldn't stop it. It was all he could do to keep from shattering like a piece of broken crockery. "Wouldn't that be the best thing?" he said. "What if I'm crazy? What if I'm dangerous? I might jump overboard. I might mutiny and try to take over the ship. Maybe I should be kept in a straitjacket? Don't you think that would be a good idea? Maybe chained to a wall?"

Marchetti grimaced as he leaned forward.

"Doc, calm down. Listen to me. This didn't just come out of left field, you know. It was your letters to the generals and admirals that did it. The shit hit the fan. Kenney himself ordered the checkup."

Doc had no doubt what the verdict would be. What better way to get rid of an enemy than to have him declared insane, send him home on a Section Eight, and lock him up for the rest of his life? From now on, nothing Doc could say would be taken seriously. So be it, Doc thought. His work as the Emissary was done, his mission accomplished. The evidence was in other hands now. Not everybody was blind, corrupt, or stupid. Somewhere, someday, somebody would see the truth of Doc's discovery. He, personally, was expendable. But his personal future terrified him. He remembered the sickly smell of a veterans' hospital he'd worked in as plainly as if he were standing in one of the locked wards. The sweat of frightened men, urine, rotting teeth, stale tobacco smoke, disinfectant, and every so often the mockery of a nurse's perfume. He remembered the bolted doors, the window screens like a cross-hatching of bars. He would be in such a prison for the rest of his life. Courtenay and his conspiracy would keep him there for their own protection. Doc wanted to scream at Laird and Marchetti, *Don't you see what you're doing?* But he twitched instead. He had to be even more cunning now, hold himself together. Screaming would only make them think they were right.

"Am I relieved of duty?"

Marchetti wrinkled his forehead at Laird.

Laird succeeded in looking depressed.

"I guess that's about the size of it. I'm sorry, Doc. We'll miss you."

"I don't suppose I could use my jeep till tomorrow?" Doc said. "There are some people I'd like to say goodbye to."

"The new flight surgeon has it," Marchetti said. "I don't think he'll need it."

"Take mine," Laird said. "It's parked in front of my tent."

While the squadron landed, Doc sweated under his hot tent roof, packing. In the distance he could hear the thunder and snarl of the landing pitch-out. The planes dived four abreast toward the runway, then pulled up quickly one after the other into a steep, climbing turn back to the runway again with barely time to get wheels down before they touched the ground. It was a sight Doc would probably never see again. As he was about to leave the tent, Steve appeared in the doorway.

"Doc, I need to talk to you."

"Good," Doc said. "Tell me where they're hiding Courtenay."

"That's why I came to see you, Doc. He'd still be alive if I hadn't—"

Doc snorted.

"I don't care what they told you to say, Steve. Do you know what's in my letters?"

Steve looked blank.

"I heard you wrote to some generals and admirals."

"Would you like to know what I said?"

"Sure, I guess."

Doc withdrew from his shirt pocket a typed version of his discovery.

Doc smiled as Steve read. Nobody could argue with his numbers—they were flawless.

"Now do you understand?"

There was an odd look on Steve's face.

"You sent this to MacArthur?"

"I sent it to everybody. Congress. Heads of state. Well?"

"Well, gee, Doc, I don't know. . . ."

"Where is he, Steve?"

"He's dead, Doc. Like I told you. It was my fault. I was his wingman."

Steve's gray eyes were so wide and sincere that Doc was tempted to believe him.

"Are you one of them, Steve?"

"One of whom?"

"They're trying to take over the world."

"Who is? What are you talking about?"

"I've done my part, Steve. Now it's up to the rest of you."

"Doc, this is crazy. . . ."

Doc was getting angry. "It's not going to do a damn bit of good, is it? As soon as they get me locked up, Courtenay will come out of hiding and nobody will even try to stop him."

Steve reached out as if to touch Doc's shoulder, but Doc jumped back out of reach.

"Doc, listen to me. Courtenay bailed out and pulled his rip cord too soon. A Jap cut his legs off with his propeller. I saw it happen."

"Don't lie to me, Steve!" Doc yelled. "Everybody's lying to me! Of all people, I never thought I'd hear it from you!" He snatched his calculations from Steve's hand, shoved past him in the doorway, and ran to Laird's jeep. Doc started the motor and threw the shift into gear and yelled over his shoulder, "They're sending me home in a padded cell, Steve! I'm psychotic! Did you know that?" The jeep sprayed red gravel as Doc made a U-turn and headed down the squadron street.

As Doc raced toward the field, he had misgivings about the way he'd talked to Steve. Doc stopped the jeep near the opening to a revetment. Was he crazy? Maybe he really was crazy. He was sorry he'd yelled at Steve. Steve had always seemed more like a son to him, the son he'd never had. Maybe he should think about this. He shouldn't have said that about the padded cell. Steve had stood in the doorway with a stricken look as Doc drove away. Doc wondered what it would be like in a padded cell. Doc hadn't seen a look like that on Steve's face since his best friend Buster was killed. The door to a padded cell had a little tiny window with thick, unbreakable glass. For a twenty-year-old, Steve had always seemed so cool and self-possessed, sure of where he stood. Padded cells had thick metal doors, powerful locks, often a steel bar from one side of the door to the other on the outside because some insane people had the strength of three or four men. Doc had once stepped inside an empty padded cell and shuddered, thinking if he was ever put in a place like that and was not crazy, he soon would be.

Doc had been staring at a P-38 inside the revetment. It was a dented old plane with six Jap flags painted on it and the name "Humper" peeling off the nose. It was a spare, fueled and armed, ready to fly in case a pilot had a mechanical failure before takeoff and there was no other plane available. It was a plane Doc sometimes climbed into and started the engines and imagined himself taking off, flying across the Owen Stanley Mountains with his squadron. Doc pulled the jeep into the revetment and parked it. He got out and climbed up on the wing and popped the hatch and got into the cockpit. Without a parachute pack under him, he sat too low. He levered the seat up to the highest notch so his head rose above the sill. He primed and started the engines. He might never again hear Allison in-line engines singing on either side of him. When the engine temperature gauges rose enough, Doc leaned the fuel mix, depressed the brake pedals, and pushed the wheel forward to keep the nose on the ground while he increased the throttle setting. He felt the bird tremble. It wanted to fly. Doc had never taxied a P-38, but he'd taxied other planes. All flight surgeons received some flight training. He switched off the engines and climbed out of the plane. He pulled the chocks from under the wheels and threw them over by the jeep. He climbed back into the cockpit, buckled his safety belt, adjusted his pith helmet, and restarted the engines. He began working the throttles and rudder pedals to guide the plane out onto the taxi strip.

Humper was normally parked in the revetment closest to the landing strip, to be available for a fast takeoff. Doc soon found himself at the end of the taxi strip and moving out onto the end of the runway. He swung the plane around and stopped with the nose centered on the far end where the runway tapered to a point. As he usually did before his imaginary flights, Doc pulled the checklist out of its pocket and ran through the takeoff procedure. He set the propeller pitch, adjusted the fuel mix, and tightened his safety belt as if he were about to take off. He closed the hatch.

In the corner of his eye, Doc saw a jeep and a fire truck pull out from behind the radio shack. Another jeep was racing down the taxi strip toward Doc's end of the runway. A red light flashed repeatedly in the tower. Doc twisted to look at the sky behind him and around the field. There was no other plane in the air. They were coming to get him out of the cockpit. Probably the controller in the tower had been yelling at him that he had no clearance for takeoff, but Doc could not hear because he hadn't brought his earphones. Soon the ambulance would come racing down the road with Klemmer and the new flight surgeon. A fire truck or two. Another jeep with Marchetti and Laird. Maybe Courtenay would come out of hiding.

Doc watched, fascinated, as his left hand advanced the throttles until they stood full forward. He released the brakes. The acceleration shoved him back against the seat with his heart pounding. The runway lights began to streak past, the ground blurred, the control tower whipped past. Doc concentrated on the rudder pedals that kept the plane centered on the runway. His eyes flicked to the airspeed indicator and back to the runway. Doc kept a gentle forward pressure on the yoke to hold the nose down and the tail up until he felt a lightness in the yoke. Then the vibration of the wheels on the metal mesh ceased and the plane left the ground of its own accord and became a creature of another element and dimension rising above the trees.

Doc pulled the landing gear lever and felt the plane lift faster as the wheels came up. He retracted the flaps and adjusted the propeller pitch and began a careful turn toward the Owen Stanleys. He was getting the feel of the controls. The plane was sensitive, even more so than the C-47 transport he sometimes flew as copilot. He would be all right as long as he kept well above stalling speed and did not try any fancy maneuvers. He banked the plane toward the Owen Stanleys with the throttles full forward, and leveled off a few hundred feet above the jungle. When he roared past the tower, he'd seen men running toward Laird's red-nosed P-38. Doc could be a long way from Port Moresby and hard to find by the time Laird got airborne.

Only now did Doc allow himself to look at what he'd done. Maybe he was crazy after all. If he tried to land, he would kill himself. He knew nothing about landing a plane with tricycle gear, especially a fighter. He would freeze at the controls or overcompensate or forget to flip some critical switch. Nobody would be able to talk him in like Courtenay had talked Buster in, because Doc had not brought his earphones. He had no parachute and therefore he could not bail out. He had not planned this, it had been totally impulsive, out of character. Who was in control? Who had shoved the throttles forward? It had been like watching somebody else's hand in slow motion. Doc shivered, but managed to hold the plane on course and altitude.

Doc could fly all the way to Rabaul or the Admiralty Islands if he wanted to and still return home. Nothing was decided yet, nothing was irrevocable. Doc told his body this. But he also told it, suppose we manage to land without killing ourselves. Then what? Are we ready for a straitjacket, a lifetime in a padded cell or a locked ward? The body became even more afraid. When Doc had pushed the throttles forward, he remembered the Emissary helping. The two of them together had overcome the body. Maybe the Emissary was still with him. Did the Emissary know where they were going? What were its intentions? Why didn't it speak now?

There were times when Doc's body shook so hard that the plane nearly went out of control. The last time his body did this and Doc had got the plane back on course, a red-nosed P-38 dropped down from the sky above and took a position in formation alongside. Doc ignored it. He felt himself being studied. He refused to look, except for a stealthy creeping of his eyeballs. There was a thump and Doc's wings tilted slightly. The other plane had tapped Doc's wingtip with its own. Doc was startled into looking at the pilot. It was somebody he used to know. Steve Larkin. Steve was flying the plane of one who had gone over to the enemy. It did not surprise Doc that they were in collusion. The time had passed when there was anyone Doc could trust.

The other plane pulled ahead and the pilot looked back. It flew underneath and the pilot looked up. It flew above, inverted, and the pilot looked through the top of his own canopy, down into

Doc's cockpit. The other plane stayed alongside until Doc had crossed the Bismarck Sea and was flying almost due north. Between the Admiralty Islands and New Ireland, Doc turned northwest into the Pacific. The plane beside him jinked, bouncing up and down so violently that Doc was again tricked into looking. The pilot gestured with his hand, *Follow me.* Doc shook his head. The pilot pointed to his own chest, then back toward Port Moresby. Doc understood. The other plane had no belly tank. It would have to turn back or risk running out of fuel before it got home. Doc felt himself being studied a few seconds longer, then the other pilot raised his hand to his forehead in salute. The red-nosed plane did a wingover and disappeared.

Ahead of Doc was empty ocean for more than a thousand miles to the Marshall Islands. The sun was low on the horizon, still hot against Doc's neck. The fuel needles hovered near one-half. He would have to make a decision soon. What was there to decide? Was he crazy? All his life he had done his best and it had never been enough. This time, his best had made him dangerous to those with power and they had to silence him.

Just as the fuel needles stood at one-half, Doc heard a scream. "No!" somebody cried, and tore the controls away from Doc, trying to turn the plane back. For a moment, Doc conceded, then he screamed, himself, and fought to regain control. He felt the Emissary helping. The Emissary was not afraid. It was empty-calm. It had never been afraid. Doc remembered it from his childhood (he had not known it as the Emissary then) when he'd learned how his mother had died. The Emissary lived in a small space of absolute calm inside Doc's chest. It had appeared also when Doc's first and only adult love left him. It was not to be confused with the calm of morphine—morphine deadened all of life in order to deaden pain, but the empty space sucked the pain in and somehow dissolved it.

The Emissary was here now with him, in him, around him—he felt it looking after him.

In the red light of sunset, Doc saw islands beneath his wing. He did not know what they were. He found a worn map in the map case. He unfolded the map on his knees and against the control column. He tried to match island shapes with what he saw on the map. Suddenly he grabbed the map from both sides and crushed it between his hands. What did it matter what the map said? He knew where he was going, all of him—Doc, the body, the Tourette's twitches, the Emissary, and any other hitchhikers and hangers-on. What did he need with a map? He rolled down the starboard window and the blast of air nearly knocked his pith helmet off. He threw the map, and there was a brittle crash as the map whipped out the window and vanished in the slipstream. Doc felt a sudden release, a wild freedom. He threw his head back and began to howl with the engines. Then he began to sing. He'd always kept silent when the pilots sang. He'd hated singing ever since kindergarten, when he'd been forced to sing. He had a terrible singing voice, like belching or a frog croaking. He couldn't keep a tune. He couldn't keep time. People laughed. But he sang now, with only the ocean and the sky and the plane to hear. He sang at the fullest power of his voice the songs of the pilots that he'd heard a thousand times. He didn't care how he sounded, he opened both side windows and tried to outsing the engines and the roar of the atmosphere as he passed through it. He switched on the instrument panel light so he could stay on course and watch the fuel gauges as they slowly fell toward zero. He sang as the sky grew dark and the stars came out and glittered on the glassy sea beneath him so he could not be sure which was sky and which was ocean without his instruments to guide him. He sang on, into the night.

PATSY

Steve approached Berkeley from behind the hills to minimize his chance of being reported over the no-fly zone. Above Grizzly Peak, he dumped the nose of his AT-6, shoved the throttle forward, and set the propeller pitch for maximum noise. Steve had timed his arrival for a few minutes after noon. His airspeed indicator read 300 miles per hour as he flashed past the campanile and banked so he could look down from the side window of the cockpit at Wheeler Hall, where students poured out onto the broad front steps on their way to lunch. He was low enough to see them waving, throwing papers and notebooks into the air, girls with skirts flying, jumping like cheerleaders. Steve made a steep, climbing turn back toward the hills at full throttle. He'd promised himself only one pass in order to give some officious citizen less time to run for his binoculars and read the ID numbers on the plane. But he couldn't resist, seeing all those people, some of them his friends. To hell with the no-fly zone and the one thousand foot minimum-altitude rule and officious citizens in general. When he roared down the slopes of Grizzly Peak on his second pass, the crowd was even bigger, waiting for him. He gave them a little show this time, rolling over on his back as he neared the campanile, looking up through the canopy and saluting as he passed above the crowd, then rolling out and using his great speed to streak back up over the hills and out of sight.

As Steve parked on the ramp at Hamilton Field and climbed out of the cockpit with his parachute, a jeep pulled up alongside. The sergeant at the wheel yelled that Steve was wanted in the CO's office. Somebody had read his number over Berkeley.

The CO was a major with a wrestler's neck who sat like a boulder in his desk chair. He'd done a bit of exciting low-level flying himself, he said. He'd once flown his P-47 through a French roundhouse to put a final burst into a German locomotive. In combat, that was the way you were supposed to fly. He knew how it was with hotshots just back from the war. The country would allow them a little time to get it out of their system, then they had to face the fact that the war was over. You can't get away with that stuff anymore, he said, ace or no ace. At least not over populated areas. The next time Steve was caught, there would be a court-martial. He would also be asked to resign from the Reserves and lose his commission. No more free flying. No more flight pay. The major stared as if to see whether that had sunk in. Steve looked appropriately contrite. It brought back the time when he and Bix and Danovich were threatened with court martial for giving their Aussie girlfriends a ride in the P-38s they were supposed to be ferrying back to Port Moresby. On that occasion, too, Steve could have sworn he saw a glitter of envy in the CO's eyes.

At a party not long after he buzzed the campus, Steve spotted a girl across the room with blue-flame eyes scanning the crowd. Her eyes met Steve's and she started across the room toward him. She had long, slender legs and a tangle of curly black hair that suggested gale winds and bed. Her name was Patsy. She'd asked around to find his name. He was the pilot of that plane, wasn't he? When she was a little girl, her father had taken her to an airshow. Ever since, she said, she'd wanted to fly. When Steve had roared over campus upside down a few feet above her head, she knew she had to meet the man who could fly like that.

"There are plenty of us," Steve said. "All the guys I flew with."

"I wouldn't know what to do with more than one of you," she said.

A week later, Steve moved into Patsy's studio south of campus. The better he knew her, the more he liked her. She'd tried to enlist in the Women's Army Air Corps, but the Army had discovered her criminal record. The night before she left for college, as a parting judgment on her Nebraska hometown, she had stolen a fully loaded manure spreader and distributed its contents evenly from curb to curb the length of a deserted main street. Then, in Berkeley, she'd borrowed a Pacific Gas and Electric lineman's gear and challenged an ex-Army captain by the name of Roger Falk to climb eucalyptus trees with her on Grizzly Peak during a storm.

Another week went by, and Patsy observed that Steve hadn't even mentioned the war. Until he met Patsy, Steve had hung out with guys who hardly ever spoke of it. At a party or a bar, somebody might ask if you were in Europe or the Pacific. You might hear that somebody was Army or Navy, drove a tank in Africa, or served on a destroyer or flew a bomber. You might get ten or fifteen more words from them before they ordered another drink and changed the subject. Steve would sit with a beer in one hand and sometimes a girl's hand in the other, and he'd notice his knee bouncing about four beats per second and the rest of his body tensed up as if preparing to slam the controls around in a live-or-die maneuver to escape the bullet stream from an enemy fighter.

Patsy noticed right away, and put her hand on his knee to calm the jumpy leg.

"You're supposed to talk about it. You can tell me, you know. I won't shrivel up and blow away."

But the guys who did talk abut it always sounded as if they were bragging or feeling sorry for themselves. He told her some of the easy stuff, how he loved the flying but could have done without the shooting. He told about Jennifer, the crazy Aussie girl who had thrown his racetrack winnings on the street, about Courtenay's alcoholic parrot, and the time he and Bix and Danovich had taken the Aussie girls for a ride. The trouble was, one thing led to another and the pressure would build up like water behind a dam and Patsy would say, "You're jumping again," and that night he might have a nightmare.

He wanted to tell her about his duel with the Japanese ace Ishigawa, but that would open doors to places he didn't want to return to. For a while after the duel, he'd felt invincible. Yet his old friend and mentor Bix had seemed invincible, too, until the day Bix had disappeared over New Britain. With enough bullets flying around you and enough shells exploding, it didn't make any difference how good you were. There had been a time when he knew he'd come home alive, then a time when he wondered, then a time when he was sure he'd leave his bones at the bottom of some alien ocean along with the bones of Bix and his enemy Ishigawa and all the others.

Steve suspected he'd gone a bit mad, flying his last few missions, waiting for the bullet that would finish it for him. During the long hours to the target, Steve's dead friends crowded into the cockpit with him, and sometimes even Bix's girlfriend, Addie, who'd been like a sister to him, and Rachael, an Aussie girl he'd really liked, and he could feel the heat of their bodies pressing around, a comfort he hoped he could hold until the very last instant when he hit the ocean like a wall of concrete. But he hadn't hit the ocean. The trouble was, he still felt as if he expected to.

• • •

Patsy introduced Steve to her friends. Patsy was Steve's age. She'd stayed in school while Steve was away at war, and she'd had time to collect characters around her as offbeat in their own way as some of the pilots Steve had flown with. One was a surrealist poet, one a Trotskyite cell leader, another a niece of Sigmund Freud who ate apples in bed during sex. There was a teenage physicist who had made a discovery based on a verse in a Vedic sutra. There was Louie Lamontia, who had lied about his age, joined the Merchant Marine, and had three ships torpedoed out from under him. And square-jawed, ape-shouldered Roger Falk, who had climbed the eucalyptus trees with Patsy. Falk had parachuted behind enemy lines in Burma to set up an Allied spy network. They met almost every day at Toby's restaurant on Telegraph Avenue at one of the big round oak tables they called Patsy's Table, downstairs in the coffee shop. The floor was covered with sawdust—a tradition, Falk said, from a time not so long ago when bar and restaurant patrons spat tobacco juice and other effluents on the floor. The walls were covered with photos of famous and not-so-famous patrons who had come there as students.

The first time Steve sat down at the table, Falk had his chair tipped back against the wall and his thick arms on display over his chest. He regarded Steve through half-shut eyes while he was being introduced.

"I hear you're an ace," he said.

"Yep."

"How many kills?"

"Eleven."

"Ever been shot down?"

"Once."

Falk seemed to wait for more.

"He doesn't talk about it," Patsy said.

"Hey, no problem," Falk said, generously. "I couldn't talk about that shit for a while, myself."

Apparently, Falk had made a full recovery, for Steve heard twice in the same day about Falk's technique of sneaking up behind an enemy sentry and slipping a piano-wire garotte over his head. How Falk had been equipped with a hollow tooth full of cyanide like the German general Erwin Rommel, so he could commit suicide if captured. Falk often mentioned his 165 IQ, and he tapped his square-tipped fingers as if waiting impatiently for another person to finish talking since he could predict where the story would end anyway. He spoke in an inflectionless drone that seemed to say, if you looked away while he was talking, he might tighten the garotte. Walking home with Patsy, Steve said he wondered if he was going to have trouble with Falk.

"You don't have to like any of them," Patsy said, "as long as you like me."

Ever since Steve had told Patsy about taking the Aussie girls flying, she'd been asking questions about it. How did the girls like it? What kind of flying stunts had they done? How had they avoided being caught? For as long as she could remember, she'd dreamed of flying a real plane. Did Steve think he could smuggle her into an AT-6? Her friends applauded the idea and offered strategies for getting her onto the field and into a plane. Lamontia suggested she could wear one of Steve's flight suits and tuck her hair up under a canvas helmet. From Steve's description, Falk drew a diagram of the field and made suggestions. He'd be glad to help. He probably wouldn't strangle a sentry, but he knew plenty of diversionary tactics.

Steve explained that he was already on probation for flying at nearly ground level over campus, not to mention violating the no-fly zone and performing maneuvers forbidden by the AT-6 operating manual. Things had been different in the combat zone. Hot pilots were needed there. You could get away with stuff they'd lock you up for here. But Falk's offer seemed to encourage Patsy.

"It's peacetime now," she said. "Maybe they don't have sentries."

"It can't be done," Steve said. "I wouldn't be able to get a parachute for you."

"People fly all the time in airliners without a parachute," Patsy said.

"Airliners don't loop and roll and spin."

"We don't have to loop and roll and spin. I just want to fly with you."

"It's no fun if you don't loop and roll and spin," Steve said. "It's boring."

"Then for heaven's sake, let's loop and roll and spin. What's the worst that can happen?"

"A wing could come off."

Falk looked surprised.

"Aren't those planes made to take it?"

Steve resented Falk's entry into the argument.

"The manual has a list of maneuvers an AT-6 is not supposed to do."

"But you do them anyway."

"We have parachutes in case the plane comes apart."

"Steve," Patsy said, "I'm willing to take my chances."

"Give me a break, Patsy. Do you think I could bail out and let you go down with the plane?"

"What would you do?" Patsy said. "Stay in the plane so we'd both die?" She seemed almost entertained by the thought.

"I'd probably keep trying to land until it was too late to bail out."

"Land—with one wing gone?"

It was beginning to feel like the struggle to get Ishigawa off his tail.

Upstairs, somebody held the door open, and a streetcar rattled past with its bell clanging. Falk grinned.

"What the hell, Steve, take her up. It's not exactly as if you're aiding and abetting the enemy. What can they do to you, anyway?"

"I could be court-martialed. Kicked out of the Reserves."

"So?"

"So I like to fly."

"So fly anyway."

"Money, Falk. Do you know what it costs to keep a military plane in the air, even a little old advanced trainer?"

Falk's shrug suggested that he, Falk, would not be deterred by such petty considerations.

Falk had been a light-heavyweight boxer in school before the war. He had had more training than Steve and was ten or fifteen pounds heavier. The way he stood and walked suggested that there wasn't much he was afraid of. Maybe it would be different with a gun pointed at him. And maybe not.

In spite of himself, Steve found Falk entertaining. In his controlled, droning voice, Falk repeated to the crowd at the table the bizarre data he ferreted out of the locked stacks he had access to as a graduate student. The sexual peculiarities, for example, of the people studied by Havelock Ellis. The lunatic laws and penalties. One afternoon at the crowded table, he declared that the United States was one of the most sexually repressed countries in the world. Did they know that in Minnesota there was a law on the books making it a felony to have intercourse with a dead fowl? Before she could get a napkin to her face, Patsy sprayed coffee across the table and shrieked with appreciation. In a judicial drone, Falk proceeded to probe deeper meanings. Was dead-fowl fucking really such a threat to the health and welfare of our country? Even without the law, who would be drawn to it? The surest sign of creeping fascism, he said, was the proliferation of unnecessary laws. Did the assembled company know that every year in the United States over a thousand new laws were added to the books, and almost none were repealed?

Steve noticed Patsy's rapt attention.

"It's nothing to worry about," she told Steve, after Falk had left. "He's just an interesting character. Berkeley is full of them."

"Have you slept with him?"

"Don't even think it. For one thing, he's a natural killer."

"So am I."

She laughed.

"You're not a killer, you're a lover. That's your whole problem."

It was Steve's second semester back at school, and his academic record was nothing to brag about. He'd start with a full fifteen units, get bored with his courses, and drop all but the few units required to keep his GI bill checks arriving. Falk made sure everybody knew that he'd signed up for twenty units every semester, himself, dropped none, and finished with straight A's.

One day between classes, Steve was lying on a lawn near the library, with his head in Patsy's lap.

"Maybe I'm not smart enough for college," he said.

"Don't be silly," she said. "You're as smart as anybody I know."

"Even Falk?"

"Even Falk."

"I don't have an IQ of one hundred sixty-five."

"An IQ test only measures certain things," she said. "Plenty of so-called geniuses didn't get to be pilots. You had to be very nearly perfect." She leaned closer and tapped the tip of his nose with her forefinger.

"Did you know that, Mister Ace?"

Steve had known her only a couple of months, and already it was hard to imagine life without her. But he needed to come home from the war. In classes, in sleep, even in making love to Patsy, some part of him was always up there, locked in battle.

They were sitting around Patsy's Table at Toby's one rainy spring afternoon, with the room redolent of wet wool, perfume, piney sawdust, and the occasional steaming coffee. Falk said if Steve couldn't take Patsy flying, they could all chip in and buy her an hour at some local airport for her birthday. Of course, he said, it would mean flying in some little putt-putt, not a hot military plane like the ones Steve flew. Steve studied Falk's expressionless face. Was he suggesting that the ace with eleven kills was too timid to give his girlfriend the experience of a lifetime? Patsy had already told Steve it had been a bad idea and she would stop nagging him, but Falk seemed determined to keep her mind on flying in general. Along with his encyclopedic knowledge of many subjects, Falk had collected a headful of aeronautical lore and data. The performance of World War II aircraft, Allied and Axis. The exploits of famous fliers like Lindbergh, Wiley Post, Amelia Earhart. The inside story of Howard Hughes, who, Falk said, had designed the Zero and sold it to the Japanese because the United States was not interested. Falk would ask Steve about some obscure event or number, and smile tolerantly when Steve could not match Falk's photographic memory. The crowd at the table learned that Falk had done a bit of flying, himself. He'd had to strangle two sentries and steal a Japanese observation plane to escape when one of his Burmese agents betrayed him.

"I didn't know you were a pilot," said somebody at the table.

"Oh, not like Steve!" Falk protested, hand raised in overdone modesty. "I'd never flown a plane in my life, but when it's a matter of survival it's surprising what you can learn on a moment's notice." Taking off had been the easy part, Falk said. He was a complete dunce about landing. He had stalled too high, did a belly flop and wiped out the landing gear, which probably saved his life because he was headed straight for the jungle wall. His tolerant chuckle suggested that a person so intelligent that he could fly a plane at first try could be allowed a mistake or two.

Falk stared across the table and began lamenting Steve's reluctance to talk about the war. "I'll bet you could really tell us some stories, huh, Steve?"

"I'm sure they couldn't match yours, Roger."

"Hey," Falk said, "there's no need to be modest at this table. Nobody else is." He winked at Lamontia, then planted his thick elbows on the table and leaned forward with his face a picture of humble curiosity. "What's it like, really? I can only imagine what you went through, with a few thousand tracers streaking past the cockpit windows. I bet you saw some of your best friends blasted, right? Empty cots in the tents? Empty seats in the mess hall? Seen them go down burning, exploding, hitting the ground before they could get out? What's it like when you can't twist out of the bullet stream? I've heard guys talk about that. They say they nearly jumped out of their skin when they heard the rattle of bullets stitching the plane, headed for the cockpit or the gas tanks. They sat there waiting for the engine to quit or their guts to explode all over the cockpit."

Steve felt dizzy. He got up and went to the men's room and splashed cold water on his face. When he came back, Falk was looking at him with overdone concern.

"Steve, are you all right?"

"I'm fine." Steve picked up his books. Patsy followed.

"Did I say something?" Falk yelled as they started up the stairs.

Outside on the street, Steve turned his face up to the spring drizzle and filled his lungs with cool, moist air. Patsy opened her umbrella over them.

"Don't mind him, Steve. He's just oblivious."

"The hell he is. He knows exactly what he's doing."

They walked to the corner and waited for the light to change. Rain dripped from store awnings, tires hissed on wet pavement, the bell of a streetcar clanged.

"It sounds to me," Patsy said, "as if what he's doing is trying to get you to talk."

"He's trying to come between you and me."

They had just crossed the street and stepped up onto the curb. Patsy stopped and peered up into Steve's face.

"It's not working, as far as I'm concerned. Is it, as far as you're concerned?"

"Don't be silly," he said.

She gripped his arm and gave it a little shake. "I don't like to see you like this. You are so much bigger than Falk."

When he mentioned Falk coming between them, he'd heard a whine in his voice that jolted him. He remembered breaking up with a girlfriend in high school. The more he'd whined and tried to hang on to her, the more he'd driven her away.

"Anyway, the heck with Falk," Patsy said. "As far as I'm concerned, if you don't want to talk, then don't."

"The amateur psychiatrists are telling me I'm supposed to."

"We don't all work the same way."

Steve began to simmer down. He'd really found something when he met Patsy. He wished he could satisfy her dream of flying. He remembered how many times he'd seen the blue sparkle in her eyes when she told friends about watching him fly over Wheeler Hall upside down, saluting as if to her. It occurred to him that he might be able to give her something almost as good. He could give

Patsy her own personal airshow someplace like the open rangeland north of Fairfield, far from people and no-fly zones. He knew the country up north, he would pick a spot on the map, and three or four carloads of their friends could drive up and have a picnic, and Steve would arrive at a prearranged time. He'd be able to stretch out up there. He'd show her some real flying.

Steve flew due north in a sky of robin's-egg blue. The little cross-road towns two miles below the plane had given way to open country, and the earth beneath him was now an unbroken green carpet undulating toward the coast range in the west, and disappearing in the east toward snowcapped peaks low on the horizon. The only thing Steve might have added to this perfect flying day would have been Patsy in the rear cockpit and a few fleecy clouds to chase for a sense of speed.

Several flashes of light ahead of the plane caught Steve's eye. They came no doubt from Falk, who had found his way into the act with his trusty signaling mirror. Steve pitched the plane forward as he advanced the throttle and dived toward a cluster of cars centered over the engine cowling. He leveled off, roared across the cars, and pulled up in a steep climb, then over onto his back in a loop that brought him down near ground level again. He cut power, lowered the flaps, and drifted past the cars at nearly landing speed with his canopy open. He could make out Lamontia's pipe-stem legs in Levi's, Patsy with her flag of wild black hair, Falk with his ape shoulders that seemed oddly foreign to his 165 IQ. Other friends waved a tablecloth, bottles, shirts. Patsy ran parallel with the plane's path for a few yards, holding up a beer bottle, while Steve, with the plane on its side, pretended to reach down for it. For a second or two, Steve was on the verge of setting the plane down on the field near the cars, but a little flicker of sanity reminded him of marshy spots in the spring grass that could wreck the landing gear.

Steve advanced the throttle, raised the flaps, and began a climbing turn at full power. He watched the cars shrink to the size of bugs. At ten thousand feet, he did a wingover and dived to gain speed, pulled out in a series of rolls, split-S's, vertical climbs that became vertical rolls and ended in hammerhead stalls that turned into spins, power dives, loops, Immelmans, and every maneuver that Steve knew an AT-6 could survive, or barely survive, in spite of what the manual said. For a moment he could almost believe he was flying his favorite P-38, the one in which he'd dueled with Ishigawa.

Steve's fuel gauge told him he should start home soon. He put the plane into a final dive toward the cars with the engine wide open, then pulled straight up until the plane was hanging from the propeller. As the controls lost authority, he kicked the rudder pedal. The plane fell over into a hammerhead stall that turned into a spin. Steve pushed the stick forward, kicked the rudder pedal again, stopped the spin, and accelerated toward the cars. His plan was to zoom over them at the highest speed yet, pull up, roll, and head for home. As he hauled back on the stick and felt the pullout slam him down into his seat at four or five gravities, there was a sickening crack, the plane staggered, and a hurricane of cold air tried to tear him out of the cockpit. Steve looked down to see green hills through the bare tubes of the framework. The panel covering the whole right side of the plane was gone.

Almost in a single motion, he pulled the throttle back, dropped flaps, and eased the stick forward to bring the plane out of the dive as gently as possible. He kicked the right rudder pedal and pulled the stick to the left, so he was flying at an angle sideways to the left, shielding the open right side from the blast of air that could build up inside the fuselage and blow the tail off. He set the trim tabs, eased the throttle forward enough to maintain flying speed, and began a gingerly turn in the direction of Hamilton Field. Finally, he opened the canopy. If the tail fell off, he could be tossed around inside the tumbling cockpit so violently that he might not be able to get hold of the release handle.

Except for a minor vibration, the plane seemed to behave as it should. Steve allowed himself to notice his pounding heart, and the half sick feeling in his stomach he remembered from close calls in combat. What scared him even more was the thought that Patsy would have seen him die. He remembered the pain that had shot through his body once when she cut her finger slicing onions. If it was like that for her, too, what would she have felt, seeing him crash?

Steve would have to concoct a story for his CO, but he couldn't worry about that now. He had a plane to get home. When he got closer to Hamilton he'd radio ahead for the ambulance and crash and fire trucks. It brought to mind all the times he'd radioed ahead with one engine out and the other leaking oil or gas, or radioed ahead for a friend who was wounded or down in the ocean or whose radio had been shot out. He remembered Courtenay calling in for Buster, and Buster's blood still dripping out through holes in the belly of the plane after Doc and his medics hauled the body away in the ambulance. Buster's face and the remains of his body as it looked in the infirmary when Doc pulled the sheet down to show Steve. Maybe he shouldn't have done that. He heard Doc's voice, some of the things Doc had said before he'd stolen the P-38 and flown off, mad as a goony bird, to disappear somewhere over the Pacific Ocean. Steve saw a flicker of light and turned his head, he could have sworn he'd seen Bix's plane off his right wingtip, then a voice that sounded like Addie, he could swear he'd felt her sisterly touch on the back of his hand he looked the other way and saw the Monk's crazy grin and heard his signature remark, Nothing is ever exactly the way you think it is, and then they were all in the cockpit crowded around him as they'd been on those last few missions, even Rachael the Aussie girl he'd liked so well and had taken away from Danovich, and his boyhood friends the Hurlingames, Todd who was still alive, and Blake whose plane had exploded over Manila, even Courtenay was there, even Ishigawa, who in some strange way had become a dead comrade not an enemy, Steve wondered if this was at last the end, a message, he didn't even feel very sad about it, but then he saw Patsy's face through all the others and he thought maybe he'd better pull himself together long enough to get his airplane on the ground in one piece, give Patsy a phone call, maybe that's what this was all about, Patsy was there to bring him home, maybe that's why the others had been there, too, his guardian angels.

Steve closed the switches and watched the propeller spin down, becoming visible, then stop. It had been a very close call. Steve hadn't wanted to think how close it was while he was flying. Once he'd shot the tail off a Zero with a half-second burst, and a Zero was a much stronger plane than an AT-6. As he flashed past the tumbling plane, he'd seen the look on the face of the pilot struggling to get the canopy open before he hit the water. Steve had never told Patsy about it. Maybe the time had come to tell her about some of these things.

Patsy was crying when she answered the phone. She said she'd never been so scared in her whole life. At first, they thought maybe Steve had fallen out of the plane, then they'd thought surely he would crash with such a large piece of the plane missing. They'd watched him become a little speck and disappear in the sky, and Falk said it looked as if he'd get back to Hamilton okay, but the next problem would be landing it in one piece.

"Well, here I am in one piece," Steve said, "except for the panel." The CO hadn't even given him a lecture, he'd merely shrugged and said he was ashamed to have his top guns flying trainers anyway, one of these days they'd have P-51 Mustangs, let them try to tear a Mustang apart.

"Oh, that's wonderful," Patsy said. "You'll be able to do the kind of flying you love best."

"I've been thinking about that," Steve said. "I need to talk to you about it."

"Yes," Patsy said. "Come home and we'll talk about it. I'll have dinner ready."

"I think I need to talk about the war, Patsy."

"Anytime you want to, Steve."

"We'll talk about it, okay?"

"Oh, yes. It's time."

"I think maybe those amateur psychiatrists are right."

"I think so, too," Patsy said.

"I mean, who can I trust with it if I can't trust you?"

"You can trust me, Steve."

"Even to hear the horrible stuff I've done?"

"Yes, even the horrible stuff."

"I don't know. I saw my twenty-millimeter cannon blast a pilot's body parts all over his cockpit, Patsy. His head blew out through the canopy."

"Come home, Stevie," she said. "You can't tell me in a phone booth. Come home and tell me."